MODERN GREEK WRITERS

THE COURTYARD

ANDREAS FRANGHIAS

THE COURTYARD

Translation
MARTIN MCKINSEY

KEDROS

The translation costs of this book have been covered by the Greek Ministry of Culture.

Typeset in Greece
by Photokyttaro Ltd.
14, Armodiou St., Athens 105 52
and printed by
H. & G. Zaharopoulos & D. Sitaras
Moskato, Athens
For
Kedros Publishers, S.A.,
3, G. Gennadiou St., Athens 106 78,
Tel. 38.09.712 - Fax 38.31.981
October 1995
2nd reprint March 1997
Cover design by
Dimitris Kalokyris

Cover photo by
Sotiris Kadinopoulos

ISBN 960-04-0914-5

CHAPTER 1

EACH MORNING, when he was finished at work and ready to head home, Stathis would pause at the door of the printing press, rub his hands together, and button his coat all the way up, as if reluctant to set out. The deserted streets and dissolving shadows of the last hours of night frightened him. The light from the printing press fell on the buildings across the narrow street, their windows shut and gratings down: Oils and Tallows, Ready-to-Wear, the late-night café. It was all old and familiar, but farther on stretched long segments of night, city blocks without end, the occasional drowsing street lamp, the sleeping population ... Suddenly the roar and clatter of the printing press swept over everything. Successive waves of dense sound, in quickening rotations, thrust Stathis away from the door. The newspaper was being printed, the day was beginning even before it dawned. And unprepared, he would set forth on his small journey, that ended in a courtyard lined with rooms. He would walk the same, never-familiar streets alone, he would cross the whole of the night during its most ambiguous hour. As he neared his home, day would begin to break – a transformation that made the journey seem that much longer. As always, dawn came as an indistinct glow that rose from the quiet rooftops and the streets to enfold the houses.

Stathis always tried to slip in as lightly as he could through the iron gate out front, which creaked at the slightest nudge. He would hold it open barely a crack, then glide in sideways. Everyone else would still be asleep, the things around him as yet undefined. He'd unhook his key from its nail, ready to let the world drop then and there, like an old newspaper he had read and reread. If his room's green door had been any lower, he would have bumped his head going in every morning, he didn't have the strength left to stoop.

Today too, he would make it home without being stopped. He was always on his guard, especially going around corners. A vague dread crept over his body like wet air. Anything could happen at any moment – the main thing was to escape notice. He closed the iron gate and drew a deep breath. It wasn't such a major feat to have reached home safely.

Before he'd made it through the long passageway, he heard hurried steps coming down the winding staircase that led to the roof. Ismene, the girl living on the first floor of the front house, came up to him and took him by the arm.

"Do you have today's paper," she asked in an anxious whisper.

Stathis was taken aback. What could she want it for?

"I left just as it was going to press ... Why, has anything happened?"

"No, I just wanted to see something."

He took a few more steps past her toward his door and the end of his long trek. But Ismene came right behind him, bringing her mouth up to his ear and whispering something even more softly.

Stathis scowled, struggling to understand her words through his surprise. Ismene waited. She knew that if he had news to tell her, it would be bad news. She repeated her question:

"Was there anything in the paper about him, did you see his name?"

"No ..."

"Think hard ..."

Stathis clutched his hand to his forehead, and it all came back. The image of his old friend Angelos suddenly loomed before him, followed by a whirlwind of panic that shattered whatever sturdiness the walls had begun to assume.

"He hasn't been picked up, has he?"

"That's what I'm trying to find out ... I thought maybe in the newspaper ..."

"I'd have noticed if there was something ... No, I didn't see his name ..."

"Did you notice anything unusual in the street?"

Stathis again replied no and unhitched his key, eager to open his door and call it a day. Sleep and fatigue weighed heavier on him than ever. If Ismene didn't believe him, she could read the papers when they hit the streets in a couple of hours. He turned to his door, on the verge of telling her good-night, but Ismene wouldn't let him go.

"There's something I have to talk to you about ..."

"Go on," he said with a sigh.

He had opened his hands, that hung down at his sides, to let her know what a sacrifice it was for him to remain upright, though he would hear her out if it was for a good reason. Ismene immediately launched into a long and timeworn story, one that fortunately Stathis already knew, knew intimately in fact, so he did not have to listen. He himself had typeset the court proceedings and verdict in Angelos' trial. Letter by letter those terrible words – "sentenced to death in absentia" – had passed through his fingers. He could feel them searing into his eyes, his fingertips, his blood. The metal troughs of molten lead had reeled, the iron shafts of the press had shrieked and clashed and all but shattered. He remembered, all right. It had been winter, a rainy night – yes, February of '47 – and the rattle of the dies had drowned out the sound of falling rain. When the bulletin had come in – Angelos sentenced to death! – everything had stood still. But many years had passed since then – an even seven – and there had been no sequel to that brief but terrible news item. Ismene was in love with him before that, Stathis had often seen them sitting together and talking on the winding staircase up to the roof. But it took courage for her to go on waiting for him. Fear should have been second nature to her by now, she should have had nerves of steel.

As the daylight spread, the girl's face grew clearer and paler. Her eyes widened as she tried to make him see that she could no longer take the anguished waiting, the shadowy, unrelenting fear. Stathis realized that all she wanted was a sympathetic ear. He could see her lips quivering. Her coal-black hair was in tangles, her fingers were gaunt from year after year of numbing fear. She spoke in gasps, as if she wanted to get it all out in the same breath. The morning's transparent silence amplified her whispers, and though everyone seemed to be asleep, there's no telling what goes on behind closed shutters. Ismene stood so close to him now he could feel her warm breath on his cheek.

As she spoke, Stathis edged nearer his door, and once there, latched onto the doorframe. But she stayed with him, and again asked him to try to remember whether he had seen Angelos' name in the newspaper anywhere.

"No, I told you ... Now why not go and get some sleep? After all these years ..."

Ismene glared at him. She curtly informed him that she was not in the least bit tired of waiting, what she couldn't bear was the never-ending threat that hung over Angelos' head. As if not a single day had passed ... If only she'd had some word of him, just so she could know for a fact he was alive.

"Why are you telling me all this?"

"You're his friend. You're the only one who asks about him."

Stathis stood motionless, more intent on remembering than listening.

"I'd like to see Angelos ... You know I'm always there at the printing press. Have him give me a call some night."

"But I never see him, I don't know where he is," said.Ismene.

"When you see him, tell him hello for me ..."

"You haven't heard a word I've said, have you? You're not listening."

"I was too listening ... So, you don't see him?"

"Not once in five years."

"Strange!"

It was clear Stathis didn't believe her. She was right to say she didn't see him, but she shouldn't go so far as to believe it herself ...

"Why's he been hiding all this time, anyway?"

Ismene wondered at the absurdity of his question.

"To save himself," she answered simply. "What else could he do?"

Light suffused the sky above the buildings, and Ismene's features were clearly visible now. She flounced out her black hair. Her eyes had lost none of their clarity and sparkle. Stathis took advantage of her surprise to unlock his door. His room always gave off a musty odor, mingled with the smell of unwashed clothes.

"Good-night, Ismene ..."

He went in and closed the door behind him. Ismene stood

there for a while, staring at the door with its green paint, its knob and keyhole. There was ample light in the courtyard now, but its walls seemed to be all but touching. The passageway out to the street opened before her like an avenue of escape. She went as far as the front gate. From there, she examined the street closely, on the lookout for anything suspicious or unusual. At that hour, all those who set off for work in darkness moved along the walls in the direction of town. With small steps the buildings hurriedly formed into a line, standing shoulder to shoulder. Redeemed from the unruliness of night, they stood, abrupt and perfectly straight, facing the quarter of the sky where the light was breaking. The desolation of the streets was sharpened by the shiver of cold that ran through the morning. Stathis had not understood Ismene's anxiety. He had looked at her distractedly, as if his eyes were turned around so that only the whites showed – as with marble statues. "Fear for Angelos' life may be old news for others," Ismene thought, "but for me it's still vivid and undiminished." She shuddered. There were times when she came to the conclusion that there was no point to it all, that everything had been over for a long time without her knowing. But how could she ever accept that? It would be like another death sentence.

Danger, inexorable and unaccountable, thickened the air. A few blocks down, a large building was going up – a movie theater, or a parking garage. A sign giving the engineer's name was hanging from the scaffolding. When would Angelos be able to hang his own sign from a tall building – like one of those he had spent his nights designing while at the University?

Ismene ran her eyes carefully up and down the street one last time, then went back into the courtyard and sat down on the kitchen landing. She smoothed her skirt down over her knees, and sat trying to take up as little space as possible. The courtyard, with its red and white tiles, its drab, scaling walls, was deserted. Angelos' mother had arranged flowerpots along the top of the wall, along the ledges, and on the winding stairs up to the roof, but she had let them go when her son was convicted. She no longer even went out to look at them. Ismene had decided to water them herself, not out of any special fondness for flowers, but because it would have been a kind of mourning to have that many withered plants around. Angelos was alive, the certainty of it filled her the way light came to fill the new day, the way objects reaffirmed their solidity. Yes, she would wait for him. And despite her fear, despite how cold she felt in that mute confusion, she knew he was alive.

She rested her forehead against the iron railing. The others still slept: peace-loving people who had found their niche, who knew when their day began and when it ended. Another day was dawning. Would Angelos live through it? She'd be better off never mentioning his name. The more people remembered him, the greater his danger.

For Stathis, each morning marked the end of the previous day. His room was nothing but a roof and a mattress where he could cast his body. Once across the threshold, it was all over. He knew what everyone else would be reading in the papers later on, and he could rest easy. But today, certain memories had welled up in him. Maybe that was why it took longer than usual for his shoes to clunk on the floor, as he tossed them off in his stupor.

To the others, it was a sign that the day had begun.

IT WAS TIME FOR ANDONIS, sleeping in the next room, to get up. His wife, Vangelia, gave him a nudge, but he muttered something about not being asleep, and wanting to be left alone a little longer.

"It's just you said you had to leave early."

"When I have something to do, I don't need anybody to wake me."

"So why not turn over so we can talk?"

"There's something I need to think through. I'll be done in a minute ..."

Andonis had no more time for discussion. Vangelia's voice sounded melodic in his ears, but there was no point his letting on that he'd heard. The gray light that seeped down the wall like a damp stain was slowly turning red – which meant it was already late. If the air lost its filminess, if the voices in the courtyard were joined by the sounds of traffic and people in the street, and he still hadn't completed his thought, it would be an irretrievable loss. Vangelia could wait, that radiance in her eyes would still be there for him tomorrow, but this was no help to him now in figuring out what he had to do to make the most of his day. Hence he had to take full advantage of the indefinite interim that remained to him. Were it a question of hard work or self-sacrifice, he would have known the answer. But by now, the day was already underway.

"It won't be today either ..." he thought despairingly.

Andonis had turned his back to Vangelia, watching as the light took hold on things, secretly hoping it would have a change of heart and turn back, or even just linger a while, thus granting him a small reprieve. All he needed was enough time to figure out where to begin.

"Andonis, turn over and let's talk. I have something important to tell you."

"Not now. I haven't got time. Anyway, nothing's more important than what I'm thinking about."

"But what if there is?"

"We can talk about it later ..."

Vangelia's eyes became clouded. She curled up behind Andonis' back, trying to retain that sense of springtime she felt diffused about her. The whole world had converged in the two rooms of her home, in whatever her eyes beheld. Outside, the courtyard was deserted as yet, though fragrant with Ismene's flowers. Spring soundlessly penetrated the shutters and cracks, spreading over her pillow, over the side of the wardrobe, over Andonis' brow and closed eyelids. Vangelia stroked his hair so lightly she might not even have touched him, but he waved his hand as if brushing away a gnat. Then Vangelia raised herself on one elbow, resting her chin on his shoulder.

"I have something to tell you ..."

"So tell me and get it over with."

But seeing his features harden, she changed her mind and broke off.

"So out with it. I haven't got all day."

"Have you noticed how sweet the flowers smell?" she asked him, because it came easier to her tongue.

This was too much for Andonis. He started ranting about how at critical moments she always came out with the most ridiculous drivel. She curled into a ball behind him and held her breath, like a naughty child hiding.

"So say it!" he shouted.

"When you calm down ..." she murmured.

"No – when I have time."

Andonis would have liked to take her face in his hands and, peering deep into her brown eyes, tell her straight out that he had been running himself ragged to no purpose, that all his splendid business efforts had only succeeded in wearing him out, that not one of them was solid enough to allow him a moment's rest. What could one possibly have on one's mind that was more important, more difficult than that? "I run around from morning till night knocking myself out," he wanted to tell her. "I never stop talking, never stop walking, chasing down thousands of possible deals – and at the end of the day what have I got? We could be evicted, I could even be thrown in prison. Imagine me going to prison for debt! They might even repossess our bed. Anything could happen. I don't even know what's in store for us today. And because anything's possible – even probable – there's still a chance we'll get lucky. That's why I haven't said anything. I couldn't stand to see you worry all the time. So for now I'll go on running myself into the ground and wracking my brains. At least if I were hit by a car and spent a couple of months in a cast, I'd have an excuse to sit and rethink things from the beginning. As it is, I never have the time. I need a loan: a time-loan. I'll steal it from you by telling you lies, and from other people by snatching it right out of their hands. That's what everyone does these days. Want to know something else? The highest interest rates are on loans of time. It's the most expensive commodity there is. (Not bad, that! But who's listening?) So, interest is a function of time – no, it is time. But what interest can there be on time, when time is life itself? It's not capital I need, it's time, and I'll pay any price to get it."

When Andonis opened his eyes, he saw Vangelia sitting looking at him from the foot of the bed.

"I think the first bus just went by," she told him.

"That was a truck, I heard it. Damn, why did I lose my watch? What are you doing up, anyway?"

Vangelia realized she would get nowhere by pleading. What she had to tell him had nothing to do with business. It wasn't something you just tossed out, as if you were spitting on the street. She had to catch him at a good moment, when he wasn't wearing that scowl. She wanted him to take full pleasure in the news. Now his eyes had closed again, and his lips moved silently, as if he were mouthing a prayer. Then he abruptly rolled over and plunged his face into the pillow.

A cart was going by on the street. Andonis noted that one of its wheels must have been broken, the way it hobbled along as if gnashing the asphalt with a single tooth. If the man pushing it were to count how many times the offending spoke struck the ground, he would find the exact distance he'd traveled – granted, of course, he knew the wheel's circumference (diameter times 3.14). But no, the man would calculate the distance he had covered, afterwards, by how much money he'd made. If your job was pushing a cart, you knew your work would be measured in terms of distance and weight. "That's the kind of work I'd like, something you can measure down to the decimal point," Andonis mumbled, and sank his face deeper into the pillow, annoyed with himself for wasting time on such trivial thoughts. Whatever takes up your time robs you of life. If Vangelia could only get that one simple notion through her head, instead of pestering him to talk.

Now day pressed in on all sides. The street had come to life, and everything seemed to be on its way somewhere. But Andonis was plagued by the thought of Yeoryiou's unpaid draft, which had come due. If his only concern had been how to fix things to keep his debtors at bay, he would be a common crook who played fast and loose with other people's money. But he had to pay it back. He wanted to make sure he never found himself wanted for debt.

Vangelia still sat watching him. It made thinking more difficult. Her wrinkled nightgown clung to her, almost as if she had nothing on. Around her head was a delicate line of light that wove through her fine, chestnut hair, then curved down around her neck and arms. If she were to join her hands, it would have formed a complete, enclosing circle. Vangelia, of course, had no inkling of what was going on with him, and her innocence served him as precious capital.

"What was it you wanted to tell me?" he asked her distractedly.

"Something ... Now's not the time."

"I agree, it's late already," he said, and his lips reverted to their mumbled calculations.

Suddenly someone started shouting in the courtyard. It was

Eftihis. Eftihis lived in the two next rooms, just before the passageway, with his mother and his younger brother. He was ordering them to clear out all of their things. The others refused, so Eftihis heaved out a couple of chairs, and an old framed picture that shattered noisily on the tiles. Then he furiously pushed out a table, and took all their clothing and covers and threw them in a heap. Mihalis, his kid-brother, came out half-dressed, Eftihis having yanked away his covers. Eftihis gave him a good whack on the head, and told him to stop whining, what he said went. Hadn't he been telling them for days to move their things out in an orderly fashion? It was time to give the place a good whitewashing, they were being buried alive in filth. But he must have had something else up his sleeve too.

With all the racket, Andonis couldn't follow his thoughts. He sprang to his feet in exasperation. Just his luck that that deadbeat had chosen today to do his spring cleaning.

"What time would you say it is, Vangelia?"

"Hasn't your friend fixed our radio yet? If we had the radio, we could ..."

"We should just buy ourselves another one," Andonis answered quickly. "That one's such a wreck, it'd be more to fix it than to buy another one. They sell these great little ones these days. Cheap too ... As soon as I get the chance ..."

Vangelia threw on a robe and went out to ask the time. She saw Eftihis, his face flushed deep red, still throwing things around. His mother was shrieking that she had never heard of anyone making such a stink over a little whitewashing. Vangelia went past them toward Ismene, who was again standing at the front gate. She stepped softly up to her and asked what time it was.

"Ten to seven," Ismene replied curtly.

"Could I pick two or three carnations from your pots?" Vangelia asked as she turned to go.

"You can pick them all, for all I care," said Ismene.

Vangelia didn't dare to pick any. Standing there in the passageway, all she could feel was how alone she was. In the courtyard, Eftihis continued to add to the pile. She caught a glimpse of Andonis at the kitchen window, bent over the sink splashing water on his face. How distant he had been as of late! Always worried and at such loose ends. He never understood what you told him, you had to scream if you wanted him to hear you.

Instead of going inside, Vangelia turned and tiptoed up to Ismene.

"Don't let that business with Angelos get to you," she told her.

Ismene gave a start. A spark of anger flashed in her eyes.

"And how do you know about Angelos?"

"I heard you asking Stathis about him this morning. You don't have to act like that, I wasn't eavesdropping or anything. You know, Andonis often goes away without telling me. If he loves you, there's nothing to worry about. Just be patient ..."

"What else did you hear?"

"What else? Only that you were worried and frightened. You have every right to be, but there's nothing you can do about it."

Vangelia started to leave, but hesitated again, and asked as simply as she could:

"Are you expecting a child? Is that why you've been so anxious?"

"What gave you that idea?"

"Well, you told Stathis you couldn't wait. If it was something like that, you'd feel a real need to tell somebody. That's all."

"Well, I'm not," Ismene said. "It'd be better if I were ... I haven't seen him in five years."

"I'm pregnant," Vangelia went on simply. "You're the first to know."

"What about Andonis?"

"I want him to be calm when I tell him. He's got so much on his mind these days, he's always on the run."

Her eyes lit up with a smile. There, she had said it, she had told someone. She looked at Ismene again.

"That's why I asked about the carnations."

But when she saw the same bitter and forlorn expression on Ismene's face, she again asked the time and went off, gathering up her hair with a sense of relief. In the courtyard, she saw Eftihis frantically pushing his mother's bed out the door, with its mattress and covers still on. His mother, bracing herself in the doorway, was trying to hold it back by the iron headboard. Just then Eftihis gave a grunt and pushed with all his might, as if to rip out the doorframe and dislodge his mother, who was wedged between.

"Hey, pull from that end," he shouted at Vangelia.

Vangelia gasped. She gently rested her hand on her stomach, asking:

"Are you talking to me?"

"Yes, I was. Give a pull from that end and help me get this thing out of here."

Eftihis' mother cast her a poisonous look.

"Come on," Eftihis bellowed.

Vangelia didn't move.

"Quit prissing around and pull."

"I can't. I'm not well."

Vangelia looked over at the window where Andonis had been washing his face a few seconds before, but he was gone.

"Come on, Vangelia," Eftihis said angrily.

"I told you, I can't."

"But you two can still ask for loans, eh? Pull on the bed, I need your help ..."

Vangelia stood paralyzed. She looked uncertainly at Eftihis, with his bulging eyes, and wanted to ask what he had meant by that, but at that moment Eftihis gritted his teeth and with a sudden jolt dislodged the old lady from the doorway, dragging her and the bed out together. Her hands, caught between the bed and the doorframe, had been skinned. Once out in the courtyard, Eftihis turned disdainfully to Vangelia:

"I don't need you now. And you can tell your husband I'm no dummy ... I know that when someone borrows from you, they help you out if they don't have the money to pay you back."

Vangelia went inside and found Andonis standing at the table, utterly absorbed in sorting through his briefcase. He had spread out all of his papers and calculations before him. He pretended not to notice her, and went on with his search. Then he set his briefcase on the floor, without having found what he was looking for, and began scribbling down a complex multiplication problem.

"Andonis, did you hear what Eftihis said to me?"

"Just a second, I'm in the middle of something," said Andonis, raising his palm to indicate she was not to disturb him.

"You mean you didn't hear him?"

"That'll be the day, when I start paying attention to Eftihis' family squabbles when I've got so many other things to think about."

While he went on pretending to be working, a hard knot bulged under his ear. His forehead – a network of swollen veins – was transected by a deep furrow that plunged between his eyebrows.

"So what was Eftihis shouting about?"

"Oh, nothing. He's just having another of his fights with his mother," Vangelia said indifferently.

"And there I was thinking ... Anyway, what do you expect with a bum like that?"

Andonis abruptly thrust back his chair and stood up, still avoiding his wife's eyes. He gently shut their door. Then he went over to the mirror and began combing his hair. That way he could watch his wife without meeting her gaze. He had never before lavished such attention on getting his part straight. He stood for some time with his face up against the glass.

Why was Vangelia silent? He looked in the mirror but couldn't see her anywhere. So did she know everything now? What time was it, anyway? If only the earth's axis remained at a constant angle to the elliptic, people wouldn't need watches to tell the time. He laughed aloud at the silliness of his thought.

"I'm not cut out for this work," he murmured to himself.

"What work's that?" came Vangelia's voice, like an arrow pinning him in place.

"You heard that? I said it out loud? Tell me what you think I meant by it. Out with it!"

"Only that you have too many worries and too much to do. You're worn out. What you'd like to have is work that's both challenging and regular ..."

"That's it! Not that I can't handle it, of course. I hope you realize that when it comes to work, there's no holding me back. All I'd like is ..."

"And all *I'd* like is not to be left by myself all the time."

"Just be patient. You'll see ... You have to understand, Vangelia, that in business you don't choose the company you keep. You get mixed up with all types. One guy robs you blind, the next curses you till he's blue in the face ... You just have to stick it out ..."

"Yes, I know ..." said Vangelia.

"Some day, Vangelia, I'll explain the meaning of time in the economic sphere. It just might be the biggest factor of all. You're making coffee? I thought we were all out. So, the time-factor plays a critical role. I'll tell you about it sometime ..."

"I have something else to tell you, too ..."

"Not now, though. Someday when we have more time to spare. If you don't mind ..."

Andonis mechanically got dressed and sat back down at the table, with the invoices, receipts and accounts spread before him. An old acquaintance of theirs, a sharp operator named Thodoros, had proposed that he try to sell a shipment of smuggled goods. It was the only sure means he had to get out of the hole on the interest payments for the draft, and earn an extension. Of course, the last thing he wanted was to become a salesman, especially of smuggled goods. But he would consider the ethical dimension later, on the bus.

He sensed Vangelia across from him, and broke off his figurings. If she brought up something to do with Eftihis, he would have trouble answering. He went back to rummaging among his papers.

"Do you know if anything happened to Ismene's friend Angelos?" he asked. "She was up and down the stairs all night. You don't think they ... I knew him, you know, he was a friend of mine. A good friend. Did Ismene say anything to you?"

"No. I just asked what time it was ..."

Vangelia went into the kitchen. Eftihis was still shouting in the courtyard, so Andonis crouched there, a prisoner of his own two rooms. He had to slip out without running into that deadbeat, that *saltodoros*, otherwise he would have no choice but to give him a piece of his mind ... And who knew what might come out of that loser's mouth? Imagine insulting a woman because her husband happened to owe you five drachmas, or five zillion drachmas. Besides, Andonis had given him his radio a few days before to cover some of the loan, but Eftihis had been less than overjoyed. "This old thing?" he'd remarked. Andonis concocted the story about having it repaired just to throw Vangelia off the track. But now she would be suspicious of any and everything, wondering what else he was keeping from her. She would make a mountain out of a mole hill, and worry herself sick, thus robbing Andonis of the peace and quiet he required if he were to think and act to good effect. Why had he remained glued to his seat instead of going out and giving the bastard a couple of good slaps across the face?

When Vangelia brought in his coffee, she leaned over him from behind. She was about to put her arms around him, but the instant Andonis felt her breath on his neck, he sprang up, grabbed his briefcase and shoveled in all his papers. He hurriedly stamped his cigarette out on the floor, and started for the door. Vangelia went and leaned against it, however, lest he slip out as he had on other days. But when Andonis saw her lying in wait, he remembered that he'd left his pencil somewhere. He ransacked the room in search of it, then shuffled around like someone with nowhere to go. He was afraid to say anything to Vangelia, because he knew that once he got started, there'd be no holding back: he would have to tell her everything. He went over by the door and shot a glance through the window to see if Eftihis was still there. The coast was clear. Vangelia stopped him to straighten his collar. Her hand being raised, she slipped it around his neck and leaned against him with her whole body.

"Let me kiss you," she said. He drew back.

"Not now. That was just back when I was at the company."

"Will you be home for lunch?"

"I don't know. Don't wait for me ..."

Vangelia stood aside to let him pass. When she looked down, her arms were empty. Andonis opened the door a crack. No one was in the courtyard. He waited a moment or two, then, darting out on tiptoe, jumped over Eftihis' things, and reached the front gate. There he paused. He looked up and down the street, as if deciding on the spot which way to go. Then he scampered off, as if chasing something the wind had blown out of his hand.

As the bus flashed past the narrow opening of the passageway, Vangelia saw only his leather briefcase, suspended over the heads of those clinging to the bus door.

AS SOON AS THE CORNER NEWSSTAND opened, Ismene rushed down to buy the newspaper. She had been doing it for years, and the man behind the counter had gotten to know her, and handed her the paper before even saying hello.

"A little early today, aren't we, Miss?"

Ismene took the newspaper and darted back in. Inside the

gate, she hurriedly scanned all the pages. Then she folded it up again and climbed the winding stairs that led to the kitchen. Harilaos, Angelos' father, awaited her as he did every morning. He wore his glasses, and sat ready in the designated seat. He sat up straight and began reading the moment Ismene spread the newspaper on the worn sprigged oil-cloth that covered the table. They skimmed each and every column, even the most trivial news items, to see if there was anything having to do with Angelos. In recent days, Ismene had been searching with particular intensity. She hadn't mentioned it to anyone, but she had noted some suspicious happenings: a man she didn't recognize followed her all the way to work, and there were often people watching the house. The previous evening, a woman living in the neighborhood, out of the blue, asked after Angelos. But everything was so fragile in that household, the littlest thing was enough to cause a major disturbance.

No one said a word while they read. Ioanna, Angelos' mother, sat wrapped in her shawl at the far end of the table. Every so often she would reach over to smooth out the pages, but she really just wanted to touch them, because for her the newspaper was, in some indefinable way, a daily letter from her son. Every morning Ismene lived in terror that the dreaded news would leap out at her. Still, reading the paper was the only way to learn anything – though any news would have been bad news.

Whenever her hand brushed that of Angelos' father, she felt instantly calmer, because he had a tranquil conviction that everything would ultimately return to its proper course. "It's a temporary aberration," he liked to say. "A mere digression ..."

Angelos' sister Lucia slipped soundlessly into the kitchen. She edged forward, her back to the wall, until she was standing behind her mother. Since her arrival five days earlier, she hadn't shown the least interest in their silent search through the papers. Ismene could feel her eyes coolly judging her. She had begun to wonder if there was still room for her there, now that Lucia regulated life in the household. A few days before she'd said, "We should keep the kitchen door locked," which was no doubt her way of expressing her displeasure at Ismene's right to come and go at will. But that was the least of it. She had been living out of town with her husband for years, and had forgotten that, here at least, certain routines still took precedence over her whims.

In the morning, everyone waited in suspense while the newspaper was being read. Every day began the same way, and nothing mattered until they were sure that Angelos' name was nowhere to be found. The house felt old, as if everything had remained exactly as it had been on that day in February 1947 when they read that Angelos had been sentenced to death. Seven whole years had gone by. The sprigged oil-cloth had more holes in it now, the pans and cannisters in the kitchen were black with grease, and Ioanna's hand had a tremble to it. "Read the small print, too," she would say. "Don't skip anything." "A real newspaper," Harilaos had once said, "shouldn't only tell what's happened, but what hasn't happened too, just so you could be sure. Sometimes what didn't happen may be even more important than what did." But what newspaper could assure them on a daily basis that Angelos was still alive? Lucia noisily opened a cabinet door, and started humming. Then she put the *briki* on the stove for coffee, keeping aloof of their daily ritual. A few mornings she hadn't appeared at all.

Once they had gone through the paper thoroughly – including the tiniest classified – Harilaos took his glasses off and said, with a note of relief,

"So good, there's nothing."

Then Lucia spoke up, as if she'd been waiting for that moment.

"How long are you going to keep up this ridiculous pantomime? Aren't you sick of it?"

"What did you say?" Ismene said in disbelief.

Ioanna immediately got up and closed the kitchen door so they wouldn't be heard in the next apartment. The ferocious look in Ismene's eye alarmed her. She begged Lucia to stop. But Lucia went on:

"I said you can't keep this up forever. You should just face up to the fact."

"What fact?" asked Ismene.

"That he might be in prison, or worse ... Whichever it is, you can't keep this up ..."

Her father gazed at her thunderstruck, the color draining from his face, as if confronted for the first time with something incomprehensible.

"I can't believe what I'm hearing ..."

Lucia flushed with anger, backing up to the wall as if wanting something solid behind her.

"Well, you should. Seven years is a long time ... He could have left the country, or maybe he's even been ..."

"Impossible," her father interrupted, preventing her from uttering the ghastly continuation.

"What makes you so sure?"

"Even if he's been arrested," Harilaos said calmly, "there's a standard procedure to follow. He would have the right to an attorney, he could file a caveat, he'd notify someone ... After thirty-five years as a judge, I know about these matters ..."

"What's probably happened," Lucia doggedly went on, "is that he's set himself up nice and safe somewhere, and has simply written you all off ... Would it have been so hard for him to get in touch, to send us some word after all this time?"

"She's right, Harilaos," Ioanna put in. "Just a word or two, some sign that he's alive ..."

"I'm sure he has good reason," said Ismene. "He knows better than we do what he should and shouldn't do."

"Nonsense. Name one good reason for him not to. You're just making excuses for him because it suits your purposes."

"What does?"

"To think he's coming back."

Ioanna started to cry. She cried at the drop of a hat. Lucia's coffee boiled over. Harilaos looked at them all.

"Angelos is all right," he flatly stated, "and he's going to come home. And I can assure you it will be sooner than you think ..."

"But, Father, you said that the day his trial was over ..."

"Well, I believed it then too ... But it's different now. Even if my efforts come to nothing ... Angelos is all right. There's not a doubt in my mind."

"That's exactly what I was saying," mocked Lucia. "He's so all right that he doesn't give a damn about any of you."

Ismene saw the malice flare up again in Lucia's eyes. Ismene's voice became unbearably hard as she asked her, her white teeth flashing,

"What are you so angry about? No one's done anything to you. What's it to you what we do, anyway?"

She stood at Harilaos' side and emphasized the word "we." Lucia had to be made to see that she wasn't one of them, she had no right to mock them.

"I wonder ..." her father said. "We accuse Angelos as if it were his fault. Since he's all right, all the rest ..."

"How do you know he's all right?" his wife demanded. "Have you heard something?"

"Yes, Ioanna, I know for a fact."

"So you've seen him with your own eyes?" Lucia let fly like a poisoned shaft.

"He wouldn't say it if he didn't have good reason," Ismene snapped at her.

"How about you? Do you see him?"

"Not once in five years ..."

"There's a fiancé for you! Suppose he's found somebody else? And here you are scouring all the papers!"

"That's my business. Does it offend you?"

"Offend me? You're the one torturing yourself for nothing," Lucia said with a shrug. "It's so romantic ..."

Ioanna was blubbering again. What were they doing fighting over her son? As long as he was all right, it didn't matter if he stayed in hiding for a hundred years.

"Ismene loves him," said Harilaos with suppressed emotion. "Let's just say that she's sitting in for him here. If they'd had a chance to marry ... This is her home, Lucia."

"If that's what she wants to believe, it's all right by me. No one's going to kick her out. But it's about time you people decided what you're going to do about this whole mess. And that goes for Angelos, too."

"Angelos can't very well decide what he's going to do. It's not up to him ..."

Interrupting her crying, Ioanna went over to her husband.

"You mean you saw him and didn't tell me?"

"Don't ask me to explain, Ioanna," said Harilaos. "It's a very delicate matter. Let my personal assurance suffice ..."

"Did you really see him?" Ioanna persisted. "Say something, for heaven's sake."

"Yes, I saw him."

They were all struck dumb. For perhaps the first time, Harilaos saw himself in the role of the accused. Ismene tried unsuccessfully to read what was in his faded blue eyes. Ioanna began wailing that no one ever considered her feelings, keeping her in the dark even when it came to her own son. "I'm his mother, after all ..."

Lucia went up to her father and peered into his eyes.

"Are you telling the truth, Father?" she said with a smile.

"I am," Harilaos replied without flinching. "I can't say any more. Just take my word for it, he's all right ..."

This satisfied no one. Ismene tried to discern where Lucia's outburst had come from, and why Angelos' father was trying so hard to persuade them that Angelos was all right. Prior to that moment, there had been no indication whatsoever that they were meeting, and Harilaos' interest in reading the newspaper hadn't flagged for so much as a day. On the contrary, he was always anxious for Ismene to say something optimistic, and had even sent her two or three times to see old friends or classmates of Angelos' when he found out where they were living. On the other hand, maybe he *was* seeing him. In recent days, he often disappeared from the house, and would return home strangely perturbed. He would sit for hours without saying anything. But his eyes never lost their luminous serenity.

"Tell us about my boy, Harilaos ..." his wife pleaded.

"There's nothing more to tell you ..."

At that, he opened up the newspaper to read it at his leisure, as everyone did when they wanted to find out what was going on in the world, without being fixed on a single burning issue.

Lucia chose that moment to start whistling. She put the *briki* back on to make coffee, and the saucepan to make tea. She took the newspaper from her father to see what movies were playing, then banged around looking for the sugar cannister.

"You're out of your minds, all of you ..."

Ismene could take no more. She braced herself against the back of Harilaos' chair and demanded,

"So what do you think? Is Angelos alive or not?"

"What's it matter what I think?"

"I'd just like to know," Ismene persisted.

"I don't know, leave me alone."

"You mean you really don't know, or you'd just rather not think about it?"

"Both. What's so strange about that?"

Lucia looked at them each in turn, as if inwardly mocking them.

"Is that how you spend your time around here? Asking each other what you think about Angelos?... Since he's written us off, I've done the same to him ... You're right, I don't want to think about him, I don't give a damn ..."

"That answers my question," said Ismene.

"Don't give me that, you poor creature. And with such a straight face!... What are you having, coffee or tea? You're not planning to go tell him what I think about him, are you?"

"I never see him ..."

"Oh, sure. You're all seeing him, you're just not telling me. I knew it from the moment I arrived. You think I'll give him away or something?"

Harilaos lowered his paper slightly to watch this unexpectedly rabid outburst on Lucia's part.

"But I'll find him on my own," she went on. "That's what I came to Athens for. This time I'll root him out, I don't care where he's hiding. I need him for something ..."

"That won't be easy, Lucia," said her father. "Not to mention rather dangerous."

She straightened her hair and gave her father a scornful smile.

"What I do is my business ..."

"You have no right," cried Ismene. "After all these years it would be horrible if something were to happen to him just because of your being so spiteful."

"So tell me where he is," Lucia demanded. "You know, Father, don't you."

"It's out of the question," Harilaos whispered, rattling his paper uneasily. "It's not my secret to divulge. I'm sorry, Lucia."

Lucia cackled, but her tone instantly changed.

"I've had it with all your stupidities," she said indifferently.

"So now we're stupid, just because we happen to think about someone ..." Here Ismene looked around, then very softly added, "... someone we love."

She checked to make sure no one had heard. Lucia sat silent and spent in the corner, as if her words had taken everything out of her. Her hand shook, spilling coffee on her saucer. Then she put everything down and went into the back room. What did she want with Angelos? Why was she always so tense when she talked about him? Harilaos opened the paper again and hid behind it, pale as death. "Apparently, when it comes to belief," he thought to himself, "the hardest thing is for humans not to automatically assume the worst." Ismene sat stricken with fear. Every time Angelos' name came up, she was terrified it would somehow curse him. For so many years they'd had a silent understanding not to say his name out loud. What did Lucia want with him? Not once since her arrival had she asked about him, as if she'd forgotten the other person who used to live there. Yet even the bed she slept in was his. Ioanna had insisted on keeping it made. When the sheets grew musty, she would change them when no one was looking. His books still stood behind the door, covered with a piece of cloth to keep off the dust. All his drawings were on top of the wardrobe, rolled up and bound with a string. There were, of course, no pictures of him in the house. Ismene had the foresight to tear them up – another precaution. Thus only those who loved him kept his image alive.

"So, Harilaos," Ioanna asked abruptly, "you still won't tell us anything?"

"Such as?"

"What harm could it possibly do him for me to know?"

Once again Harilaos kept silent, and his wife angrily pushed aside her coffee cup. Ismene pretended to be reading the paper. Ioanna demanded that she be told.

"I never say anything just for the sake of talking, Ioanna," her husband replied, without looking up. "You of all people should know that. During my entire judicial career, not once did anyone find grounds to question my credibility. So let me assure you one more time: Angelos is all right."

Nothing could diminish the thick anguish that had been building up in that house for years. All their strength had crumbled away, leaving only dust to remind them of how old everything was. Surely the house looked different from the outside, too: its facade wrinkled, its roof sagging – like some ruin from the war no one had bothered to fix or tear down. The landlord had reclaimed the front rooms that looked out onto the street. He locked the frosted glass sliding-doors in the middle and confined the family to the back rooms, saying they didn't need all that space now that Angelos had left and Lucia had gotten married. Now they could only use the winding stairs in back that went up to the roof. It was better that way. Turned toward the inside, people would see and remember them less. They just had to keep their voices down when discussing certain crucial subjects, lest the strangers living next door overheard.

Harilaos lay the newspaper on the floor and stepped lightly into the back room. He had learned to pick out the sound of muffled crying, which was a regular feature of the house. He found Lucia lying face down on the bed, a handkerchief clenched in her teeth.

"You must think that ..."

"I didn't say anything, Lucia."

"Did anyone else hear?"

"No. Relax ..."

Lucia bit her lip, trying to stifle her sobs. It would only give Ismene satisfaction. Harilaos stood above her, as if waiting to perform an autopsy on an especially intriguing case.

"Leave me alone," Lucia managed at last. "I don't need any of you."

Harilaos went back into the kitchen. Ismene was bent over the paper. The two of them were able to talk more calmly. As if taking up where he had left off, he told her:

"In just a few more days I hope to have assembled all the evidence needed to establish his innocence in any courtroom in the country. Then he'll be able to request his own caveat. As a former judge, I still believe in justice ..."

"And I believe that he's alive," said Ismene.

It was time for her to leave for work. She'd be reported as late again, and things at the office were tight as it was.

"Be extra careful if you're planning to meet him anytime soon. I've noticed some strange goings-on in the neighborhood ..."

"I have to speed things up. We must be prepared for any new development. This afternoon I will be meeting that material witness I told you about. Thank you, Ismene ..."

Lucia appeared at the door, her eyes red. She grimaced at the sight of her father and Ismene conferring in undertones. Not this again! Would they always be carrying on in whispers and nods, shutting her out altogether?

Ismene hurried down the winding stairs. Seven years was a long time. The flowers filled the courtyard with their sweetness. "I'll wait for him," she told herself.

NOW THE DAY WAS IN FULL SWING. Out on the street, windows had been thrown open, people were on the move, trucks barreled past loaded with boxes and sacks, tires squealing on the asphalt ...

Eftihis cast a disdainful look at the beds, the rickety tables, the scattered clothing and rags they had collected over the years. It had been a mere half-hour's work – hardly worth all the fuss. Then he strolled through their two empty rooms, going from one end to the other because he liked how his shoes sounded on the bare boards. He examined the walls and the cracks, ran his finger over the windowsill, and scowled when it came away caked with cobwebs and dust. He looked all around, as if gauging something, then started walking again, bringing his heels down even more loudly. His mother came and stood across the room, trying to catch his eye, but Eftihis avoided her gaze and shouted out to his kid-brother Mihalis to drum up a bucket someplace and go fetch some whitewash.

"Get with it. Suddenly all you guys want is to loaf around dreaming the day away. I'm telling you, come hell or high water, this place is going to get whitewashed. I want the holes patched, the whole place fixed up. You can't set foot in here without the worms and cockroaches eating you."

As they just stood there staring at him, he made them a proposition.

"I'll pay you. So go on, do what I told you to."

His mother sat back down on her bed, looking wretched, as if she'd been tossed out on the street. But what do you want, old ladies always found something to get upset about.

"I'll pay," Eftihis repeated. "How much would a woman charge if I had her come in and mop?"

"What are you up to?" asked the old woman

"You'll find out soon enough. Right now I just want us to whitewash. Have Mihalis patch the holes first, then sand it down. He'll manage ... And I want you to mop the floors and to wash the windows. That's woman's work, right?"

But his mother just sat there lost in thought, her arms clasped around the headboard of the bed.

"If you make this much noise about whitewashing a house, I can't wait to see what you're like when it comes to building one."

"I'll do that some day, too," Eftihis was quick to respond.

He put on his coat and, without realizing what he was doing, found himself at Vangelia's door. She was sitting in a chair with her hands laying open in her lap. She looked at him in fright.

"Pardon me," he told her. "I said some things I shouldn't have earlier. Old ladies can really get to you when they set their minds to it."

"Does Andonis owe you lots of money?" she asked him simply.

"You still thinking of that? I know, I can be a real bastard when I lose my temper. I always tell myself, Eftihis, you have to control yourself, but I never manage to. All I wanted was you to help."

"How much does he owe you?" Vangelia repeated her question.

Eftihis saw the color rising to her cheeks.

"Now I've gone and upset you ... What a shame – you looking so pretty today and all."

He laughed when he saw her surprise. He leaned in the doorway, adding mischievously:

"Or do you think your being pretty means you can turn your nose up at a neighbor when he asks you to help?"

"I shouldn't be lifting anything heavy ..."

"Are you sick?"

Vangelia again asked how much Andonis owed, but she looked so sad and lovely that Eftihis couldn't bear to worry her any more than she already was.

"What's the big deal? I'm in business, too. Sometimes I owe him something, sometimes he owes me. He must have really been mad this morning ... I'm a stinker, all right!"

"He wasn't here," Vangelia stammered. "He left early today."

"I have respect for Andonis," said Eftihis.

"Why won't you tell me how much he owes you?"

"Hold on, you're making me dizzy ... No more money questions!"

Vangelia started to say something, but Eftihis had already gone back into the courtyard, where he kicked over an old stool.

"I ought to just throw this stuff out," he told his mother.

"Why?" the old lady asked uneasily.

Eftihis regretted saying more than he'd intended. Aliki and her sister Urania came out of the front downstairs apartment. Eftihis greeted them almost chivalrously. He couldn't take his eyes off of Aliki. She was a tasty number, all right. And Urania always smiled when you said something to her. She had snow-white skin, and her eyes were big and round.

"So tell me, girls, I didn't scare you with all my shouting, did I?"

Aliki smiled at him meaningfully, as if to say she was in on his secret. "You're not going to escape my clutches," Eftihis thought to himself. "Some day when I get you alone ..." He had been saying that for a long time now, but what with all the worrying and running all over town he had to do, he never had a chance to appreciate the beauties around him. But it was downright stupid to let a girl like that – from his own courtyard no less – run around with a joker like Pericles. Just because he rode a motorcycle, and was always showing off.

"Taking the bus by any chance, girls? I'll keep you company if you are."

"No," the two girls said.

"Too bad ..."

When they were almost to the front gate, Eftihis asked Aliki:

"Is Pericles coming by tonight?"

"He said he would."

Eftihis immediately shouted to his mother, who was standing helplessly in the middle of the courtyard:

"Leave everything there till I get back. Have Mihalis do the walls, and you scrub the floors ..."

He opened the gate and let the girls go out ahead of him, then slammed it shut.

CHAPTER 2

THE GATE CREAKED WHENEVER anyone went through it. If it was someone in a hurry, they'd push it hard, and the sheet iron would clatter against the wall. Later in the day, when everyone was awake, the gate remained open and the courtyard quieted down.

Eftihis raced over to Monastiraki, as he did every morning, to meet his people. For years they had been setting out together from an old warehouse and hitting the streets, selling whatever merchandise happened to come their way that day. But street-peddling had become trickier, you had to be a real pro if you wanted to sell knitwear one day, combs the next, undershirts, pens, plates, whatever. They had to dash madly from corner to corner, wracked with anxiety, to somehow make enough for all five of them.

His friends were waiting at the door to the warehouse. He counted them even before saying hello, and noted the absence of a certain brunette head. Once again, Elpida hadn't come. They immediately asked what he'd set up for the day. Eftihis raised himself to his full height.

"Nothing," he informed them.

The others fixed their eyes on him in bewilderment and disbelief, then exchanged looks. Before they could speak, however, Eftihis went on:

"We're taking the day off. I'm hunting around for something better."

"You should have told us," Simos said. "Now our whole day's shot."

"You couldn't find anything to sell, or you just didn't feel like it?" asked Iordanis.

"I'm working on something better," snapped Eftihis.

"So why don't you let us in on it?" Fanis said.

"In other words, until you find this 'something better,' we're out of a job?"

As he gazed at the three men standing before him, they began to look more and more like a whole mob of people – their heads all but welded together, their eyes – thousands of them – staring back at him. If they started going over it now, it would only make for bad blood, without accomplishing anything. So as not to leave them with their doubts amid that uneasy whispering of eyes, Eftihis announced:

"Whoever wants to is free to set out on his own."

"So we won't have any way of knowing whether you feel like it or not," Fanis muttered. "It'll all depend on your mood. You want us to ask you every day?"

"Supposing I got sick ... Did I ever promise you I'd always be healthy?"

"Cut the bull," Simos said angrily.

"Maybe it's just time we made a clean break."

A peculiar silence followed Eftihis' words. All at once their heads were no longer so close together. Each went his separate way, and began pacing the half-dark of the empty warehouse. Its roof gaped; shafts of sunlight fell between the beams. Assorted odds and ends had been abandoned here and there: market carts, unsold merchandise stored under tarpaulin, cardboard boxes. Big puddles formed whenever it rained, and the place smelled of mold. Eftihis' three partners continued to follow their diverging paths, each sunk in his thoughts. Apparently the crazy bastard had fixed himself up somewhere else and was dying to get rid of them. He sounded like a boss who wanted them to get down on their knees and beg for a job. What was that "something better" of his? If he was really on the level, why wouldn't he tell them? No, it was clear he'd lined something up for himself on the sly, and now was telling them they could go cut their throats for all he cared. For three years they had been on their feet nonstop, gasping for breath, run ragged by fear and the need to chase down a few measly bucks. But their greatest fear was to be at the mercy of some slob who jerked them around whenever it suited him.

Their silent pacing started to make Eftihis uneasy. He almost made a nasty remark, but thought better of it.

"So you want me to look for somebody else when I get my business going?"

"Easy, friend," said Fanis, whose eyes were always as red as open wounds. "What's that supposed to be, a threat? Why not just tell us straight out that you want to end our partnership here and now?"

Eftihis nearly clobbered him for that one. Reining in his anger, however, he calmly told them all:

"Can't you give me one measly morning? Let's just say I'm asking you as a favor. This could be the break we've been waiting for."

Then, since he had nothing concrete to tell them should they ask, he began to act as if he were in a hurry, anxious to get moving on that better deal he had promised.

"So, see you here tomorrow," he told them on his way out.

In the doorway he stopped again, and stood looking out on the narrow street with its old shops, as if waiting for something. Those bastards didn't believe him. If only Elpida were there. But to escape the sounds of mute shuffling behind him in the warehouse, he went to the coffeehouse next door, which had two or three tables out on the sidewalk. He grabbed a chair at the farthest one, and sat gazing down the street. But soon Fanis came and parked himself next to him.

"So, is this what your big hurry was all about? Couldn't wait to plop yourself down here?"

"I just got tired of looking at you all," Eftihis answered. "Next thing you know you would have been asking me to compensate you for your lost time."

"We should have," Fanis told him. "It's a waste of a day. But, hell, what do you expect from dopes like us ... Once I get work in textiles, you'll see. I've got a skill, you know, I'm a knotter. You don't think I used to go around selling lottery tickets on the street, do you?"

Fanis saw that Eftihis was unimpressed. As if he even knew what a knotter was. Fanis stayed there next to him, the two of them looking off down the street. He spat, then nudged Eftihis with his elbow.

"So, what's your plan? You're holding out on us."

"Like I told you, I'm working on something better."

"That's a lot of bull, Eftihis, and you know it. You just want to keep us quiet. I think you're fixing up something just for yourself."

"It's for all of us, I told you."

"I don't buy it."

"I mean it, it's for all of us. On my life!"

"Bullshit ..." Fanis drawled, his dry mouth filling with bitter saliva.

That did it for Eftihis.

"Are you calling my life shit? Do you know what you just said? *Your* life may be shit, because you never once had to put it on the line. But just ask me what I had to go through to be sitting here in one piece today."

"All right, all right, calm down," Fanis said. "I didn't mean it that way. But why won't you tell me what you've got up your sleeve?"

"Because it's my idea, and if I told you guys, you'd just start pissing and moaning and spoil it for me. I know how you guys work ..."

"Fine. So at least tell me who you're waiting for now."

"Elpida," said Eftihis. "Of course none of you wondered why she hasn't showed up in three days."

Elpida was the girl who worked with them. You always needed a female around – someone to pretend to be buying something, to keep an eye peeled for the cops, to make sure people paid. Eftihis had had more than a few arguments with the other three, trying to get it through their thick skulls that Elpida was indispensable in their line of work, and deserved full wages. What did they do that was so much more important? He even warned them to keep an eye out for her, to watch their filthy mouths around her and keep their hands to themselves – or they could kiss their asses good-by. They all sniggered over that one. Eftihis swore at them. "What, you can't have a woman in the same room as you without turning into pigs?" But yell as he might, none of them doubted for a moment that he simply wanted the girl for himself. The fact was Elpida offered little to their operation. She wasn't as slick an operator as some of the women out there. She would look at you with timid eyes, speak in a whisper, and for all the times they had seen her smile, her laughter was like a wilted flower. But she could spot danger coming, and wasn't easy to fool, and she kept a sharp eye on the customers. Eftihis liked knowing Elpida was somewhere nearby. No one had ever seen them spending time outside of work together, or noticed any funny business. Eftihis always addressed her in a friendly manner, without ever getting syrupy, and he never chewed her out as he would if she were his girl. Hence no one had dared to suggest that Eftihis was dragging his girl along and giving her a full cut of the take, just because he knew the others depended on him. Once, when divvying up their earnings at that very table, Simos had ventured the complaint that it was time for Eftihis to stop wringing Elpida's share out of them. Eftihis had brought his fist down hard on the marble table-top, spilling their wine and water glasses. "That's it," he'd shouted. "We're through!" Luckily, Elpida wasn't there, or she would have been upset. Eftihis could imagine nothing worse than seeing Elpida cry.

"What have you guys got against me?" he asked Fanis now.

"Nothing, it's just you've written us off."

"We're square, aren't we? Don't I always make sure there's something for us to sell?"

Fanis put his hand on Eftihis' arm and regarded him fixedly. It wouldn't have been half so bad if his eyes weren't as red as a rabbit's, or if he didn't suck his teeth that way every so often.

"Be honest, Eftihis. Why do you go so far out of your way for Elpida?"

"I've known her since we were kids, I was best friends with her brother."

"And where's this brother now?"

"He got killed. Why?"

"Just wondering."

Eftihis sprang to his feet.

"Is there something between you two? Speak up."

"What if there was?"

"Then you better tell me. Go on."

"Tell you what?" Fanis said evasively.

"Why this sudden interest? And don't try hiding anything from me either. Otherwise, I'll ask her to tell me in front of you."

"Don't go doing anything as dumb as that. There's nothing between us."

"Well, anyway, I'll find out."

"That'd be a dumb thing to do. You'd just upset her. I give you my word ..."

"You love her, though," Eftihis said sternly. "That's obvious enough. But you don't touch her, you don't so much as talk to her or get ideas without coming to me first. That girl is ... Never mind what she is ... Understand? I don't care if you go along with it or not – what I say goes in this."

"Just don't say anything to her ... Please ..."

"You don't really think I'd help you out just because you're chicken, do you? If I said something to her, it'd just make it that much easier for you ..."

Fanis stopped sucking his teeth. Eftihis got up to go.

"See you later. And don't forget what I said. Don't let me catch you trying anything behind my back."

He went down the street and checked both ways to see if Elpida was coming. He wanted to see her. He had a whole slew of things to take care of today that were more problematic than selling a few undershirts on Stadiou Street. His mood turned gloomy at the thought that something might have happened to her. He would have felt better had he known for a fact that somebody – even Fanis – was truly in love with her. He thought how bitter the spit in Fanis' mouth must be. If he were to kiss her, she'd have to wipe her mouth instantly. What a shame she would have to put up with that rancid taste.

He wandered for a while, killing time on the streets. He'd never really done it before, walking along as if he were simply out on a stroll. The world was a lovely place, all right, when you didn't have a pile of scarfs and pens to sell! And it wasn't bad being alive, either, just being able to see and to breathe.

Eftihis slowly strolled along. At Ayia Irini he remembered that Phillip's shop was on a sidestreet nearby. During the war, Phillip had sold currant-cakes in Vathi Square. Later a goldsmith took him into his workshop to teach him the trade. Phillip used to steal small pieces of gold by swallowing them, then taking castor oil when he got home to help them come out. He messed up his intestines in the process. It hurt like hell, and he ended up having an operation for it later on. Once he was in a panic because, despite the purgative, he hadn't found a gold chain he'd swallowed days before. "Imagine if they bury me with that gold inside me!" he told Eftihis. He'd become skin and bones, and could barely walk. One evening, Eftihis went by the workshop and they left together. As they were quietly heading down to their neighborhood, Phillip's pace quickened. He had a stomach ache and wanted to get home on the double – if he used some other bathroom, he'd lose the gold. There were tears in his eyes from his effort, and he finally set off in a mad dash against the clock.

Now Phillip picked up unclaimed jewelry at pawnshop auctions. Some of them he would just melt down. Others he would put in velvet boxes and sell door to door.

Without beating around the bush, Eftihis asked what the gimmick was. Phillip became coy and evasive.

"Hey, cut the rigmarole and just tell me flat out. Is there money in it or not? I want to know."

"You got capital, there's money. Gold goes by weight, it's not made out of air."

"So how much does it take to get a business going? I'm expecting some money."

"How much?" Phillip asked.

"How's a hundred sound?"

"If you've got a hundred in cash, you can buy enough to make five. Everybody wants gold these days, because even if there's a war, you can melt it down and sew it into your underwear."

"Yeah, you're right, it doesn't lose its value," Eftihis remarked. "But what do I know?..."

"You don't have to – that's what I'm here for. You'll pick it up soon enough ..."

"I'll think about it," Eftihis said.

"What's there to think about? There's no mystery in gold. It speaks for itself. Look, you just rub it against this black stone, add a bit of juice from this bottle here, and there you have it. Of course, the customer doesn't come in carrying scales and little bottles. If a girl likes a piece of jewelry, you can sell her bronze and she'll still be crazy about it. A piece of jewelry is worth whatever a customer wants to pay for it. That's where a salesman proves his worth – by knowing how bad someone wants to buy a luxury item, and what he's willing to fork out for it ... Besides, now the war's over, everyone wants a ring or bracelet of their own to show off, or maybe they're getting married, or buying a present, or they've got a girlfriend. And so you get them smack dab between the eyes – never for less than double its value. Then there are the others ... Someone who's killing something he loves isn't doing business, he's asking your help. So you buy it from him at less than half what it's worth ... But what are you giving up working the streets for?"

"I'm just tired of it. I want a sure thing, something I don't have to be worrying about day in and day out. I don't want to go to my grave still making the rounds."

"So come hook up with me," Phillip suggested. "If I'd had any money during the war, I'd have my own shop by now. You remember back then?... There was that friend of ours, too. Kostis, wasn't that his name?"

"Right. A German truck ran him over."

"He had a sister, didn't he?"

"Elpida. She works with me now."

"Remember how you used to tell me I should come truck-hopping with you? Some truck would have probably run me over too ..."

"But look at me, *I'm* alive!" said Eftihis proudly.

"So you were lucky ..."

"You know, I think about it every time I look at Elpida. It's no small thing, being alive ... But what would you know about it ..."

Eftihis took hold of a gold chain with a rosette in the middle, held it up with two fingers. He asked Phillip:

"How much is something like this?"

"You really interested?"

"Sure."

"Don't be a dope, buy her gold-plate. All women care about is making an impression."

Eftihis irritably let the necklace drop, and headed for the door.

"In your book, everything's a fake ..."

"So, Eftihis, what do you say? Are you going to put up some money?" Phillip asked impatiently. "Gold's good business ..."

"I'll get back to you," answered Eftihis, as he gloomily went out the door.

He asked a lot of people, but still couldn't make up his mind. If his plans bore fruit, and he suddenly found himself with money to burn, he had to know what to do with it, he didn't want it just wasting away in his pocket. He went all over town. They were all *making* things. And Eftihis cursed his clumsy hands, that had never mastered a practical skill. The fact is, he was all thumbs when it came to such things. If he'd only had time to learn a trade, he wouldn't have to go around asking for anybody's help. Scratching his head, he answered them all the same way: "I'll think it over and let you know." Before anything else, however, he had to make sure about the money.

Once again the movement and noise of the street drew him on. There was nothing finer than being able to stroll along without a care in the world, making up plans for yourself.

On Athinas Street, he paused to watch the street-hawkers. A bus thundered right past him, and came to a stop a little farther on. He took off running and caught it. He got off at Thision. A few blocks more and he was at Mary's door. He whistled and waited. A girl's head, with short curly hair and pimples on her pale white face, popped out of a window.

Eftihis put his hands on his hips, cocked his head, and took a few steps back to get a better look at her. Mary smiled to let him know how pleased she was that he'd come by to see her so early. But Eftihis kept right on considering her with his probing eye, as if to establish the value of an unknown quantity. "She's going to be my wife," he thought to himself, which brought on an odd feeling of wonder. "My wife ..." It was still early, he was in a hurry, Mary was smiling, and he didn't have a chance to form a clear opinion of the girl standing at the window. It wasn't easy getting used to the idea that someone was going to be your wife ...

"Why aren't you saying anything? What did you want?"

Eftihis just kept looking at her.

"Are you coming in?" she asked.

He shook his head.

"Are we going somewhere? Just a sec while I get dressed ..."

"We're not going anywhere. I just came by to let you know I'm going to see your dad tonight ... Do whatever you can so we can get this over with."

"What should I tell him?"

"Just give him a hard time ... A little weeping and moaning never hurt ... Or you know, tell him how you love me and can't live without me ... How happy we'll be together ... Old folk go for that sort of thing."

"But I ... All that's true for me, Eftihis."

"I didn't ask you if was true or not. Just say it. It'll be up to us to find out later what part of it's true and what isn't."

"Why are you talking like that?"

"I'll catch you later. Do like I said. Hang tough with the old guy, and let's get this business out of the way ..."

"Will I see you tonight?"

"I don't know, I'm pretty busy ... See you."

ANDONIS WAS THE FIRST ONE out of the elevator. He sprinted down the front steps, waved at someone he knew from afar – of no economic interest to speak of – and plunged back in among the crowds in order to get to the bank before it closed. Who had time for small talk anymore – "How's work, how's everyone at home?" – now that each hour rode hard on the next, now that the clocks ticked on and life was measured by what you had managed to accomplish in the bump and grind of useable time. Everything else was a dead loss. He still had not had a chance to properly and systematically think through how to proceed. For the time being, he would have to follow the frantic foot-race imposed on him by his business affairs.

He ran from Omonia to Syntagma, then over to Customs – was it possible there could be so many mindless nit-picking officials in the world? – then to the Revenue Office with its rickety stairs, the Ministry, the electrical supply store, then by his customers. He had talked his mouth dry, and worked his brain raw with numbers.

Then he remembered that he had to make a call to Loukis. Contacts with people who had close ties to major business ventures were useful. He stopped at the first newsstand with a telephone.

"I didn't wake you, did I?" Andonis said quite naturally, as if recognizing the other's right to sleep until noon. I'm at the Stock Exchange, looking into that matter you asked me about."

The street noise kept him from catching everything on the other end.

"I'm gonna need you," Loukis shouted encouragingly into the phone. "That deal with the group of investors is coming along ... I'll need your help ... You've got some terrific ideas."

"Terrific, eh?"

"It's a real opportunity ... Maybe later this week."

"I've got other good ideas too ... I'll come by so we can discuss ..."

"Not today, though ... I'll be expecting you."

"So they liked my ideas?"

The phone clicked off with a "'bye" and Andonis wiped his forehead contentedly. His briefcase suddenly felt lighter in his hand. All around him, like a swarm of bees, buzzed the hit-and-miss speculators of the Exchange: ignorant, sly little creatures who fed on the fringe of supply-and-demand, jingling a few gold coins in their palms. These poor scavengers scattered at the first gust of wind, without ever suspecting the economic forces they served. That business with Loukis was another promising prospect. A group of capital-holders were interested in making some profitable investments. Loukis was in thick with them – women, late nights, fancy cars. But Loukis only knew how to dance with the ladies and make conversation in the salon, which is why he had enlisted – quite wisely, too – Andonis' aid. And so Andonis went around making inquiries and getting facts, laying the groundwork for a financial partnership with unlimited horizons. It took hours of explaining before Loukis understood how the affair should be handled. In the modern world, the trick was to set up and manage business ventures with other people's money. "Organization is the flip side of skill," Andonis thought, going up the front steps of a building.

It was fortuitous he had thought to stop by. It gave him a chance to drop in on Sotiris, the tailor. Three months earlier he had left some fabric for a suit, and he still hadn't had a chance to have his measurements taken. Andonis paused on the stairs to catch his breath. "I'm always waiting for something, but I haven't yet defined what it is," he thought to himself, as he went down the dimly lit hallway with its doors and its signs. "Maybe success will come easier once I figure out what I'm aiming for. I must accept the fact that I'm still only at the beginning, in order to give myself the right to wait for things to come to fruition" – a shrewd thought, to be sure, like a dose of tonics "to help my legs put up with all my running around." But his knees suddenly went weak as a new thought stung him: "What if this 'beginning' lasts forever? A beginning that drags on indefinitely, without a follow-up, is sure disaster ..."

He hastened into the tailor's. Sotiris was arguing with a thin schoolteacher, a regular of his. The teacher was maintaining that he had suffered more during the war, because he had spent two and a half years in Dachau. Sotiris, a fifty year old with white, bristly hair, was regarding him with scorn, because in his view no camp had been worse than Haidari.

"Tell him, Andonis, what we went through ..."

Andonis was still standing in the door with his briefcase at his side, waiting for them to finish their curious debate. How was he to judge which had suffered more? It wasn't a question of justice, it wasn't something you could measure.

"Why don't you say something," said Sotiris, flushed red with anger. "Tell him how nice it was to wake up each morning, waiting to hear your name called ...."

Still Andonis didn't speak, and Sotiris, incensed by his silence, glared at him. "Say something ..."

"Forgive me," said the teacher, "but the air was filled with smoke from the ovens ..."

Sotiris pleaded with Andonis to answer, lest he be forced to heap more curses on this old fool who was trying – of all things – to pass off his suffering as greater than his own.

"The smell from the crematorium ...." the teacher murmured.

"I'm not saying another word," Sotiris thundered. "My friend Andonis is here, and I'll let him tell you. We were in the same barracks."

Andonis went over to the bench and told them:

"The war's been over for ten years now, and you want me to tell you who suffered more? I came to get a suit made ..."

The two men stared at him furiously. The look in the teacher's eye as he left expressed the vast gulf separating them. Once they were alone, Sotiris became even more vehement.

"So you've forgotten it all, have you? The mornings, and the hard-labor, and the list of names, and the machine-gun outside the walls? Have you also forgotten that time you went nuts and wrapped yourself in the covers so you didn't have to listen to it?"

"I'd like you to make me that suit ... I need it," Andonis said dryly.

"So you've forgotten everything?"

"Come on, take my measurements, I'm in a hurry."

Sotiris sputtered and wheezed, unable to find words to curse either Andonis or the teacher as they deserved.

"I thought he was my friend, that's the thing. I even bought him coffee everyday ... And you – you didn't say a word. As if you'd forgotten the whole thing ..."

"I haven't forgotten anything," Andonis said softly. "Now come on, let's get going ..."

He stood admiring himself in the mirror. Being constantly on the move from one business meeting to another took the polish off one. Andonis tried to shape his mouth into a smile, aware that dust, numbers, and the ceaseless pursuit of hope gave one a desperate look. "I've been letting my appearance slip lately, which is inexcusable for someone who spends his every waking hour seeking out new clients and making deals," he thought, and asked Sotiris to get his suit made without delay. "I've got an important meeting coming up ... This week, maybe next ..." He looked himself over again. "Could I trust someone who looked like that?" he wondered. "Would I invest in his ideas?"

Sotiris began taking his measurements while Andonis described the type of suit he wanted.

"I'd like to request you to use every ounce of your skill. I don't want it to look overly fastidious. The trick is for it not to smell of petty bourgeois hardship, as if it were my one and only good suit, the one I keep in the back of my closet and only get out on Sundays. But also I don't want it cut to the latest fashion. Men of taste always follow the preceding one. It should be comfortable and well-made, without looking fussy. And I don't want something that, say, a factory-owner would wear. Have you got all that? It's not for formal meetings. It should look like it's something I wear every day. Like just one of my suits ..."

"I understand," Sotiris said somewhat guardedly.

"And of course I'll pay you as soon as I get the chance ... But

I'd like it to be exactly as I described it ... What, say, a financial consultant would wear, or a ... Would you like me to give you a breakdown of the social, economic, and class-standing of the individual it's intended for?"

"You mean it's not for you?" asked Sotiris dubiously.

"Practically ... I want it for a particular occasion ..."

Andonis, knowing how much his friend liked hearing such things, began explaining that a new social stratum was being formed – namely, of technical managers, specialists, financial consultants. Capital had become invisible, faceless, the conveyor of it no longer participated in the production itself. Now it was expressed via people who understood the workings of the economy ...

"I've heard tell about it ..."

"Step on it, I'm in a hurry. So, that's the kind of person I want it for. Any questions?"

Sotiris, who had shared a blanket with him at Haidari, took his measurements. On other visits they had discussed the international situation, exchanging overviews, forecasts and conclusions. Today they had nothing to say on the subject. Andonis was in a hurry to get his unusual suit. He already owed money for the material, and now he would owe money for the tailoring ... They would discuss political developments another day.

"I'll come try it on tomorrow. I need it by this Saturday."

Soon Andonis was back on the street. "There are innumerable ways to exploit the conflicts inherent in the economic system itself," he thought as he wove among the shiny new cars. And he didn't mean swindles and scams, but legitimate means, on the up-and-up. Somewhere in all this must be the break he was looking for. Once you spotted it, it was yours for the taking. Opportunities abounded, but everything was hazy as yet, like the galactic nebula. And yet that diffuse light consisted of billions of bright stars – 150 billion, if he wasn't mistaken. Of course, it was the savvy operators that attracted the really big deals, the way honey drew flies. "I'm not there yet," Andonis thought to himself, "but it's only a matter of time."

AS THE DAY PROGRESSES, THE STREETS change in appearance,

like living faces. Different people brush past, but the same river of asphalt follows you, encircles you. You are nothing but a moving point in a moving world, whose rhythms remain hidden.

In order to determine his own trajectory, he had to plot the movements of everything around him. But why was it that, for all his mastery of the science of economics, he had such trouble uncovering the secret – indeed, was in danger of being eliminated by the very economic laws he had studied? How was it that so many others seemed to have cracked the code? And if it was something definite, like the solution to a mathematical equation, then it wouldn't have been a secret, there would have been a formula that everyone knew. This should have been the case, but it wasn't. But these thoughts cost him dearly, they were a certain loss, a disaster waiting to happen. He couldn't even sort out all the factors involved in his own problem, there on Aristidou Street, plagued as he was by the memory of the outstanding drafts, the money he owed Eftihis, the time he was wasting, Vangelia – who knew yet didn't know – and finally himself, with his plans reproducing themselves endlessly, while the flames of panic lapped around him.

From one angle, the protested drafts could be seen as a sign that he was in some way dependent on the system, caught in a web of interlocking interests, and thus not a wholly isolated individual with nothing to offer but ideas.

The streets had been overrun with apartment buildings – he had foreseen that too, in '48 – with refrigerators, radios, beautiful women, people on the go. In the capitalist system, everyone wracks his brains trying to figure out how the next guy makes his money. If you don't pay off your debts, it's prison. This was an ancient law, in existence since the advent of private ownership. "Just you wait and see. If I go to prison for debt, everyone'll start looking up to me," he told himself with a chortle. A few days before, a certain shark had confided in him – as if revealing the secret of the atom bomb – "If you want any special favors, find out who the boss' girlfriend is." "But that's blackmail, fraud!" Andonis had responded in disgust. "Boy, are you underdeveloped!" the other had said, erupting into contemptuous laughter.

Andonis raced onward to get to some ministry or other before it closed. He stopped in at two or three shops to put their tax forms in order, knocked on doors – ever wearing a smile – to collect payment, met with potential clients, and generously handed out advice ... Then he remembered Vangelia. She was still so unformed, and so full of tenderness ... She truly believed that he was doing something worthwhile and productive ... He would have to educate her, but not yet, it would be too much, too soon. Once there was light at the end of the tunnel ...

He went by an importer and was paid for some complicated matter he had taken care of down at Customs. He counted the money with considerable pride, and felt instantly lighter on his feet. Now he would be able to think through his options with a certain amount of clarity. The streets ran in straight lines, people had "things to do," the system still managed to function in the unity bestowed on it by the chaotic conflict of its individual cases. "I'm a 'case' myself – and a rather common one at that," Andonis reflected, and decided to spend more time analyzing his problem, once he managed to save up some peace of mind.

AT TWO-FIFTEEN, HE ARRIVED PANTING at the coffeehouse in Omonia where he was to meet Thodoros. He hesitated out on the sidewalk, however, for he saw Thodoros talking to an elderly gentleman. He looked at himself in a shop window, and tried to assume a calmer air. People with merchandise – even smuggled goods like Thodoros' – conducted business from coffeehouses or plush armchairs in their offices. They had no respect for sweaty salesmen. Andonis circled the sidewalk a few times, because the person talking to Thodoros looked familiar. He got a better look at him through the far door. It was Angelos' father, the retired appeals judge living in the front house. Thodoros was eyeing him mistrustfully, his bulging eyes pulling him down into a stoop. The judge was discussing a very grave matter, you could tell by his demeanor. "Just think, this man used to pass judgement – the hardest job in the world," thought Andonis, studying the judge's calm demeanor. He wondered what had become of Angelos. He went down to the newsstand and read the headlines of the afternoon papers. He exchanged no more than a brusque hello with Angelos' father when they happened to meet at the front gate; it wouldn't have been wise, for any number of reasons, to let the other find out that he had close business dealings with an ex-collaborator like Thodoros.

Andonis walked back to the coffeehouse. Harilaos had risen, and was taking leave of Thodoros with utmost courtesy. The latter was looking at him with glazed eyes, as if unable to make things out. Then the judge went out, glancing behind him on the street as he bought a paper.

The coffeehouse was buzzing with noise. Andonis went up and stood before Thodoros, even tapped him lightly on the shoulder, because there was no doubt in his mind that otherwise he wouldn't see him.

"Sit down," Thodoros ordered him, "and don't say a word."

Andonis sat down, drank a glass of water that was on the table, and contemplated the large, blackened paintings in gilt frames that adorned the walls. One was an old-fashioned idyllic landscape in which a shabbily clad, lightly-stepping, and sickeningly romantic lass was scattering flowers from a basket. Mercifully, cigarette smoke, dust and flies had coated the canvas. The waiters shouted unnecessarily, loafers and gawkers wandered in and out. Thodoros seemed to be watching something that was taking place far away, and Andonis didn't dare ask how long that silence was to last. He studied the next painting – animals drinking at a river – then a gentleman on a couch reading his paper. But sitting there was a complete waste of time. Who knew when and if Thodoros would clear up the muddled thoughts that occupied him. Once again the newspapers were filled with stories about bombs, and nuclear wars, and crimes, and deceptive economic policies, and new security measures. Nevertheless those unsettled times of theirs, that rolled by without history, like some dreary Middle Ages, were brimming with profitable business opportunities.

"Well? Did you decide to take the stuff today?" Thodoros asked abruptly.

Andonis, not having an answer ready, hemmed and hawed while he thought of how best to begin. When, for perhaps the first time in his life, he drew a blank, he quickly opened his briefcase and drew forth a piece of paper with figures on it.

"I did a thoroughgoing analysis of the job," he said.

Thodoros took the sheet of paper, and without further ado tore it to little pieces. Evidently something was eating him. In any case, was a detailed analysis of a job involving smuggled goods really necessary? Andonis hadn't thought of that. Unnerved, he began frantically gesticulating, trying to explain everything all at once.

"Maybe that analysis wasn't the best idea, but it's nevertheless indispensable. Everything, no matter what, needs to be systematized, to be put in some kind of order. I wrote down the prices, the demand for each item, the discounts ..."

"Why are you acting like an idiot, Andonis?"

"The marketplace isn't some gypsy fair. You have to be familiar with prevailing conditions before making an investment. The import business is a science unto itself."

"The stuff's waiting. What I need is someone who's going to move it, and move it fast – not an economist."

"But I'm not a salesman," Andonis said. "You need someone who knows, someone who follows the market ... I have a few ideas ..."

"I got it," Thodoros said sharply. "You've got moral qualms ... You don't like that it's black market ..."

This humiliating characterization was like a slap in the face. The buzz of the coffeehouse roared in Andonis' ears. Everyone was talking, talking and bargaining.

"No, Thodoros, no, I swear. My reluctance has only to do with cold calculations, believe me. Everyone has to look out for himself ... I'm trying to develop a good credit rating out there ... Call it a trust-rating ... Take you, for example. You offered me this job because you knew I'd sooner be hanged than ..."

"In other words you refuse ... Just say it ... In business, it's gumption, not heroism, that counts ..."

The buzz in the coffeehouse swelled. The bags sagged under Thodoros' eyes. Andonis had to keep himself from paying Thodoros back in kind, calling him a traitor, a collaborator who'd licked the boots of every last invader, who'd sold his hide to the highest bidder ... He kept his mouth shut, however, for he was a businessman in the broadest sense of the term. No matter how much abuse Thodoros heaped on him, it would have been unwise to alienate a promising client. He looked at the people around him, the blackened paintings, the filthy, fly-crumbed chandeliers, the cigarette smoke and the seconds rising and disappearing, the glasses coming and going, Thodoros' bloated fingers lying on the marble tabletop like lifeless pieces of meat.

"An old appeals judge who was just in here was saying something along those same lines ... how I should 'consult my conscience ...'"

"About some business deal?" Andonis asked, burning with curiosity.

"No, something else. He said he knew in his heart that my conscience ..."

"But I wasn't asking you to do that," Andonis protested. "I was only saying that you needed someone with ideas and insight, someone to follow the market and study shifts in the economy ... That's all I was saying, Thodoros ..."

"So are you taking the job or not?"

"It's not in my interest ..."

"Why'd the company fire you, Andonis?"

"What's that got to do with it? If I'd wanted to stay, it would have been the easiest thing in the world. It wasn't for misuse of funds or incompetence."

"You mean you consulted your conscience, like the old man ..."

"If that's how you choose to view it. It was a personal matter ... Imagine spending your whole life as an accountant. These days," Andonis went on bravely, "I make a living by the services I render. It's not a matter of being compensated for things done under duress ..."

"Who do you think you're talking to? You're just a salesman up to your ears in debt, running around from store to store ... When they stick you in prison ..."

Suddenly the coffeehouse fell silent, the paintings disappeared beneath the thick grime of the walls. Water sparkled in glasses, people gestured soundlessly, opening and closing their mouths out of habit. Someone bumped Andonis going by, almost knocking him from his chair. "If you think about it," he said to himself amid that overwhelming silence, "my reservations are not entirely of an ethical nature. With so many outstanding debts and protested drafts, it would be monumentally stupid of me to compromise myself further in a deal involving smuggled goods. Besides, even if I work myself to death, it'll never be enough to satisfy someone who thinks he's degrading me by calling me a salesman." He reached into his pocket for a handkerchief, and touched the money the importer had given him earlier.

"So, have you talked it over with your conscience?" Thodoros asked wryly.

"It's not in my best interest," Andonis answered. "I know full well that the nature of merchandise doesn't change just because some tariff or other hasn't been paid."

"So what's the big problem?"

"I'm working on something else that looks promising ... There's a group of venture capitalists ..."

Thodoros tuned out Andonis' talk of the profitable investments he was lining up. His eyes were glued to the door, but he seemed to be watching something hard to make out that was taking place far away. Then, as if he could sit still no longer, he got to his feet and guided his lumbering body through the clutter of chairs.

"Think it over. I'll be here again tomorrow," he said over his shoulder.

Andonis remained seated, awash amid buzzing voices and bustling people. Yet the deal with the smuggled goods did represent a chance to clear up the mess with the overdue drafts. When he realized that he had spent more time in the coffeehouse than was justified by what was after all only a minor perplexity, he gulped down a glass of water and was back on the street. No matter how beat you were, sitting down was an unforgivable luxury. That much, at least, was beyond dispute. The deal had fallen through – all else was immaterial. And he quickened his pace so as not to be late.

CHAPTER 3

THOUSANDS OF PEOPLE walked down that street, yet nobody's walk resembled his. Shading her eyes, Ismene fixed every passerby with a gaze sharp as a hawk's, hoping to discover some familiar trait. The winter sun warmed her body and glinted in her coal-black hair. The street was a busy one, it started miles and miles away, at the very edge of the world. Those who made it this far were sure to be headed somewhere; one by one the side-streets, the doorways, the shops swallowed them up.

Aliki, the pretty girl living in the rooms up front, had just gotten back from work. On the way home she'd joked with the tobacconist, flashed a smile at the young men in the coffeehouse, waved across the street at a girlfriend.

"Waiting for someone?" she asked Ismene as she breezed in through the gate, humming to herself.

"No," Ismene stammered.

The people waiting out on the sidewalk for the bus were calm, clean and orderly. "For people all over the world," she was thinking, "every hour of the day had its own rhythm. We're the only ones who never managed to move on; for us, it's as if the war never ended." Ismene knew it was a waste of time to wait there at the gate, but she still didn't move. It was nice to think it *could* happen, even though she knew it wouldn't. Apart from that, however, she wanted to see what was going on in the neighborhood, to keep an eye out for anything suspicious. Somewhere in that huge, boisterous city, with its thousands of doors, its numberless windows, its pedestrians and mute walls, she knew that Angelos existed, besieged by danger and fear. For he was never alone, there was always that inexorable threat hanging over his head. They had become one. If anything ever happened to him, she would learn of it. Bad news travels fast. Angelos was alive, but she knew nothing about him.

As soon as she got back from work, she went upstairs and asked Lucia if Harilaos had come home. Lucia answered, with as little interest as possible, that no, the old man hadn't shown up yet. Lucia had to make them understand that she couldn't care less about all their clandestine carryings-on, so long as they let her be. Ismene never knew what to say to her. A bit later, however, Lucia made it clear that she'd put their morning flare-up behind her. Couldn't they talk about something else for a change? She invited Ismene to sit down, and asked if her work tired her out.

"Don't all those numbers make you dizzy? What made you decide to go work for the company?"

"I had no choice. It was the only thing I could find ..."

"But you used to love to draw, I remember."

Ismene was at a loss. She looked around the room, at the covered books behind the door, the frazzled straw of her chair.

"Stay and have dinner with us," Lucia all but implored her.

Angelos' mother was worried. Harilaos was later than usual, he hadn't even said where he was going.

"Do you by any chance know where he went, Ismene?" she asked.

"He's around some place, he'll be back," Lucia said. "Do we have to start wringing our hands about *Father* now?"

Lucia was wearing a tight-fitting dress and as she spoke, she cast sidelong glances at herself in the mirror. She straightened her body, then arched her back and took a mincing step with her hands on her hips. She'd been away for years, that's why she'd changed so much. But even when she was living at home she never really spent time with the rest. She didn't have the same friends, didn't laugh at the same jokes. She'd start sulking over nothing, then go off by herself or lock herself in her room.

"Aren't you going to wait to talk things over with Father?"

"Well, it's only that ..."

"Why don't you get your hair cut short, like everybody else these days? You'd look better with it short."

“I don’t know. I never gave it much thought.”

“Oof, everybody’s gotten so serious around here. Were you always this way?”

What more was there to say?

“Hey, why don’t we go to the movies?” Lucia suddenly proposed.

“I can’t. I have to ...”

“Come on,” Lucia persisted, “it’s a musical. I didn’t come to Athens just to sit around at home. You people are worse than out in the country!”

As Ismene went back down the winding stairs, she could hear Lucia singing. There was a certain doggedness to her voice, as if she were doing her best to keep up a perky tune.

The scarlet sun was hammered in place at the end of the street. If Angelos were truly all right, and simply wasn’t concerned whether Ismene worried about him or not, it meant that he no longer cared. Maybe Lucia was right after all when she said that he’d forgotten them all. Ismene’s face grew hard. It was as if he’d told her he would meet her there without fail, and she was angry with him for making her wait. She felt an impulse to shout at the people walking past, asking them what right they had to look so calm. They were all against her – the pedestrians, the cars and the people in their houses, the newspapers and coffeehouses – they were all part of a mute and savage Nature, since they permitted and even contributed to the darkness that engulfed her. Now the afternoon winter sun made her shiver. Evidently she would have to wait forever, just like during the war, when she was in utter agony until she heard his footsteps, his key turning in the door. Then wondering when he would send word from the mountains, or whether he would find somewhere to hide and to sleep. Ismene had loved him ever since she used to go upstairs, notebook in hand, to have him work out her geometry problems. Once she even kissed him instead of saying thank you, when he had solved an especially difficult one ... Later, when they met once in Faliron, while Angelos was in hiding, he told her: “I want you to hear this, and to believe it: I love you with all of my being.” But why did he think it necessary to remind her of his love that night? Did he believe Ismene loved him any less? “No need to say it, or even to think it.” It’s just something that is, like the green of a leaf, or the weight of a rock. One afternoon before the war, Ismene and Angelos were watching a solar eclipse through smoked glass. How quickly that dazzling, savage darkness had spread. The birds and the neighborhood dogs were frightened, you could feel things tremble at some approaching end. Angelos put his arm around her and she huddled against him in fear. "What if everything just stood still, and it stayed like this?" she asked. "That could never happen," he solemnly informed her. And when the sun reappeared in its entirety, and the world took on its old aspect, Ismene clapped her hands in delight and Angelos gave a loud laugh. "What did I tell you?" he said with a certain pride, as if the resumption of life were his own doing.

There were a lot of garages, warehouses and metal-works in the area that made use of blow torches. At the coffeehouse across the street, the games of backgammon had already begun. A tall man in a felt hat had been standing at the corner with his eye on something for quite a while. The bus collected the people waiting at the stop. At the lumberyard on the first cross-street, they were sawing up logs. An incessant whine rose from the chainsaw, you could feel its steel tearing through the wood. Its myriad teeth whirred round at high speed, turning red-hot as it sundered whatever crossed its path. The cut of that snake-like blade was straight and sure. The truck rumbled past, loaded with lumber. A young man reading the newspapers pinned up on the side of the newsstand suddenly frowned and walked away, as if wanting to put distance between himself and something he had read. A young girl in a checkered dress darted off after making a quick call at the counter. The tall man was still there at the corner.

EFTIHIS STORMED IN FROM THE STREET and told his mother to hurry up and get him his dinner. But the old lady just sat there on the bed in the middle of the courtyard, her fingers wrapped around the iron headboard, and made no move to carry out his command. Eftihis could see where her hands were scraped from the fracas that morning and felt mildly ashamed, until he decided the old woman's obstinacy was as much to blame as anything. He told her in a loud voice that he'd been running around all day and was dead tired.

"You seem to have forgotten that you kicked us out," she said.

"Are you telling me there's nothing to eat?"

"All you told me to do was clean the place up. Go see for yourself – it's clean as a whistle."

Eftihis was beginning to lose patience with her hard-headedness. Just because he wanted to give the place a thorough cleaning, did that mean she had to glower at him through the iron bars of the headboard? Her face was all bones, just like her ravaged hands clutching the bars.

"What are you staring at me like that for?" he demanded.

"I'm just trying to figure out what you're up to."

"You too?" he said, throwing up his hands. "Everyone keeps trying to get me to tell them what I'm up to. You of all people, Mother, should be more understanding. Why didn't you fix anything to eat?"

"When I asked why you had to go and toss all our things out here in a heap, you told me it was just to clean the place up, as if I was some gullible child ..."

"You mean if I'd told you what my plans were you'd have made us dinner? In other words, you're starving me as a form of punishment."

"This morning you asked me to clean house, as if I were someone you'd hired off the street. When people have a cleaning lady they make it their business to feed her. I know, I've been one."

Eftihis felt an impulse to start smashing things. You just couldn't talk sense to old people. When it came right down to it, he expected his family to be willing to do him a favor without making a big stink. But a few moments later he sat down next to his mother, and talked to her more gently:

"You think it's me I'm concerned about? I could live on chicken-feed if I had to. It's no big deal. I should have brought something for us to eat from the grill. If I yelled at you just now, it was for your sake ... You went hungry just to spite me, you started panicking just because I ..."

Before he could finish, he dashed inside to inspect the walls.

"I don't like the color," he said when he saw it. "Did you see it? – pink! Pink walls!"

"Mihalis thought it would look nice. He did a good job."

"Tell him to do it over again. He should throw a bit of ochre in next time to get rid of the pink. And look, it's all streaked and runny ..."

"He did a fine job," his mother repeated.

"I want it to be nicer ..."

He stretched out on the bed that stood in the middle of the courtyard. He closed his eyes, folded his arms on his chest, and lay still. But a moment later he sprang up and asked for his nice white shirt. The old lady still refused to stir. He went through the trunk himself. When he found it, it was all crumpled up, and he let loose a stream of curses. Jesus Christ and Mother of God, this wasn't a home, it was a national disaster. He nearly tore it to shreds, then remembered he didn't have another one. He bunched it into a ball and pounded on the kitchen door of the apartment in front. Aliki poked her head out and was startled by how agitated he was.

"Aliki dear," Eftihis said in his sweetest voice, "be an angel and run an iron over this for me, will you? Just here along the front, and the tips of the collar. That's no big deal, is it?"

Eftihis noticed her smile at him as though she already knew what he wanted the shirt for.

"I've got somewhere to be tonight," he added, looking down at the ground.

Aliki took the shirt from him.

"You're a sweetheart ..."

The good-natured girl closed her door with a smile on her face. Her sister Urania was waiting for her inside, and they instantly burst into giggles. Urania took the shirt to do the ironing herself, and Aliki stood before the mirror and combed out her hair. Occasionally she'd steal glances out at the street, toward the corner coffeehouse. She still couldn't see Pericles' motorcycle parked on the sidewalk. It was early yet, and nobody goes on dates while the sun's still up. Aliki would be going for a ride with Pericles again tonight. How she loved racing along on the back of his bike! She held on to him tightly, her arms wrapped around him. The wind whistled in her ears and whipped through her hair as she huddled down behind him. Sure, he acted tough, but he was considerate, and always took her home when she asked. He was courteous too, clean and well-groomed, not like the other men at the coffeehouse. He had supposedly gotten a good deal on the bike, and would have to scrimp and save until it was paid off. "But who cares about the money, the important thing is that you like it," he had said the other day, on their way back from Dafni.

Her sister was ironing the shirt with great care. At one point she even appeared to be stroking the fabric, across the chest and under the arms.

"Before long he'll have a wife to iron his shirts for him," Aliki said with a note of finality. "He won't need any of us." She continued combing out her hair. Urania stared at her in the mirror.

"Eftihis is getting married?" she asked.

"Sure. That's why he's been making such a fuss out there," Aliki answered simply.

"How do you know about it?"

"Pericles told me. Just you wait, he said. Eftihis will end up getting hitched to Mary."

"That tall girl with the pimples?"

"That's the one. She may not be much to look at, but she's got a good body – or so Pericles tells me."

"And how does Pericles know what kind of body she has?"

"He just does. They broke up when we started going out together."

"And what about Eftihis?"

"Don't worry, Pericles told him everything. Don't feel you have to go and let the cat out of the bag ..."

"Why should I care who Eftihis marries?" said Urania, pressing down on the iron. "If he still wants to marry her, that means he must love her."

"That must be it," Aliki said evasively.

And she went on to relate how Pericles came to tell her about it. A few days before, they had gone to a forest in Dafni on his motorcycle. When they got there, Pericles pulled his bike off the road, and they continued on foot under the pine-trees. When they had gone a ways, Pericles leaned his motorcycle against a tree, which freed up his hands; he'd been pushing the bike up till then. He spread a newspaper on the ground and told her to sit down, putting his arm around her waist. But it had rained, and Aliki was wearing her good skirt. They walked on a bit. Aliki was cold. She didn't sit down. She's quite sure of that, she remembers it all perfectly. Pericles didn't insist either. He was pushing his motorcycle along again. Just before they reached the road, he pointed to another tree and said, "It was under that tree that ..."

"That what?"

"One night," he said, "Mary and I sat down there together ..."

Urania let out a shriek.

"And did you sit with him under the same tree?"

"We were just walking," Aliki protested. "We didn't sit down anywhere, it was too wet. Plus he was pushing his motorcycle the whole time. Careful or you'll burn his shirt."

"Look at me, Aliki ... Tell me the truth ..."

"The truth is we didn't stop anywhere. I was cold and I told him I wanted go."

"And then?"

"And then we got back on his bike and came home. All I could see was his back. I was huddled down out of the wind. When he let me off down the street here a ways, he was grouchy. 'Get off here,' he told me. 'And next time ...'"

"And you're getting ready to go out with him again?" asked Urania with fright in her eyes.

"I'm not like Mary. Besides ..."

Eftihis knocked on the window and yelled,

"What's taking you, girls? It's not like it's my Sunday suit. You don't have to go putting creases in it."

Urania carefully held it out to him, without daring to look him in the face. She only saw his hand as he reached for it.

"I hope it's all right ..."

"Couldn't be better! It's just I didn't want it looking like an old rag."

He quickly threw it on right there in the courtyard and again sternly warned his mother not to move anything back inside until he returned.

When Urania went back into the room, she stopped short and looked in alarm at Aliki's hands, which were gently moving the iron back and forth over her good skirt.

"You're not going to wear that tonight are you?" she asked.

"Why not?"

"But it hasn't rained today, the ground will be dry ..."

Aliki looked out the window toward the coffeehouse on the corner. Pericles' motorcycle was nowhere to be seen.

"Say what you like," Urania said, "but I think Eftihis is all right. He's marrying that girl because he loves her, even though she ..."

Urania brought her face up to the window that looked out onto the passageway. She motioned Aliki to come over. Through the slits of the closed shutter they could see Ismene's dark head leaning against the inside of the gate.

"Is she crying?"

"She's such a grump," said Aliki, and went back to her ironing.

The two of them agreed that Ismene made herself miserable out of some quirk of character. Maybe she even enjoyed it. She worked for a large company, got paid a regular salary as an accountant. She claimed she hadn't seen her fiancé in years, but no one believed her ... She was right, though, that way no one would track her to his hide-out. It was anyone's guess where they met ... The judge's son was that tall partisan who showed up one day with a thick black beard. He shook with laughter and practically pulled your hand out of its socket when he shook it. But that was a long time ago. Of course they saw each other on the sly, and no doubt he loved her. Buy why did her eyes always look so desperate? Why was she always so upset?

"So are you going to Dafni again tonight?"

"I don't know," Aliki answered meditatively.

ISMENE GREW WEARY OF WATCHING the street and the people on it. The chain-saw buzzed more sharply now. More people had collected at the bus stop. Hereabouts there was always the sound of wheels and pinions turning, of men hammering iron and doing auto repairs. The whole neighborhood had been transformed. "What's happened to all our old friends?" Ismene wondered. Most of them had left, some had simply disappeared, and if you ran into them you didn't even say hello, you weren't sure whether they would remember you. "Everyone's taken care to bring their corner of the war to a close. But what about us, who are already so far behind? How can we make our own little peace knowing Angelos' life is still endangered? Come to think of it, how many times has spring come in all these years?"

Angelos' father turned the corner. He strode up to the gate

and whispered into Ismene's ear:

"I have some important news ..."

When they entered the courtyard, Eftihis' mother stood up and stopped them before they could climb the stairs.

"Did he have any right to throw us out into the courtyard like this, Mister Harilaos? You were a judge for so many years, tell me what you think. Did he have any right to do that? He didn't even give us a good reason."

"Which bothers you more," Harilaos asked. "Finding yourself out here, or not being given a good reason?"

"Shouldn't he have told his own mother what he's up to?"

"So it would have made a difference to you if he'd confided in you?"

"He simply ordered us to do what he said ..."

"You have every right to be upset," the judge said. "But since you've already done what he wanted you to ..."

"What could we do, he's the one who threw all this out here. Did he have any right to do that?"

"It seems that nowadays we've come to believe that people have the right to do whatever they can get away with."

"If you were the judge, what would you decide?"

"Your son believes he has the right to make his own decisions, and you're right in wanting to know his purposes. But for you to sit out here makes it look like you're obeying him. Be patient and he'll tell you what he intends to do. He has no other choice."

Eftihis' mother wasn't satisfied with the judge's answer. With confusing speeches like that they cast people in prison. Angelos' father took leave of her and gingerly climbed the stairs, as if he were afraid of wakening someone.

"Did he have any right?" Eftihis' mother shouted from below. "Tell me, did he?"

The judge smiled at her and went into his house, while the old lady, fuming, plumped back down on the bed in the middle of the courtyard.

Lucia was about to leave to go to a movie.

"Don't go yet," her father told her. "Have a seat. There's something I want you to hear."

His wife was uneasy and asked if anything bad had happened. Harilaos informed them with obvious joy that he had found the man upon whom Angelos' life depended. He had been seeking him for years, and had finally met with him today at a coffeehouse in Omonia Square.

"He's the only one who gave evidence against Angelos. The decision was based largely on his testimony. He's a government insider who collaborated with the Germans economically, possibly even as an informer. Now he's a merchant who's involved in all kinds of odd business dealings. He listened closely to what I had to tell him, he didn't remember anything ..."

"And what did he say?"

"He said he'd think about it. I'll be seeing him the day after tomorrow. I'm certain I can convince him."

"That doesn't mean anything," his wife put in.

"You're mistaken, Ioanna. He personally had nothing to gain by lying. I laid everything before him and I gathered he had no real objections. Others put him up to it. Once he's talked it over with his conscience ..."

"And if you convince him?" Lucia asked.

"I asked him to withdraw his testimony. If that happens, Angelos will no longer be in danger. He could even appear in court. We'll enter an appeal ..."

"And he'd be able to come home, Harilaos?"

"Most likely, Ioanna."

"You guys are living in a fantasy world," Lucia blurted out sarcastically.

Her father instantly froze, then dropped exhausted into his desk chair. Lucia looked at them all with a certain satisfaction, as if pleased her words had hit home.

"I'm bored. I'm going to the movies ..."

Her father pretended not to hear. He drew his son's brief – in its familiar faded bluish folder – out from its drawer and with great concentration began to read through an old typewritten sheet of paper. Soon the kitchen door slammed, and Lucia's high heels clattered down the stairs. What did she have to gripe about? She had her husband and her own house and the right to live however she liked. "I consider myself a guest here, so let me know if I'm getting on your nerves and I'll leave," she'd said the other day, even though she was the one who seemed to be annoyed by the least little thing. She hadn't mentioned her husband once, as if there were no other person in her life. She had married out of the blue, shortly after Angelos' conviction, as if she'd been waiting for that before making up her mind. She married someone none of them knew, a teacher at a high school somewhere in Macedonia. She brought him by one night, he had a talk with her father, a week later they held the wedding, and three days after that they left for Xanthi. The following year she wrote them a couple of lines from Karditsa, then from Komotini. "I'll just be staying a couple of days," she said when she arrived, then quickly added, "If you'll have me, of course ..." Her mother, nonplussed, took her small bag from her. An hour later it was as if she'd never left. Her old sullen air, as if she were holding something against them all.

"I can't help thinking it'll be like the trial all over again, Harilaos," Angelos' mother said. "Someday you'll have to acknowledge that you were wrong ... It's a good thing the boy didn't listen to you then ..."

"We've said all there is to be said on that topic, Ioanna. Must we rake over the coals?"

"But you were convinced then too that he would be found innocent. You even said he should appear for the trial," Ioanna persisted.

Harilaos explained that it was different now. "If that fat man with the bags under his eyes comes through ..."

During the trial, Angelos' father had also believed that he had taken the appropriate steps and was convinced his son would be acquitted. He had sought out the judges, who were former colleagues of his, and told them: "I'm not asking for any special favors. Judge him as your conscience sees fit. I believe in his innocence, but you must render a decision without outside interference." He returned home that day proud of himself, and informed the family, "It's the most honorable thing I could have done. If I had discussed the case with them, I would have been acting like a common trial lawyer defending his client, whereas this way I put Angelos' life before them as a guarantee of my belief in him and a standard for their consciences. It's not an easy thing for a father to do. Those judges know me, they'll draw their own conclusions." He was even of the opinion that if Angelos were there in person, they'd have had even more reason to acquit him. Ismene, who was seeing Angelos at the time, communicated his father's view, but

Angelos didn't appear. It would have been suicide. At the trial, his father remained out in the hall throughout, lest the judges think he was trying to influence them. To the very end he believed that they would make his case an exception. The decision was handed down well past midnight; Harilaos returned home crushed. He tapped on Ismene's window. "I was wrong," he told her, and crept up the stairs like a burglar. They agreed to tell Ioanna his trial had been postponed pending additional evidence. They even hid the newspapers hoping she would forget the whole matter. Lucia read the notice, however, and started screaming. Something between weeping and rage. Thinking they'd already executed her son, Ioanna fell stricken. Ismene raced over to Stavros' house, where Angelos was hiding. There she was told that he had high-tailed it first thing that morning, as soon as he'd read the verdict in the papers. She didn't see him again for a month. She found him at Aunt Evanthia's house. Angelos was *afraid*! During that period, he moved between four or five houses, all belonging to friends and colleagues. At the time, no one thought the witch-hunt would last. With the passage of time, he grew bolder, and they would occasionally meet. Almost two years went by like that, full of uncertainty and frantic activity. Toward the end he was staying with Manolis, in Marousi. One day he didn't show up at their meeting place. Nor the next. Ismene went to the house and it was all locked up. She went back two or three times, but still no one answered. Finally a neighbor told her they had all gone away. She hadn't seen him since.

Angelos' mother again asked Harilaos to explain the importance of his meeting that afternoon.

"Oh, it's important all right. Extremely important. You'll see."

His optimism hadn't convinced Ismene either. That bothered him most. If Ismene lost hope, all would be lost. "The fact that a young girl is still waiting for him means that he'll be back. If Ismene had the slightest doubt, she wouldn't base her whole life on the idea of his returning ... Isn't that proof enough for you, Ioanna?" he'd said to his wife some time before. That's why he often peered deep into Ismene's eyes. He wanted to know what was going on inside her. "But why is it," he wondered, "our children are so shorn of hope that they have to look to us old folk for support?"

The setting sun, burning red and gold, fell full on Harilaos' face. His deep blue eyes were shining.

"I'd also like to establish that when I assured the judges of his innocence, I wasn't asking them to do me a favor ... What do you think? Tell me the truth."

"He'll be back," Ismene pronounced with conviction.

"You're right, he will. That came from your heart, Ismene. Thank you."

HARILAOS QUIETLY SET OFF from his house. His even gait carried him in the direction of town. Ismene left soon after, as if she were simply going to the corner store, or someplace nearby. She tailed him, careful not to get too close. The late afternoon was sunlit and quiet. Before going out, Harilaos had been strangely agitated, though he'd tried to hide it. He had taken a long time getting ready, and kept looking at his watch. He had gone through his desk drawers, and removed some papers from Angelos' brief. Then he counted the money in his wallet, and asked Ismene if she'd noticed any suspicious movements around the house.

The whole way Ismene, with as casual an air as possible, watched to make sure no one was following either of them. The judge never glanced around or altered his pace. With the streets as crowded as they were, it would have been impossible to spot anyone suspicious-looking. Ismene regarded with resentment all the people who were able to walk around at large, without a sentence hanging over their heads. Thousands of days had already gone by, and who knew how many more would pass in exactly the same manner. There had been thousands of buildings built, but Angelos had yet to build a single one. It didn't matter if he never built one, as long as he just survived. It didn't matter if he'd forgotten that some place there were people who loved him, as long as he was safe and at peace and free of care. When Angelos left to join the resistance forces in the mountains, Ismene was still wearing her black school pinafore. She met him on the stairs the night he came to bid farewell to his family. They set out in silence. What was there to say? They moved along the dark streets with difficulty, as if the night were a material they had to rip their way through. After they had gone a ways, Ismene couldn't stand it anymore, she threw her arms around Angelos' neck, stricken by the immense burden she felt weighing on her the whole way. They said nothing; all was understood. They kissed in the shadow of the warehouse behind the station. When a German truck rumbled down the next street, Ismene had clung even more tightly to him. She lost all sense of time. Then she said, "Good-by," and loosened her grip, because she knew that he had to go. From then on, he would be on his own. She stood watching him go, until even his shadow was gone. The taste of that kiss stayed with her throughout that hot summer – the summer of her high school graduation, and of the mass demonstrations.

Angelos' father crossed Patission Street. He looked at his watch again. Ismene could feel the sensation of that kiss welling up in her even now. What if she were to meet him tonight? When Angelos came back from the mountains, he had a dark tan and a full black beard. Then too she'd flung her arms around his neck. During those glory days of cheering and flags and songs, they had walked the streets together and Ismene, filled with wonder and yearning, realized that what she was feeling must have been what people called happiness. One day, they spontaneously began skipping and prancing along the street. When they realized what they were doing, they looked at each other and burst out laughing. It wasn't long before the persecutions began, but Ismene, like everyone else, believed things would right themselves in no time. Angelos threw himself into his studies, planning on getting his degree. "It's something left over from before the war," he'd said. "The sooner I get it out of the way the better." After taking a good many precautions he went to the University, and the whole time he was in taking the exam, Ismene waited outside on the marble steps, her heart pounding. When he finished he came bounding down the steps, elated. He squeezed her arm and they decided to celebrate with friends. It wasn't to be, however, because two days later some men came and asked for him at his house. His father learned that he and a few others were being charged for something that had taken place during the war. That's when they realized that the war wasn't really over. Ismene never paused to think what course of action to follow now that Angelos was a wanted man. She never once doubted the inevitability of waiting; it had seemed natural and self-evident to her. Even now she couldn't say to herself: "I'm waiting." She didn't think of it as waiting, it wasn't a matter of choice.

They arrived at the park. Harilaos continued down its narrow pathways, passing up a number of empty benches. He was headed for one that was out of the way, as if he already knew where he wanted to sit. He immediately unfolded his newspaper, and cast searching glances on all sides. Ismene ducked down behind a bush. So this was where they met! Harilaos knew what he was talking about after all when he assured them that Angelos was all right. In any case, he was incapable of telling a lie. Ismene moved off to one side, keeping close watch around her. To think that, any minute now, Angelos would appear! It would be enough just to lay eyes on him, to see him before her in the flesh, because, as vividly as he lived on in her memory, there were times when she discovered, to her horror, that his image had begun to fade. No, she remembered everything, she knew his every gesture and expression, how he raised his eyebrow when he was pulling your leg, how many wrinkles creased his forehead when he was doing geometry problems, how he squeezed her hand in his warm palm. What she couldn't conceive was how he would look today. Had his eyes lost that fearless glint? Five whole years was a long time. Even longer, when you've led an existence like Angelos'. Harilaos glanced at his watch again, then moved to one end of the bench, as if leaving room for somebody else. Ismene wasn't sure she'd be able to hold herself back. She crouched behind a thick shrub. The green leaves shone placidly in the late sun. People strolled past on their way through the park. Now someone was coming with a steady gait down the path! No, it was a stranger. Two kids played tag in the planter-beds. Some school girls went by, whispering among themselves. He would be coming by one of those paths, emerging from the trees, from somewhere far off and unknown, somewhere fraught with terrifying shadows. Angelos would be wiser than all of them now, filled with strength and conviction. He would look upon them as sedate, complacent, spineless people who had no idea which direction the sun rose from. What could one say to him after so much time? It had to be something comparable to what he'd been through, something in his own language. It wouldn't be as easy as back when they used to walk hand in hand, Angelos gazing deep into her eyes and then at last taking her in his arms as she laughed with pleasure. Things were so different back then. He used to whistle as he turned into the courtyard, and she would come to her door and they'd sit on the winding stairs late into the summer evenings.

Something was happening. Angelos' father lowered his newspaper and peered down the shadowy path. Steps! No, it was another stranger. He went by without stopping.

Ismene finally sat down on a bench. It was better that way. If she continued to creep about through the shrubbery, someone would get suspicious. She tilted her head up to see. Harilaos was still sitting there, alone. Yet he appeared calm, patient. What if Angelos came from this direction and caught sight of her first? A couple sat on the bench beside her. Ismene moved over, then got up to let the pair murmur to each other in privacy. She went around to one side and peeked: the space next to Harilaos was still unoccupied. She made a big circle and came out behind the bench. She would be happy to see the back of his head, his shoulders. Beyond the thick, cropped foliage she could make out Angelos' father. Perhaps now that it was dark, Angelos would come. He would be sure to come, since he'd said he would. Evidently he and Harilaos met quite often. Then why couldn't he send her a message, just a word to say he hadn't forgotten her? But he always knew what he was doing, he would have thought everything out and decided that it was for the best. A single glimpse of him was all she asked! She wouldn't move from her spot, she'd hold herself back, since that seemed to be what the situation demanded.

It was already night. The shadows had descended, the light had drained from the sky. The whispering and slow lingering steps multiplied, while the chill and gloom of night came on through the trees. Harilaos folded up his paper. He checked his watch and started to get up, then thought better of it. Once again Ismene was filled by the sensation of that kiss, together with an awful shudder that ran through her body and made her fingers tremble. Why was he late? Something must have happened. Perhaps the danger that surrounded him, claiming him for its own, had once again tightened its noose.

Some time later, Angelos' father rose and slowly walked away, plainly distraught. The park benches had filled with couples and secret murmurings. The light coming from the street lamps was frigid, the trees looked unreal. Angelos had not come.

EFTIHIS APPEARED AT THE DOOR of the coffeehouse in his clean white shirt, freshly shaven, wearing a tie and polished shoes. He paused at a table where they were playing cards, then went over and watched a game of backgammon. Then he went back out front on the sidewalk. He was punching the palm of his hand with his fist, looking up and down the street. One or two of the boys said something to him, but he made it clear he wasn't in the mood to talk. All they knew how to do was shoot off their mouths, he thought to himself. It made you wonder if they'd ever had to make a single decision in their entire lives.

Then he heard the sound of a motorcycle. Pericles came wheeling around the corner. He pulled up, shut off his bike, and parked it on the sidewalk. The new neon lights gave off an eerie white glow, and Pericles could see how pale and nervous Eftihis' face appeared. He removed his motorcycle gloves, revealing his heavy gold ring, and slowly lit a cigarette. He looked down the street at Aliki's window. Then he smoothed his mustache and smiled self-contentedly, exposing a row of white teeth. Eftihis imagined how much fun it would be to punch him in the face and spoil those good looks.

"How's your gas?" Eftihis asked curtly.

"I've got a bit."

"I want you to take me over to Thision."

"What's wrong with the bus?"

"I want you to take me."

"But at eight I've got ..." Pericles looked back toward Aliki's window.

"Let's go, I'm in a hurry."

Pericles made a face. Eftihis was always stubborn as a mule when it came to getting his way.

"I'll pay you for the gas," Eftihis told him.

Right then, Andonis came around the corner. When he saw Eftihis, he gave a start, but realizing there was no escape, he put his hand on Eftihis' shoulder and told him he needed him for something very big. Pericles was all set to get going.

"I've been looking for you," Andonis said.

"Now?" Eftihis asked and got off the motorcycle. "This morning I had a slight misunderstanding with your wife. I was a bit out of line ... Did she say anything?"

"No, I haven't been home yet."

"I wanted her to help me with something. I hope she's not angry."

Andonis decided it was a chance to offer Eftihis something in return for the money he owed him. It was also a way to get him to keep his mouth shut.

"So, Eftihis, I've got a sure thing for you. Good money too. Are you in?"

"You better believe it."

Andonis quickly filled him in on the merchandise Thodoros was looking to get rid of. "You're just the man for the job. When he told me you were the first one I thought of ..."

"I got you," Eftihis said. "Black market stuff."

"It's not up my alley, but I wanted to help the guy out."

"When do you want to go see him?"

"Let's make it for the day after tomorrow, ten a.m. in Omonia," Andonis said as he strode off.

Eftihis jumped back on the motorcycle and ordered Pericles to get a move on. The latter started it up without enthusiasm, but it wasn't running smoothly, one thing after another needed adjusting. Eftihis began to lose patience. Pericles kept looking toward Aliki's window, mumbling that he didn't buy the damn thing to cart other people around on their errands. At some point he saw Aliki's face at the window and was about to dismount, but Eftihis grabbed him by the collar.

"Cut the crap and let's get a move on, I'm in a hurry."

They set off. Pericles went by Aliki's window and made a gesture telling her he'd be right back. Then he sped off to dispense with his chore.

"Did that fellow with the briefcase weasel another loan out of you?" he asked Eftihis.

"That's my business."

"I asked you for a little something the other day and you dragged your feet."

"I'm gonna need Andonis' help one of these days," Eftihis said. "Step on it ..."

"What, and you don't need mine?"

"Give it some gas and let's get by this truck ..."

"Get yourself a chauffeur if you want to start giving orders."

"I just might ... Watch the bumps, you almost threw me back there."

When they reached Thision, Pericles slowed down and pulled over to the curb.

"Turn down the little street on the right, to Mary's father's place," Eftihis ordered him.

They went on a short ways and Pericles stopped at the corner. He said he didn't want the old man to see him.

"But I want him to, that's why I brought you. What do you care, anyway?"

Pericles submitted. He stopped in front of a small shop with a sign that read "Plumbing."

"Wait here. I'll be right back," Eftihis told him as he went in.

Mary's father was using a wooden mallet to bend a sheet of metal around a horizontal cylinder, shaping it into a funnel or a duct. He caught sight of Eftihis over his wire-rimmed glasses and instantly stopped what he was doing. Eftihis walked in with his hands in his pockets, saying "Evening" and closing the door behind him with his elbow. Pericles tried to make out what they were saying through the glass, but then the old man started pounding the metal again. Pericles soon lost interest; what was the point of getting mixed up in other people's problems anyway? He'd dumped Mary, and if that sap Eftihis wanted to get mixed up with her, he wished him all the luck. Pericles had done his duty as a friend and warned him – Eftihis would have to take it from there. He wondered if he'd gotten her pregnant and had things to settle with her father.

Pericles made a rather lewd crack to a couple of girls who happened by. Why not, no one knew him thereabouts. Then he ambled down to the corner, lit a cigarette, walked up and down a bit, went back and looked through the window, then started up his bike to let Eftihis know it was time. Eftihis however, pigheaded as ever, acted like he'd hired a limousine and went on gabbing away. Mary's father kept hammering on the metal. At one point the old man wrinkled his forehead; he lay down his hammer, looked Eftihis in the eye, smiled, shook his hand, and thumped him on the shoulder. But Eftihis didn't long hold that genial stance. He shoved his hands back in his pockets and, pushing open the door, said to the old man,

"The rest is up to you."

"All right, you'll get what you want," the old man replied, taking up his hammer again.

Until they rode off, they could hear his hammer banging away, faster and louder than before. Once they were underway, Pericles asked Eftihis if he'd rented the bike by the hour, but the latter ignored him and instead cautioned him not to leave him in some pothole.

"I'm getting married this Saturday," he casually let drop as they sped along.

"Too bad, I'll be busy all day."

"Even if you weren't, you wouldn't be invited. I don't want anyone there."

Getting it out all at once like that made Eftihis instantly feel better. It was a good moment too, they were heading down Pireos Street and Pericles, keeping an eye out for traffic, didn't have a chance to think about it or to ask questions. And Eftihis didn't have to see his reaction either, it was almost like he was addressing thin air.

"So it's all set with her old man?"

"Watch it, there's a truck behind us."

"Mary's a good girl," Pericles said.

When they got back, Eftihis jumped off and stormed inside, slamming the iron gate behind him. Pericles left his bike running so Aliki could hear. Then he coasted down to the small orchard where they always met. Tonight, with the moon, they'd be taking a wonderful little walk. He had brought along loads of newspapers this time, so they could sit under a tree. But Aliki didn't come out. Pericles went back and stood under her window.

Eftihis paced up and down in the courtyard. His mother and his brother Mihalis weren't there. He went inside and stood in the dark for a little, then went around and switched on the lights. The room, empty and pink, didn't please him in the least. Their things were still heaped up in the middle of the courtyard. The light bothered him, so he turned it out. In the dark again, he sat on the bed, but he still couldn't relax, because the spasmodic flashes of sharp white light from the metal-works in back hurt his eyes.

When his mother appeared in the doorway he bellowed at her to go find Mihalis. He had something important to tell them both.

"I'll be back in a quarter of an hour," he said and went out.

He dashed over to Mary's place. He whistled under her window and waited at the corner. He made sure he never went into her house. He couldn't be bothered exchanging formalities with his future in-laws. He'd even told Mary to inform her family that he would be marrying – if they went along with it – just her, not the entire clan. Now Mary was sad she couldn't take a walk with him because her mother was sick.

"That's not what I came about. Your father promised to come up with everything I asked for. Now you have to do your bit so we can get it all over with."

"Like how?"

"He dragged his feet a bit, but he finally came around. So, does that make you happy?"

"Which part?"

"If you do your share, we can get married on Saturday."

"This Saturday?"

"What do you think, next year?"

Mary gave him a fleeting kiss, but since it wasn't the time to be mushy and starry-eyed, he told her not to let up on her father for an instant about the money. Girls lose it when you start stroking their hair, all they can think about is a castle built on clouds. So Eftihis was somewhat abrupt with her that evening. "You've got to keep after the old man, otherwise ..." And he left her there before she could pester him with questions. Like it or not, they would have to tie things up as quickly as possible.

Back home, he found his mother over in a corner of the courtyard, with Mihalis beside her. Eftihis went into the first room and switched on the light, clapping his hands as if he wanted everyone there to hear what he had to say. The room looked even emptier now, the electric overhead bulb hung drowsy and bare. He clapped his hands again and his mother and Mihalis came in and stood anxiously before him. Their shadows fell on the pink wall. Lit from above as they were, their eyes were in shadow, which bothered Eftihis, who wanted to see their precise reaction to the news. After a few moments of heavy silence, he mustered up his courage and said:

"So, I've decided to get married. Maybe even this week. And for obvious reasons, I want you out of the house. I want us to live alone."

Eftihis acted like he hadn't heard their murmurs of surprise, and went on:

"You know what a pain it is to always have other people in your hair. When my wife moves in, she's not going to want to have you guys underfoot, just like I don't want to have anything to do with her family. That's all I had to tell you. Now go get a good night's sleep and think about what you're going to do." Eftihis ended abruptly, relaxing his stance to let them know he was through and they could break up. His mother, however, didn't move. She was staring at him.

"What about me?"

"You'll go live with the oldest. They've got room for your bed there."

The old lady couldn't believe her ears. What, was she now to become a servant for that stuck-up daughter-in-law of hers? She went crying into the small kitchen, as she had always done when she had a fight with her husband or her sons. But now the kitchen was empty, and there was nowhere else for her to go. Mihalis started whining that he wasn't going anywhere, how it was their father who'd gotten this place. No one had the right to just boot him out like that.

"Don't be a jackass," Eftihis told him. "You can sleep at the machine shop. I already talked to the foreman about it. It's time to cut the bullshit and get on with our own lives."

Mihalis gave him a wily smile and said:

"I've been thinking about giving you the slip for a long time now. I don't much like it at the shop, but I'll do it just for my own peace of mind."

"There's no way they'll lay you off now, you'll be like a cog in their machine. They'll even up your salary."

"That's a lot of crap," Mihalis said more seriously. "They'll give me a few whacks on the head, roll down the grating, and there I'll be, stuck inside ... I'm no fool. No, I'll go because I want to, on account of your ..."

But Eftihis had finished with him, and was busy surveying the patches in the wall. He got out a cigarette and, without even realizing it, for the first time in his life offered one to his brother. The boy took it and wasted no time lighting up, now that he was his own man and didn't have to answer to anyone.

"That whitewash you mixed is ugly as hell," Eftihis told him, as if addressing a house-painter.

"If you'd been here you could have told me exactly how you wanted it," Mihalis shrugged. "Anyway, you don't know what you're talking about. It's perfect!"

"She won't like it," Eftihis said under his breath and looked around at the walls again to see what impression the room as a whole made.

His younger brother went outside to smoke his cigarette in peace. Eftihis, he thought, was a tough boss to please. Maybe he didn't like the color, but it was just the thing for newly-weds. It was almost like Mihalis had known, and had thrown in a bit of extra pink on purpose.

Soon Eftihis yelled for them to help him take the beds back inside. Only the beds. And not too close to the walls either, because the paint was still wet and they'd mess it up. Mihalis gave him a hand and they lugged them into the front room. Once the other two were in bed, Eftihis sat on the doorstep to clear his head a bit, despite the bursts of light that erupted every so often from the metal-works. Soon Ismene came back, climbed the winding stairs, and was gone. There was light in Vangelia's window. Everyone else was either asleep or out.

Eftihis climbed into bed with his clothes on. But still he couldn't settle down. His mother was crying without letup under her covers. He had no choice but to drag his bed into the next room, peevishly closing the door in between. But try as he may, he couldn't help hearing the stifled sobs from the next room. He got up wearing only his shorts, went next door and shook his mother by the shoulder.

"That's enough! You're acting just like somebody died."

The old woman went on crying and Eftihis roared,

"So how much will it take to make you shut up?"

"Keep your money," Mihalis said without turning his head from the wall. "It doesn't make it here."

Eftihis may have felt ashamed. He immediately turned out the light and went back to bed, leaving the door open. He was back before long, however, feeling in the dark for the headboard of his mother's bed. Then he sat down beside her, leaned over and said in a whisper:

"Is that all you can think about, yourself? What about me? You didn't even ask who I'm marrying ..."

His mother stopped momentarily and he took advantage of it to tell her:

"You don't have to worry. I'll take care of you, you'll have everything you need. Food, clothes, spending money. We'll keep in touch. It's just a couple of blocks away from here. You can do that much for me, can't you? So I can be alone, now when we're just setting out ..."

ANDONIS CAME BACK LATE. Coming through the door, he saw Vangelia sitting at the table embroidering with colored thread. There was a vase of flowers next to her. She greeted him, then continued slowly stitching out the pattern. Andonis pretended not to notice the flowers: he knew how dangerous it was once she started in on her hopes and dreams. All he wanted was to comprehend what was happening in that room, where everything seemed so peaceful and orderly. Vangelia picked out the colored threads with studied care. She was waiting for Andonis to ask her what she was embroidering and why.

"Are you feeling contented tonight?"

"About what?"

"About what you've been doing all day."

"More or less. I mean things look promising. I'm just coming from this fellow who makes neon signs. He wants us to work together ... Advertising's good business, it's got a future ... Imagine lighting up a whole street! ... Did anyone come by asking for me by any chance?"

"No."

"Were you out at all?"

"No, I've been here embroidering all day."

Andonis was exhausted and wanted to drop into a chair. The flowers and the embroidery could have been a well-laid trap. Perhaps Vangelia knew everything and was just acting so matter-of-factly so he would say something first. If that was the case, no matter what he said he would come out looking foolish. He must have looked pretty ridiculous to her as it was. He set down his briefcase and stood awkwardly in the middle of the room, as if there were nowhere for him to sit. The house was so neat, you didn't dare move anything.

"So no one came looking for me? That's odd."

Andonis sat across from Vangelia at the table. As casually as possible, he moved the vase to one side so as to block his view of her. Then he took out an accounts book and started writing. Someone who dealt in electrical appliances, the fellow with the neon signs, had asked him to bring his books up to date. Andonis had brought them home with him. He tried to make his figures as shapely as possible, to show care and diligence. But his hand moved automatically, while he tried to figure out what was going on around him.

"We used to have friends who came by," said Vangelia "Now ..."

"It's because I'm so busy," Andonis said. "They know I'm out in the evening. Anyway, like who?"

"We don't even see that Mr. Yeoryiou anymore," Vangelia went on simply. "We used to get together and have a laugh ... Put all that stuff away and let's talk ..."

Andonis left his papers where they lay and stood up. He could sense a crisis approaching. He had to keep a grip on himself. The art of the deal meant keeping a poker face.

"Are you sure Yeoryiou wasn't by tonight?"

"No, nobody came by."

"Eftihis?"

"No, but he must be here, I heard shouting a while ago. Sit down and let's talk, since you're in a good mood tonight."

"I've got to go out again," Andonis said a little guiltily. "I just remembered something ..."

"Why didn't you go straight there?"

"I wanted to see you first."

"So why don't you ask me what I've been doing? Why not just sit here with me? Where are you running off to at this time of night, anyway?"

"I have to ..."

He could hear the storm approaching. That glow in Vangelia's eyes was the most dangerous thing of all. Disaster was only seconds away.

"Wait till tomorrow," she told him. "We'll lock the door and turn out the lights. Just the two of us ..."

"No, I have to run ... I've got to be somewhere ..."

He made a show of pulling out a number of hundred drachma notes, telling Vangelia:

"Take these, to cover our expenses."

"You won't be home tonight?"

"You might already be asleep. It's just so you don't worry. And so I can relax too. You need more than that?"

He hurriedly dropped the money on the table. It was chilly out in the courtyard. Andonis thought to himself that, aside from his need to escape, it was idiotic to spend so many hours sitting around the table and lying in bed. All those hours sleeping were a waste – as if you were just tossing yourself into a state of nonexistence. Apparently Vangelia knew how things stood, and was just having him on with those artful smiles of hers.

As he headed out the gate, a motorcycle stopped on the sidewalk with its motor running grated on his nerves. Who was that anyway? Why did the fellow keep the motor running when he was just sitting there?

Andonis glanced at the face of the young man on the bike and decided he was harmless. Yes, neon signs were a good business to get into. "See that sign there?" you'd say. "I put that up." At night you would be able to see it from the other side of town.

He changed his mind and went back inside. He banged on Eftihis' door and even shouted his name loud enough for Vangelia to hear. Eftihis grumpily stepped out in his undershorts.

"What's up?"

"I stopped by to give you the low-down on the job I told you about."

"Not now. Tomorrow."

"No, better now. Come on out so we can talk it over."

Andonis spoke in a loud voice and turned to see whether Vangelia had come to the door. He wanted to prove to her that he wasn't afraid to talk to Eftihis.

"It's good work," he said pompously. "There's no question of my doing it, of course. I'm up to here in work as it is. It's not my specialty either. He'll give you a good cut, too. He wants to get rid of the stuff."

Before Eftihis could respond, Andonis ran over to his own door and shouted triumphantly in to Vangelia:

"I'm out here, Vangelia. I'm talking to Eftihis!"

"Why don't you two come inside, it's cold out there," Vangelia said.

Thinking it was too late, or else overtaken by a sudden fit of gentility – hinting one shouldn't show oneself before a lady without his pants on – Eftihis threw on an old overcoat he used as a blanket and stepped back out into the courtyard.

"You'll make good money," Andonis repeated loudly. "You'll be good at it too – I thought of you the instant he asked if I knew anyone for the job. I vouched for your character ... I know that Thodoros. He thinks I'm honest to the point of stupidity, and I reinforce that impression because it serves my purpose. He asks my opinion and always does whatever I tell him to ... It shouldn't matter much to you, though."

"It's not like it's the first time something's been sold illegally," Eftihis laughed. "So, tomorrow at ten in Omonia?"

There was nothing more to discuss. The job Andonis was offering Eftihis was like interest on his loan. And the money he had given Vangelia earlier was interest on an extension of her ignorance. In a sense, Vangelia was capital that was being made to wait. And the rule is you always have to pay to have something wait.

Before Eftihis went back inside, he said to Andonis:

"Try to get that ... that cash back to me as soon as possible. I'm up to my neck in expenses these days ... By the way, your radio's a piece of junk, I couldn't even get a nickel for it ..."

"Shhh ..." Andonis said, panic-stricken, putting his finger to his lips and then pointing to his window.

"I'm just telling you in case you think this makes us quits ..."

Could Vangelia have heard? Their window was still lit, and the door was ajar.

"Vangelia," Andonis said, in a voice louder than Eftihis had used when he'd mentioned the radio.

She didn't come out. He said her name again, even louder this time. Nothing. He wished Eftihis good-night, but the latter seemed to have remembered something.

"Listen, do you have a moment?"

"As much as you like. Let's go over here."

They stood in the angle of the wall and Eftihis hurriedly let him in on the fact that in a few days he was expecting to have gotten a good bit of money together and was on the lookout for a lucrative, fail-safe business investment.

"I asked a slew of people what they thought and all I got was confused."

"I bet they all sang the praises of their own business, and stressed the need for capital ..."

"How'd you guess?"

"Business is my world."

"So what do you think? What's the best bet?"

"You can work out the particulars later. For now you have to decide which it's going to be, manufacturing or sales."

"I can't say I'm crazy about sales. You're always worrying about something, and I've had about enough of that. My problem is I don't have any skills, I can't even drive in a nail."

"Don't worry, manufacturing doesn't mean you have to do the work yourself. Far from it! You need machinery and people. You want me to be frank with you? Human labor is what generates value – and don't let anyone tell you otherwise. The hands of a worker are the best bargain in town – reliable, inexhaustible, in constant supply. While the price of everything else keeps going up and up, the price of labor stays the same. It always gives back more that you put in. You rent an entire person who does nothing but work for you all day long. He generates wealth – for you ..."

"You really think so? But I've heard ..."

"You shouldn't be so surprised. It's no secret. In the society we live in, the only people who turn a profit are the ones who own the means of production, the ones who hire the power of labor. That's the law. Since you're going to have the capital, why shouldn't you benefit from it too. There, you asked me my opinion and I told you the truth."

"It's just not what I expected to hear from you," Eftihis said. "All I want is to get something good going. It's the only time in my life I'll have my hands on that kind of money. I won't have a second chance."

“There’s no better way. You’ll pay the legal rate, no need to cut corners there, the laws were made by people who make labor their business. So why shouldn’t you purchase the same cheap commodity, the only one with a controlled price, the only one that reproduces. Take my word for it, you’ll come out ahead.”

Eftihis yawned and mumbled,

“Most likely I’ll do something like that ...”

“Think it over and you’ll see. We’ll discuss the details some other time,” Andonis told him, and went inside, pleased with himself.

CHAPTER 4

FOR SOME DAYS NOW, Lucia had seemed preoccupied and on edge. She would throw on her clothes and run out of the house as if she had somewhere in particular to be. Of course, no one asked her where she was going. She was free to do as she liked so long as she didn't bother anyone. She had stopped her commentary on the morning reading of the paper, she now considered it a natural and useful activity. In fact, she would even appear relieved when her father put his glasses away in their case and would say, "Good, there's nothing." She had begun to enter the rhythm of the house: she no longer sang when the others were silent, or remark sarcastically on the least flicker of hope. Everyone felt more at ease, and no one paid her peculiarities any mind. One morning Lucia even watered the flowers on the stairs. "I feel wonderful today," she told Ismene, and they set off together, almost cheerfully. Even Ismene was getting used to her. Of course, they never discussed Angelos. Lucia was more concerned about her old friends, girls she knew from around there or from school. She asked who'd gotten married, how many children they had, whether they were happy with their husbands, which of the boys she'd known had made it through the war. Ismene couldn't tell her much. All their childhood friends had gone their separate ways, they led their own lives now. Some had moved away, of course, and a good number had simply disappeared. Lucia was particularly insistent when it came to certain of them, but Ismene could only shrug. A day or two before, Lucia had suddenly remembered an old friend as she was rummaging through her suitcase.

"How about Vassilis, the doctor? What's he up to?"

"I haven't heard anything."

She didn't ask anymore. She continued to bend over her suitcase, looking for she couldn't even remember what. Vassilis had been another friend. He lived down on the courtyard, in the two rooms Vangelia and Andonis were in now. Later, as she was putting on her coat, Lucia had told Ismene:

"You don't know much about anyone, do you. It's so strange, I mean they were all friends of yours. They dropped from sight and you've made no effort to find out whether they're alive or not ... You just let go of them as if you'd never even known them ..."

She spoke without seeming to give much weight to her words. She inspected herself in the mirror, tightened her belt, and left. Ismene sat by the window, looking out at the courtyard and the nearby roofs. There were clouds gathering, darkening; sifted onto the rooftiles like a gray dust. The days began and ended with the same careless rush. Angelos' father had entrusted her to copy out some depositions, some complicated court decisions having nothing to do with Angelos, and had asked her to find out where two engineers had their offices now. Ismene had finished everything and left it on the judge's desk. It was probably all somehow connected to Angelos' case. "I must get things moving ..." he often said, looking squarely at Ismene, as if finding it hard to finish his thought. "It can't be put off ..."

Whenever Lucia went out, it was as if the house had been robbed of the breath of life. At first, Ismene was put off by her frigid smile and angered by her show of indifference. Now, however, she mostly just felt curiosity about her carryings-on, and often a touch of sadness. When she was at home, Lucia would sing, slam the cupboard doors, open and close drawers, pore over the dresses in magazine ads. Ismene liked hearing her voice, even when it was raised in anger. One afternoon, Ismene went into the bedroom and saw Lucia sitting hunched over on Angelos' bed. Her shoulders were hunched, her eyes glazed over, her hands hung lifeless between her legs. She seemed so lost in thought that she would not have noticed had the house collapsed around her. Ismene turned around and went out, quickly shutting the door behind her, and joined Angelos' mother in the next room. A few minutes later, when she realized there was someone else in the house, Lucia had suddenly appeared before them. "I just got in," she said as if justifying herself, and immediately started singing. When Ismene left, the singing abruptly stopped.

One day, during a light rain, Lucia came home wet. Halfway up the stairs, she noticed that Vangelia's door was ajar. She went back down and strode in. Vangelia, starved for company, was happy to see her.

"You're soaked ... Come on inside."

"I always see you from the window ... Is that embroidery? Can I see what you're making?" Lucia said, making a move to enter.

But she paused in the doorway and surveyed the room. She hung back until Vangelia took her coat and brought her a chair.

"It's so different in here now ..."

"Dry your hair. You can take off your shoes too if you want ... What were you doing out in this rain?"

"Can I see the other room?"

"Go ahead. Everything's a mess, though. My husband works all night and his papers are everywhere. I don't touch it, it's all book-keeping and business accounts."

"This place is so full of memories for me," Lucia said. "He had his desk here, his bed here. His mother's bed was over there. How long have you been living here?"

"Almost five years,..." Vangelia said. "At first it was only temporary, but this August it'll be five years exactly."

"Who lived here before you?"

"It was empty when we came. A seamstress, I think, with lots of brothers and sisters."

"And before them?"

"I don't know. I never heard ... Sit. You've been here for such a long time and we've never had a chance to talk ... Will you be staying long in Athens?"

"I came for a specific reason. Once that's taken care of ..."

Vangelia proudly showed her her handiwork. "I've embroidered two tablecloths, with napkins to match." Lucia looked at them without interest, she was too busy studying the walls, the door, the floor. But for Vangelia's sake she pretended to admire her taste and her fine needlework. She asked questions about the stitches, the pattern, the material.

"I remember you too," Lucia said after a bit. "Didn't you use to live in a red-brick house near the train tracks, down by the crossing? A friend of mine named Liza used to live next door, do you remember her?"

Vangelia remembered everything and they talked about their girlfriends, about the young fellow with a stammer who flirted with them, reciting lines of verse he'd learned off of his calender, and about the fat girl who used to dye her hair a different color each week. There was Mrs. Maria's daughter who ran off with the bicycle repairman, and her mother with her Greek-American friend who wore all those gold chains ... How much there was to remember!

"It's strange we never got to know each other back then. And for so many days now we've barely even said hello ... I'm by myself so much these days," Vangelia said.

"Let's go to the movies sometime ..."

"Okay. I've got loads of time on my hands ..."

The two women agreed that some day soon they'd visit the old neighborhood by the tracks, and look for their old friends. Lucia's spirits were buoyed, and Vangelia seemed almost happy that she'd finally found a nice person who wanted to spend time with her.

"I get so lonely ..."

"I got tired of being stuck out in the country too ..."

Vangelia opened a drawer.

"Here, let me show you the curtains I've been embroidering ... We're always talking about moving. But I never finished them. We won't be needing them for a while ..."

"So you think you'll be staying? Do you like it here?"

"I'll have to get used to it," Vangelia answered evenly. "Since my husband's work isn't going well, we can't really think about moving. Andonis runs around all day, but he still hasn't gotten anywhere ... He doesn't tell me the truth, he puts everything in a rosy light. But I know he's in trouble ... I act like I believe him so as not to worry him more than he already is. And I embroider the curtains for our new house ... That way he believes he's got me fooled."

"You don't find that hard to do?"

"Sometimes I almost feel like laughing when he tries to hide things from me. He goes on about these big plans of his ..."

"And what do you do?"

"I listen and pretend to go along. Yes, of course, everything'll turn out in the end, I tell him ..."

Vangelia fell silent. She folded up the unfinished curtains, and the smile returned to her face.

"But the truth is I really do believe everything will turn out," she said. "Andonis is a good man, he'll pull through. Why shouldn't I make him a gift of my certainty, since he needs it so much? Isn't that a way of helping him too?"

"I'd really like to talk to Andonis one of these days," Lucia said.

"About business?"

"No, about my brother. I heard they were friends."

"He told me that too."

"Don't say anything to Ismene. Not even my father knows they were together during the war ... Can you find out if he ever sees him? It's the biggest favor you could do me. That's why I came to Athens. I have to find him, I need him for something. And I *will* find him ..."

Vangelia promised she would learn whatever she could by some roundabout means, and Lucia started talking again about the medical student who used to live there.

"He was a friend of ours ... We all felt very close to him."

"Where is he now?"

"No one knows anything, it's as if the earth had opened up and swallowed him ..."

Lucia got up and slowly walked around the room, once again examining the walls, the window, the floor. Gently touching the door between the two rooms, she suddenly asked Vangelia:

"How did you meet Andonis?"

"He was wounded outside our door ... A bullet. We heard him groan and carried him inside. He stayed with us a few days, until he could use his leg ... So I got to know him," Vangelia said simply. "We didn't get married right away, he wanted to get set up at the company first."

"Does his leg still give him trouble?"

"He walks on it morning to night and never complains. He's probably forgotten all about it."

Suddenly the door opened and Andonis came in with his hair tousled. He was taken aback at first, but then he quickly set down his briefcase and politely greeted Lucia.

"I'm so pleased to meet you ... I recognized you right away, you're the judge's daughter ..."

"Angelos' sister," Lucia said.

"Then I'm twice as pleased! Angelos was my closest friend ... I still feel great warmth and admiration for him ..."

Lucia said nothing, and Andonis spread his hands and told Vangelia, "Good news! Remember that group of venture capitalists I was telling you about? Well, I have my first meeting with them a few days from now."

"Does that make you happy?" Vangelia asked anxiously.

"It's got real possibilities ... Of course, it still requires a good deal of care and study ..."

"I was just showing Lucia the curtains I've been making ..."

"Yes, it won't be long now ... I think I'm on the verge of a breakthrough."

He paced around the room for a few moments, talking about the great opportunities just around the corner, glancing somewhat fearfully at Vangelia, then at Lucia. Then he pulled up short in the middle of the room.

"Since you've got company tonight, Vangelia, I think I'll run out for a little while. It's a chance to tie up some unfinished business ... So, I'll say good-night," he told Lucia. "It was a real pleasure."

He grabbed his bulging briefcase and left. Lucia left shortly afterwards, still not saying anything.

HE MADE IT TO METAXURGIO. Yannis lived next to the corner store. He was an old friend who was now involved in construction. Andonis went up the marble steps. "You never know, something might come of it," he thought. He pounded on the door. He used to come here quite a lot in the old days. He knocked again. A light went on inside somewhere, then the small peephole in the door opened, and Yannis' face appeared behind the iron grating.

"Don't worry, it's me, Andonis ... I stopped by because of what we talked about. Any chance you asked those contractors about the iron and the lumber?"

Yannis opened the door and they stood talking in the hall.

"No, I didn't," he said sleepily.

"Let's get together tomorrow and go have a chat with them. We'll go fifty-fifty. We can't lose ... All you have to do is introduce me, and I'll do the rest ... Iron's going to disappear from the market, they've revoked all the permits, prices are bound to go through the roof ... I have it from a good source that there's money to be made ..."

From within came the sound of a woman's voice asking what was going on.

"Nothing, it's just a friend," Yannis said.

"You'll come out ahead," Andonis continued. "We'll sell large quantities at the old price ..."

Yannis' wife appeared in her nightgown and gave Andonis a ferocious look.

"Good evening, madam," he said with a smile. "I know I'm disturbing you but I felt it was my obligation to let my friend Yannis know of the latest developments in certain business matters he stands to profit from ... We've never had the good fortune to meet. I know Yannis from the war ..."

"And what's all this about exactly?"

"I was telling your husband here about the iron rods used in construction. If he acts now and reserves himself a substantial share, you'll have ..."

The woman showed no interest, and looked at Yannis as if to say it was time to bring the discussion to an end. Andonis instantly put on his most winning smile and stopped her.

"Perhaps, ma'am, you would be interested in a fine spring dress, some silk lingerie, nylons, blankets, sheets? Or perhaps a refrigerator, or some kitchenware? A young housewife is always in need of something ... As for the dress, you can select it from one of the shops I represent. What's twenty drachmas a week? Would you like me to stop by with some samples?"

"Let's go over it another time," Yannis suggested.

He gave Andonis a pat on the shoulder and, pushing him toward the door, said by way of closing that he'd talk to the contractors and let him know. Before Andonis had reached the bottom of the stairs the light had gone out.

As he looked up at the house, Andonis reflected on how quickly people change. Once, during the war, they'd held a meeting there.

But it all amounted to nothing now, seeing as this shrew of a woman didn't want so much as a piece of lingerie, and Yannis couldn't have cared less about iron.

Andonis slowly started home. The rain had stopped and the wet asphalt glistened. The peacefulness of walking, the clean night-air and the hush of the streets eased his nerves. It was a chance to rethink things. But where to begin? It would be a long hard winter this year, just like the last, and he'd get through it with promises, prospects, charades. Vangelia had given him an extension on a priceless line of credit, the luminous calm of her eyes, and in exchange held on to certain long-term promissory notes which Andonis had signed in a moment of thoughtless zeal. "Hold on for just one more winter. Things'll start looking up by the spring ... Trust me, it'll all start paying off ... We'll look for a better place next month." And Vangelia accepted it all with a smile. "I know things will get better too," she'd told him.

So the point was to think the whole thing through from start to finish. There wasn't time tonight. He was nearly home and besides, it was very late. You needed peace and quiet in order to think, not Yeoryiou with his overdue drafts, not this constant running around. Neon signs were good business. If you worked hard at it, you could acquire customers, you could earn a good commission. The signs would shine far into the night and illuminate the streets.

Vangelia was waiting up for him. She was still hard at work on those endless embroideries of hers, and her face was calm.

"Why aren't you asleep?" he barked at her. "It's late. I've told you a thousand times how much the thought of you waiting up hungry and sleepless bothers me."

"I'm not waiting for you, there's just something I wanted to finish up," Vangelia told him.

With that, she balled up her embroidery. She could tell by the look on his face that again it was not a good night to tell him about the child. But was it really so serious a matter that she had to wait until he was in a good mood? Yes, a child wasn't something that happened every day, like washing the dishes or signing an IOU.

"I'm not the least bit sleepy," she told him.

Andonis stiffened. Apparently Vangelia was in the mood to

talk. Her movements were slow and sure, as if she were waiting for him, as if she had boundless reserves of patience in her breast. Once again everything was in its place. If only it had been ignorance that made everything so orderly.

"I'm going to bed," he told her. "I'm beat. Can I ask you to get me up first thing? You can stay up if you like ..."

"You're not having supper?"

"Oh, I couldn't, I've got to lie down."

He fidgeted a bit, going into the kitchen for a glass of water, then hunting for something among his papers, the whole time avoiding Vangelia's eyes.

EFTIHIS ROUSED HIS HOUSEHOLD EARLY by clapping his hands. His brother immediately rolled up his things – two blankets, a pillow, a pair of old shoes, two pairs of underwear – threw a last look around the house, and set off with the bundle under his arm. "I'm off," he said. "I'll be seeing you." Thus he cut his ties without a lot of fuss. At the machine shop, he shoved his things under a bench, eager for night to fall, when he could settle in and become something like the lathe, the milling-machine, the pulley-block – and his own master. He oiled up the various parts of the lathe as he did every morning, then told the foreman that he'd be back in an hour, he had some important business to attend to. He went at once and found a pushcart, as Eftihis had told him to do, which he left outside on the sidewalk.

When he reached the house, Eftihis was calmly explaining to his mother why she would be better off with the new setup. But since she wanted no part of it, Eftihis began dismantling her bed himself, propping the iron pieces against the wall. Then he spread a blanket on the ground, and piled in whatever of hers he could find. When the old woman saw her dismembered bed, she realized that she would do best to keep quiet. Eftihis knotted the corners of the blanket crosswise, with all of her things inside, and tossed it onto the cart along with the mattress, the trunk and the iron bed-frame, and told Mihalis to take it to their older brother Pavlos' house. The old woman was crushed by the news, and chewed on her handkerchief as if the corpse of a loved one were being taken from the house. She followed the cart at a distance, leaving the old house without saying good-by to anyone. As they proceeded down the street, she cried out once or twice for Mihalis to slow down. He paid no attention, however, and bounded along behind the cart, wanting to get his chore out of the way. Still, for all his complaining to Eftihis about his kicking them out, he was truly enjoying all the uproar and commotion.

Mihalis arrived back at the house at a run and reported to Eftihis that Thalia, Pavlos' wife, had refused to let him put the old lady's things inside until Pavlos got home from work. Exasperated and swearing under his breath, Eftihis dashed over to his brother's. There he found his mother sitting on the doorstep like a beggar, and the cart loaded with her things parked on the sidewalk. Without a word to his mother he banged on the door, and when Pavlos' wife opened the peephole, ordered her to let him in. The look on his face frightened her, and she told him Pavlos was boss there, not him.

"Fine, I'll come back when he's here and we'll talk it over."

He piled his mother's things in the hallway, and told her to go on in. But the snubbing by her daughter-in-law had gotten her hackles up, and she refused to cross the threshold until Pavlos came home. She sat there on the stairs with her arms around her knees. Eftihis left her like that – he knew how impossible old people could be. He went back home.

Alone at last! He felt like shouting at the top of his voice and jumping up and down in the empty rooms. Then he stopped dead in his tracks. Maybe this whole marriage business was for the birds, maybe he'd be better off living there all by himself, throwing down a couple of rag rugs in a corner for a bed. What did he need all this fuss anyway? He thought it over for a good while, and asked himself if he truly loved Mary.

Before he could come up with an answer, however, he started going through the various things left out in the courtyard. Whatever he deemed of no use he tossed out on the sidewalk: a cabinet with small glass panes where they had kept their coffee-cups, and which every Christmas and Easter his mother decorated with newspaper garlands; the serving tray and liqueur glasses for when they had guests; an old, wobbly couch, and other rubbish. He called over a junk dealer who happened to be passing and gave them to him without haggling over the price. The rest – a few old chairs, framed pictures of various aunts and uncles, and whatever else could be burnt – he jammed into the laundry-room. All he kept were the pots and pans, since Mary wouldn't be bringing any of her own. Thus he got rid of that whole sorry mess, and he felt a great sense of relief seeing the courtyard gradually empty. Why in God's name had they held onto it all for so long? As if that house had ever been a real home, as if they had even once all sat down to eat a meal together. Their old man would stagger home drunk, his mother would be off working in the mill, or sulking in the kitchen; his brother would only show up at night, and Eftihis, as far back as he could remember, would be running around in hopes of putting a little something aside. Years went by like that, too many to count. But that was all in the past. Eftihis shouted to Mihalis that he'd need him for a few things later on, but the boy was too absorbed in contemplating his new life to pay much attention.

Eftihis' cohorts were waiting for him, as they did every day, in Monastiraki. On the way over he had decided on how he would break the news of his impending marriage, but the moment they caught sight of him they began pestering him about what he had lined up for the day.

"There's a chance we'll be getting into something different."

"You mean it's not settled?"

"It's something new, a two-or three-day job."

He looked at each of them in turn, then grimaced.

"You look like a bunch of bums. You haven't shaved and you're all scruffy. Just because we've been idle a couple of days doesn't mean you have to go around looking like beggars."

While he was surveying them, his eye fell on Elpida, who was standing off to one side. The others again asked Eftihis what the new job was all about.

"I'll let you know in an hour. In the meantime go get shaved, put on your ties and polish your shoes. This is a job for gentlemen."

He then dashed off for his meeting with Andonis, who arrived ten minutes later and began breathlessly offering excuses. On the way, he quickly told Eftihis about Thodoros, his words gasped out between breaths. He always created such a flurry around him, he reminded Eftihis of a fire-engine speeding off to a fire. The business at hand was as he'd suspected: smuggled goods. In another coffeehouse, buzzing with activity, there was a fat man waiting for them. With a certain amount of pride, Andonis presented Eftihis to Thodoros. "Here's the young man I was telling you about."

Eftihis quickly went over things with Thodoros. They immediately agreed on how to go about selling the nylons, and parted with positive feelings on both sides. "He's not such a monster," Eftihis thought to himself. "Just somebody looking out for number one."

He headed straight back to Monastiraki. His crew was waiting for him all spruced up now. He signaled them to follow him into the warehouse. He got straight to the point and told them what kind of job it was.

"Hit the merchants you know first. And use your brains. Don't go shooting off your mouth."

"Is this the new thing you were talking about?" Fanis asked.

"This is just temporary. Just so we don't sit around twiddling our thumbs. Not scared, are you?"

"Are you going to need me?" Elpida asked.

"No," Eftihis replied. "But stick around, I have something to tell you."

Once they'd gone through it all and everyone understood how to stay out of trouble, Eftihis left with Elpida. They walked together for a ways, but Eftihis couldn't bring himself to tell her his news. Elpida didn't ask, either. They went up Athinas Street, threading their way through the carts, the crowds, the automobiles and trolleys, and still Eftihis hesitated as he saw her walking along with her head bent as other people jostled past. Why was it so hard for him? If Kostis were alive, he'd be the first one Eftihis would tell about his getting married. But even if Elpida *was* Kostis' sister, it was different. Kostis had died, had been killed, rather, years before, trying to steal bread from the back of a moving German truck. As he was jumping on, he lost his grip and the truck ran him over. He was, what, twelve years old at the time? There was nothing left but bloody, mangled flesh, and the wide tread marks from the truck. Eftihis immediately jumped off, tumbling head over heels, and went back to look. They gathered Kostis up with a shovel as Eftihis watched, a loaf of bread under his arm. He went and found Elpida, without Kostis this time. He gave her the whole loaf, he wasn't even sure if she realized at the time what that sour dark loaf meant for her. Ever since, whenever Eftihis managed to put a little something aside, he would hurry over to give Elpida her brother's share, remembering that Kostis never ate all the carob beans, no matter how hungry he was. "I'll take the rest to Elpida," he would say. So, in a way Elpida was still getting Kostis' share. No one else knew about it, of course. He wasn't about to tell them, either. Eftihis always insisted that it was useful having a girl around in their line of work. "When it comes right down to it, you guys don't do any more than she does," he had said, just to let them know he could do without them if he had to. He couldn't forget what an awful end Kostis had come to, while he, Eftihis, had come out alive. And it sometimes occurred to him that Elpida should get a share, not because her brother had died, but because he, Eftihis, was alive – which was no small matter. Yet today he was having trouble forming words into a sentence to tell her that he was getting married. They were walking together, but every now and then some people – or a cart – would come between them. Elpida crossed at an intersection, and immediately a long line of cars separated them. Eftihis stopped and shouted across to her,

"I'll see you. I have to go this way."

Elpida waved good-by, and suddenly Eftihis felt like he were suffocating. He dashed across the street and caught up with her.

"Just a second, there's something I forgot to tell you."

"What?"

"Come on," he said, taking her by the arm.

The whole way, Eftihis' eyes never left the sidewalk. Why was it so hard for him to come out with it? They turned down the next street and continued walking, but still Eftihis didn't open his mouth.

They backtracked to Monastiraki. Eftihis told her to wait and went into a pawnshop. He asked the shopkeeper, a friend of his, for Andonis' radio ..."seeing as nobody bought it." Back outside, he told Elpida,

"Take this home with you."

"What for?"

"So you can listen to music. It's a worthless piece of junk, but it works ..."

"Then why don't you keep it?"

"I don't need it."

When Elpida had taken it, he told her,

"I want you to have it. To keep you company."

Then he went off. After going a ways, he stopped in his tracks. He had wasted all that time with her, and still hadn't told her.

This business with the smuggled goods reminded Eftihis of his escapades as a *saltadoros*, a "truck-hopper," back during the war. He felt a cold shiver run through him. So, did this mean more entanglements and narrow escapes? Thodoros was generous with his percentages, and Eftihis would have to do whatever came his way until he got his own business going. If all you did was worry about the risks, you'd never get anywhere. It wouldn't be the first time he'd dived right into things without knowing how it would all turn out.

That afternoon, Eftihis ordered Mihalis to take the pushcart and fetch Mary's furniture and clothes. The boy wrinkled his nose, not knowing how to behave in a strange house, but Eftihis promised to double his bonus this time. He also gave him a light kick in the pants, almost a pat, for helping out and sticking by him. Mihalis set off pushing the cart and whistling. Mary's father had promised Eftihis that, in addition to the bed, he would have a wardrobe, table and chairs, and a buffet made later on. He'd ordered them, he said, but the furniture maker would be a few days late. Hearing this, Eftihis had made it clear to the old man that he was in no hurry to hold the wedding, and what was more, he didn't care to hear about all the old man's troubles. He made an issue of it because he knew how easy it was for in-laws to make promises. They only came through with what the groom managed to get his hands on beforehand. When it came to the furniture, however, he relented. He decided that at first, anyway, they wouldn't need buffets and wardrobes, just the bed. "We won't be having anyone over," he told Mary, who was adamant about wanting drawers that locked, with keys she could put on a ring and take out of one drawer when she wanted to unlock another set of drawers. "Forget all that," Eftihis said. "You just tell your old man to come through with the cash. That's what counts."

While waiting for Mihalis to come back from Mary's, he nipped over to see how his mother was making out. Pavlos, his older brother, had come home. Eftihis found all three of them sitting around inside in silence.

"What's this all about?" Pavlos said when he caught sight of him. "You think you can just toss Mother out when it suits you?"

Eftihis told him to cool off. Did he want them to have a reasoned, orderly discussion, or to throw rocks at each other? "Is she your mother or not?" he asked.

"She's not some beach ball we can go kicking back and forth. You can't just dump her on the street because you happen to be mixed up with some girl they're in a hurry to marry off."

Before anyone could stop him, Eftihis grabbed up a chair and brought it down on his brother's head.

"That'll teach you to talk that way about my wife."

Thalia let out a shriek and their mother turned deathly pale at the sight of blood trickling down her oldest son's face. She was afraid that Pavlos, who was a hard one to read, would lose his temper and clobber Eftihis, the way he did that time to Thomas, which landed him in jail for half a year. But Pavlos didn't move. His eyes flashed briefly, then he licked the blood seeping from his nose and wiped his forehead with a handkerchief.

With Thalia running around screeching, looking all over for cotton and alcohol, bandages, gauze and iodine to treat her husband's wound, they didn't have a chance to say more. She kept asking Pavlos if it hurt, telling him to tip his head back or to lie down. Not once did she look in Eftihis' direction, she acted like Pavlos had hurt himself accidently. Their mother hadn't left her chair, but she stepped on Eftihis' foot once or twice as a reminder to hold his tongue.

"So can we talk about Mother now?" Eftihis asked.

"The best thing for you to do," Pavlos interrupted, "is to rent a place for yourself and move in with your wife, the way I did. Better yet, if they're giving you any money, build yourself a little house somewhere."

Eftihis told him to keep his ideas to himself, and said he was forgetting that for years and years he was the one who had taken responsibility for the house, while Pavlos came and went like an overnight guest.

"Tell him, Mother, did I ever once let you go without a robe or slippers? Didn't I get Dr. Asimakis to come right over whenever you got sick? Remember the coat I bought you? And that jacket? Tell him, Mother, did you ever go without food, or clothes, or medicine? And I'll go on taking care of you, just like before. It's just I don't want anyone else living with me. I don't feel like having somebody else knowing every time I kiss my wife, or smack her one. It'll be better for her, too, not having anyone else around. As for Mihalis, he'll learn the trade better living at the shop. And I'm tired of having him stumbling home at one in the morning with his pants unbuttoned. Besides, I won't be using the money I'm getting to build some shack out in the boondocks. I'm going to set up a business."

Pavlos went on grumbling that Eftihis should let their mother stay put, and go out and find his own place.

"Don't forget how I kept you fed and gave you money all those years you were broke and out of work," Eftihis told him. "I even footed the bill when you got yourself in trouble, first during the trial and then when they threw you in prison. You remember that? I hired you a lawyer and got you an appeal, and when you got out I made sure you had cigarettes, and coffee, and clean shirts. Did you ever think how much all that cost? And if it weren't for that appeal, you might still be in the slammer? Did you know I went and made sure Thomas' witnesses watered down their testimony? And how about those packages I brought you while you were inside?"

"Okay, fine ... But what about Mother here?"

"And how did you all make it through the occupation? The first thing you used to do when I walked through the door was look to see what I had in my hands. And what were you doing the whole time I was out there stealing bread? You called me a *saltadoros*, I was an embarrassment to you. Of course, that didn't prevent you from helping yourself to the tins and the *paniota* I brought home. And don't forget, they were using real bullets back then, it wasn't a game. Or I could have been run over, like Kostis. And what did you do? You skulked along the street like a dog. Some big hero."

"So what does all that have to do with ..."

"I just wanted to refresh your memory, that's all."

They weren't getting anywhere, and Eftihis concluded that there was no point in further discussion. He checked his watch and asked where they wanted to set up the old woman's bed. Thalia said it couldn't go in the drawing-room. "How could we ever have guests in when Mother was asleep?" Which left the kitchen. Eftihis reassembled the bed before leaving. He told his mother to lie down, mostly to lay claim to that small corner. They were capable of moving her into the laundry-room once he left.

"So when's the wedding?" Pavlos asked.

"This Saturday maybe, or the start of next week. I'm waiting for them to settle a few last details ..."

But he made it clear that his brother's interest meant nothing to him, he only came to help the old lady settle in. He made her bed himself, and before leaving gave her some money, telling her it was for the housework she'd done, as they'd agreed. But his mother wouldn't take it from him, and he left it on top of the covers. With the kitchen door shut, he said in his mother's ear,

"Don't worry. I want you to be happy. I won't forget about you ..."

His words trailed off as his lips brushed his mother's cheek. He may even have given her a kiss. But he quickly straightened up at the sound of Thalia's heels in the hall. He went on out, not wanting to be seen like that.

Once on the street, he felt set free. Mihalis was waiting for him in the courtyard, but the cart was empty. Mary's things weren't ready yet.

"So much the better," Eftihis said. "That's it for today. You can go."

Once again Eftihis found himself alone in the two empty rooms. He took some leftover rags from the laundry-room and spread them out in a corner. He lay down on the floor, letting his body relax as if he hadn't slept in days. Never had he felt so carefree, so independent and self-sufficient, with no one tugging at his sleeve asking for something. Yes, it was a real temptation, this solitude. What if he just chucked it all out the window and told Mary and the old man he'd changed his mind? He'd have a room with pink walls, a bed of rags, and a key. And he could come home whenever he felt like it and sleep wherever he pleased.

He lay like that for what seemed like an age, his arms and legs sprawled on the floor. "It's great to be alive!" he told himself. Then he got up to go find out what was happening with the wedding, the gold sovereigns, and Mary. "Well, I guess I'm ready," he said on his way out, leaving his door ajar.

ANDONIS WAS TIRED OUT by the time he reached Syntagma. He looked at the sky. Neon signs were a good beginning, a way to make a living while waiting for something better to come along. Besides, advertising was a necessary ingredient in a competitive free-market economy. The first person to sell out on market day is the one who shouts the loudest. Andonis would study the matter with the investors later on. He had his new suit on today, which was a step in the right direction.

Suddenly a face inserted itself between himself and the gray sky, bringing the full weight of its predatory look to bear on him. Yeoryiou! His face seemed carved out of some dark granite, his hand crushed Andonis' arm in its iron grip.

"Gotcha!" he gloated, as if snaring something he had long been stalking.

Andonis froze. Yes, it was Yeoryiou all right, and he was trying to bore into Andonis with his eyes, trying to find out what was going on inside him – a futile exercise, since it struck Andonis that he was suddenly and utterly empty, as if the sidewalk had sucked out all of his blood. Yeoryiou stepped back to get a better look at him. People, automobiles and colors streaked past behind him like drunken birds.

"I was unable to ..." Andonis whispered. "Forgive me ..."

But Yeoryiou didn't hear him, he just went on staring at him, ready to spit in his face. Andonis could see it wouldn't be easy for him to wriggle out of this one. His briefcase had become so heavy he couldn't lift it, the street coiled around him like a snake. Would they stay frozen in that position until nightfall? It was as if all of his foregoing life had been careening toward this one, terrible moment. A clock showed fourteen minutes past two. When something is coming to an end, each minute deserves to be stamped in one's memory. As Andonis took note of the exact hour, he remembered how, at critical moments in his life, he had always wanted to know what time it was.

"I'll give it to you as soon as I can ... You're right," he managed to say.

"It's my money that's right," Yeoryiou shot back.

"So call me a crook ... I was taken in too."

He instantly marveled at the ease with which the word "crook" had rolled off his tongue.

"So call me a crook ..." he said again, more loudly this time.

"You think that lets you off?"

"No, but ..."

Yeoryiou's hands were strong, and he looked angry. Everything danced in Andonis' wide-open eyes like frightened insects. "If he hits me," he thought to himself, "it'll be over with quickly." Instead of hitting him, however, Yeoryiou said:

"You've ruined me ..."

A light went on in Andonis' brain. Yeoryiou did indeed wear the look of one who'd been ruined. Maybe he really believed it. This was the critical moment. Andonis grabbed Yeoryiou by the arm, with a familiarity bordering on outright nerve.

"So let's go have an ouzo," he boldly proposed. "We're both in the same boat. Don't worry, it's on me. It's the way of the marketplace. A businessman's greatest asset is to not take his setbacks to heart ... Maybe you'd prefer a quick beer?"

Yeoryiou was taken off-guard. He didn't have time to detect Andonis' well-laid trap or to resist. Maybe he really had been ruined.

"Let's go figure out what our next step is going to be. Don't look so down in the mouth, it's not the first time this has happened to anyone. You're probably in debt to somebody else, right? So you know how I feel ..."

"It's too late," Yeoryiou said. "Too late for everything."

"Don't say that. Money never loses its value. This is just a momentary weakness, a hitch in the scheme. I can't believe that you were depending exclusively on what I owe you. As a rule, such irregularities are in the nature of business dealings. Besides, bad debts should be calculated into the balance sheet as a necessary evil, a legitimate element of the economic system ... I'm only sorry it falls to me to formulate this everyday, natural truth at your expense."

"In other words, you've become a systematic swindler, Andonis?" asked Yeoryiou in amazement.

"If that's how you choose to look at it. I simply hold that in business, someone's always bound to get hurt. Am I wrong?"

He was surprised to learn that this man, who believed himself ruined on Andonis' account, was all the more willing to follow him the more nonsense he spewed. Andonis took him by the arm, communicating a degree of geniality with his light grip, an understanding of the difficult position Yeoryiou found himself in. Andonis took care to use just the right amount of pressure for the circumstances; the most important thing was to remain in control of the situation. He led him down Stadiou Street.

"Shall we walk in the shade?"

"But the sun's not out," Yeoryiou observed.

"Right you are, but it's still better," Andonis went on.

Yeoryiou followed him – a good sign. They waited for the cars to pass. By the time they reached the other side, Andonis had started up again:

"I was taken in too, it's not like I blew it on women or lost it at cards. The whole procedure for protesting drafts is really quite absurd. It's become a fact of life in the world of small business, where everything operates according to a deadline."

"But I gave your drafts to an importer, and now I've lost his confidence ..."

"Tough luck for him, and even more for you. You shouldn't have based your credibility on a piece of paper signed by a third party."

"But you and me are friends, Andonis ... At least I thought we were ..."

"Another mistake. Had that been the case we wouldn't have had to rely on a signature," Andonis chided. "Don't think badly of me. Your problem is that you personalize business, which is what they did back when capitalism was in its early stages ... Amid all the thousands of deals being made, someone's bound to get hurt. There's just not enough profit to go around. That's the law. And for the moment, we number among the losers ..."

Andonis squeezed Yeoryiou's arm a little more firmly. Perhaps it was more than just the art of the deal. Andonis felt a genuine sympathy for this man, who in his innocence had trusted him and given him merchandise on the basis of a signature. And he was a friend, not a close one; an acquaintance, say. Yeoryiou had called Andonis a crook, but he was too late because Andonis had already accepted that fact; thus the label had no value. Yes, he *should* feel sympathy for this man who had no choice but to allow himself to be led silently along by the arm, while Andonis did his best to lay down a verbal smoke screen. One had to keep in a state of constant readiness when one's life had taken such a dangerous turn for the worse ...

The street swarmed with other men clutching briefcases, all in a greater or lesser hurry. The cars honked at them, not understanding the peril they were all in. Yeoryiou had not yet lost his temper, so Andonis decided there was room to elaborate. He spoke to him with an empathy bordering on pity, because Yeoryiou was indeed a pitiful character now, the way he all but agreed with everything Andonis said. "It's in this man's power to have me thrown in prison," Andonis reflected. "You think it's a small matter to openly acknowledge you're a crook?"

Andonis realized he had gone this way once before, when he had been picked up by the Germans. There had been a tall, sallow-faced man in glasses, a stooge of the SS, with a pistol under his trench-coat. Andonis had tried to engage him in conversation, but the traitor had told him, "Turn around one more time and you're a dead man." There were two others on his right. The wind had been icy cold that time too, and he had the same feeling of something being brought to a close. A clock showed two thirty-seven. "So this is it," Andonis had thought to himself. They had been waiting for him at the company door, the man in glasses had jumped him and jammed the pistol in his gut. "If you want to live, don't move a muscle," he had said. Andonis saw the others forming a circle around him. "So this is really it ..." He had followed them, up Stadiou, past unsuspecting passersby hunkered down in the cold. In Klafthmonos Square, they threw him in the back of a covered transport and took him to Merlin Street. A fellow student, wearing handcuffs, had also been in the truck. After exchanging glances, they acted as if they didn't know each other. Later he would remember that it had been Spiros Ioannidis, and wonder what had become of him.

"I know they pulled a fast one on you, Andonis, but that doesn't help," Yeoryiou was saying. "I told the importer's lawyer you'd been duped."

"Wrong!" Andonis protested. "Don't ever say that about me

again. Next time say that I'm a crook ... in other words, a businessman in a jam ..."

Andonis would never accept that he'd been duped. The whole thing had been his idea. What got to him was that that idiot Theophilos had messed it up. He had worked closely with Theophilos, they helped each other out, drank coffee and talked over a slew of economic opportunities in the upper level of his shop. Andonis' specialty was fabrics – to mention just one of many – and Theophilos always consulted him. One day he'd told him, "Andonis, I've lost my credibility in the market." "Well, there's always me," Andonis had replied confidently, knowing that even though he hadn't made a name for himself as a merchant, there were lots of stores out there where they knew and trusted him from his days as an accounts manager at the company. So he ended up getting merchandise from Yeoryiou in exchange for those drafts. Andonis had dubbed that period "the struggle for the acquisition of a clientele." It was the hardest and most tiring phase. He still had Theophilos' drafts in his briefcase. A few days later he had jokingly said to Thodoros, "Small-time business deals like this are a thing of the past. All people do is sit around waiting for someone to come by and justify their laziness. A truly enterprising merchant with imagination would buy merchandise on credit, sell it wholesale at a discount, then leave the country. Once across the border he would buy something else, along with a truck, which he would load up and drive back himself. He'd pay the standard customs fees, and sell the stuff off, again at a discount. He would pay off his first notes, plus a few others, to build up his reputation as a good investment. Then he'd buy something else ..." The whole time he was talking, Theophilos listened with his mouth open. A few days later Andonis went into Theophilos' store and found his shelves empty. One of his employees told him that Theophilos had gone to Salonica. So, he had put Andonis' idea into action! Andonis waited for him to come back so he could tell him how to proceed during the plan's second phase. But fifteen months passed and Theophilos hadn't shown. He sent Andonis a postcard of a winter landscape. "The Tirol's gorgeous," he'd written on the back. Then another: "Munich's fantastic," then "Paris is wild!" Meanwhile, the drafts Andonis had made over to Yeoryiou came due. He still believed in his heart that Theophilos would return to complete the cycle of trade Andonis had outlined to him. But when he received a postcard of a bullfight in Spain, he lamented the downfall of his brilliant idea at the hands of that idiot. “The biggest shortcoming in any business activity is the lack of perspective – that is, imagination,” he told himself, and wrote off his venture with Theophilos as if it had been the victim of some unforeseen accident – a fire, or death by stroke. It was too bad. As for the notes he had signed for Yeoryiou, he was still convinced he would be able to handle them. Only idiots went to prison nowadays for debt.

Yeoryiou turned and asked him why he'd stopped.

“Where was I? Oh, yes,” Andonis went on. “In every period the marketplace has its own unique characteristics. These days, only those with the widest range of prospects will survive. Everyone else will be ruined or left behind, because they represent older forms, of no use to any one ... You're a man of little means, Yeoryiou, just like me. No, I take that back. We aren't alike, because I know.”

“What do you know?”

“I know how the mechanism works, I know its secret ways. That's a source of capital you have no inkling of.”

“So why can't you get me my money then?”

“It's one thing to know how the economy works and another to have money at any specific moment. Am I wrong? One of my many different ventures is sure to come through ...”

“But will it be in time?”

“In time for what?”

“The importer ... He phoned me the other day. He said the verdict was out.”

Andonis let go of Yeoryiou's arm.

“And what is that supposed to mean?”

“You're asking me? Someone who knows the ins-and-outs of the economy should know that whoever doesn't pay goes to prison ...”

“In other words ...”

“That's right, they reached a verdict, I don't remember how many months it was for.”

“Why didn't you tell me that right at the start? Why'd you let me run on with all that drivel?”

“I like listening to you,” Yeoryiou said with a petrified smile.

"You have such a way with words ..."

Andonis quickly got hold of himself, and spoke up with pride:

"I'll be seeing you, Yeoryiou, I've got to run. I'll buy you that ouzo another time. But mark my words: I will never go to jail on account of debt."

He left Yeoryiou to plod along behind, and dodged out into traffic. So that ashen-faced man had gone along with him purely for his own amusement, and thus Andonis had wasted a brilliant maneuver for just such difficult moments. But he instantly congratulated himself on his new suit, he straightened his tie and continued walking with unflinching eyes, because he understood that he had reached that critical moment when you either go down the tubes, or start working your way up. And he immediately made a telephone call to find out about that important business deal with the investors.

THE CORNER COFFEEHOUSE attracted a good-sized crowd in the afternoon. Some of the customers played backgammon, while others just hung around marking time. A few of them, however, were rolling in cash. The man in the pin-stripe jacket, for instance, had five trucks operating in the market. He just sat in a chair and they brought the money to him. The man sitting next to him bought scrap iron by the ton and sold it as if it were gold bullion.

Who had ordered the double ouzos? Ah, it must have been Andonis, the accountant sitting across from them. He had been trying for some time to convince two partners from somewhere out in the sticks to entrust him with their business transactions. He clicked open his briefcase, showed them assorted accounts and invoices, talked nonstop, and sweated profusely. The other two listened to him in silence with their arms folded. His tongue rattled on, his eyes darted nervously, his long slender fingers never stopped moving, as if he were trying to grasp something that kept eluding him.

"Just give me the opportunity to work with you and you'll see that there's still such a thing as honesty in the world. Simply put, you'll come out ahead ..."

Andonis immediately offered to buy the partners ouzo. He signaled the waiter that it was on him. All he drank was a gulp of water. His saliva had thickened and gathered at the corners of his mouth.

Before he could go on, he caught sight of Ismene at the corner. He excused himself and hurried outside.

"Ismene! Ismene!" he called to her in as genial a tone as he could muster. "I have a favor to ask ... Since you're at home so much more than I am ... If some stranger comes asking for me, could you tell them I'm out of town ... Have you got that?"

"Of course, don't worry."

"You know how these things are ... You see, there are certain financial matters pending I'd like to avoid if possible ... And if you don't mind, if you can swing it somehow, I'd just as soon Vangelia didn't find out ..."

Ismene understood perfectly. Andonis thanked her and went back to the two merchants, whose posture remained unchanged. He immediately took up where he'd left off.

"So, before buying anything, you need to consult me, otherwise the sharpers'll skin you alive. Everything's synthetic these days, grease, fabric, rubber, you name it. You buy linen and it turns out it's made out of straw, or wood, or, who knows, milk. They wouldn't dare pull something like that on me. And I know how much an item costs at the factory level, I know the ins-and-outs of cost accounting, imports, tariffs, duties. The world of business is incredibly complicated nowadays. Everyone's trying to extract the yoke before selling the egg ..."

"And what's in it for you?" one of them roguishly asked.

"For our first transaction, I want no monetary or in-kind payment. All you have to do is give me a percentage of the difference between my prices and what you find out on the market. The money, the price lists – it'll all be right there in front of you."

This didn't seem to go over very well. Maybe they didn't understand. They exchanged looks.

"Look, you come down here to Athens," he went on, "and you worry about getting your wallet stolen. But thieves don't pick your pocket these days. They take your money and stick you with worthless merchandise. But there's a better way of doing business, more honorable and lucrative than pilferage ..."

"Want to go?" one of the partners proposed to the other.

"I will sell you my integrity at an unbeatable price," Andonis hastily added, without knowing for sure whether they heard.

"Yeah, let's go," the other said.

"But we haven't said when we'll meet again," Andonis said in dismay. "You only stand to gain ..."

"And who'll protect us from you?" the first of the two said, as if this natural uncertainty had just dawned on him.

Andonis' mouth dropped. The world flashed before him, then darkened. Had he heard right? Andonis managed to laugh almost instantaneously, however, so quickly the two partners didn't have time to notice his reaction to that unendurable insult. He immediately turned it into a joke and said with utter naturalness,

"Why, me, of course!"

They still didn't understand, but they did see him laughing. The faintest hint of a smile showed on their lips – a good sign.

"But since I don't have a spare moment tomorrow," he said self-importantly, "let's meet the day after, in Syntagma. At Zaharatos'. I'll be there at ten p.m."

"Fine," one of them said.

He didn't wait around to hear what the other had to say. He took his leave and went out. No sooner did he turn the corner, however, than he paused to catch his breath, and began walking at a more leisurely pace. He was in no hurry to be anywhere. Though his house was right across the street, he was reluctant to go in. He had better lay low for a few days, until that ridiculous business with the drafts was resolved. "Right now I'm at a decisive point," he said to himself, and strolled around the block to give some thought to the things he hadn't had time for all day. "You can spend your life that way, without a minute to think ... In the world we live in, you've got to be prepared for anything, even success." Without realizing it, he'd come back to the corner where his house was.

Stathis was setting out for work with light, diffident steps. Crossing the street, he was pinned between two trucks. He stood frozen in place, his eyes fastened shut. He narrowly escaped being rolled like a cigarette between two iron hands.

CHAPTER 5

FROM THE MOMENT SHE WALKED through the door, Ismene knew it wasn't business as usual at the company office ... She felt a chill in the empty corridor. The receptionist gave her a sour look: "You picked a fine day to be late." Typewriter keys clacked. Everyone was bent over the papers on their desks, as if it were forbidden to raise one's eyes any farther. Ismene was out of breath by the time she reached her desk. She opened a thick ledger, mostly to have a chance to collect her thoughts.

"Act busy," the woman next to her said under her breath.

Clio came down the long corridor and everyone did their best to avoid her gaze. Her wide skirt fluttered, a thick bunch of keys jangled in her hand. Not a whisper came from the adjoining office. Telephones rang unanswered. The employees wore dour looks, their hands were like dry sticks. Their elbows and knees refused to move, the numbers, hopelessly mute and slippery, grew blurred before their eyes in sharp quivering lines. The only sound was the typewriter, but if the roar filling everyone's head at that moment had been let loose, it would have swept everything before it.

"It's a ruse," Dimitris said. "They do this every time there's a strike at the factory ... Nothing new ..."

Raising their eyes, they saw Clio standing before them. Had she heard? She always wore the same ironic smile, you never knew what she was thinking. It was nothing new, yet your life hung from her hand by a thread. It would cost her nothing to add your name to the list of dismissals. She stopped before Ismene's desk.

"Miss, you will put aside whatever else you're doing and prepare the Ministry payroll. You came in late today ..."

She immediately stalked off and vanished into the director's office. If you didn't get along with her, you cleaned out your desk and left without further ado. It was a new building; business was booming. The blonde woman was on pins and needles. She went up and asked the department head if he'd heard anything regarding her. The two of them always left together after work. In the evenings they were always running off to some concert or other, and the next day they would discuss the reviews in the papers. The department head said they'd be laying off five or six, but he was more interested in the new record he'd bought the day before. The blonde walked off as if she'd never heard a piece of music in her life. Word had it they'd even notified payroll to have enough money on hand to cover compensation. The secretary finished typing out the duplicates, covered the typewriter with its cowling, and burst into tears. The young girl with circles under her eyes was in a panic because when her month's contract ran out, they told her to stop what she was doing and gave her work to the person at the next desk. The director was out of sorts, you'd do best to keep out of his way. When Ioannides grew irritable, his voice turned cold as ice, his utterances were short and harsh, his face drained of its color. Back when he was an accountant, everyone used to call him by his first name, Spiros. Today he was being excessively polite, which only increased the danger. His face was white as a sheet, making the deep scar on his forehead all the more visible. If you were to walk out of here with your last paycheck, the buildings would all look turned on their heads, the cars would be dragging past on their bellies, your legs would feel like they'd been lopped off a little below the knee. "In my village they say an animal that is spared the blade becomes twice as handsome and healthy. If I make it through this, just you watch how hardworking I'll be." "The balance of the stock is credit. Yes, make a cross-entry." "Don't tell anyone you've got a fever." "Did you get a permanent?" "How was I supposed to know? You think it'll make a difference that I went to the hairdresser's? Makis said he was going to take me to meet his mother today, but the moment he mentioned me to her, the old lady came down sick." "So now what are you going to do?" "We'll wait until she dies, then get married. What else can we do?" "Shh. Hand me the invoices ..."

Ismene took a sheet of paper and walked down the deserted corridor to the office at the end. Not a sound came from within, as if it were empty. It was full of metal desks, file-cabinets, employees holding their breath, a window looking out onto an airshaft. She returned to her desk. Dimitris, sitting in the corner, made a show of gathering up his papers.

"That's it, no more work for me today. I don't care if they do fire me."

"But you're friends with Boufas! I heard you calling him Dino one day."

"That's why I'm sure they're going to give me the boot, because I know him so well."

"And to think I was going to ask you to put in a good word for me ..."

She bent over her papers again. "What if they do fire me?" she wondered. She never wanted to have to ask her family for help. None of them understood that her life had been in a state of suspension for years, and they were all too ready to pass out facile advice. Even her mother had remarried with a retired officer, and hadn't shown her face since. Her older brother, a department head in a ministry, believed that the entire world depended on his signature, and patronized Ismene. Her younger sister Voula married a confectioner and all she could talk about was her pretty dresses. Ismene stayed on in the old house with Aunt Amalia. "Don't worry about me, just let me be," she would yell when they went on about how it was time she got some sense and thought about her future. "I never bothered any of you."

"The director would like the payrolls now," the office-boy told her.

The numbers danced before her eyes and dissolved amid clattering typewriters, shuffling papers, the disarray of fear.

"I'll be right with you. Two minutes."

Spiros was shouting into the phone that there was no point in having the workers' committee come up to the office because the chief was out. He was the only one who could discuss their demands. He would inform them the moment he returned. Clio understood his stratagem and came running over. They conferred in low voices, then Spiros said, "All right, tell them to come on up."

Several employees overheard the conversation and understood. Dimitris was bent over his papers, making child-like drawings of ships. His hands were ice-cold, and the ships began to toss on a stormy sea. Addition was a superb exercise, the production index an excellent indicator, the rattle of a typewriter like music to the ears. What he would give to have a little peace and quiet, to be able to get some rest. "I want to be able to work like a dog, but to have the right not to be worried sick while I'm doing it." "Where are you going?" "I'm going to tell them straight out: you can lay me off, but you have no right to torture me." "Save the heroics, Dimitris, and just make pretend you're writing something," the man next to him said, holding him back. The adding machine was spitting out a steady stream of numbers. The man operating it had lost his rhythm and was calculating whatever popped into his mind. He counted how many times the girl with the new permanent sitting across from him blinked in the space of a minute, and thus figured out how many times one blinks in one's lifetime. But then he realized his calculations might not be accurate, since the girl was in tears. Everyone was waiting for Boufas. The walls maintained an impenetrable silence. Back when Spiros, the manager, had been one of their colleagues, he used to rant and rave about how shameful wage labor was. If they could get through these critical hours, they just might make it. Still, it was absurd to think of layoffs as a factor of time. Time was unchanging. But that wasn't right either. Time was something that happened, an event which at the moment Clio held in her hands. No, it was the *situation* that granted her the power to create disturbances in your life. "What of it?" "Hand me the customer accounts. Not that one, the one with the green spine." "Good morning, Mr. Mitsos!" And the old man in the next office with the dyed hair grumbled, "Save your 'good mornings' for some other day." The phones never stopped ringing. The orders had to be delivered on time. Strikes are blackmail, plain and simple, according to Clio. "But how can you start all over again?" "You think the café-owner knows something? No, don't ask him, I owe him for five coffees." "What would he know, anyway?"

The office-boy took the payroll from Ismene. Almost immediately she was called into the manager's office.

"There's an error here!" he coldly informed her. "I am indeed sorry to see that in your carelessness you managed to put the good name of our operation in jeopardy. You should have had a more responsible attitude toward the task you were entrusted with."

Clio immediately came in and started making a fuss about the delay. As Ismene stood silently listening to them discuss her error, her ear made out a voice wafting through the offices.

"Phone call for Ismene!"

Without pausing to think, she left the two of them there. She scurried down the hall and grabbed the waiting receiver.

"Is this really Ismene?" a voice asked.

"Yes, it is. May I help you?"

"This is ... Angelos ..."

"Who?"

"I didn't mean to scare you ... Really, it's me, Angelos."

"Who is this? Please, tell me."

"It's Angelos. Now you tell me something so I know you're Ismene ..." the voice at the other end asked.

Very softly, Ismene said into the receiver:

"Five years ... It's me ... Is that enough?"

"I want to see you tonight. Can you make it?"

"Why not now? Where are you? I can come right now ..."

"Impossible. Tonight."

"Where? Where will you be?"

But the voice wasn't there. The receiver had gone dead.

"Tell me, A ..." she began, but caught herself. Alarmed, she looked around to see if anyone had overheard. Clio was standing in the doorway watching, jiggling her keys.

"Tell me," Ismene demanded of the mouthpiece, as if she were demanding an answer of the world itself.

"At the entrance to the Gardens," said Angelos softly.

"What time?"

"Nine o'clock. Tonight at nine. Be very careful ..."

There was a click on the line, followed by silence. Ismene carefully replaced the receiver, despite her hand's violent shaking. She turned and began walking through an endless silence. Clio was waiting at the door. As they went down the corridor, Clio paused to let Ismene, who was following her with her head lowered, to catch up.

"How long since you've seen him?" she asked her gently.

Ismene controlled herself, but her cheeks were flame red as her head jerked up in fright.

"Will you be seeing him tonight?" Clio asked again.

A "yes" escaped her.

She bit her lip, reminding herself that Angelos' safety meant much more than anyone's curiosity. Why had he said to be careful? Clio went into an office and slammed the door behind her. Ismene slowly proceeded to her desk, looking at each of the other employees in turn, as if seeing them for the first time, then sat down. Angelos' faraway voice drowned out everything else. The turmoil in the office, the anxiety and disruption caused by the factory strike, existed in some remote land, where the hunched employees breathed an icy air fraught with confusion and uncertainty. To Ismene, however, everything stood out clear and unequivocal. The building across the street was new, its lines perfectly balanced. Each cloud had found its true place in the sky, the unending street cries rose once more to her ears from below. Angelos was alive!

She got up from her desk and went over to the window to see how the things of the Earth looked, now that she had received the most important piece of information the world contained. Angelos was somewhere close by, he too felt the touch of this light that united all living beings. Such a revelation couldn't fit into the narrow confines of the company offices, which were filled with the terrified countenances of people who believed their lives depended on someone else's good will. Ismene leaned her elbows on the windowsill. She sensed Clio passing behind her. She didn't care anymore. Today, she had become a human being again, someone who occupied a specific amount of space. For years, she had been forced to expend a large part of herself just to keep alive the conviction that all was not lost.

Then she went back to her desk, flipped shut the ledger, and stuffed all her papers in a drawer.

"I'm leaving," she said to those sitting near her.

They all looked at her aghast. Surely she was looking to lose her job. They noticed a strange tremor in her hands as she tried to button her coat. Dimitris got up and asked what she was doing. But she couldn't bear to hear friendly words now, nor take the trouble to explain herself. "It's nothing, really. Thank you ..."

There was a fluster in her body, a churning inside her that had communicated itself to the things around her. "It's a personal matter," she said. "I'll be all right ..."

On her way out she saw Clio angrily pounding on Spiros' door. She came up to Ismene and said:

"Now that you've gotten over your excitement about the phone call, do you think you can do the payroll correctly for us?"

"No, I have to leave ..." she answered without stopping.

"But you're seeing him tonight ... Where are you going?"

Ismene couldn't make out what Clio was saying, only a malevolent hissing, "All right then, go!" The office receded behind her, with its bated breath, its furtive looks, its eerie, oppressive silence and fear.

Out on the street, she peered insatiably into the faces of everyone she passed. She would run up to someone, then turn back, stepping into the street and dodging through traffic to get a better look at someone on the other side. No, it was two college students, laughing. She recrossed the street. Maybe he was waiting down at the bus terminus. She hastened along through the gutter to get ahead of everyone. It was impossible to take in those moving throngs at a glance. Even if you shouted, no one would hear. The faster you try to move through a crowd, the more packed together it seems, you want to fill the gap between them with your stride, to pull them closer with your momentum. Angelos wouldn't be wandering around aimlessly, in hopes Ismene's avid gaze would unearth him. A single sweep of her eyes embraced and rejected thousands of faces, successive waves of eyes, foreheads, backs, hair. It was enough to glimpse a certain movement, a sliver of arm, an elbow. Angelos was all right, that was no longer in doubt. His voice had been a little shaky perhaps, but that must have been from the phone. The newspaper sellers were louder than usual, the streets were busier, as if some event had taken place, as if some momentous piece of news were making its way through the entire crowd. After all, five whole years had been condensed into a single instant.

Suddenly she stopped. She realized there was no point in running around aimlessly like that. She would be meeting Angelos that evening. She leaned against a wall, and gradually saw through her yearning and impatience. She retraced her steps to her office. “This is how it has to be,” she said to herself as she climbed the stairs. “It’s different now.”

“Back already?” Clio asked her in the corridor.

“Yes. Can I have those payrolls? I’ll do them right this time ...”

“You know, other people are in love too, but they don’t carry on like this ... So it’s been a long time since you’ve seen him?”

“Can I have those payrolls now?”

She sat back down at her desk and began doing the calculations all over again.

ONCE IT WAS DARK, ISMENE quietly climbed up to the roof and peered out over the ledge to see whether anyone was watching the house. She may also have known how difficult it would be for her to keep her secret. Tonight, Angelos’ life depended on all these factors. On the clouds, on the cold wind, on the feeble streetlights, the screeching of the trains, on wary looks and dark shutters. They would often sit up there on the roof. They would get boxes and chairs out of the small shed, which now was locked and used only for storage, and they’d sit talking till late. His friend Vassilis used to come up too at first, and sometimes even Lucia, who’d sit without saying anything.

Ismene went back down on tiptoe. She saw Vangelia in her room with the light on; Eftihis’ place was all closed up. The light from a blow torch flickered on the walls, and in one of the flashes she saw Harilaos climbing the stairs. He looked deeply disturbed, the sharp light gave his features an anxious expression. They went into the kitchen together, and in a low voice he told her that someone had shadowed him the whole way.

“I felt sick just knowing he was there behind me ... He was waiting for me, and when I came out, he followed me all the way here ... Could you get me some water?”

“They followed you here?” Ismene asked uneasily.

“If they’re at all competent, let them find him for themselves. I have the right to do everything I can to try and save him. I’m not breaking any laws. It’s despicable, yes, despicable, to follow a father in order to kill his child ...”

He flung open his coat as if shaking off contaminated dust. He unbuttoned his collar and took a deep breath.

“Any reputable judge would have to consider an arrest arising from the parents being followed as invalid,” Harilaos said once more.

Ismene listened wide-eyed. They would no doubt follow her as well. But she had to keep from telling even his father.

“Are you going out?” Harilaos asked.

“Yes, something quick I have to do. Today at the office ...” she said without looking at him.

“From one angle, it’s good that they’re following us,” Harilaos went on in his agitation, “since they won’t find out anything that way ...”

“You mean ...”

“You can rest easy, Ismene. He’s not in any greater danger for their having followed me.”

Ismene took note of all this but refrained from asking what he was implying. Harilaos realized that in his anger he’d spoken without thinking, and at once went on to say that there was no need to worry because none of them would be meeting Angelos any time soon. He sat down at his desk and opened up the brief. Ismene looked at him with a touch of sorrow. She started to leave, but hesitated out of a sense of guilt – or perhaps it was fear that held her there. Angelos’ father knew nothing about her meeting later that night, or of her having followed him the other night to the park. Then he looked up from the file and fixed his eyes on her. Now it was impossible for her to move.

But then Lucia came into the room, and Ismene was able to get up and softly bid them good-night. Lucia stopped her at the kitchen door, saying,

“So, you’re meeting someone tonight.”

“How’d you guess?” Ismene laughed nervously.

“You just look ... You might as well be shouting it ...”

Ismene started down the stairs, but Lucia gripped her firmly.

“Just a second.”

“What?”

“I’m coming with you.”

“You must be joking.”

“No, I mean it. I want to see him ... I promise not to bother you, I’ll just tell him a thing or two, ask his advice on something, then leave ...”

"What gave you the idea that?..."

"Don't try to hide it, you're seeing him tonight."

"You're wrong," said Ismene.

"Then you're meeting someone else. So what difference does it make? I'll keep a distance, and when I see it's not him, I'll leave ..."

"Wherever I'm going, you have no business coming with me. Have I ever asked you where you're going? Now if you don't mind, let me go."

"I'm coming with you," Lucia persisted.

"Forget it. You have no right ..."

"Don't make me laugh ... I ruined my life because of all your lunacies," Lucia almost whispered, and immediately regretted it.

"Why are you being so hateful? Don't you feel any love for him at all?"

"I love what I lost," Lucia answered curtly. "Anyway, what do you care? Why are all of you so bent on keeping me from seeing him?"

"Good-by, Lucia, and don't do anything foolish ..."

Ismene went down the stairs and slammed her door. Let her wait, she thought. It was early yet, there was plenty of time. Inside, it was quiet. Aunt Amalia sat knitting, without suspecting a thing. Ismene looked at herself in the mirror again. How had Lucia known? All she'd done had been to wash her hair and comb it a little more carefully than usual. "I wonder how I'll seem to him?" She looked herself over one more time, then smiled at herself. "That's just who I am, I can't change a thing ..." She took all the money she had in her drawer, put her coat on and went out.

In the passageway, she stopped and stood on tip-toe at the gate, peering over its wrought iron out onto the street. She heard steps on the stairs. At the same moment the bus pulled up, and she dashed out and jumped on. But there was someone running behind her who managed to grab onto the door before it closed. Ismene pretended not to notice anything, she took her time getting out her change and sat down behind the other person. She studied his skin, his eyebrows, his hands, trying to surmise if he was someone to fear. She looked at her reflection in the bus window. "He'll think I'm a wreck. A nobody ..."

Without warning, she got off at one of the stops, but she

instantly sensed the same person beside her. Her legs stiffened on the sidewalk. The person came nearer. Now what was she to do? She stared straight ahead at a pharmacy across the street. She sensed the person's icy nearness, but she couldn't see the face, couldn't interrogate its gaze ... She concentrated all her strength and began walking. She turned a corner and stopped. It was an old, narrow street. A light went on in a window. A woman with a net bag disappeared in a doorway. Ismene waited a little longer, but everything was quiet. She set out down the block, keeping to the shadows the whole way. If something bad were to happen on her account, it'd be as if she herself had doomed him. And that, of course, was something Ismene could never have lived with.

Lucia! Yes, it was Lucia who suddenly rounded the corner and pounced on her.

"Ha! I found you. I don't know why you tried to give me the slip. I told you I was coming with you."

"Get away from me or I'll hit you," Ismene shouted at her.

"Just try ... Scream all you want, but I'm coming with you ... I'm not going to be made to suffer on your account again."

"What have I ever done to you?"

"Back then too, after the trial, you were hiding him. I begged you a thousand times, but you wouldn't let me see him."

"I wasn't seeing him either ... It was a good month before ..."

"Liar! Just like now ... You thought he was your own personal property."

"And what harm did it do you?"

"I got married. I *needed* him then. I had to talk to him ..."

"Don't cry, Lucia ..."

"I'm not crying, you just think I am ... I need him now too."

"So go find him," Ismene said with feigned indifference. "Just leave me alone. I'm in a hurry."

"Well what do you know ... A love-sick school girl on her way to a tryst ..."

Ismene abruptly turned around and started running. The look in Lucia's eye had scared her. How long were they going to stand there talking? And what if she was late? She kept switching directions, and came out at the railroad tracks. She hid behind a tree and waited. A shadow darted out. Was it Lucia or the stranger on the bus? A whistle blew, and a train pulled into view. The figure –

a woman – was drawing nearer. Her halting steps made it clear she was looking for something. The moment the train's beam fell on her, she would be sure to be seen. They were walking parallel with the train. Ismene sprang across the tracks a few yards ahead of the engine. The train screeched past behind her with its rhythmic click-clack, a ponderous, all-powerful barrier between her and danger. Its loaded cars lurched slowly past, as Ismene checked to make sure no one else had managed to cross. She plunged down a dark street, took a tangle of side-alleys, ducked a car's headlights, and gasped for breath until she reached a bus stop. When she got on the bus, she tried to conceal her heavy panting. She looked at the other passengers. Could she relax now? What about the car behind them? Or the lady with the wrinkles? Or that well-dressed young fellow with the mustache? Nowhere was safe. Fear invested the very air, like a creeping disease, like a murderously sharp object whose very touch meant death. A snake's hissing filled her ears. Should she turn back? "He needs me," she thought. "I must go, no matter what."

CHAPTER 6

BEHIND THE WROUGHT-IRON FENCE, the trees of the Gardens cast thick shadows beneath a damp rustling of leaves. Those hurrying under the full pepper-trees were cold. Ismene slowly walked the near empty streets, among silent cars and dark, alien, incomprehensible buildings. Her whole life had been a lesson in waiting; those extra ten minutes she had to wait now were nothing. The wind whistled in the trees, the asphalt glistened, the road curved away under the street lamps. A car crept up to the curb and stopped. Frightened, Ismene moved away, but the car followed her. A voice called to her from the car window. The door opened. A white hand gestured to her.

"Ismene!"

It was Angelos. She climbed in and tumbled right on top of him. The car pulled away. She hugged him with all her might, she caressed his neck, his chest, his hair, his arms. She could feel his warm breath full on her cheek. When she raised her eyes, his face flickered a thousand different shades from the neon signs. He was unchanged – a little thinner than before, no, really about the same. "Let me get a good look at you." Ismene couldn't hold back her tears. "None of that," he whispered. And she stopped at once, remembering the driver. "So how have you been?" There was no reply. "You're all right, I can tell, I always knew you would be." The lights swiftly changed and his face broke into that old smile of placid joy. Now it was the same old Angelos ... They looked at each other, then she laughed, and lowered her head back to his chest.

The taxi was speeding down Panepistimiou Street. "Let us off here," Angelos told the driver. "At the movie theater."

His voice was the same too, deep and warm. A little shakier perhaps.

"Let us off here," he told the driver again.

"Here?" Ismene asked.

"Yes, come on."

He paid the driver, took her hand, and they found themselves on the sidewalk among people pouring out of a movie theater. Ismene clung to his arm and tried to pull him to one side, but he stood rooted amid the outflow of people. His coat was shabby and slightly too small for him. He wore a dun-colored wool scarf that covered his throat and chest. His face looked bonier – but it was Angelos all right.

"Angelos ... Angelos ..."

He didn't hear, didn't turn to look at her. He was greedily watching the steady stream of people. A few of them bumped into him, but he just moved more into the thick of things. He was always like that, rash and a little pigheaded.

"Quit tugging at me," he told her.

"Please, can't we go down a little ways ..."

"I want to see all the people."

"But ..."

Angelos stood gazing at the signs, at the billboards, at the lights, at the women going by, the pictures on the walls. This was crazy, Ismene thought. She dragged him along, trembling with fear.

"Just a second," he told her.

The crowd thinned out. No one paid any attention to him. A group of people came up and stood right in front of them. She must have been grabbing his arm too hard.

"What do you keep pushing and pulling me for?" he asked her angrily. "If you're afraid, just say so."

"Let's just go down a ways so we can talk. I haven't seen you in such a long time ..."

"*Are* you afraid?" he asked.

"Have they let you off?" she asked. "Why didn't you tell me?"

Angelos soon moved along on his own.

"Tell me, Angelos, are they still after you or not? Are you a free man?"

His laughter rang harshly in her ears. He tried to be calm as he told her, "Me, free? Hardly."

He pressed his fingers against his temples, and as he walked he covered his eyes with the palms of his hands, as if bothered by all the lights. Ismene followed after him. Angelos had come back tonight from a far distant journey, from a mysterious land without sun, a realm of ambiguity and fear. But perhaps the fear was all in her head, since he didn't seem worried about anything. How could she protect him surrounded by so many people?

"Where are we going?"

"Wherever you like," he told her.

Ismene came around in front of him and stopped, and Angelos widened his eyes and put a finger to his forehead, as he did when having a brainstorm.

"What do you say I buy you an ice cream? Or maybe you'd rather see a movie?"

"Let's go somewhere where we can be alone, where I can look at you," Ismene told him.

They went into a pastry shop and sat down in the corner behind a pillar. They gazed into each other's eyes. "So ..." No, such a conversation needed no such lame beginning. She gave his hand a squeeze. She wanted to engrave that moment in her mind, make it last forever. Five whole years! She was still dazed by the enormity of it all. She always knew he was all right. She hadn't doubted it for a second.

"Are your eyes still hurting you?"

"No. So what would you like?"

Between them was the marble tabletop, and around them mirrors that multiplied the customers' faces and the soft lights. The other couples also spoke in whispers. And beyond, past the windows of the shop's facade, a city of inconceivable breadth and unutterable possibilities sprawled beneath the night sky. Angelos probed Ismene with his gaze, as if trying to fathom who he had sitting across from him. It was no longer the school girl who'd hung laughing from his arm. As much as he may have loved that hardened face with its dark, intense eyes, there was something unknown there as well.

"Don't look at me like that ... Now tell me clearly: are you a free man?"

Angelos smiled. He acted as if her question surprised him.

"Tonight, I am," he solemnly told her. "So why not, let's say that I am ..."

"And you're all right?"

"Don't I seem all right to you?"

That was just how he used to act when she came up to him with her school binder and ask him to solve her math problems. He always insisted it would be better if he just explained them to her and had her work them out for herself. But Ismene would beg him to tell her the answers. "Come on, what difference does it make to you? Write down the answers for me and I'll do whatever you want me to." But he had never asked her to do anything for him – he wasn't one to ask favors of anybody. "So, if we assume that ..." he would begin. "Accurate data always contains its own solution ..."

"Not like that," she said now. "Tell me so I can understand."

"Tonight I am a free man. Honest ..." Angelos huddled in the corner behind the pillar. He tightened his scarf and turned up his coat collar as if he felt a chill ... He wanted to relish that sweet experience of fear that reminded him he was alive ... Yes, he was free, since he'd very nearly been ... There was nothing to worry about, no one would think it strange to see him hunched over like that, fascinated by the emotional expressions of this girl who marveled to find him near her.

"You mean you've been waiting for me?"

"Have you been waiting for yourself?"

Angelos didn't immediately see what she meant. He repeated his question.

"What I mean is," she explained, "I didn't once ask myself whether I should wait for you or not. It's all I thought about. What happened, happened to us both ..."

"In other words you've been going through the same things?"

"Not exactly."

"That didn't wear you out?"

"You wouldn't believe ..." answered Ismene.

Angelos shuddered and quickly turned the conversation to everyday matters. He asked her about her job, then about his family – "aside from you, of course." Before she could answer, he went on almost hurriedly, as if time were running out:

"You mean even more to me than myself ... Thank you for helping me all those years."

"Me? What did I do?"

He didn't explain. Where were they to begin at this difficult juncture? How could he be sure he wasn't in danger there, where anyone at all could walk in? The glass doors squeaked unnervingly whenever someone entered. Still, it was better that way, you could keep tabs on things. He resumed fiddling with his scarf, his collar, the sleeves of his coat that were too short. Ismene's eyes were like gates thrown open to receive his image. She told him that everyone at home was fine.

"Do you want us to leave?" she asked.

"Not at all. Calm down. Do you like compote?"

"No, I want you to tell me how you are."

"I'm fine, that's all. I'm alive."

"I can see that, and I'm so happy. Tell me what I can do for you. I want to help. You'd be surprised, I'm better at things now than when you knew me."

Angelos started to say something, but broke off. It wouldn't be easy to tell her that he had called her to ask her help in finding a place to hide.

"So what are we going to do, Angelos?"

While waiting for his answer, Ismene smiled into the mirror on the wall behind him. She wondered how Angelos saw her now. He was leaning forward on his elbows, which were resting on the marble tabletop. His shoulders were hunched.

"It won't be easy finding anything we *can* do. I'm only afraid it'll wear you out even more ... I don't even have the right to make you any promises ..."

"I wasn't complaining. I'm not asking anything of you ..."

"Still, it's not enough for me."

Ismene felt half afraid. Never before had Angelos spoken to her so obscurely, so haltingly, as if short of breath.

"You have to save yourself, Angelos ... You have to keep your guard up ..."

"I'm doing my best. But for how long? If only there were something that depended on my existing ... Every morning I tell myself: I lived through yesterday ..."

"That's the most important thing!" Ismene cried joyfully.

"You've got to get away so we can start living ..."

Angelos' chest swelled as if he wanted to take it all in with a single breath. It hadn't escaped his notice that she had said "we." It meant a willingness to share, but it was also a demand on her part. He felt like putting his arms around her, but held back because of the other people around. And there was that cold marble between them too. Ismene was tired – and with good reason. He didn't put his arms around her, nor even reach his hand toward her, because it occurred to him that he might not have had the right. After all, he had nothing to offer her, not one certainty, much less some promise corresponding to her "so we can start living."

"So you think that's enough?"

Ismene laughed. Surely he was joking again. What could be more important than being alive? She looked at him for a while as if he were some kind of oddity. The fact was, Angelos did not resemble the other men sitting at the surrounding tables. Just look at his eyes – what they must have seen! – his hands, his mouth, his hair. What answer could there be to the question "How long?" He kept tightening his collar as if he were cold.

"Why don't you say something? Tell me what we have to do."

Angelos shrugged.

"I'm afraid," Ismene said. "What else can I give you? Since there isn't anything, why don't you let me buy you a pastry? Which do you like, chocolate or vanilla?"

"A little water's all," replied Angelos.

"Bring us two of those," she told the waiter, "and lots of water."

Her troubled smile and forced humor dissolved. Angelos cast furtive glances at the people coming in or talking at the surrounding tables.

"At least tell me how you spent that 'yesterday' of yours. I can sum up mine in four words: 'I waited for you.' How about you?"

"I played cards."

"Cards!"

"That's right. Cards and nothing else, day and night."

"For five years?"

"For four whole years."

Ismene's face froze as if she'd just heard something horrifying.

"That's all you did?"
"That's all."
"You never went out?"
"Not once."
Since she couldn't understand, he went on:
"After I left Manolis' place – I'll tell you about that some other time, though you wouldn't be missing anything if I didn't – I went and lived with a retired major. His son Alkis had been a friend of mine, a literary type with glasses who was executed right at the start, in Haidari. The major took me in, and from the very first night we played cards. From eight in the morning until twelve midnight. The old man got grumpy the one or two times I made it clear I was bored, and I was afraid that would be the end of his hospitality. I even used to be the one to suggest we play, just to make him happy. He couldn't stand to be alone, but he didn't want to talk about anything but cards. I spent four years that way, one day at a time, with a deck of cards in my hand. God knows how many thousands of games we must have played. I love that old geezer, because he prolonged my life. I let him cheat, he felt so proud of himself when he beat me. Isn't that a riot? Winters and summers came and went, and the two of us played cards in an empty house. That's how I managed to survive ... Then I woke up one morning not long ago and when the old man sat down across from me to play, I couldn't take anymore, I ripped up the deck ... He kicked me out the same day."
Ismene gave his hand a squeeze, then opened up his palm there on the cold marble, and lowered her face into it. Angelos held her head, as his hand grew wet. Her sobbing continued.
"Picture it, Ismene ... But I told you all that to make you laugh ..."
Ismene went on crying. Someone on their way out gave them a look, and the waiter smiled as he wiped off a nearby table. Her sobs troubled Angelos. He had come to ask for her help tonight, he needed her strength.
"Ismene," he pleaded. "Don't worry, Ismene, everything will turn out."
"I'm not crying about that."
"About what then? Don't give up, things are bound to get better ..."

"I'm so sick of hearing that ..."

Outside lay the whole vast city, the streets he once loved to walk – and there he sat inside, unprotected, watching in awe as the girl who'd waited so many years for him wept. A whirlwind of panic whipped around him, and he felt utterly lost. How could he convince her he was telling the truth, when he himself couldn't believe in his own destruction. "Please," he silently told her, "lift your head, you've got to help me. Only for tonight. You do want to, don't you? I still have a certainty deep inside me, that's what I struggle to hold on to. And for me, who even the newspapers write about, it is a terrible struggle. Just think, there are people out there whose job it is to carry out the sentence. I wanted to live, that's all I could think about ..."

"When are things going to get better, Angelos?"

He couldn't give her the temporal framework she demanded. He still saw her as that school girl in her black pinafore, clinging to his neck as he swung her around in the courtyard. How had she come to such despair?

She lifted up her eyes, wiping them with the back of her hand.

"I'm sorry," she said. "I was crying because I love you, and I'm afraid for you, but that's no help to you at all."

"You think I'm any less afraid? All this time I've never stopped being afraid, Ismene. I want to be truthful with you. It was like a trembling that rose out of my bowels and paralyzed my whole body ..."

"And all you did was play cards?"

"For four years."

Ismene's eyes grew damp again.

The waiter came over and told them they were closing. They suddenly found themselves surrounded by stacked-up chairs. Angelos gave the waiter a pleading look, hoping he'd let them stay in that quiet corner a little longer, but the waiter told him, "Unfortunately, we do have to close."

Outside, the street was dark, with only a few people scattered about.

"Where shall we go?" Ismene asked.

"Wherever you like ... Want to walk a bit?"

"But what if ..."

"Don't worry. I feel like a free man tonight. Just imagine if it were really true. Will you keep me company?"

"What time do you have to be back?"

He hesitated, wanting to put things as simply as he could:

"They've been letting me stay on the condition that I never go out. It's a bit like prison. They left on a trip this morning, they'll be gone a few days. I took advantage of their being away and slipped out."

"But this morning you told me it was something important ..."

"It was. For me to see you ... to spend some time with you."

"Is it safe for you to be walking around this late?"

"Relax. No one's paying us any attention. The streets are full of people, they can't arrest everyone. Slow down, I'm out of breath."

"So that's all, you only wanted the company?"

Angelos looked up at the buildings while holding Ismene by the arm; he seemed not to have heard the question.

"I can't believe how much this street has changed ..."

THEY WALKED DOWN other streets, turning corners at random, and lost themselves in the stillness. Ismene clung to his arm and peered uneasily into the shadows. The arm she clutched was uncertain, some nameless fear threatened to take Angelos from her. Yet she didn't dare remind him, nor ask the purpose of their aimless walk. She tried to act as if everything were as simple as he would have liked – and as full of happiness too, as they walked along together after so long. Could it be that their lives really had entered a new phase, now that Angelos strolled along whistling, with his arm around her?

But it was getting late, and Angelos' fear began to bear down on him. Would he frighten her too much if he told her he had nowhere to go? He had escaped by means of an airshaft, and there was no going back.

"What would you say, Ismene, to my going home to the old house tonight. No one would see me. And boy, would it ever be a surprise. I'd really like to see my mother and father ..."

"No!" Ismene cried in alarm. "Lucia's there too, and she doesn't love you. She told me as much. Besides, on our street ..."

"Don't worry, I was just kidding. I meant just to see their surprise. I've been away so many years, no one would ever suspect I'd gone there ..."

"You'd be better off going someplace you know is safe ..."

He tried explaining to her that in the uncertainty in which they lived, probabilities increased in direct proportion to the tightening of the circle of possible situations. But he wasn't about to begin lecturing her now.

"We shouldn't be afraid of words, Ismene. You'll get used to the idea too. You already should be by now ... I can almost stomach it myself, but it's still not that easy."

"You're not leaving, are you?" Ismene asked, frightened. "No, I won't let you."

Angelos turned and faced her on the sidewalk. He asked her plainly:

"Do you know anywhere I can stay tonight?"

"Why? What's wrong with where you were?"

"Let's suppose I'm tired of it, or maybe I had a fight with the people there ..."

Ismene panicked. The night and the surrounding buildings were tightening their grip, and she had no idea how to help him.

"Let's walk down a bit. It's so nice out. And no one's even bothered us! What do you say we push all the buzzers in this building then run around the corner and hide?"

Ismene stared at him in disbelief. She pulled him down the street a ways, and Angelos reached out and rang the bell on a bicycle parked outside a dairy shop. A man came storming out demanding to know who'd done it.

"I did!" Angelos proudly announced. "Just for the hell of it ..."

Ismene was frightened. Things weren't as simple as he tried to make out. After they'd gone a ways, he asked about their old friends. "Do you ever do anything with them?" "No, I don't see any of them." "Do you think Tasos would take me in for a couple of days?" "But he's doing his residency at a hospital." "Which one?" "I'll ask tomorrow and let you know." "Don't bother. How about Stamatis?" "I saw him the other day, he's starting work on some contract out in the country somewhere." "Did he ask about me?" "No, he just told me what he was up to."

"So nobody's asked about me?"

"Nobody – fortunately," Ismene answered with satisfaction.

"No one cares whether I'm alive or not?..."

"At first, a lot of people asked, but fewer and fewer. Lately, only Stathis, the typesetter who lives in the courtyard ... He says he's your friend and would like to see you ..."

"Do you know which press he's working at?" Angelos quickly asked.

"Yes. And he always works the night shift."

"Let's go find him."

Angelos took her hand and they hurried back the way they came. Ismene told him how the more people forgot about him, the easier she breathed. She shuddered every time someone mentioned his name.

"In other words, no one ever says anything."

"You should be glad."

A little farther on he asked:

"I hope my books at least are all right."

Ismene assured him they were safely stored behind the door.

Back in the center of town, with the lights and the traffic, Angelos strode boldly down the street, past the all-night cafés.

When they arrived at the printing press, Angelos asked Ismene to go let Stathis know that he was waiting downstairs. He stood in the entrance among the rolls of paper, listening to the rhythmic drumming of the presses. Every click meant another letter. Everything continued to function, the world was alive and well. Its news was trumpeted in the papers, and everything rolled forward into the new day and the day after, with a quickening rhythm that was new to him. He alone had been cut off from things, gnawed by an unequivocal fear that transformed everything into yesterday. No matter where he penetrated the sphere of silence that enveloped him, he was met by the same cold wind of danger, the ambiguity that fenced him in. It was as if the world had come to a standstill that distant morning, when in small print the newspapers published the news: condemned twice to death in absentia. And suddenly everything, including himself, existed only "in absentia."

Stathis raced down the steps. A friend! He went up to Angelos and gave him a bear-hug with his ink-smeared arms. Ismene saw Angelos' face light up, but she wondered what Stathis' warm smile concealed.

"And you told me you never saw him ..." Stathis said light-heartedly.

Angelos, however, had something important to tell him.

"Do you mind if I have a word with Stathis alone," he asked Ismene, then walked with his friend down to the end of the corridor. Angelos hid behind Stathis back.

"I could be arrested any moment. This morning ... I have nowhere to stay. I've been wandering around the streets. I don't dare tell Ismene."

"Do you need money?" asked Stathis in alarm.

"No, somewhere to stay, even if just for a night ... a day or two."

Stathis shrugged, thrown by Angelos' unexpected request. His eyes grew tiny with fear.

"It's not that easy, Angelos, out of the blue like this ..."

"They don't notify you in advance ... You're the one person who can save me ..."

"How? By dong what?"

"Is there anyone living with you?" Angelos asked abruptly.

"But everyone there knows you ... It's right next to your old house."

"Listen, Stathis. If I keep roaming around on the streets like this, it's as good as giving up. I might as well go turn myself in. And I couldn't keep it up for much longer."

"How could we work it? I'm expecting my sister any day now ..."

"Tell me straight out, Stathis Do you want to help or not?"

"Fine, you can come ..." Stathis whispered. "Three days from now."

"Give me the key. No one'll know, not even Ismene."

"I always leave it hanging from a nail just to the right of the door ... I still think it's too dangerous ... I get off just before daybreak."

"Thanks, Stathis. I'll be there in a couple of days. That is, if they don't pick me up first ..."

They went back down to where Ismene was standing. Angelos seemed more relaxed. Stathis stared at him listlessly. He said it had been a strange night. Every cable was worse than the last.

They kept talking about war, the Bomb ...

"Do you want to walk some more, Ismene?"

Heavy drops had begun falling outside. It had been years since he'd felt the rain on his face. He again asked Ismene if she had to be home, whether they would be worried about her at home. He spoke to her as if nothing had changed, just like when they used to go for walks together. How easy everything could be again! They stopped at a street corner, swallowed up in stillness and the quietly falling rain. Ismene put her arms around him, but he was slow to respond. "Let's walk a little farther ..." he said. They turned up a new street, unfamiliar territory. Neither of them said anything about where they were going, or how long they would go on walking. Ismene kissed him. The rain came down harder now.

THEY TOOK SHELTER under a tin canopy and huddled against the wall. Water and darkness washed over everything. What if someone asked them what they were doing? Had he come out of hiding after five years just so they could spend the night getting soaked to the bone under a leaky tin roof? Angelos seemed *older* tonight somehow; heavier, more stooped. Maybe it was only his fear and the rain.

The rain was coming down harder, pooling at their feet. They pressed together against the wall, as rainwater streamed past. Angelos suddenly asked her when she had to be at work in the morning.

"Why are you shaking," he asked. "Can't you see that I'm not afraid? Who else in my shoes would be out walking at this time of night?"

"That's what I've been wondering the whole time. How long are we going to stay out here? You're taking a real risk."

"That's nothing new. Six years now. And you were angry I didn't tell you? There's nothing I care about keeping secret anymore. Come on, the rain's letting up."

He took her by the arm and started to go, but Ismene wouldn't move.

"I'm leaving right this second unless you tell me what's going on with you."

"What's there to tell? You know all there is to know."

They walked along the street under the downpour. A taxi drove past and splashed them. Someone ran by with his hands in his pockets, unafraid. The rain lashed the sides of the buildings. Angelos avoided meeting her eyes, which didn't escape Ismene's notice. The water streamed down her body, her clothes clung to her skin as if she were naked. Angelos pulled her behind a half-open door in an unlit entry. Somebody hurried past.

"Don't go, it'll be day soon."

"Why would I want to leave?"

"You're tired, I can tell. Just hold out a little longer, it may not take much more ..."

"What's that supposed to mean? No, don't tell me, I don't want to know. I'll stay with you as long as you want. As long as you need me ..."

"I didn't mean anything bad by that. Something good might happen. The war has to end someday, even for people like me."

"Your father thinks so too. He's gathering evidence to prove your innocence. He even tracked down an important witness ..."

Angelos laughed, and the dark, unexplored doorway echoed with the sound. His laughter ended as abruptly as it had begun. "To prove my innocence ..."

"Did he pass on my greeting when he saw you?"

"When he saw me?"

"At first he hid the fact that you two were meeting, but then we forced him to tell everything. Now don't you go trying to hide it from me ... One day I sensed something in the way he was acting, and I followed him. That time you'd agreed to meet in the park ... I wanted to see you, even if only from a distance ..."

"And did you?" Angelos laughed.

"But you didn't come! He waited till after it was dark."

A light went on in the stairwell and the two of them continued on down the flooded street.

"I never saw him."

"Never?"

"Not once."

They soon found themselves in a small square with trees. They ducked under a pine-tree. They rested their cheeks on its wet bark. They were two children again, just like in the old days. "We never had time for play, for falling in love ..." "I've never once stopped loving you. I feel as though if I did, something bad would happen to you. All those years I never doubted you were alive ..." Then Ismene laughed.

"I've got plenty to complain about, though. Not one letter ..."

"I thought of writing you so many times, and I even did, but I tore them up."

"Why?"

"I was afraid that by the time they reached you, everything would be finished."

"Isn't that the way it always is with letters?"

"Not exactly. When other people write letters, they know that they'll still be around when it arrives."

He looked at those two shining, quick-moving eyes so close to his own. Ismene reached out her hand and touched him, as if wanting to support herself against the tree trunk. Her hand was so pale and frightened. She rested it against him. Once again Angelos didn't dare to take her in his arms, because he knew she expected something from him he couldn't offer. What right had he to make her promises about their life together?

"I didn't write because I didn't want to remind you of any bond there may have been between us ... I wanted you to be free. I tore them all up because I realized I couldn't ask anything of you, not even for you to remember me ..."

"Yet I never doubted you were all right ..."

"Listen to me, Ismene. The fact is, two people form an attachment only when they know that they can plan some kind of future together. That's just how it is. Life is a question of being reasonably certain that you'll still be alive in an hour's time. You might die before then, but at least when you start off you have some kind of plan ..."

"But we're together now. Isn't that enough?"

"It's just that we don't know what's going to happen between here and the next corner ... Don't forget that I read my own death sentence in the papers, and I've lived through every detail in my mind, right down to the bitter end ... Make that a little before the end."

Ismene was crying now, but with the rain her face was streaming with teardrops anyway. She kissed him. Drops ran down his face too.

"Think about it," he laughed. "It's the only thing about my life I can really be sure of ..."

They had gotten used to the rain. Ismene leaned her head on his chest and closed her eyes. She felt his hand resting lightly on her hair. Angelos gazed at the surrounding buildings, trying to understand how the city could live and sleep as it sprawled unprotected beneath this dark rain. How could it hide its dreams, which overflowed and spilled screaming into the streets? Earlier, Stathis had said the news worried him. Would Ismene be able to hold up if another war broke out? The hydrogen bomb! "With all my troubles," Angelos thought to himself, "I've never had a chance to study nuclear physics. All I cared about was not getting caught. I've defended myself thousands of times, in a thousand courtrooms. Not for the charge they brought against me – I never found out what that was – but against whatever it was that was smothering me. I called it fear just so I'd be able to speak to it. The only ones who remember me now are people who want to carry out an old sentence written on a piece of paper yellow with age. Which is why I'm still at war, cut off at the critical stage of an ongoing battle. For me, the war is being fought with silence; for others, it's with the hydrogen atom. Would it be easier for me if I were read up on nuclear reactions and atomic fission? Life can't exist in utter silence. Everyone needs a future. There's not going to be a war, of course, but the odds are I'll be arrested in the end."

"It's kind of ridiculous, isn't it," Angelos said, "our standing here huddled under this tree?"

"But it's raining ..."

Ismene held him even more tightly, as if she were trying to support herself. Her hand slipped under his jacket and touched his chest.

"You don't have a shirt on!"

"I know," Angelos said, trying to make it seem natural. "I didn't have time to get dressed, I was in a big hurry ..."

Ismene caressed his wet, bare chest and said nothing. Angelos shivered, as if he'd just discovered he'd come out without a shirt or socks.

"You can't go back there?" Ismene asked. "Are they after you?"

Angelos looked up at the sky, at the rooftops, at the tree over their heads.

"It'll be light soon. I'll figure out what I'll do in the morning."

LIGHT SUDDENLY ROSE UP AROUND THEM. The sky gradually became ash-blue, the needles of the pine-tree that sheltered them turned green, the streets began acquiring depth. The first pedestrian went by. Everything was poised to begin. Ismene still had both her arms around him, a hold that Angelos realized only made his situation that much more difficult, now that day was breaking. What would the new day bring? How could he stop that slow wedge of daylight coming between them? That faint transparent glow that had overspread his face would soon become the full glare of day, and then Angelos would leave her. She looked at him with a face brimming with supplication and surprise. How many years had it been since she'd seen his eyes so clearly? Danger, which the new light always brought back with renewed vigor, kept her from speaking. After six years, they were right back where they had started. Back then, at least, they thought everything would change, that it would only be for a short while. Now his sodden jacket, his bare ankles, the panic tearing at him in this sudden onslaught of dawn cast them into a new realm. Angelos carried the war with him, a leftover from the past. The thing she found hardest to grasp was that Angelos was afraid! Ismene knew she could no longer endure the voiceless despair that would again gnaw at her, day and night – the despair of not knowing, of living without news of this man who had done all he could, for one whole night, to convince her that it was nothing more than a stroll in the rain.

The small bushes with their freshly washed leaves no longer hid them. The light welled up as if on waves of some inexorable breathing. The buildings acquired features and mass, the dirt became dirt again and Ismene no longer confused the swollen bark of the tree with Angelos' chest. Surely the city was lined with doors only too ready to receive Angelos, but he didn't know where they were. It was all still out there ... There were hordes of people who cared about your life, who would have liked to protect it, it was just a little hard for them to find you.

They left the shelter of the tree. The streets were open and exposed, they increased in length as Angelos and Ismene moved along them. Someone eyed them wonderingly, seeing their wet clothes and hair. Ismene was afraid that the moment had arrived.

"I'm coming with you," she said, clutching his hand.

"You can't, it's obvious now ..."

"Wherever you go, I'll come with you."

"That'd be easy if I knew where to go."

"Well then?"

"I don't know, I'll find somewhere I guess. I've got to live ..."

Angelos jerked his hand away and broke free.

"Good-by. And thank you ..."

He gave her a glancing kiss on the cheek and went off like a hunted animal. Ismene hesitated. She had known all along he would leave. Then she ran after him a little ways, but couldn't catch up. Out of breath, she stood watching Angelos mingle with the other few early morning pedestrians, until he turned a corner and disappeared.

CHAPTER 7

EFTIHIS FOUND THODOROS at the Omonia coffeehouse and filled him in on the results. Thodoros seemed pleased.

"We'll work wonders together, you and me," Thodoros said. "I've been looking for someone like you. That Andonis talks too much. I get dizzy."

They agreed on distribution, and Eftihis spent all morning wrangling with wily shop owners. Then he went home to wash up and change. He'd be meeting Mary's father in the evening and he didn't want the old man to think he was dealing with some guttersnipe. You need to get tough and nasty with sticklers like him. Not shouting and tantrums – tactics. That's why he'd gone to the body shop with Pericles last time. The old man knew that Mary used to run around with him. Just in case he tried passing her off as some hot-house flower, someone who'd never seen the light of day. As for Pericles – most of what he told you was a lot of crap. If you took his word for it he'd laid every woman in town. Besides, what girl hadn't taken a spin with some guy? All that was certain about Mary was that she'd been on Pericles' bike two or three times. There was no way of knowing about the rest. Apparently Eftihis had been right to bring Pericles along that night. The old man had seen him through the window all right. He began by offering only fifty gold pieces. He was hoping to get off easy, and started in about how he was a poor man, all he did was bash metal all day, and was that any way to make money? – and especially now with his phlebitis he couldn't be on his feet for that many hours a day. As if Eftihis were a doctor or a tax collector or something. "Fine, so we'll talk it over some other time, what's the big rush anyway?" Eftihis told him, as if he didn't much care one way or the other. At that point the old man had upped it to seventy, but Eftihis made a face and acted bored. When it reached a hundred they'd agreed on August 15th, the Feast of the Virgin, at a hundred and thirty they'd made it for Easter. But when he'd seen the old man's eyes light up at this, Eftihis lowered his head and said, "Let me think about it." "You don't think my daughter's in any hurry, do you? It's not like she's pregnant ..." "That's what I'm saying, let's both just give it some more thought and we'll talk about it another time," Eftihis had mumbled. "So how much do you want?" "Two hundred and we'll get married by the end of March," Eftihis replied curtly. The old man listened to the motorcycle running out on the street, looked at Eftihis over the rim of his glasses, and let off some steam by giving the sheet of metal in front of him a whack with his hammer. Then, without giving it much thought, he'd said, "All right, you've got it." "When?" Eftihis asked. "If it's this week we can hold the wedding on Saturday." The old man had gone along.

Eftihis set out, ready for anything. He purposely wasted time on the way, he took the long way around just so they'd have to wait a bit, then stopped at a barbershop for a shave. He had to make it clear to them that he had all sorts of things going, one of which – indeed the most bothersome of which – was the marriage.

He found Mary and her father in the coffeehouse in Omonia, their eyes glued to the door. Mary was in her best clothes, her face was flushed with anticipation, her pimples stood out more than ever. As soon as he joined them, Eftihis clapped his hands for the waiter, then, remembering he didn't have any cigarettes, went out to buy some. Coming back in, he gave Thodoros a call, and when he sat down again he turned his head to scan the headlines of the paper someone next to him was holding. No need to hurry the matter.

"Well?" the old man asked.

"I'm waiting to hear from you," Eftihis answered unconcernedly.

"I brought you eighty. I'll have the rest in two days."

"Keep it. I thought you were a man of your word ..."

The old man flinched at this, and guiltily tried to make excuses, saying how poor he was, and swore, trembling, that he would come up with the rest if it killed him, since he had made a promise. He pleaded with Eftihis to believe him. He had never in his life cheated anyone, he always kept his word.

Eftihis waited for him to finish, making it clear he wasn't interested in all his double-talk. Very slowly, he drew forth the marriage papers from his pocket and showed them to the old man.

"These are the permits ... If the other business had been taken care of ..."

He crumpled the paper up in a ball, to show how easily it could all go to pieces. Mary turned pale, and the old man began to lose it.

"But I gave you my word ..."

Eftihis cut him off:

"There's a big yard behind your house, right? Practically a whole lot. Why not put it in Mary's name? After all, it's yours, not something you have to go out and borrow."

The old man thought it was a good solution. It hadn't occurred to him. It may have been small, but it looked out on an alley in the back. Mary revived somewhat, her eyes and mouth came back to life. She poked her father with her elbow.

"What'll you do with it? Build?"

"I don't know, are you offering it?"

"I guess so."

"All right, let's get a move on."

Eftihis found them all a taxi, went with them to their place for the papers, and with the same taxi took them to a notary where the old man put the empty lot in Mary's name. While they were drawing up the papers Eftihis stayed out in the corridor smoking and strolling around as if their family affairs were of no concern to him. When it was over, however, he asked how much it had all cost and immediately covered the expenses. On the stairs, the old man came abreast of Eftihis.

"So, you're not marrying my Mary out of love?" he asked.

"That's my business. If I love her it'll be better for both of us, for her and for me. It's not something you should be trying to cash in on. You could have made out that lot to her without my having to tell you ..."

"I thought you were only interested in sovereigns. I never thought of it."

"That's what I'm saying. My old man wasn't thinking of me either when he stayed out all night at the taverna ... Your daughter shouldn't have to lose out just because I happen to like her ... Of all the things," Eftihis said in amazement. "Trying to use my feelings to save a few sovereigns on your daughter."

"That's not what I meant, but don't go putting a noose around my neck either ... I took her mother with just the dress she had on ..."

They were out on the street now and Mary joined them. Eftihis gripped her arm tightly. When they reached an intersection, he stopped her and shouted to her father:

"We're turning here," and he pointed down one of the streets. "As for the rest, I'll be expecting you at my place. As soon as you've got the two hundred come on by. I'm not setting up any more meetings."

They left her old man at the corner and were swallowed up by the crowd. Mary walked along at his side, aware of nothing but his hand clutching her arm, as if guiding her through all the noise and commotion.

"Where are we going?"

"Taking a walk is all. I wanted to give the old man the slip. He's some whiner."

Mary told him how her father nearly had a stroke that afternoon when the fellow who'd promised him the money pulled a fast one on him.

"Can it, kiddo," he snapped. "I see you've picked up a few pointers from the old man. What, you think I want it for pitching pennies on street corners? It'll be yours anyway. I guess you still haven't realized who you're dealing with. I'd be happy living in a tree if I had to ... As it is I sleep on the floor."

"Well, then?"

"It's for you, dummy. I mean for both of us. We're going into business, we'll have good times, and we won't need any son-of-a-bitch's help ... You'll see ..."

Mary's eyelids drooped slightly as she gave herself up to this vision. The colorful lights lining the street became a wonderful jumble, and it was as if the crowds pushing past, and the people calling to her, and the cars, the bright shops, and all the bustle were wafting her far away. Eftihis understood how dangerous it was to put such ideas into a woman's head, so he went on:

"But first you've got to be ready to put your nose to the grindstone. You're going to have to work like hell, day and night, just like I will. What were you thinking with that silly little brain of yours, that we'd be spending all our time looking into each other's eyes?"

When they found themselves on a street with only a few people on it, he plunged his fingers into her short curly hair, forced her head back and gave her a kiss. Then they returned to the street bustling with lights, people and noise, and Eftihis observed her at length out of the corner of his eye. She seemed intoxicated. As he watched her face changed with the shifting colors from the neon signs, Eftihis wondered who that girl was, walking beside him as if lost in her own world.

"Mary ..."

She tried to see who had called to her from the throng of passersby, but Eftihis gave her arm a shake.

"Tell your father to make it snappy."

"I will."

As they waited at a corner to let the cars go by, she leaned her head on his shoulder and, half closing her eyes, whispered,

"I never loved anybody but you."

"Save that stuff for later," he told her bluntly.

When they reached her neighborhood, he left her at her door and rushed back to his place. In the passageway he bumped into Aliki. She drew back, but Eftihis blocked her path. She was damn tempting, that girl.

"All alone? What's the big hurry? Let's have a chat."

"What about?"

"Anything, just to talk ..."

Aliki went on into the courtyard, but Eftihis made a lunge for her under the stairs. He pressed her body to him, and was beside himself. Aliki, however, grabbed hold of the wrought iron, and wiggled out of his grasp like an eel. She opened her door laughing, and Eftihis hid in the shadow because Urania asked her who she was talking to. "No one," Aliki said between breaths. He sat down on his doorstep and waited. "If she comes out again," he thought, "she won't get away." But after a while he started getting restless. Soon he heard Pericles' motorcycle pull up outside at the curb. Eftihis went to the front gate to find out whether Aliki would be going out with him. He strutted out, and tossed Pericles a brusque hello.

"No point in your waiting around," Eftihis told him. "She's not going out with you tonight."

"What makes you so sure? Maybe she's not back yet."

"She just went in. She's inside."

Then he cackled at the other's inanities, and went across to the coffeehouse. His mind was abuzz with all of his new activities. "Am I really in love with Mary?" he asked himself. But that was a whole other matter. Pericles came through the door. There were some hopeless types in there who envied Pericles because he tooled around the neighborhood and got the girls' attention. "I have a job too, but I don't have a nice pair of pants, a ring or a girlfriend, or wavy hair like his," one of them complained to Eftihis. "Keep away from me, stupidity's catching. If that's what you want, go out and get it," Eftihis said, getting up so that the other would know he had no patience for that kind of drivel. He wandered among the tables, looked out at the deserted street, and since he knew he wouldn't be able to sleep, he asked Prodromos, the owner, for a couple of old newspapers to read till he drowsed off. Prodromos told him again what a big mistake it was to send his brother over to the "blacksmith's," since he made more money at the coffeehouse, "he always managed to pocket a bit of everyone's change." Eftihis gave him a bored stare because he'd heard it all, in the same words, many times before ... Apparently it took people a long time to switch the record they put on for any given occasion, he thought to himself as he looked at Prodromos' tiny eyes. He took three or four newspapers with him and left.

He closed his door behind him and stretched out on his mattress. He must have lain there reading a long time, however, because his eyes began hurting and his throat felt dry. When he got up to get the water pitcher, he noticed a bluish glow at the shutters. What he had read in the papers had extinguished all desire for sleep. Could it be that war was going to break out, right when he was about to get a business going and get his hands on two hundred gold sovereigns? If something like that happened, did it mean he'd have to start jumping trucks to steal bread again? And who was to say that next time he wouldn't be the one they scraped off the road with a shovel. On the other hand, the newspapers were a month old. He tried to remember what he'd been doing on the days they came out. He couldn't remember anything in particular. He sleepily resumed reading. What everyone feared the week before might still be an issue, or even nearer at hand. He swept the ragged newsprint aside and lay down to sleep. "I'll read today's paper at the newsstand to get the latest," he said to himself, and realized that in the world we live in, everyone had to tend to his own affairs, and what mattered most was to get Mary's father to come up with those two hundred gold pieces. Yet he couldn't shake the fear that had seeped into the paper along with the ink, no matter how passé it may have seemed. Empty as it was, the bedroom was a regular prison cell. "Apparently the old man's made up his mind I'm in love with his girl, and now he wants to make me jump through hoops. Just as long as war doesn't break out ... I want a chance to show him what I'm worth."

Eftihis went out as soon as it got light and bought a paper. It confused him even more. Through the window of the kitchen next to his he heard Andonis telling Vangelia, as he splashed water on his face, that he'd stayed up all night going over the figures the investors had asked him for. "They might contact me any day now, and I better be ready."

"Does that make you happy?" Vangelia asked anxiously.

"I don't know, I haven't had a chance to think about it. I'll tell you in a couple of days. I won't have time to think about anything before that ..."

Eftihis went over to his window. He saw Vangelia putting her arms around Andonis' neck, about to give him a kiss. "Mary'll do that every morning," he thought to himself, then jerked back because they caught sight of him. Andonis uneasily poked his head out the window.

"It's nothing," Eftihis reassured him. "If you're leaving now we can go together."

Within seconds, Andonis was in the courtyard, as if he'd safely escaped a tight fix. The whole way, he went on about the fluidity of contemporary life. "God help you if you think you know where you'll be tomorrow. If you do, it means you've been left behind, a fossil. Am I wrong?" Receiving no answer, he set into an endless sermon on import permits, price indicators, terms of credit and the punitive laws that capitalism enforced to extirpate the victims of its contradictions.

"I'm not interested in that stuff," Eftihis told him. "But what do you think, are we going to have a war?" "Not a chance," Andonis declared without hesitation, as if he'd had the answer ready. "All indications are that one's getting closer, but in the end ..."

"In the end, what?"

"Nothing. They'll figure out that it's unnecessary. Capitalism ..."

"Does Vangelia kiss you that way every morning?" Eftihis asked. "Nice!"

"It's nice when you're not feeling harried. But these days ... Let's go down to the next corner ... As I was saying, Eftihis, capitalism's a competitive form of economy. Ultimately all those who stumble are cast into prison, the inevitable and indispensable victims needed for the system to work. Without them, the whole thing would come to a grinding halt. Funny thing, huh?"

"Sure is," Eftihis agreed, "but I was asking about the war ..."

"Isn't that a kind of war?" Andonis asked in dismay. "And a vicious one at that. Just think, at any moment you could suddenly find yourself ruined ..."

"What are you getting so worked up about? We're not at war. You yourself said it couldn't happen ..."

Andonis' eyes were glazed over with fear, his lips had drained of color.

"You never know, it could happen at any moment ..."

Eftihis seemed to have guessed what was on Andonis' mind. He addressed him humbly:

"I know you've got some big business deals in the works. But see if you can give me a little help on the side. I'm expecting to get two hundred gold pieces, that money I was telling you about the other night. What do you think, is that enough to get something worthwhile going?"

"Anything's possible. You have to study the matter first ..."

"You want us to do it together?" Eftihis proposed. "I've been thinking about you all along ..."

"Let's talk about it another time, Eftihis. At the moment ..."

Eftihis took his leave and headed off. He understood that one needed peace and quiet, and a good deal of discussion, before embarking on such endeavors. He walked down a deserted morning street, with closed shutters lining both sides. He went up onto the overpass and gazed out at the waking city, which looked refreshed and beautiful. A cool breeze caressed the old rooftiles, dusting off the night's soot and rousing them to meet the new day. Brightly colored laundry rippled on a rooftop clothesline, smoke rose from a smokestack. A couple went by. The man was looking at the woman tenderly, feelingly. A train pulled up at a station. People got out. Eftihis moved along with the crowd, rubbing his palms together. "Life is wonderful, all right," he said, and began whistling the same tune he did when he wanted Mary to come to the window.

THE BUS WAS PACKED FULL. Andonis ran up and held out a finger to tell the driver to stop, as if the world were at his command. The people waiting on the street crowded on in a crush of bodies. The street was full of pot-holes, despite the millions of drachmas being spent on improvements. This time of day, all the riders were employees trying to make it to work on time. Why should a single minute make such a difference in the life of a human being? "I have nowhere in particular to be, but I'm in the biggest hurry of all. I should have been there yesterday, or the day before. Or last year," thought Andonis bitterly, watching as one last person grabbed onto the pole in the doorway.

Those who managed to get a window seat pressed their faces to the glass, thinking their own thoughts and staring out at the road. In the press of bodies, Andonis was hampered by his bulging briefcase. Yet it was an essential tool of his trade, it contained his memory, his ideas, his hopes. The bus crept along. The tall eucalyptus trees hung with a few sparse leaves in the square, their tops lit by the sun as it passed over the roofs of buildings. No one had the right to play games with someone else's time. Who could say how much a minute was worth? At that hour, the windows of the buildings had a damp sheen, and people's faces were more careworn than usual. Andonis ducked his head slightly to see the sidewalk and the sides of the buildings, trying to figure out where they were. Then he cast a furtive glance at the watch of someone who was holding onto the overhead handrail. "What makes him any better than I am?" he wondered. The face of the street changed continuously. No one building resembled the next. The bus had picked up speed. "If I were still employed by the company ..." No, that was just wishful thinking. A few days before, an old friend of his had suggested he do the accounting for a trucking cooperative, but Andonis had laughed and flaunted his fat briefcase under the other's nose. His friend had stammered an apology, and Andonis had magnanimously forgiven him. He had to carry through with what he had begun. "I'm not afraid of hunger, only of failure," he reflected, and his thoughts quickly turned to his many promising prospects.

The bus was hurrying along now. The way they were all packed in there, you would think they were headed for the same destination. Your nose bumped the cheek of the person next to you, while he bored into you with his gimlet eye, wanting to see how deep he could probe. The breath of strangers mingled with your own, it was impossible to collect your thoughts. "While I still have something of a margin," Andonis reflected, "I have to work myself without letup ... It seems that up until now I've been holding back, which is why I'm still at square one." This struck him as quite brilliant, and he smiled to himself contentedly.

Suddenly a shriek tore through the bus.

"Stop! I have to get off!"

The bus lurched slightly, and everyone pitched forward.

"Stop right this minute!"

Andonis saw that it was Lucia, screaming as if she'd gone out of her mind.

"Open the door, it's an emergency."

But the bus started moving again, and Lucia pounded on the metal door with her fists.

"There's no stop here," the bus driver snapped.

"Then open the door and I'll jump out, it's an emergency."

"Don't! Don't!" a few of the passengers shouted.

"I can't, you'd be killed," the driver told her again.

"So what?" Lucia screamed back. "What's it matter to you?"

"It matters ..."

And he instantly speeded up, as if just to spite her. There was no one in front of him on the road. Andonis shouted up to the driver,

"Why don't you let her off since it's obviously an emergency? What are we, your prisoners?"

The driver gave no answer. He kept his eye fixed on the road, and couldn't see how Lucia's eyes flashed with anger.

Andonis went over to calm her down.

"Did you see him?" Lucia asked.

"See who?"

"Angelos! He went by right next to the bus."

The door opened at the next stop, but Lucia didn't get off. There was no point now that they were so far past where she had sighted him. A number of people commented on it, and the driver quipped, "A bus has regular stops, it's not a mule, it doesn't do door-to-door service. What if I got a ticket? What if everybody wanted to get off outside their office, their store? She probably saw a friend she wanted to say hello to. So why doesn't the young lady get off if she's in such a big hurry?"

"There's no point now," Lucia told him stonily.

She saw the driver grinning in his overhead mirror, and decided he had the most despicable eyes she'd ever seen.

"Take it easy," Andonis told her.

She didn't answer. Angelos wouldn't be anywhere thereabouts anymore. He had appeared for only a instant, and in a particular spot. He couldn't be everywhere at once. She had seen him though, however briefly, walking so close to the bus that it had almost struck him. He was wearing a black overcoat, his eyes looked unfocused, as if he'd just awoken, or as if all the people frightened him ...

She got off at the Academy stop. Andonis hopped off after her and she stopped him.

"You're his friend, you've got to help me find him," she told him. "Everyone else is trying to keep me from him. You'd think I was going to hurt him or something ..."

"I haven't seen him," Andonis told her. "Not since ..."

"How much do you want?" Lucia asked.

"But how am I supposed to find him?"

"I know you're in a tight spot financially ... I can see it in your eyes, and by the way you act ... You know how to find him ... I won't cause him any trouble ... He's my brother, I need his help ..."

"I mean it, it's been years since ..."

"Ask his friends ... How much do you want for it?"

"But, Lucia ..."

"Yes or no? I'll make it worth your while."

"I'll see what I can find out," Andonis whispered, and he hurried away.

TWO DAYS LATER, Angelos was still roaming the streets. He halted in his tracks, as if a statement like that required a moment's pause. "They haven't caught me yet!" he said aloud in amazement, but no one paid any attention. A number of people jostled past on their way to work. Someone carrying a big load quite naturally yelled at him to move out of the way. The pushing and shouting of the morning rush had thrown him off balance. But he loved it all so very dearly that he felt like thanking everyone who bumped into him or elbowed him aside, thinking him just another pedestrian. "Maybe things aren't so bad after all." He'd believed that the moment he set foot on the sidewalk they'd arrest him. So he was wrong there too. Things would have been easier if his coat hadn't been so small. He caught one or two people eyeing him curiously, but luckily they kept on going. Who knows, maybe they were people he used to know. By and large the streets were filled with new faces, unfamiliar for the most part. A bus went by right in front of him, narrowly missing him. He sprang onto the sidewalk, glad to have escaped danger of a different sort. He plunged his hands into his pockets and resumed his original course.

He circled the block, reassessing his situation without coming up with anything new ... A little farther on he came to a square that had changed completely in appearance. Now it was lined with automobiles, newly opened stores, fresh buildings going up. He continued on and explored the first unfamiliar street he came to. His gaze wandered over the newspapers on display, the facades of apartment buildings, the shop windows. All in all, everything looked slicker, catchier. These changes were a yardstick of how far he'd lagged behind. Still, it wasn't an easy thing to measure. In another hour and a half he would be burying himself in the darkness of a movie theater. Before him lay an endless expanse of time, filled with infinite possibilities: "In other words, one," he thought. "My being arrested."

That possibility allowed him to walk with a freer gait. There was no need for him to buy newspapers. On other days he had wanted to learn what was going on in the world in case there was anything that had a bearing on his situation. But now it was all right there in front of him – the people, the streets – and he was exposed to any and every danger. As he walked among the coffee-houses and the traffic and the serious-looking businessmen, he couldn't believe that he had forgotten about them for so many years. Everything was so familiar, even though he felt like he was seeing them for the first time. And to think that a good half of the people on the street were his friends.

He walked briskly in the direction of Ismene's office. He would feel better being near her. Her large, somber eyes created a whole new space for him. The difficulty was that she expected so much from him. When he reached the door of the building, he stopped abruptly. If they met again, he wouldn't be able to leave her. It was more dangerous for him when he was with her. Her face would light up again, but somewhere deep below the warm protectiveness that flowed from her eyes was an expectation. And what had he to offer her? "I still haven't reached the stage yet where I can accept her love," he said to himself. A glass shop on the ground floor caught his eye. A girl was dusting some crystal. Her slender fingers were firm yet delicate. What was that unkempt fellow in the window staring at? Next door was a photography studio. He clenched his teeth, as he did when poring over a geometric figure, trying to work out the answer. The point was to find "the necessary and fit conditions ..." Only his own problem couldn't be mapped out in lines ... In order to say that a problem was unanswerable, however, your proof had to be every bit as unshakable as for an actual solution. "And I do want to go on living. Therefore there must be a solution." That observation allowed him to keep going.

A passerby peered into his face. A car pulled to a stop at the curb. Two men were talking at the corner. A woman coming out of a shop almost ran into him. Angelos stood to one side and just watched. The people kept coming, there was no end to them, walking, standing still – laying siege.

Ismene had let him go the other day, as if she had understood that that was how it had to be. Angelos had run without knowing where he was going. The daylight that suddenly caught them in its web had frightened him – as had Ismene's trying to cling to him. He had wandered around aimlessly, then was suddenly stunned by the realization that nothing had happened. "There is no salvation," he thought while looking at the stills outside the movie theater. Then he realized how idiotic that was. "I'm alive, aren't I? That's my salvation. It means I can keep on going." He counted out his money and went in. With the warmth and all the people inside, his clothes quickly dried. He bought a small bag of roasted chick-peas at intermission. When the lights came back on, he hid in the men's room, then moved over to the other side of the theater. He slept for a while, so he missed half the movie. He woke with a start when there was gunfire, and immediately changed seats. During the next showing, he tried to follow the movie, jumping again when there were gunshots, but he paid more attention to the people around him, and was alarmed every time the usher pointed her flashlight in his direction. Once she even held it on his face while making change, and he sank down in his seat. "Sorry," she'd said as she went off. When the lights came on again, he bent down to tie his shoe, so no one would see him. "I should never have torn up that pack of cards," he thought to himself, but instantly remembered Ismene's tears when he'd told her his funny story. Then too he had had nowhere to go. He'd felt comfortable in that house. Whenever he lost patience with the cards, he would take the clipping about his death sentence out of his pocket, and start dealing again. It was the only piece of I.D. he carried with him. Sometime later he added a second clipping, about the two others who had been convicted along with him being put to death. The movie was totally inane, but who cared?

When everyone got up, he knew the movie was over and went out. It was dark now, but the streets were well lit – needlessly, for there were few people about. "There's no point in my being careful," he said to himself, and immediately felt his lungs struggling for breath, as if there were an iron band being tightened around his chest. He hurried to get off the main streets. "I must have taken a wrong step somewhere," he thought. "Why else would I be in such a mess?"

He went up to a construction site. The boards across the entrance had been left open, and he squeezed past. He moved gingerly among bricks, plaster, scaffolding. He found the stairs and went up. They'd poured the posts and the slab-work as far up as the fourth floor. Angelos curled up in a corner, but sleep didn't come easily. He got up again and inspected the building. The light from a neon sign allowed him to duck the wooden supports for the freshly poured beams. "I wonder when I'll ever get to build something." He studied where his fellow engineer had situated the posts, he looked over the cantilevers, the beams, the slabs. If there had been more light, he would have tried to figure out the various stresses. He fell asleep on some boards, beside some sacks of cement that sheltered him from the wind.

He left in the morning before the workers arrived. "One's calculations must be correct at every point," he reflected as he attempted a clear-sighted review of his situation. "A large safety coefficient must be factored in, with no stinting on material. I have to make it through till Thursday night." He cast one last look at the cement skeleton of the building, then set out, as if leaving behind something that belonged to him. On just such a morning, in the early spring of '48, they'd led those who'd been sentenced with him to "the accustomed place." They would have given the solid stone walls of the prison just such a look as they left. Angelos hadn't known any of them, but in the endless hours of his solitude he had often tried to engage them in conversation, to tell them that they shouldn't judge him too harshly for having managed to escape. He wrapped himself in his scarf and continued walking. "Thursday night," he repeated to himself, and it was as if he had said, "next year."

He counted his money again. There was enough for two more movies, with three drachmas left over. That meant one bag of chick-peas a day. Once he'd settled that, he walked with the step of someone with something specific to do. One attracted less attention that way. When it finally came time, he ducked into a different movie theater. It was the same routine all over again: changing places at intermission, hiding in the men's room, tying his shoelaces, sleeping – everything in a calculated order. The movie was better this time. That night he went back to the same building. Once again the boards across the entrance had been left open. Angelos took careful stock of things and went up the stairs. He noted the new casings, the scaffolding, what progress had been made. He couldn't get to sleep. He was terribly hungry, but that wasn't something one should waste time on. "Imagine living your whole life this way," he thought. The movies would become like the major's deck of cards. The next day was Thursday. When he had left the building that morning, he hadn't turned around to look. There was a hand somewhere out there, waiting to grab him by the shoulder. It was the last day that he'd be able to go to the movies. He would be out of money, with only one drachma left.

He hurried away from Ismene's office. She would instantly have seen how scared he was, and he couldn't allow that. Time was passing, automobiles and people barreled past. He slowed his pace because he remembered he wasn't wearing any socks, and when he walked fast, his bare ankles showed. He needed a shave too. His eyes drooped, his head felt heavy, and there was a sharp pain at the base of his neck that made him hunch his shoulders. "Until Thursday ..."

He went into another theater. He sat down next to a column so he could lean his body against it. Soon the lights went out and the music started up. He sank into the darkness and slept. Before long the person beside him gave him a nudge.

"Just you wait and see, the fellow with the mole's going to kill that tall guy."

"What makes you say that?" Angelos asked in alarm.

"Because he's got to, otherwise the movie's a piece of junk."

"Have you seen it before?"

"No, I just figured it out. What do you say, think he'll kill him?"

"He could get away," Angelos said quietly. "It wouldn't make any sense for them to let him get killed, since it's so obvious."

"Not a chance," the other said. "It'll happen just like I said."

"You really think so?"

"It's a foregone conclusion. It doesn't matter what he does, the other guy'll get him ..."

The man beside him was sure it would all turn out exactly as he said. Maybe he really knew. Besides, in a movie, you couldn't change anything. If Angelos had been paying attention, perhaps he would have figured it out earlier. Now, however, it was time to switch seats. The conviction of death voiced by this man with a hook nose and curly gray hair troubled him. He glanced over at him: a middle-aged man with sunken eyes, he was absorbed in the movie, eager for his prediction to come true. Angelos quietly slipped away. He wandered a bit until he found a new seat. The same sweet drowsiness weighed down his eyelids. "Maybe he'll escape," was his last thought before his eyes closed. The dark theater was filled with people anxiously waiting to find out what would happen to someone who someone else was trying to kill. There were sirens, screams, running feet, panting, and silence. Nothing had been decided yet ... Then more shouts and footsteps. It was pitch-black, your eyes wouldn't open. Alone and unknown, a living relic ... And everything was closing in, as if in anticipation of your certain demise. No, there was nothing that *had* to happen. It wasn't like in the movies, things could turn out differently. It was impossible to know how things would turn out right from the start, there were other forces at work ... He had to get away. He had to *live*. There was no sordid, insidious truth forbidding it ... The audience let out its breath; a respite. Angelos fell asleep, and saw none of it. At the intermission he went out and studied the mugshots of the actors on the wall. The people milling around in the lobby smoking knew how the movie had turned out. He couldn't look at them. Everything seemed suspicious. There were some odd characters in the crowd, people talking in whispers, someone came up and stood beside him. But how could he leave? It was worse out on the street. He had only one drachma left, but instead of buying the bag of roasted chick-peas as planned from the shaven-headed boy selling candy and cookies, Angelos went over to the public phone. He dialed and asked for Ismene. Soon her voice came clearly over the line.

"Don't be afraid ... I just called to say hello. Didn't I promise?" he said in a low voice.

"Are you all right? Where are you?" asked Ismene.

"I'm fine. Really. I'll be seeing you real soon."

"Tonight, at the same place?"

"No, not today. I can't ... You know how it is ... I only wanted to ask you something ... The other day, I was afraid that maybe you thought ... But now I'm fine ..."

He bent to the mouthpiece and whispered,

" ... and I love you as much as ever. You'll see me again, don't worry. Maybe even ..."

"Maybe what?" Ismene asked anxiously.

"Maybe it'll be better ..."

"Go on – better how?"

"Not now, I'll tell you another time. Good-by ..."

"Be careful, all right? Careful you don't get sick ... and watch your step ... Good-by ..."

"Thank you," Angelos put in softly before hanging up.

He paid his last drachma and slipped back into the darkened hall. "I'll see the conclusion of the movie later," he said to himself, and dropped off to sleep.

SUCCESS WAS FLITTERING NEARBY, he could feel it. Andonis, sitting in a deep plush chair, sensed that the air was thick with promise. The shiny parquet and the deep carpet and the curtains and pictures and the chandeliers and the serious faces he had before him were all clear indications that he was approaching the critical phase in this major transaction. Loukis had unexpectedly announced that the investors would be meeting that day. So Andonis had polished his shoes and shaved, then grabbed his brightest smile and gone right over. Loukis introduced him as an important economist. And Andonis had accepted it. "A good consultant is worth his weight in gold," someone had let drop, and Andonis smiled in agreement and stationed himself contentedly in the armchair. He took a deep breath and relaxed, because he felt like he had arrived somewhere.

While they waited for the others, Loukis asked what they'd have and brought out a whole collection of bottles, crystal glasses and silver platters. They were all men loaded with money and connections. Contracting, importing, stocks, they went out every night, swapped girlfriends and chatted in a casual drawl about dizzying sums of money. Circumstances were highly favorable for these gentlemen at present. They considered it ludicrous to exert themselves to make a profit, since everything was offered to them on a platter. They never asked each other how they came into their money. "If only the reverse were true," Andonis thought. "That is, when you *didn't* have any money ..." He sat patiently in his chair waiting for them to finish talking about some minor marital infidelity they all seemed to think was terribly funny. Their drinking and banter dragged on, however, and Andonis began to worry that their time would be up without anything of substance having been said about the important matter at hand. It was an accomplishment just to be in a place like that, all the legwork in the world didn't get you there. He studied their faces and could think of nothing relevant to say, so he contented himself with smiling. One of them was telling about some magnificent nudes he'd seen in Hamburg, and someone else about what happened to him one night at a New York cabaret. "Who cares?" Andonis found himself wondering. The conversation was running on dangerously, one person glanced at his watch. Andonis tried to show approval or surprise at the various things being said. Then he pretended that until that moment his existence had been without meaning since he had been living in ignorance of certain new gadgets one young man had just had installed on his yacht – the son of an industrialist whose father had spent years funding a certain laughable politician, and now sent flowers every morning by plane to a dancer in London. "She's just wild about gardenias!..."

At some point they decided to get down to business, and a look of gloom suddenly settled on all their faces, as if it were a tedious but unavoidable digression that would have to be gotten through as painlessly as possible. They all waited, cocktail in hand. Loukis gestured to Andonis, who began speaking. One well-fed boob across from him sat with his mouth hanging open. In a single breath, Andonis threw a whole lecture on lucrative investments of recent years at them. He defined goals and outlined current prospects, showered them numbers, statistics, indices ... What a grasp of the facts! Not a lot of theoretical claptrap – he gave them straight talk, meaty and to the point. He stunned and stupefied them with his meticulous verbal needlework outlining the science of instant profits – they all broke into simultaneous smiles – and proceeded to a detailed analysis of financial scams as reconfigured by current political-economic realities in a system of extortionist business practices. The investors beamed like freshly opened daisies, and the further Andonis delved into his figurings of probable profits, the more their faces came to resemble the angelic backsides of babies. Ah, what happiness! "What we desperately need is money, and lots of it," he said at one point, and they all piped up with utmost satisfaction, as if it were the easiest thing in the world. "They'll give it to us ... We'll get loans ... It'll be a breeze!" Apparently they were only too eager to undertake a government contract of some sort. They'd make a rock-bottom bid, and later seek additional expenses. They also discussed a large open bid with commission. Everything was splendid!

Thank God for his briefcase, which contained all anyone would ever need. His eye caught Loukis gazing at him proudly. "The latest London closing was ..." He bowled them over on imports. The capital would come of its own, like water down an irrigation channel. "You must act now, however, while the doors of opportunity are wide open," he told them, and they all agreed. This whole meeting was the work of Loukis, who by all appearances had the least to offer. They had entrusted him to look the matter over, and he had passed on a clutter of papers for Andonis to sort through and complete a study on. And Andonis went all out to show them what was involved in a true economic analysis. His presentation dazzled them, they were convinced of his expertise. Despite his fatigue, the words flowed from his tongue, his intellect sparkled in a felicitous display of boundless knowledge. "Everyone knows the trick of turning a profit, so don't try to pass yourselves off as anybody special," Andonis thought to himself without pausing. He'd demonstrated to the gentlemen that he too knew the secret, so what if he was scrambling for a buck. Sitting in that deep, warm and above all solid armchair, ideas came to him in droves, his eye quickened, his mind moved in leaps and bounds. His throat grew inflamed, and he drank water from a glass of cut crystal. The cool breeze of success whirled about his ears. From here on in, everything would hinge on his expertise. Maybe he already had the game won. And lest there be any lingering doubt, he unleashed a flood of numbers at them before they could catch their breath. Tariffs, freight costs, international pricing, seasonal fluctuations, all these were useful and significant indicators.

"What do *you* think?" asked a man with a small moustache.

"How you want to apply these principles is up to you ..."

Then they agreed among themselves that it was absurd to discuss the matter of capital. Everything would be taken care of.

"When it comes right down to it, we'll bribe 'em." To them, such details were like delightful, uncomplicated toys. They spoke of someone who ran four separate gambling clubs, how he would line up girls for anyone who asked. Then they went on at great length about some confused business involving photographs, thefts, forgeries, adolescent girls, blackmail and other equally uproarious matters. Andonis didn't know the first thing about all this, which had nothing to do with economics. He discreetly shut his briefcase, lest someone notice his samples, which were the nuts and bolts of the salesman's lowly trade.

The discussion wandered off again. The gentlemen would be playing cards that evening. Andonis did his best to get them back on track, shrewdly starting in on the profits to be made by undertaking some government project. One of them, an engineer in fact, excitedly assured the others that Andonis' calculations were right on the mark.

The industrialist's son had reservations about the wisdom of making large investments when, as he'd heard from his father, war was just around the corner.

Andonis grew livid. That was nonsense. He told them of all those who stood to benefit by fanning such fears. It was propaganda meant for the gullible masses, God save us if investors like them were influenced as well. "We can safely bet on peace, that's the most probable scenario," he said with conviction.

However, this subject was dropped the moment the gentleman with the mustache reminded them that the whole enterprise hinged on one thing: financing.

"What we need's a man of action," the engineer counseled. "Someone to get the job done right ... The rest is easy."

Andonis was overwhelmed. Now was his big moment. He sprang up with the readiness of someone who had been waiting years, and looked at each of them in turn, holding his breath, engulfed in total and eternal silence. They became hulking shapes with sealed lips and secret, inviolable wills. He besought their consent, attempting with his piercing look to extract the endorsement that would mean his salvation.

"As soon as we find him, we can get started," the engineer repeated.

Then came the same asphyxiating silence, the same vacant

expressions, fleshy faces, inertia, lifeless fingers. Andonis, in a final attempt to transcend the chaos bearing down on him, said in a firm voice:

"I'm your man!"

But once again no one said anything, almost as if they hadn't heard.

"Let's call it a day," someone without a face said. "We'll arrange the whole affair some other time ..."

They remained in their seats, enjoying that giddy feeling that comes with having dealt with a multitude of bothersome yet gainful matters. They'd grown weary of listening and talking. Andonis sat in his armchair, crushed, still hoping to extract some promise that the whole thing wasn't going to end then and there. He gazed with infinite sorrow at the crystal glasses, the cigarette butts, the carpet, his briefcase resting on the floor. He downed a glass of strong spirits and told them,

"Please don't feel in any way beholden to me. I looked over your numbers and brought a variety of issues to your attention. That's my job ... You see, we belong to such different categories ..."

Loukis smelled a lurking danger in this sudden outburst, and cut Andonis short, skillfully maneuvering the discussion back to the important topic of night clubs. He related a juicy tidbit, and they all burst into laughter.

"In underdeveloped economies, the contractors are the one's in charge," Andonis pressed on determinedly. "Today's business no longer adheres to the classical but slow-moving method of accumulating surplus-value ... They want to get their hands on the sum total of the national wealth ..."

Andonis felt a chill as the others continued chuckling over the preceding anecdote, as if they hadn't heard a word he'd said. Andonis fell silent.

"Pleased to have met you, Mr. Stefanidis," the gentleman with the moustache said in a formal manner.

"Hope to see you again," the industrialist's son murmured.

"When?" asked Andonis anxiously.

Most of them, mere faces lacking identity or features, glided out into the hall. There had been no commitment, not even for a follow-up. Yet they'd all looked him in the eye while he spoke. At the very least someone should have offered him a reason, any shabby little excuse would have done, something for him to go on in the difficult hours ahead. He stood off to one side, because he couldn't bring himself to leave. Soon two others made for the door. Which were they? That left only Loukis, and Rapas, the engineer, his sole ally.

"You and I speak the same language," he told Andonis.

"I'll be sure to stop by," he said with a flicker of optimism. "Soon, too."

Then he took his leave with the polite forthrightness of someone who feels comfortable speaking in surroundings where he is understood. So that was it, then? He found himself on the street without knowing how he got there, or where he was going.

On Korai Street he bumped into Phaidon Yiannopoulos.

"I'm still waiting for that article of yours ... I need it for the next issue."

"You'll have it in a couple of days," Andonis promised.

"Three pages – it'll be a snap for you ... I always said you should devote yourself to theoretical studies."

"You really think so? I'd like to too, but ..."

"So, I'll be expecting it."

"You bet. The day after tomorrow at your office. See you then."

Yiannopoulos put out a magazine on economics, with no circulation of course, but it did afford him all sorts of connections. Andonis felt publishing his article there right then would have great significance. "I'll be sure to finish it up tonight," he promised himself.

THAT AFTERNOON AFTER WORK, Ismene bounded up the winding stairs and, without thinking, asked Lucia if "Father" was back. Lucia fixed her with a stare and said nothing. Ever since her meeting with Angelos, Ismene had avoided her. When she came home afterwards at dawn, drenched, she had quickly changed, dried her hair, and headed straight for the office. The whole day she'd had the shivers, and that night was burning up with fever, but she didn't tell anyone. Ever since that night she'd been filled with an intense joy. She knew he was alive, that he existed just like everyone else, and that he loved her. She knew it for a fact, her eyes and her hands and clothes and hair radiated that certainty. Often, however, such thoughts would break off, and her knees would grow weak as she remembered the danger Angelos was in. Even so, it was better than the dead silence that had tormented her for so long. The clenching knot in her stomach had been untied, that formless dread without beginning or end. She had seen him, held him, kissed him. The strangest thing of all was that Angelos had been afraid. Even today, when he called, she could tell he still was. It was better that way, it would make him more cautious. There was no need for heroics now. What would anyone else have done in his shoes?

As soon as she finished at the office, Ismene went to an old friend of Angelos', an agronomist, whom Harilaos had wanted her to ask about certain crucial dates. "We'll be able to show," he'd told her, "that he was someplace else, and couldn't have been involved in the incidents named in the indictment." Ismene tracked him down in a travel bureau, where it was his job to answer the questions of foreign tourists. When she said Angelos' name, he gave a start.

"You too? A woman was in here yesterday asking if I ever saw him, and where she could find him. She said she was his sister ... What's going on anyway? Who are you?"

Two foreigners approached and he began speaking to them in French. Ismene left. So, Lucia had uncovered all his old acquaintances and was trying to get them to tell her where Angelos was. Ismene would have to let her father know, and leave it to him to give her the scolding she deserved. She would have to be made to realize how dangerous to Angelos this search of hers was.

That afternoon, Ismene went out to water the flowerpots. The flowers had to be taken care off. Someday the house would come back to life and Angelos would be pleased to learn that no one had ever doubted his return.

The moment Harilaos came through the door, Ismene gave him a hug.

"Angelos' safe. He called me today," she burst out.

His mother immediately came over and asked was it really him, did she recognize his voice, and what did he say. His father gazed into Ismene's eyes, trying to determine if she was telling the truth. After all, hadn't he assured them that he himself had seen him? Whenever he felt compelled to lie like that, however, he would look at the ground or pretend to be occupied with something else because he was afraid his eyes would give him away. But there was nothing clouding Ismene's eyes, she wasn't hiding anything. He studied her, weighed her credibility, and asked:

"Is he in any danger?"

"He said everything was just fine."

Ioanna, his mother, wanted to know where he'd been all that time, and why he hadn't written, complaining that he'd forgotten her. "What's that boy doing wandering the streets like that?"

"He didn't say much, just said to say hello to everyone and that he hoped that someday soon ..."

"How's his morale?" Harilaos asked

"Great – as always," Ismene said.

"He looked frightened and sick to me," Lucia interrupted, "like he was shaking, all slouched down and wary ..."

"What?"

"That's right, I saw him too! He was wearing a black coat that was too small for him, and a scarf. He hadn't shaved and he kept his head hunched down on his shoulders ..."

"So you *did* see him."

"I've got my secrets too ... As if you tell *me* anything ..." Lucia said as she left the room, smiling bitterly.

THE MOTORCYCLE HAD BEEN rumbling for some time out on the sidewalk. Aliki turned out her light and stood beside the curtain. Pericles let the motor run and went on waiting. As long as that rhythmic throbbing called to her, she used all her strength to stay put at the window. Pericles apparently lost patience, because at one point he peeled away, purposely making a racket. The sound of his motor vanished the moment he turned the corner.

The motorcycle came back. Aliki's window didn't open. Lucia appeared on the sidewalk. She looked at Pericles, her hand on the gate.

"So you're the one making all the noise."

"I'm not bothering you now, Miss, am I?" he asked with the utmost charm.

"Of course you are, making such a racket ..."

"Then I apologize ... What would you like me to do?"

"Tell your girlfriend to get on out here ... What, is she standing you up tonight?"

"I'm just waiting for a friend of mine ..."

Lucia stepped back down from the step. She looked at his bike and asked, in all simplicity,

"Does it go very fast?"

"Sure, if I want it to. Hop on and I'll show you," Pericles suddenly said.

Lucia laughed.

"You'll love it," Pericles went on.

Without thinking what she was doing, Lucia sat down behind him and said, "Let's go."

They promptly set off, taking the road for Dafni. Lucia huddled down and felt the air whistling past her ears. Speed made everything shrink to nothing in the night. All that was left was the roar of the engine and this unknown man's back. The road stretched before them, glistening and straight. "It's not like I'm doing anything so terrible," she thought to herself. "I've always been so alone." She couldn't go on living in her father's house. It was worse than out in the country. Lucia couldn't count the number of unbearable small-town squares she had come to know, all those stifling Sundays in blearily lit cafés, all those wagon roads with mud so deep you sank in past your ankles. And all this with a querulous, pettifogging schoolteacher who was perpetually dozing off. "What do I care," she thought, "since no one'll go anywhere with me?" Had anyone asked her what kind of life she'd led up there all that time? To get back at them, she wouldn't tell them anything about life in the provinces. That night she had gone to see a wonderful movie. She wouldn't even tell them what a good time she'd had. In any case, no one would ask.

"Faster!" she yelled at Pericles.

There were fewer houses now, the night was impenetrable. "I love what I gave up more," she said to herself. It was better not to start complaining, that became a form of surrender. All she had found here was a high-strung mother who never left the house, an insufferably formal ex-judge, a brother condemned to death, and Ismene. It was the same old routine, the same things being said, the same oppressive silence. As if it hadn't driven her crazy the first time through! Her father reviewing law decisions, her brother preparing for the University, God forbid anyone make noise or try to sing ... Then there was Ismene, as willful as ever. What was she always whispering to Lucia's father about? Angelos, of course. It was always Angelos! Back when he was studying, then later with the resistance, and now too, they couldn't stop talking about him. Was every family like that?

Pericles slowed down. They'd come to a pitch-dark area with pine-trees. Lucia could hear the wind in the needles. A light twinkled somewhere in the distance, as if rocked by waves.

"You like it here?" Pericles asked.

Lucia ordered him to keep going, and Pericles obeyed. He would do her bidding – the first time. She loved racing along like that at breakneck speeds. How else could she get the mud off her, get rid of that feeling of suffocation? Kostas, her husband, was always sleepy and spent hours on end trying to cover his bald spot with a tuft of hair. Why did he bother? He would be coming into town in a few days to try to get the government ministry to take action on his promotion. Then Lucia would have to go back with him. They might even transfer him. "What do I care? I've lost everything – though I'll make sure no one else finds out." Like back during the war. She remembered that first day when the sirens sounded. Vassilis, the boy living with his mother down in the courtyard, immediately came up to their place. He and Angelos had felt a strange excitement, which kept erupting into laughter. Her father said nothing. Lucia got into a bad mood and went and sulked off by herself. She could smell trouble. That summer she finished high school, and one night her father asked her if she would be taking the examination to study literature. He was up to his ears in casework at the time, and he propped his glasses on his forehead and held his fingers over his eyes to soothe them. "No, I don't like literature," Lucia had answered. "What do you like, then?" "Dance," Lucia said firmly. "That won't do. Find something else you want to study," the judge had replied without missing a beat, and bent back over the court briefs. That fall marked the start of the famine, and Lucia never found anything she liked as much as dance. She'd bought wool tights – she still had them somewhere – and would do dance exercises when no one was home. New faces had started showing up, friends of Angelos', and would disappear into his room. What could they be spending so much time talking about? They'd quickly slip inside and shut the door, then leave the room two at a time without saying a word. Angelos' room would be filled with smoke and scraps of paper, which Angelos would burn immediately afterwards. "Your friends aren't very polite," his mother complained. "They've never even introduced themselves." She'd invite them to sit down in the parlor so they could talk, even to have their mothers over "so we can pass the afternoon together." Alkis, a blond fellow with glasses, was the only one who ever talked to her, or even smiled, on his way through the kitchen. "Good-night," he whispered to her the last time, and lingered a little longer than usual on the top step. "Good-night, Alkis," Lucia had said. He never returned. Later she learned that he had been arrested and executed. That was when she realized the nature of their endless conversations behind the closed door. Vassilis would come in with a big smile on his face, whistling, teasing Angelos about his equations, and shouting with indignation, "I'm hungry!" The others had given themselves over to silence and somber looks. Vassilis was always somewhat boisterous, he'd lift the lid on the pot to see what Ioanna was cooking, and on his way out he would say, shaking with laughter, "We've got a lot of work to do. You see, what we want is to rebuild things from the ground up." And the funny thing was that he truly believed it. She remembered one evening when she had gone with Angelos and Vassilis to find out the examination results at the University. They lit matches to read the list of names on a board with a wire screen in front. It was windy and their matches kept going out. In the flickering matchlight she was the first to catch sight of the name "Dimitriadis, Vassilios" on the bulletin, and she excitedly told them to hurry up and strike another match. She had jumped up and down, grabbing both of them by the arms, then solemnly shook Vassilis' hand and said: "Congratulations, Doctor." Once they'd made sure, Vassilis offered to buy them a beer. From that evening on, they called him "Doctor," which he seemed to like. And their mother would always leave out a plate of food "for the doctor," and Harilaos would ask his opinion about certain minor irritations he was having in the area of his heart. Once Lucia fell sick with a bad flu. They had Vassilis come take a look at her, and it was the first time he arrived looking so serious, with his black bag in tow. He put on his stethoscope and Lucia realized that she was expected to bare her breast so he could listen. He moved the cold metal carefully along her flesh, which was feverish and laboring from shortness of breath. His fingers barely touched her. His face wore a look of concentration and responsibility. Then he gave her an injection in the arm and wiped the sweat from her brow with his palm. He came by every afternoon: "How's my patient," he'd ask her mother. He'd put his hand to her forehead to check her fever, but it felt more like a caress.

"What are you stopping for?" Lucia angrily shouted at Pericles.

"So we can sit a while. It's out of the wind here."

"Take me home," she bid him sternly.

"But it's so nice here ..."

"Take me home, *now*."

Pericles didn't insist. Spreading out before them was a wild wooded area. Perhaps he too was a little afraid to go in among the shadows, with an unknown woman sitting behind him.

"What did we come for then?" he asked her.

"Get moving," Lucia shouted.

He turned around and let out the throttle on the downhill stretch. Lucia held her head up, and her eyes stung from the wind. Did anybody love her? No one had ever asked for her advice or her help. She had to show them all that she *liked* being along. The night she introduced Kostas to her father, it was as if she were telling him, "Are you happy now? Do you prefer it this way?" It had all come to nothing. Angelos was condemned to death, it was only a matter of time before they would hear that the sentence had been carried out ... Vassilis never reappeared. And Lucia had elected to go to the provinces with Kostas. She even pretended she was glad to be going. And it was better to have them giving her those dirty looks whenever she tried to flush them out of their arid and bitter despair. Back then it had been a self-destructive perverseness, almost an act of vengeance, for which she had paid dearly. She didn't know how much longer she'd be able to hold out, if she didn't clear matters up at once. She had to decide before Kostas' arrival. Lucia could feel the mud of small-town life weighing down her feet. Yet once upon a time they'd felt like they had wings. Like that time at a party the doctor had taken them to. They had danced and exchanged banter, and at one moment Lucia found herself spinning around in the middle of the room by herself. How had she ever gotten up the nerve? Everyone else stood back to give her room. She was blind to her surroundings, glowing with happiness, and soaring with an unfailing sense of rhythm. Everybody applauded wildly. It was the only time she'd felt so much enthusiasm around her, and such a fluttering in her breast. They all wanted her to go on, but someone said it was almost curfew. The patrol went by outside. A few days later they came to arrest Angelos, but he escaped by leaping over the rooftops of the neighboring houses. And Lucia never again danced in front of others. Vassilis rarely came home at night, then he stopped altogether. Then Angelos joined the resistance fighters in the mountains. Her father announced it to them one evening, with utmost gravity. Apparently Ismene had known about it too, but had kept it a secret. The house was all but empty now. Then came all the other troubles. Who felt like dancing? And now, after all these years, they hadn't changed a jot.

"Stop!" she shouted in Pericles' ear.

"Why?"

"Just stop. I want to get off."

Pericles stopped abruptly and Lucia climbed off.

"I'll go the rest of the way myself."

Pericles looked at her, stroked his mustache, and smiled.

"You sure now?... A nice little ride, eh? Some other time we'll get to know each other ..."

"Get lost."

Lucia jumped over a ditch at the side of the road and disappeared.

THE COFFEEHOUSE AT THE CORNER has closed, otherwise it wouldn't be a coffeehouse. Everything closes at night: windows, shops, eyelids. All that's left is the asphalt of the street, which only goes to show it's made out of tar. It's like some overworked black, laboring under the footsteps and tires that trundle down it day in and day out. Because the street works too, just like everything else in existence. The bus is making its last run of the day. Later on, the asphalt will curl up in a ball, or stretch out to its full length, whichever feels most comfortable. There are fewer and fewer footsteps; people have closed their doors, and everything is settling into an infinite disorderliness. The light from a shop sign lifts a corner of the night from the street up to its own height, like a tent whose main support rests a little above your head. From there on up is solid night, with its cosmic infinitude. But the shop sign is weary. And your clothes too are weary, they long for their accustomed nail. But everything is new, even though it looks older now. Even rocks acquire experience over time. And you, after so many years and such a long, difficult journey, roam these same streets, a changed man. Whatever you wanted to accomplish today should have been done yesterday, or ages ago. We are very late, dark had overtaken us, we all but perished in the night. And it's not something you can make up for either. Maybe tomorrow. Yes, tomorrow ... You remember back when you were just starting out? It's not possible, rocks cannot deny their own solidity. They seem so close and familiar that if not for your being afraid, you would speak to them, so quietly no one else could hear, your fingers lightly touching their seams, their coating of dust. Thus you would learn more about yourself. The doors in this neighborhood don't close very tightly. They're made out of wood, you can hear what's being said next door. The room is dark, except where the wall is lit by two or three stripes from the corner street lamp. It's amazing people who walk at night aren't afraid. Returning home full of hopes and ideas, they're all but drunk, their eyelids imbued with some dream begun on the street. You count the people going by. Someone stopped at the gate. Yes, those steps halted here, then continued on in great haste. Who could it be this time of night? Everyone else is asleep. And when a feeble light flickers on, you feel like you've got a fever. You remember of course how once your two eyes weren't big enough to hold all of your dreams, and the ones left over ran down your cheeks in the form of tears. You were feverish then too, the whole world was spinning and you were drunk on its sweet vibrations. Now and then intersections crop up before you, but crooked, erratic, disheveled, as if they'd tossed and turned all night, the way you do when sleep comes hard. But you never lose your way, or only when you want to. Most of the time you find your door no matter what, as if it's been waiting for years.

STATHIS FINISHED WORK at the usual time, and stood huddled over by the door of the printing press. A young journalist named Pandelis wound through the rolls of paper strewn in the entrance, went up to him and slapped him on the back.

"So, Stathis, how'd my piece look to you today?"

"Good. Only you wrote too much. What are you doing staying this late?"

"I was behind tonight," the youth answered. "The problem is they won't give me any peace. Run here, go there, kill yourself for the hot story. All they know how to do is complain, they still haven't seen an article worth getting worked up about. There's no pleasing them. Every night Nikolaidis asks me: 'So, mate, what earthshaking bit of news have you got for us tonight?' And he pulls a face when I tell him. How am I supposed to come up with something earthshaking when nothing impresses them? I want to find something to really knock their socks off."

"Everything's earthshaking," Stathis told him.

"You know of something?"

"Plenty."

"Such as?" the journalist asked.

"Everything's earthshaking when you stop and think about it."

The young man took this as a joke and laughed. He told Stathis that he was going to find that story if it killed him.

The streets were the same every night: the glistening asphalt, with empty tracks furrowing its length; the shops with their grating rolled down, and a long line of carts at a corner, with chains through their wheels; the tall, threadbare eucalyptus trees in the small square, the small grocery stores with their grimy slabs on the empty pavement; last year's posters on the front of a summer movie house; the kiosk, the bakery, the train crossing, the pitch-black factory and the cross streets. Stathis counted the street lamps going off into the distance, to figure out where his turn was. Tonight too the news of the world had been poured into molten lead, then cooled into headlines. Deliberations on the Berlin crisis, the war in Indochina, the hydrogen bomb hanging over everyone's head. Demonstrations, workers' demands, then the atomic panic again, and unemployment, and political intrigues.

As Stathis neared home, he could see dawn starting to come from far off. A few steps more, and he turned down the passageway. At his door, he went to take the key from its nail, but it was gone. Something seemed to come back to him, and he quickly turned the knob and went in. Before him, on the chair, someone sat waiting for him. His face was only dimly visible in the half-light. Stathis closed the door behind him and whispered,

"Good morning, Angelos."

CHAPTER 8

AFTER TWO DAYS IN STATHIS' cramped room, Angelos felt even more in the grip of danger than before. He was surrounded by familiar faces, almost all of them people he'd grown up with. The slightest sign of his being there would be enough to give himself away.

His first thought upon entering had been to find the bed and lie down. He groped in the dark, afraid of bumping into something and making noise. Fortunately, a few flashes from a welder's torch lit up the courtyard and helped him find a chair. He'd worn himself out just reaching the house, he'd had to take long detours around adjoining blocks, drenched in a cold sweat. No sooner had he sat down than he was asleep. Stathis came home exhausted in the morning and took the whole bed for himself. They couldn't talk because even whispers could be heard next door, but Stathis gave him to understand that they'd have plenty of time to talk later on. And so Angelos was alone, utterly alone. He moved his chair as carefully as he could over by the window so he could see the courtyard of his house, and the members of his family, who would soon be coming down the winding stair. But it was still too early and he had seen no one. When Stathis left for work in the afternoon, he saw Angelos sleeping with his head slumped on his shoulder. He gave him a nudge, and whispered in his ear that he was leaving, but Angelos didn't hear, so he picked him up, half-asleep as he was, and laid him on the bed. He locked the door and carefully slipped the key in his pocket, as if it were something precious.

They couldn't talk the next morning either. As soon as he

came in, Stathis indicated with his finger that silence was imperative. Then, as if to avoid him, he opened a parcel of food he had left on the table. And Angelos had submitted. "He must know what he's doing," he thought. He ate the cheese and bread, the eggs and potatoes. For the first time he felt their nourishing substance as it was greedily sucked up by every last cell. He wondered if nourishment was a cure for fear. After eating his fill, he nudged Stathis and told him "Thanks," but the latter was angry he'd woken him. Then Angelos tried to read the headlines in the newspaper by the half-light. The room was cramped, with a bed, a table, one trunk, and newspapers stacked in the corner, as if the events themselves had silted up there. Maybe Stathis believed that not even a single day had gone by, which was why he didn't ask Angelos what he'd been doing for the last six years. Nothing interested him, as if he knew it all in advance. Was it asking too much of him to give up a bit of his sleep? They didn't even have to say anything. Or maybe Stathis was right, coming home tired from work as he did. The covers awaited him, warm and deep on the bed. Angelos knew nothing about this other person's habits. And what he'd already given him, this chair and the roof over his head, was no small matter.

Angelos brought his eyes up close to the shutters. The courtyard hadn't changed, it only seemed a little smaller than he remembered, and somewhat timeworn. When he saw the others living there, free from persecution, maybe he would finally be able to surmise what the real world was like. First and foremost, however, he had to heed the various suspicious noises, the bangings and the cries that might have a bearing on your life. It had become second nature to him. For so many years now his ears and eyes had been trained to ascertain the character of all such phenomena.

He wore the same dark scarf around his neck, his feet were still sockless, and under his coat he wore only a thin undershirt. His fingers dug into thick, uncombed hair ... He would have liked to sleep for days on end. He felt the pull of the floorboards, the urge to stretch out on the ground and lay his heavy head back. His beard must have been much longer. Stathis was asleep.

A young woman went by the window. He studied her more closely. Her eyelashes were damp, her blue robe was half open, her chestnut-brown hair hastily bound up, and her throat very white. Why was she crying? She didn't used to live there. His friend Vassilis had lived in the rooms next to these. "When Stathis wakes up, I'll ask him where Vassilis is." Remember those nights when they used to sit on the roof talking about the Spanish Civil War and about girls? One evening, when Vassilis was talking admiringly of the Asturian demolitionists and Angelos was maintaining that socialism was mathematically inevitable, Ismene slipped soundlessly onto the roof, saying, "I hope I'm not disturbing you." Vassilis suggested they organize some kind of outing, and Ismene had looked at Angelos and said: "You should go, too, you've been wearing yourself out, reading day and night the way you do ..." He was studying for the University and he stayed up till all hours. Ismene would often steal up the spiral stairs at night and see him through the open window, working on his math problems. The light fell only on his papers, as he drew straight lines free-hand. Once she wished him good-night, and he raised his eyes out of the light and said hi to her. "Build the biggest, most beautiful building in all the world," she told him breathlessly, then hurried back down the stairs. Those words had never stopped ringing in his ears: "Build ..."

The courtyard was still empty.

Then there was a creaking out on the stairs. Angelos slowly opened the glass pane and peered through the shutter. Two legs slowly came down the stairs – a man's legs. Then he saw the hands on the railing – frail and white, thinner, bonier. It was his father! His step was halting, as if he weren't sure the stairs would hold him. He was tall and gaunt. Did he realize how much he had aged? His blue eyes had been bleached of their color, they gleamed dully, as in small cases, screwed tightly into their sockets. He went down the stairs, and had no idea ... What a terrible thing ignorance was! What a dark abyss such clear eyes could contain! To be sure, they still had that glint of equanimity that compelled others to keep their voices down, to always say "please." He sedately crossed the courtyard, and it was clear he took in everything without turning his head or showing the least curiosity. Everything, that is, but Angelos. They were separated by a shutter, and twenty-five feet of morning sunlight. "He's assembling evidence to establish my innocence. Was he right when he advised me to appear at the trial? I wonder what he would say if he saw me here now?" But no one could responsibly give advice unless they had been in your shoes. "He's sure to know something valuable about me. He'll have reached his own verdict ..." When Angelos had informed his father that he was joining the resistance, Harilaos had put on his glasses and said: "Make sure you've thought it all through. There'll be no backing down." Angelos assured him that his mind was made up, and it was as if he had promised never to be afraid, never to back down. He had kept that promise to the very end, but his death sentence changed all that. The truth was, you were only worth what you were capable of at any given moment. Fear and cowardice were not, of course, the same thing. And even now, when your guts had turned to jelly and appalling waves of fear came bubbling up inside you, not once had you considered backing down. Before, you had believed it possible to die a simple and quiet death, an untroubled one, even in the heat of some savage battle. Even to give your life eagerly, without it being any great achievement. Ever since the trial, however, there was a worm tirelessly gnawing at your entrails. You had no choice but to extract life from silence and the acquiescence of others. Stathis was still sleeping.

The pretty woman in the blue robe went by crying again. Then Eftihis came barging out of his room. "Would he turn me in?" Angelos wondered. "How'd that little brat ever turn out so serious anyway?" He would have to study his face more closely tomorrow. Eftihis had grown up so suddenly, there was no way of knowing what that quick little kid from the war years had become. "I stole another loaf of bread today, Mr. Angelos," he'd say, glowing with his success.

Now everything was quiet. Didn't anyone else live in the courtyard anymore? Where was Ismene? He had lived there for so many years, in that courtyard lined with flowers. Strange how fresh those flowers still were. He wondered when his mother would be out to water them. Stathis had worked as a typesetter for a newspaper back then too. He spoke slowly, as if every word were a struggle. It still wasn't easy for them to talk. "Worst of all is to think I'm here to stay," Angelos reflected. "Better to just keep my mouth shut, and be grateful I'm here at all. If it weren't for Stathis, I'd be locked up for sure, with the inevitable sequel

..." Vassilis had pinned a large map of Spain to a piece of plywood, that he kept next to his bed. Every day he would move the little flags in accordance with the latest news reports, and he would get furious whenever the black ones advanced. One night in January he had banged on Angelos' door, ranting about how Barcelona had fallen. He took to the streets in the rain and came back late. "I heard it from someone else too: Barcelona has fallen." They sat up all night, holding a wake. Then in March – the 28th it was – Madrid fell. Vassilis tore his map into a thousand pieces, bloodying his hands on the tacks. "Maybe the time's come for me to rip up my own map, and wait for the knock on the door." It wasn't easy to accept. He had fought a lot of battles of his own, but how many had he won?

He heard more steps in the yard. His father was back, carrying a newspaper. He was always such a solid presence, without frayed edges or ambiguous shadows. At the foot of the stairs he stopped and opened up the paper to read something important. "It must be about me," Angelos murmured. His father's eyes scanned every page, and he gripped the iron railing with the same pale hand, as cautious as before, though perhaps slightly more relaxed. Right then Ismene appeared with a look of concern.

"You were late, so I went and got the paper myself today," his father told her softly.

Ismene started to offer an excuse.

"It doesn't matter ..." he stopped her.

"Is there anything?"

"No, nothing. He's all right. But what were you so frightened about?"

The two of them went up the stairs. His father's clothes were worn and a little baggy. "He's all right ..." Angelos again wondered what his father would think of him if he could see him now. "Someone has to give my case a thorough examination." His father still had that courage that came of dignity, a courage that had been tested by the weight of his many legal decisions. "If he were to look me in the eye and ask what I've been doing all this time, I would tell him right out: I was afraid; that was my only act. And he would respond, correctly, that fear was not an act. But tell me, Father, is *freeing* oneself from fear considered an action? Did you all believe I was cut out for something better than this?"

But now what difference could it ever make?

Angelos closed the window pane. All this – his father, the courtyard, Ismene's door, and the snatches of song he heard Lucia singing once or twice – seemed so far away. He felt like a sick child who longs to walk around in the room next door, which contains all of creation. Those few steps would be like crossing the vast distances separating one side of the world from the other. The front door seems the most remote place on earth. And here he was hemmed in at the window, grateful the slats of the shutter were slightly dilapidated, which left a crack for him to look out of. Now his existence boiled down to being able to steam the window pane with his breath. He wiped the steam off with his sleeve. The glass steamed back up, and he wiped it again. "Playing with my breath," he thought, and laughed to himself. It struck him as more than a little ridiculous that he had to steam up the glass as a way of affirming his existence. He sat in the chair and began to tie and untie his shoe laces. He didn't have on any socks. There are many possible combinations when it comes to tying shoes, depending on how long the laces are. Everything takes on monumental proportions when you inhabited as fragile a silence as his; hands, shoes, the wooden floor, the legs of the chair.

He heard footsteps and instantly got up. The woman next door, properly dressed now, walked down to the front gate, and the courtyard grew even emptier. It was helpful when she moved around in the next room. By following her movements, he had determined the precise layout of the room. She too was careful not to make noise, as if she were only a temporary guest. She closed the gate and went off. One after the other they were absorbed by the street and their personal freedom. The room filled with noises from the neighborhood businesses, the high-speed buzz of the chain-saw. There were millions of people out there, a clamorous, numberless, unknown multitude. Stathis would sleep through to the afternoon.

Angelos opened the newspaper. He too looked to see if there was anything about him. His father had said, "Nothing," and had seemed relieved. Otherwise, the paper told about the latest hydrogen blast in the Pacific, whose fallout was spreading panic in Japan; about battles in Indochina, about the Mau-Mau's struggle, the Suez Crisis, and the need for the Powers to sit down together.

There was no word of an amnesty. It was all a vast, entangling net, with humanity caught inside. But Angelos couldn't help thinking that his whole life shouldn't have to be devoted to going on breathing. Plants were alive too, even a chair had a kind of life. Because of his sitting there, the chair had a purpose, one could even say that it was happy. When a chair isn't in use, when it exists only to be preserved as a "chair," it no longer knows the happiness of aging through use, that is, of becoming a real chair. It's nothing but a bundle of sticks held together by nails, it doesn't even matter if it was put together right or not. He and the chair had become all but indistinguishable. He would have dearly liked to know whether by sitting there he was granting it the property of "chairness." Had he known the answer, he might have had to revise his conception of his life over the past few years. "Can you believe it – the most burning question for me has become whether I help transform these pieces of wood into a chair." But what else was there to say, since Stathis insisted on getting his sleep?

It must have been after lunch when Stathis finally woke up and began dressing. Angelos was still sitting in the chair with his shoulders hunched and his elbows propped on his knees. He immediately got up and, smiling, went over to have a word with his friend.

"What ever happened to Vassilis, the fellow who used to live next door?" he asked Stathis.

"He was killed."

"Where?"

"I don't know. All I know is he was killed ..."

"Who's living there now?"

"Andonis and Vangelia."

"What's Andonis do?"

"He's an accountant, an economist ..."

"What does that mean?"

"It means he owes me money."

"Couldn't you tell Ismene to come and see me this afternoon?"

"Not a chance."

"Why not? No one'll see her."

"Either you have a reason to be hiding out here, or cut the clowning and start walking around like a free man," Stathis told him.

"What do you think? Is there any good reason why I should still be in hiding?"

Angelos' inflamed eyes were waiting for a response. Stathis gave him to understand that there was no point in his answering. Besides, they'd already talked enough: Vangelia must have been back already, they could hear her moving around next door.

Stathis wadded up their leftovers in the paper. He would throw them out at the shop, so no one would know there had been a change in his life. He even brought home the bread in slices, and collected all the cigarette butts, because Angelos smoked a lot and there would be no way to explain all those extra butts in the trash can.

"So can you say something to Ismene?"

"No, I told you."

Stathis slowly put his coat on and silently waved good-by. But before he could leave, Angelos stopped him and shut the door again.

"Could you do me one big favor? I know I've become a burden to you. Maybe you're even sorry you took me in ..."

"What do you want?"

"If you could go to a house in Exarhia, and tell them I'm all right. That's all. I owe it to them, otherwise they'll think ..."

"Impossible."

Stathis went out wearing an expression of utter refusal. Angelos could feel the key turning in the pit of his stomach, and he saw its iron tongue steadily and inexorably entering the grooves. The door had locked!

From the window he watched Stathis' back as he moved off with his slow gait. Ismene came and stood in his path. Stathis was clearly annoyed.

"Have you seen Angelos since that night? Tell me, Stathis, please ..."

"No," Stathis answered bluntly. "I haven't seen him."

"He asked you about somewhere to stay, didn't he? What did you tell him?"

"I told him I couldn't help him ... I really wished I could but ..."

"You don't have to tell me where he went," Ismene said angrily. "Just tell me whether he found a place to stay, or if he's still on the street ..."

"I'm afraid I don't know. With any luck I'm sure he worked something out ..."

"Are you positive?"

"You worry too much. Angelos knows how to take care of himself."

"But he was so tired that night."

"Naw, he's still in good shape. I always said he could take it."

She asked him to keep an eye out for a place Angelos could stay, he just might be back asking for help. Stathis glibly promised he would and left. Ismene stood dazed, clutching the railing of the stair. But she immediately began watering the flowers, which seemed to make her feel better. Lucia came down a short time later and they exchanged a few words in lowered voices. Angelos wondered if they were talking about him. Ismene kept her attention fixed on some carnations, and all but ignored Lucia until she demanded,

"Tell me, did he ask about me?"

"No," Ismene snapped back. "Not about you, not about anything."

"Does he know I've been living out in the country?"

"How should I know, since he didn't say anything ..."

Lucia went crossly back up the stairs. Ismene continued watering the flowers. Her face always wore a troubled look, even if her lips seemed only too ready to break into a smile. That night in the rain, which now seemed so long ago, Ismene had laughed repeatedly. "Just looking at her makes me feel younger. Like an eighteen year old! We never had time to talk, we got to know each other in the middle of a whirlwind. Ismene had such grand hopes for me. Even now she does, standing there staring down at the tiles. How long can it last?" He had no promises for her, no cause for hope, lacking the basic stability required to draw a line from point A to point B. When Angelos had been in command of an entire unit during the resistance, he'd made gutsy yet responsible decisions whenever necessary. But what was necessary in the present circumstances? The solidity of the past, with its breathless excitement, had dissolved into fear. Now that he was back, it seemed like his trial had happened only yesterday. "I have no choice but to acknowledge my fear," he thought. "It's the only honorable thing to do. And then start all over again." Fear was a disease, a dampness that crept into one's nerves and turned them into a tangle of threads that enmeshed you until you were unable to move. When you build something, you must first figure out the supports in your mind, otherwise it will never remain standing. Building materials never attained balance on their own. "I still haven't learned how to buttress my own life. I've spent it one day at a time, thrown it as feed to the woodworm, so as to maintain a secret, vegetal existence. So that they could speak to me in whispers, and I could answer by nodding my head. Was I in fact carrying out the sentence myself, far from 'the accustomed place,' but with the same result?"

That morning, he'd gotten up before Stathis came home. He stood waiting for some time, until he heard his steps and the key turning in the door. He held the door half-open for an instant, taking in the entire courtyard. He inhaled deeply. But Stathis closed it and started undressing.

"Don't go right to sleep," whispered Angelos pleadingly.

"But I'm tired ..."

"Say something, talk to me."

"What do you want me to say? It's all in the papers ..."

"Something else ..."

"I don't know anything else."

Angelos had to struggle to keep himself from crying out. He reflected that the walls afforded him no protection here, thus Stathis' selfishness had won. He had every right to make demands, of course; after all, he was a free man.

"Did anyone ask about me?"

"No."

"Did you notice anything?"

"No, I said."

Stathis shut his eyes and sank into a deep sleep.

Thus Angelos was once again left alone, with the grayish window before him and an obligation not to move around because he must conceal his very breathing. Quiet filled the red and white slabs in the courtyard. Stathis slept on, dead tired. The darkness hadn't yet dispersed, and his face was no more than a stubborn, white splotch. He brought with him the dust of the streets, the dampness of night, and the morning papers. He worked to turn the day's news into lead, and now he stubbornly asserted his fatigue – which betokened an infuriating selfishness. It wouldn't kill him to give Angelos ten minutes of his time. Since he brought him food, newspapers and cigarettes, emptied the can with his urine, why did he begrudge him a bit of conversation? "If he doesn't want me here, I better leave."

Angelos went up to Stathis' bed and poked him.

"Hey, wake up," he whispered.

"What is it? What's up?" Stathis bolted upright in alarm.

"Relax. I just need you to help me. Will you please tell me what I'm doing sitting in here. Who am I benefiting?"

Stathis got angry, and with good cause.

"You're asking me? That's for you to decide."

Angelos repeated his question and said he expected an answer.

"If you think it's wrong for you to be in hiding, the door's unlocked. Just leave and let me get some sleep."

Angelos retreated sheepishly. He tiptoed over and found his chair at the window and sat back down. He looked at the door. Today, only the iron latch held it closed. A little pressure and it would open. He quietly got up and turned the key once. It locked!

That afternoon, two sinister-looking men came into the courtyard. "Here it comes!" Angelos thought, and sat waiting behind the window. The two strangers scrutinized their surroundings and came forward. "The sentence is about to be carried out ..." With their every step, movement became more impossible. The squares of the pavement were merely a means of charting his advancing doom.

Suddenly, Ismene appeared.

"Who are you looking for," she asked with perfect composure.

"Does Andonis Stefanidis live here?"

"Yes, but he's away on a trip. He'll be back in a week or so," she replied without hesitation.

"You wouldn't be trying to put anything over on us, Miss, would you? We happen to know ..."

"He may be back, but I haven't seen him in days. He does a lot of traveling ... Is he all right? Unfortunately his wife's not here either. Is there something I can tell her for you?"

"Do you live here?"

"Yes. Why, what's wrong?"

"A bit of unfinished business ..."

One of them went up to Andonis' door and pounded on it just to be sure. Fortunately no one answered. Vangelia was out. The other gave the courtyard an odd look, as if it reminded him of something.

"I feel like I've been here before, years ago ... Where did you say you lived?" he asked Ismene.

"Down there," Ismene pointed.

"I remember the flowerpots ... A judge, that's right, and his son ... And his mother was ready to faint every time she saw us come tromping through the door ... He got the death penalty. Whatever happened, did they execute him?"

"No, he's still alive," Ismene said in a firm voice.

"Come on, let's go," the other said, once he was sure Andonis wasn't there. "Wherever he is, we'll find him."

"Find who?" demanded Ismene.

"This Stefanidis fellow ..."

The two policemen left, and Ismene softly shut the gate behind them.

Angelos let out his breath. He sat down and pressed his palms to his forehead. "So, they still haven't forgotten me?"

CHAPTER 9

ANDONIS COULDN'T GO NEAR his home. Since learning from Ismene that they had come by looking for him that afternoon, the whole nature of things had changed – as if time, with the addition of this final detail, had instantaneously ceased to be. Feeling defeated and insignificant, he stood on a nearby corner, shaking with fear and keeping watch for anyone who looked suspicious. His house had become something faraway and unapproachable. Behind its old, scaling facade, in a quiet room buried deep within, like a nucleus, sat Vangelia with her gentle eyes and the vast treasure of her naivete. Now Andonis was wanted for bad debts – that's how low he had sunk.

He wandered aimlessly until it got dark. Everything looked unhealthy, ulcerous, as if sick with fever. Once more he arrived outside his house, looked carefully up and down the street, and took a deep breath. Then he made a dash down the passageway and found himself face to face with Vangelia.

"I'm leaving. I have to be at the train station in a quarter-hour."

Vangelia had her hair done up, and was wearing her good dress and high heels, as if expecting guests. She was even wearing earrings, and had put on lipstick. When she heard his steps in the courtyard, she got up to meet him at the door. Andonis left his briefcase on the floor and got his suitcase down from the closet.

"What are you staring at? Come on, get me out some clothes."

When Andonis had clicked his suitcase open on the bed, he stopped and eyed her more closely.

"What did you get all dressed up for?"

"Why shouldn't I be?"

"When did you get back from your aunt's?"

"At four."

"And you've been dressed up like that the whole time? Come on, you're acting like someone with their head in the clouds. Like there was no one else to consider but yourself."

"Isn't that how you want it?"

"But why all the jewelry? I've never seen you dressed up this way."

"I enjoy it," said Vangelia.

She smiled again.

"I did it for you too," she went on softly. "For when you got back."

"The hardest thing in the world, Vangelia, is to have a clear picture of what's going on around you ..."

"There are some things that can be understood at a glance," Vangelia added, with that sweet ingenuousness of hers that so got on his nerves.

"I have to be at the station in fifteen minutes. I don't expect I'll be gone long. I don't know myself. I have to go to Larissa, then Serres. It's a rare opportunity. Would you mind not looking at me like that? There's no time to waste. Could you see if anyone's in the courtyard, I thought I heard footsteps. I'm expecting someone who owes me money. Could you get me some shirts, some underwear, some socks, and those papers over there. It's something I'm writing for Yiannopoulos' journal, I might have time to go over it. Come on, you don't have to throw in the whole drawer. It's not like I'm going to Venezuela. That's plenty, one towel will do. So, don't you worry now. It'll just be for a week or two. What would you like me to bring you?"

He gave her a hug and a kiss, thinking, "Who knows when I'll see you again, and under what circumstances ..." He grabbed his bag and his briefcase and left. He marched ahead with a courage born of despair, ready to meet disaster head-on. A blow torch lit the courtyard with sharp flashes of light. There was no one waiting on the sidewalk in front of the house. He hailed a cab and disappeared.

No sooner had Andonis climbed out of the cab at the station than a porter hurried over to take his bag. Only then did he realize that he himself had believed that story about Larissa. Leaving the house, he had briskly told the driver to take him to the station, and on the double too, since he had a train to catch, as if he sought to validate his story to Vangelia. Apparently some need for personal honor drove one to speak the truth, for consistency sake, even when one was already wallowing in lies. Or perhaps he had compelled himself to believe he really was leaving on the train in order to make his act that much more convincing.

He stood alone with his suitcase on the sidewalk, surrounded by the din of those who really were going places. There was no longer a need for consistency. He picked up his bag and began walking down the dark street that ran along the station wall. Everything seemed to have been leveled by some devastating bombardment. It had been squashed down, flattened almost level with the ground. He himself was the only upright thing, trudging along with his briefcase and his bag. He sat down on a bench in Attiki Square to figure out where to pass the night, weighed down as he was with such a huge lie. It couldn't last, the highly charged situation he found himself in was bound to come bursting out somewhere or other. He had felt something similar on the eve of the war. He remembered how the stars had trembled when he went out and breathed the air on the little terrace outside Alekos' studio. Most of the people in that circle of friends had been killed during the war, or executed afterwards, which may have been why the stars that evening had trembled the way they did. Tonight too the lights reeled dizzily. "Disaster struck because I was unable to meet my deadlines," Andonis thought. "I've been devoured by the machinery of time. Which just goes to show I don't know all I should about how the economy works. If they discover where I am, they'll rush right over. It's a good thing I brought my clothes along. But if they don't catch me, where will I spend the night tonight, and tomorrow night, and the night after?"

EFTIHIS ARRIVED HOME TIRED. The pink barrenness of the walls smote him as he came through the door. What a joke he would become if the old man skipped out on him now. But it had been days, and the old man hadn't even come by to apologize for taking so long. "He must think his daughter's the only female on the planet," he muttered as he spread his blankets on the floor. "What the hell, one more night won't kill me." He stretched out on the ground and again began reading his newspapers. But growing restless, he went out into the courtyard. Everything was as it should be; there would be no war, no unforeseen catastrophe would strike.

"Are you alone, Vangelia?"

"Yes. Andonis is off on a trip. Something came up unexpectedly in Larissa. When are you getting married, Eftihis?"

"I'm not sure. I'm waiting to hear something ... Getting married is one hell of a big headache. Do you still love Andonis?"

"Why?"

"Mary's always telling me how she'll love me forever, but I've seen enough of women to know sometimes they're just mouthing words they picked up somewhere, like parrots, and later on they forget them just as easy. I don't fall for that kind of stuff, I tell her, I know how you women work."

"What about you? Do you love her?"

"I'm marrying her, aren't I? And you know something? When I love somebody, I'm capable of giving my life for them ..."

"Did Andonis ever pay you back?"

"You still remember that? Things change around here from one hour to the next."

"I haven't noticed any big change."

"I need someone like your husband now that I'm thinking of getting a business started ... What do you say, you think we'll have a war?"

"How should I know? Even if we did, I wouldn't have any children to worry about sending off to it. Just as long as it doesn't happen twenty years from now."

"If there is one, though, and they drop the Bomb, women'll give birth to monsters from all the radiation."

"Monsters!" cried Vangelia, clutching her stomach.

"That's what I read. With too many heads or with no head at all. With one eye or with a fish tail ... Hey, don't act so scared. I asked Andonis about it the other day and he turned white as a sheet. I want to get my business going now, before something unexpected crops up. Otherwise, I can kiss it good-by. But what are you so scared about?"

"So you think we could have a war?"

"You want me to bring you the paper where it talks about the monsters?"

"No! I don't want to hear about it ..."

"It's a riot, though, you'd get a kick out of it ... With two or three heads and a tail!"

"Stop it!"

"Just think of it, giving birth to a fish! Isn't that a laugh! Now don't get all worked up. Remember, we said *if* there's a war ..."

Eftihis had begun to get sleepy. He had nothing more to say to Vangelia. He yawned, told her good-night, and shut his door behind him.

WHAT THIS CITY NEEDS is better roads and more neon signs, Andonis thought to himself as he strolled away from his bench. The small neighborhood square had emptied of people, the drugstore had closed, and it was dangerous to sit by oneself. He was much occupied with the suitcase he'd dragged along with him. If he hadn't lied so blatantly to Vangelia, he would have an easier time of it. "My panic indicates that I'm still not ready for success. If I go around afraid all the time, it means I'm still a greenhorn, a backward, underdeveloped individual. They lock half-wits and incompetents up in prison to rid the land of those who only serve to disrupt the smooth operation of the system," he concluded, and swore because he still hadn't figured out where to spend the night.

Someone walking down the street with a careless gait unlocked the door to his house, which set Andonis' thought processes going: "Odds are that I've been isolated from the solution, and am in danger of being crushed beneath the ruins of capitalism. If I lived in ancient times, they would have thrown me in chains and taken me to the slave market. Back then there were slave uprisings, but I don't remember ever having read about uprisings of debtors and dupes ..."

He found a coffeehouse that was still open. He went directly to the phone and called Loukis.

"I had a question about our meeting. I've got this idea. What do you say I come over tonight and we discuss it. I'm yours until morning."

Upon arriving at the brightly lit marble entrance, Andonis was afraid he would look panic-crazed, so he did his best to smile. He greeted Loukis warmly. He tried to explain his suitcase by mumbling something about a trip, but Loukis paid little attention. They passed into his living-room, with its deep armchairs. Loukis was on his way out, which spoiled Andonis' plan.

"I'm waiting for a call. I have a meeting at this club about what we were talking about. I'll contact you if it works out ..."

"So you're starting to put it in action?" Andonis asked. "How did my presentation come across the other night?"

"Terrific!"

"Then why did they all freeze when it came to who would be in charge?"

"I don't think they were quite ready for that. You were rushing it," Loukis told him.

"Did you talk about it any afterwards?"

"No, maybe tonight ... A lot hinges on this meeting."

Andonis started in again about lucrative investments, stalling until he could think of somehow to justify his nocturnal intrusion. But Loukis, a man without a past, someone inseparable from the machinery of the successful scam, gazed at him through his crystal glass.

"What's important to me is where I stand in their group. As you know, I have no capital of my own. I'll offer services, connections, skillful manipulations during certain critical phases. I'll negotiate my participation with them ... I have less to offer than anyone, and I never sell my services cheap. I haggle with them. If everything goes as planned tonight ..."

Andonis took note of the lesson hidden in his words. "I'm always giving my services away for free," he thought to himself, "and that's a bad thing." He admired Loukis for having mastered that difficult art, and he lavished him with praise. Worst of all, he realized that he actually meant it.

Just then the phone rang. Loukis answered, speaking in a quiet, measured voice. Then he rose and told Andonis it was time to go.

"I'm going to need you in a couple of days ..."

Andonis realized that it would be suicide to tell him about the absurd proceedings that had been brought against him. "Will I make it till then?" he wondered.

It was drizzling outside, the streets were wet. Sitting in Loukis' car, Andonis realized there were still many hours left before daylight. He had forgotten. And here he was wasting time again, at the crucial moment. Important meetings always take place after midnight, and Loukis' agitation suggested a decisive initiative was at hand.

"And if everything goes well tonight?" Andonis asked.

The windshield filled with spatters of rain. At the Museum, Andonis asked Loukis to let him out.

"Come on, I'll give you a lift home," Loukis said.

Andonis hadn't foreseen this danger. He hemmed and hawed, and told Loukis to pull over, hinting that he too had things to tend to after midnight.

"I got you. You told the little lady you were off on a business trip, something unexpected ... I've used that one myself ..."

Andonis laughed with that feigned inanity that implies complicitous understanding.

When the car pulled away, Andonis was once again left alone with his fevered brain and his suitcase, standing on the slippery street. The slow rain continued unabated, but that was of no consequence. In the whole of that city, where he was doing everything he could to get a toehold, there was not a single house where he could go. Maybe he would be better off just turning himself in. But once he started doing time in prison, it was sayonara.

On Patission Street, he remembered that Alekos' studio, with its small terrace, wasn't far off. Maybe he was still there, though Andonis had heard that he'd left for Paris. No matter. He might be back already, but even if he wasn't, Andonis could pretend he didn't know. He quickened his pace and turned in at his door. The staircase was dark and narrow and creaky, but he easily followed its many turns, as if it had been only yesterday. At the end of the long corridor at the top, he knocked softly at the door of the small garret. Now he clearly remembered that someone had told him Alekos was away in Paris. He knocked again. No one answered. It might have been the fall of 1940, and Andonis a twenty year old. They all used to get together here. He knocked again. He picked up his suitcase and started down, but was overtaken by a fear that the staircase might never end. On the second step he stopped. No one seemed to have heard him come in, so he didn't have to leave.

He went back up and sat on the landing. Rain beat on the rooftiles. He set his suitcase down beside him, and leaned up against it. This would do. He felt as if he had found a little corner of his own, near people he knew. He had no idea what might befall him between now and morning, because just like on the eve of the war out on the terrace, he felt convinced that the seething restlessness of that rainy night was bound to erupt somewhere or somehow. He still remembered how many stars there had been that night, stars that seemed to tremble. Would war break out? His throat was dry, his temples throbbed. Everything might have changed by morning.

Andonis went up to the door out to the terrace. It was locked. Through the small square panes he saw the rain pouring down. How wide was the circle that had begun at this garret? For many of his old friends, who had died during and after the war, the circle had remained incomplete. But even for Andonis the circle had not fully closed, since he merely chanced to be hiding there tonight, wanted for debt! He found a broken pane in the door. He stuck his hand out, and tried to collect some rainwater. Then he licked his palm, hoping to quench the fire in his throat.

He sat down next to his suitcase. A searing pain shot through his leg, in the bone. It was his old wound. He hadn't felt the slightest twinge in years. He reeled with the pain and doubled over on the floor. It brought back the night they'd tangled with a patrol of *evzones* near the tracks. A bullet had passed clean through his right leg. He lost a large amount of blood and passed out. When he opened his eyes he saw Vangelia looking down at him. "Maybe it was all for the best. I'm partial to this wound," he told her, once he was able to walk again. "Why?" Vangelia had asked. "Because it's how I got to know you," he told her in all candor.

Andonis said something similar just five years ago, when he left the company: "It's all for the best, now I'm free to earn my own way." And to the board of directors, who seemed to look upon him as a victim, he had shouted: "Don't think I'll be going straight to the dogs just because you fired me." Indeed, one old fellow even gave him a solicitous pat on the shoulder, as if to console him for his inevitable plunge. Andonis had looked at them all with infinite contempt, and slammed the door behind him. When he had said his farewells to his co-workers and gone down to the street, he never once looked at the building where he had spent so many years working. Bolstered by his pride, Andonis looked at the buildings and the people as if they were an accountant's sum: "This is life, and I'm going to go out and earn it," he said to himself over and over, and he wanted to shout it to everyone. He ran home to Vangelia and announced that at last he was free of the depressing existence of a menial employee, that now he could test his mettle in the marketplace, where he was bound to succeed. "So it's all for the best?" she had asked. "Of course!" he answered, with a faith as unshakable as rock. That night they went out to eat. They had been married for six months. Vangelia gazed into his eyes and agreed with everything he said. "This is only temporary," he assured her, "a momentary fall-back in the overall forward progress of things. There's nothing to be afraid of, Vangelia, we're living in an age of awesome contradictions ..." He spoke to her about the characteristics of the economy at that stage in the system's decline, and each time he'd give her arm a harder and harder squeeze to drive home the fact that there was no cause whatsoever for alarm, and that he felt a profound joy that they would be going through this difficult period together. Afterwards, he asked if they could take a walk, because his head was bursting with plans. Vangelia concurred with his optimistic outlook, and said she would help him in whatever way she could. A little farther on she asked, "Would you like me to work with you, to be your assistant?" But that day never came. Andonis hefted his briefcase under his arm, his eyes swam with numbers, and he was forever mumbling his way through one account or another. Vangelia asked him whether his plans had begun to take shape, and when he would be entrusting some task to her. "I'll rent an office one of these days with a phone, and you'll be able to set yourself up there. We'll be together all day long." Later he started rambling on about certain profitable inventions he had come up with, and trying to convince her that corruption was the rule in business, and how in that jungle environment, unscrupulous predators won the day. "But it's different for me. I know that the system allows for a margin of legitimate profit-taking, you don't have to be crooked. The burglar and the con-artist are not acting in accordance with the laws of economics." Thus the years slipped by. "There's no need for you to know about the kinds of things that go on out there," he used to tell her. "You'd find it revolting. The marketplace resembles an arena full of ravenous beasts." Thus he dug a trench of protective silence around her. Just as out in the world of business you had to adapt yourself to each new job, each new person who stood before you, in the same way he felt he had to talk to Vangelia, his most treasured creditor of all, with a serene self-confidence, so as to appear to be holding his hopes in reserve, with supreme self-control, until they were realized. Dissembling took a lot out of him. Most of the time, when he told a lie, it was for his own benefit. And yet the circle of friends who used to meet in Alekos' room had set out in life with an absolute candor, an integrity which many had demonstrated in the ultimate fashion. "So how did I end up in such a terrible mess?" Andonis asked himself.

His leg hurt, and he could do nothing to ease the stabbing pain that reached all the way to his temple.

THINGS WERE CALM, from the look of it. There would be no war or revolution. The actual, living city pulled itself up from the street, leaving behind the tattered rags of its night to be scattered by treading feet and turning wheels. Andonis darted out onto the sidewalk with his briefcase and his bag, looked both ways, and set off. He tried to appear as calm as possible, and to guess how the world had gotten up that morning. When he determined that everything was the same as the day before, he resumed his usual haste, although slowed by the pain in his leg.

Before all else he had to get rid of his suitcase. He made straight for Sofokleous Street, where Grigoris had a shop selling canned goods.

Andonis began by telling him about the declaration he had made to the revenue service, and other small matters involving his running accounts. Then on his way out he asked Grigoris, as innocently as possible, if he could leave his bag in the corner and pick it up that evening or the next day. But Grigoris, friend though he was, eyed him suspiciously.

"What's inside?"

"Clothes for a trip."

"You're sure it's only clothes?"

"What else would I have?"

"Beats me ... all sorts of things go on around here. I'd just rather not have to worry about it," Grigoris said warily. "You haven't forgotten how we used to run guns during the war, have you? You're an ace at that sort of thing ..."

Andonis threw his suitcase open and declared:

"Underwear, old man. There, satisfied?"

With some contrition, Andonis slowly picked through the things inside – handkerchiefs, towels.

"What are all those papers?" Grigoris pointed.

"Notes for an article I was asked to write for an economics journal," Andonis said, and began reading: "'Inflationary pressures ...' I write articles too ..."

He snapped shut the suitcase and pushed it to one side. He told him a few more things concerning taxes, then left with a feeling of relief. Once outside, he glanced around to see if he had been followed. "With all the crooks there are these days, it's unlikely they'd occupy themselves with me just yet," Andonis thought. "There are so many of us around ..."

HE WOULD BE ALONE again tonight. Eftihis left the coffeehouse fuming. He'd had it with all those dimwits and their idiotic jokes. He ran into Aliki at the gate and his eyes instantly lit up.

"Going someplace?" he asked.

"Why do you ask?"

"I'm going nuts, I'm so lonely. Don't leave just yet."

"What about Mary? Why'd you leave her all alone tonight?"

"Beats me. Sometimes I'm tempted to just call the whole thing off."

"You haven't introduced us to your fiancée yet."

"You'll get your chance."

"Is she pretty?"

"Kind of – not like you of course."

"You mean that?"

"What, you think I'm so crazy about her I think she's a goddess or something? You're better-looking."

Aliki laughed and Eftihis almost took her in his arms.

"If Mary were as pretty as you, I wouldn't think twice about marrying her ..."

"Is that a fact!"

"Shhh, quit laughing."

But Aliki went on laughing, so Eftihis grabbed her by the arm and pulled her across the courtyard toward his door.

"I'm by myself here, come on."

"But ..."

He gave her a tug, and the next thing she knew they were in his room. Eftihis turned on the light. Aliki seemed confused. Why had he locked the door behind them? She looked at the rag rug and the water jug on the floor. She couldn't understand how she'd ended up following him. He slipped his arm around her waist, saying "Hmmm, you're a hot one, all right." His hot breath inflamed her cheek. She tried to get away, but it was too late. He held her so tightly she couldn't move, could scarcely breathe.

"Please, no ..." she whispered.

"Hush."

He kissed her. The lightbulb overhead and the walls around them were bare, and here he was holding this lovely girl in his arms, a girl he'd spent night after night dreaming about. So, it wasn't asking for too much after all. Her blouse fell to the floor and Eftihis went wild.

"Let me go ..."

"Not on your life," Eftihis grunted, looking crazedly from the fresh white flesh before him to the covers spread on the floor in the corner. The girl shut her eyes and gave in, without resisting.

Suddenly there were footsteps in the courtyard. Eftihis froze. He picked her up in his arms and took her into the unlit room next door. The footsteps approached his door. "It's him," Eftihis said, cursing. He left Aliki there in the empty room. "Stay here. I'll get rid of him."

There was a knock at the door. Eftihis kicked the blouse over into the corner and covered it with a newspaper, then opened the door. Mary's father came into the room without making a sound. "Why look who's here," Eftihis said.

"Are you alone?"

"Sure am."

"I thought I heard voices ..."

"It could be," Eftihis said. "That little stunt you pulled has me talking to myself. So you're a man of your word after all! I'd made up my mind to let you know tomorrow it was off, I'd had about all I could take."

"I brought it with me," the old man proudly announced, and showed him a small parcel.

"All of it?"

"Yessir."

Eftihis sat down on the floor and told the old man to have a seat on the small mat, which he did. He took out a cigarette and offered one to his son-in-law, then sat back as if he himself were a young man who'd gotten together with a friend for a serious talk.

"All right," Eftihis said brusquely, not wanting the old man to get started.

"So, are you satisfied? Mary'll jump for joy when I tell her. When do you figure we'll hold it?"

"Thursday," said Eftihis, picking a day at random, just to show he was a man of his word.

"This Thursday?"

"Yep."

The old man put the sovereigns on the floor. It was a small package wrapped in newspaper and tied with a string.

"I counted them one by one, ten times over."

Then he leaned back against the wall as if he felt a load taken off his shoulders. Eftihis made no move to touch the package. He left it there on the floor. The old man was feeling on top of the world. He said he felt like a young man again, and he'd work like a demon to pay the loan off. Why, that very evening he had worked until just moments ago, and the next morning he would be off to a construction site at crack of dawn to work on the plumbing. And he would find other jobs too, yes, his hammer would be pounding away day and night.

"Fine. So, Thursday it is," Eftihis said, hoping to shut the old man up.

Eftihis made it clear he wasn't overly pleased with the other's visit. Some time went by without either of them saying anything. The old man even leaned on Eftihis' blanket with his elbow. After all, wasn't Eftihis his son now? And it's not like friends had to say something every moment. In fact, that's what it meant to be friends: each left to his own thoughts, without worrying about the silences. No sound came from the other room, not even breathing.

"But you know something?" Eftihis said thoughtfully.

"What?"

"I'm not going to be playing heads or tails with those sovereigns. I'm not going to bury them either. I want them for doing business."

"So?"

"So, just so I don't have to cash in even one of them, what do you say you give me a few more as a loan for living expenses. Things like that end up costing a pretty penny. Could you get me twenty or so more?"

The old man scratched his cheek, looking at him in astonishment.

"Fine, they're yours. Just don't think you're putting anything over on me."

"Listen, gramps," Eftihis told him severely. "They'll be put to good use. If you think you're just throwing your money away, paying me off, then forget it, I don't want it. You've given me enough trouble already ..."

Mary's father laughed. He didn't buy Eftihis' anger for an instant.

"You're a feisty fellow," he told him. "I like it when you do your tough-guy routine ... I'll get you the other twenty, just so you'll know ..."

"No, if you don't trust me, I don't want it. Keep them all." Eftihis shoved the packet wrapped in newspaper over to the old man. That's when he discovered how heavy it was.

"I've been scrambling for a living for years now, ever since I was little, and you won't get anyone to say I ever stole a drachma from them ..."

The old man pushed the package back over to Eftihis.

"A deal's a deal. I know you need it. So, what do you think, are we going to make Mary happy?"

"I can't promise anything. Happiness isn't something you go buy at the market ..." Eftihis said gravely.

"So, Thursday is it?"

"That's what I said. Make sure you have the extra twenty by

then. And if you don't mind, let's keep down the crowds and fuss and tearful farewells ..."

"Whatever you want," the old man assured him, getting up.

"Tell me your honest opinion, what do you think of the color of these walls? I'm considering changing it," Eftihis said.

"It looks good ..."

The old man left with a smile on his face, feeling light as a bird. When he heard the iron gate close, Eftihis went into the next room and found Aliki huddled in the corner, her hands over her face.

"Sugar, time to get up," he said in as kindly a voice as he could.

Aliki just stared down at the floor. Eftihis gently put his arm around her and led her into the room with the light. He kicked away the newspaper, picked up her blouse, and politely helped her into it.

"He picked a fine time to turn up. What's the matter?"

"Nothing," the girl managed to say without raising her face.

When she'd buttoned her top, Eftihis tenderly straightened her hair and slowly led her to the door. He stepped over the package which was still sitting on the floor.

"Good-night," he told her, opening the door. "A tough break. There's something I've got to take care of by myself ... Don't feel bad, nothing happened ... You're such a sweet ..."

Aliki went off before he could finish, as if, struck deaf and dumb all of a sudden, she hadn't understood a word he was saying. A pity. It had all been so easy. Eftihis cursed his luck, then locked the door again.

Now he was alone with the sovereigns. He dropped to his knees on his bedding and counted them out one by one. Just so he wouldn't have to worry about it. Then he arranged them in rows, stacked them and scattered them, pushed them into a pile, scooped them up in his palms and let them fall through his fingers. When he realized how late it was, he wrapped them back up in the newspaper, put them under his pillow and tried to sleep, calm and content in the knowledge that he had actually pulled it off. But the two hundred gold pieces were like a boulder under his pillow. There was little chance of his getting to sleep. He sat up, undid the package, recounted them, caressed them, held them over his head and let them rain down onto the blanket, scrambled them and stacked them up over and over – in short, he wrestled with them for a long, long time, so that his hands would learn to handle those dazzling coins without a trace of awe. He'd never had so much money in front of him before. "It's mine because it's here with me. I got it because I'm marrying Mary, but I'd be marrying her even if she didn't have a penny. So, the sovereigns are mine, I won them in a game. Just listen how they ring when you let them shower down all at once. If it wasn't for this big leap forward, I'd spend my whole life on the go, wearing my throat raw yelling at people to come buy some cheap junk out of my basket."

He looked at the gold sovereigns again, scooped them up and let them run through his fingers onto his bedding. He looked at his hands. They were living things, a virtual miracle. And his body, stretched full-length on the floor, had come out healthy and intact in spite of the many times he'd staked it on the toss of a coin. You didn't have a prayer in the world if you didn't hoard your loaf of bread. Nothing could save you. Eftihis remembered how proud he had felt whenever he came home with something. The others were more concerned about what he had in his hands, but he was just as glad to have made it back through the front gate in one piece. Years had gone by that way, full of anxiety and dread. He had even watched the girls from a distance, he never had a chance to talk to them, with each day born of uncertainty.

He stretched out again with his head next to the coins, so he could see them close up. Each lay glittering on the rag rug. Gold was a marvelous thing. Eftihis lay on his back, thinking. "Yes, they all deserve our respect and admiration – money, pretty girls like Aliki. But what I love most is my heartbeat, my breathing, my eyes." He reached over, took one of the gold coins from the pile and examined it with intense curiosity.

WHEN IT GOT LIGHT OUT, Eftihis picked up the coins one at a time, wrapped them in the newspaper with the story about monsters caused by radiation, and pushed his blankets into the corner with his foot. He threw open the door and the window. He stood in the doorway for a long time, holding the small but heavy package. The courtyard was quiet. Everything looked clean and fresh. His lungs swelled with air, his legs felt strong beneath him, his eyes saw with renewed clarity. He set off, neither hurrying nor dragging his feet. Today he would be able to take note of everything. He had no more worries, now that he had acquired the means to lay down plans and move ahead. If Kostis were alive, he would tell him: "We've got two hundred gold sovereigns, let's get something going where we don't have to put our lives on the line every day."

He first went by Phillip the goldsmith's workshop. He found him at the front workbench melting down gold on a gas burner and blowing into a tube. When he caught sight of Eftihis, Phillip asked if he'd made up his mind about their becoming partners.

"Nope."

"Still haven't gotten the money yet, eh?"

"Oh, I've got it all right – every bit of it," Eftihis gloated, hiding the parcel with the sovereigns behind his back. "I've got it, but I don't like your line of work."

"That's what you came to tell me?"

"No, I want something gold, for a gift. And I mean real gold."

"It looks like someone's got your number," Phillip muttered.

"I'm in a hurry," Eftihis answered coldly.

Phillip opened a number of different boxes and Eftihis picked out a chain necklace.

"It's not cheap. How's twelve hundred sound?"

Eftihis held his package under his arm, counted out six hundred drachmas, lay them on Phillip's workbench and told him:

"Take these and be grateful it's that much. If it's fake, I'll string it through your nose ..."

He dropped the necklace into his pocket and left. He headed over to Petralona, to Elpida's. There by the subway tracks, he knocked on the low window of her basement apartment, and she opened the door with beads of water on her face. She'd just woken up. Some light-hearted music was playing on Andonis' beat-up old radio. Eftihis went down the steps. The room was unchanged, with its picture of Kostis, its worn bedclothes, the wardrobe missing a mirror, the chest draped with ill-matched patchwork, the old chairs. Eftihis did his best to conceal his package, fidgeting and squirming because he couldn't think how to begin. As Elpida dried her face with a towel, Eftihis looked at her trying to decide what to say.

“Why are your eyes all red? You just have to find a new place, that’s all there is to it ... It’s damp in here, the walls are soaked ... I’ll try to find you something better ... You need a new coat too ...”

But Eftihis couldn’t make the leap from Elpida’s living situation and red eyes to the matter he had come to talk about. He circled the table, closely examining everything, and managed to mumble something about happening to be in the neighborhood. But he immediately corrected himself and said in a loud voice:

“I came by to see how you’re making out. How’d you get by all this time? Where’ve you been?”

“Here.”

“Why haven’t you been by to see me? Just to see how I’m doing, I mean ... Who knows, I could have died.”

Eftihis was taken aback by the look that instantly came over Elpida.

“No, please, don’t ever say that ...”

He would have to change tack. He circled the room again, inspecting everything, and looked at her out of the corner of his eye, but still didn’t know where to begin. A moment later he shut off the radio and abruptly asked:

“So tell me, are you in love with anyone?”

“Why?” Elpida asked in alarm.

“What’s so strange about that? It’s not like it’s something girls don’t think about. There’s always someone who’s flirted with them a bit, maybe asked them out ... You’re a girl, aren’t you? If you’re planning something, if anything’s going on, let me know and I’ll see what we can do ...”

“But there isn’t anything.”

“Come on, there must be. Isn’t there someone you have a soft spot for? Someone who’s smiled at you in a certain way?”

“Not that I’ve noticed,” Elpida informed him with a touch of regret, and shrugged.

Eftihis turned the radio back on. He asked her if the apartment had leaked during the last rains; looked at some legs striding past on the sidewalk; lit a cigarette. Elpida, with the towel in her hand, stood expectantly, which made it all the harder for Eftihis. He turned off the radio again and asked her:

“Come on, there must be somebody ...”

“But ...”

"Tell me this very instant."

Elpida batted her eyes and told him softly:

"Except for you ..."

"Anyone else?"

"No one," she said so simply that Eftihis felt the ground under his feet give way.

"So it's me then?"

"Is that so bad?"

"I know, I love you too," he told her. "But I'm asking whether there's anyone you love in a different sort of way. Whether ..."

Elpida remained silent, and Eftihis felt extremely awkward down there in that basement apartment with all its old things and that girl who was looking at him steadily. He started moving toward the door. It was no good, he couldn't tell her. On the first step, however, he stopped. He had to get it over with quickly. He went back down and asked her, as if he were just then coming in,

"Will you do something for me?"

"If I can. Is it something difficult?"

"Will you hold onto some money for me? Some gold sovereigns I don't want to keep at home. Just until I ask for them back, without letting anyone else know."

"From something good?"

"You could call it that."

Elpida sensed his unwillingness to answer.

"It's from the first phase of my big plan. I'm working on something really promising. I plan to include you too, just in case you thought I might forget you."

"But I never asked you ..."

"That just goes to show how little I mean to you," Eftihis exclaimed angrily. "You're not even curious where I got all that money, or what I plan to do with it. Don't you care about me at all? Suppose I stole it and the law was after me, I might have robbed somebody and be looking at a prison term."

"I'd never believe it ..."

"But what if it's true?"

"Whatever you do, I won't stop ..."

"Won't stop what? Say it."

" ... loving you, since I already told you."

She hid her face in the towel.

"But what if I did something really awful? What if you found out that ..."

"Whatever it was, it wouldn't change a thing."

Elpida lowered the towel and Eftihis looked into her eyes.

"And if I were getting married? What if I told you I'm getting married?"

"Really? When?"

Eftihis could no longer hold back and gave her a kiss. Elpida looked surprised. He'd never kissed her before, and he couldn't remember ever seeing her face so radiant. Was she truly happy for him? "Here's someone," he thought to himself, "who would never hold my good fortune against me." She reached out and held his head in her hand, and gave him a kiss on the cheek.

"I wish you all the best," she told him softly.

Eftihis felt on the verge of tears. A wave rose up from his chest to his eyes, choking him, but he bit his lip and clenched his teeth. Elpida's blessing meant the world to him. He pulled the necklace out of his pocket and swiftly dropped it in her palm.

"A little something ..."

He stepped back to watch the expression on her face when she opened her hand. The gold chain glinted in fingers that were unsure what to do with it.

"Put it around your neck so I can see it," Eftihis told her.

"For me! Have you given your wife something too?"

"Not yet. Her I'm going to marry."

"Now what can I give you?"

"You've given me plenty already ... Put it on."

But since Elpida just stood there holding and fondling it, Eftihis had to put it around her neck himself. But why were his fingers shaking? Why did he have such a hard time fastening the one little ring to the other? When he finally succeeded, he stood back and gazed at her, but in truth saw only her eyes. Elpida didn't go looking for a mirror to admire herself, or even touch the gold hanging at her throat.

"What can I give you?"

"I still have a lot more giving to do before we're even," he said without looking at her. "What have I ever given you before?"

"Let's not keep accounts," she told him. "So, when is it set for?"

"Thursday, at six. Will you be there?"

"How could I not be?"

Eftihis turned the radio on again and the room reverted to its original state. Concerning the gold sovereigns that had been left unattended on the table, he told her, "I'll need them in a week or two." She didn't ask how many there were, and it never crossed his mind to tell her.

"Take the radio you gave me," Elpida remembered to say. "You'll need it."

"It's yours."

"Are you buying a new one for your house?"

"So, this Thursday at six. I'll be expecting you."

He went back up the stairs and waved good-by to Elpida, who stood in the doorway, the gold necklace still around her throat.

THE AFTERNOON WAS MILD and bright, the sky a deep, luminous blue. Eftihis took care of the final details. He sent Mihalis to bring Mary's things back to the house while he himself trotted off to Monastiraki to announce to his friends that he would be getting married in a couple of days. He found them at the coffeehouse next to the warehouse, watching a dancing monkey. A gypsy was beating a tambourine, and everyone was thoroughly amused. He stood across from them but they all ignored him.

"Everything's all set!" he told them triumphantly.

Simos gestured for him to move over, he was blocking his view of the monkey.

"Get ready for the new business I've been telling you about," he repeated.

They all laughed, probably at some trick of the monkey's. Eftihis tried to catch Fanis' eye. The latter was looking down, he must not have seen him. He spit and rubbed his hands together.

"In just a few days ..." Eftihis said.

"Great. Come and tell us when it happens," Simos said, just to get rid of him.

"I've got some big news ... There's something I want to tell you guys ..."

Nobody stirred.

"I want to have a word with you," Eftihis repeated, poised to make his announcement. But at the last moment he changed his mind and instead, to get their attention, said:

"I got my hands on some capital!"

"Congratulations ..." Simos muttered.

They seemed unimpressed with the news. They didn't even ask where the money had come from, or what kind of work it would be. He wanted to tell them everything, even invite them to the wedding and maybe go out and drink some wine with them. It was a day for talking things over and making plans. Fanis was watching with his wounded eyes. Maybe he was thinking about Elpida. "If only I could be sure there was someone who really loved her, even if it was Fanis," Eftihis thought.

He all but slunk out behind their backs. They were still absorbed in the monkey's performance.

He went home. Mihalis had brought Mary's things. Eftihis left them piled up in the room, locked the door and went out again.

It was a quiet and calm evening. He went by Mary's house and whistled at her window. She promptly stuck her head out.

"Come on out."

"I've got things to do. I'm ironing."

"Leave it, I want to see you."

Mary came out.

"Let's take a walk."

He led her up the street. As of Thursday, she'd be his wife, and it was high time she cut out all the fancy stuff. What could be more important than the walk he happened to be in the mood for tonight?

"We're not getting married so you can tell me how you've got ironing to do over here, washing over there. Get that into your head, kiddo, and drop the routine."

"So you want us to sleep on rumpled sheets?"

"You got it."

Mary bit her tongue and followed him. He wouldn't think twice about dumping her and walking away. They set off toward the Acropolis. Eftihis became absorbed looking at the things around him, at the trees, the marble ruins, the sky, then at Mary, the street, the rocks, the stars faintly visible overhead.

"Unless some son-of-a-bitch comes along to screw things up, there'll be no stopping me ... If you only knew what I've gone through for you," he told her. "When I love somebody ..."

"Oh, so you love me then?"

"I'm marrying you, aren't I?"

"You never said me you loved me."

"That's funny. It must have slipped my mind."

He took her hand and they walked for quite a ways. The street lamps and the lights in shop windows were coming on. Eftihis was lost in thought, a vague, pleasurable feeling of giddiness. He was taking the biggest step of his life. He had made up his mind, and there could be no turning back. Mary was still a stranger to him, an unknown entity.

"We're going to get one fine business going," he told her.

"What's it going to be?" asked Mary, as simply as a child.

"I don't know yet. I only know that when it comes to my own business, nothing's going to get in my way."

"Who'll be at the wedding?"

"I only invited one person. Elpida."

"I don't know her. Who is she?"

"You'll find out."

They walked for a ways without saying anything. Then Mary started saying how they needed to buy this and that – curtains, tablecloths, and a zillion other indispensable items – but Eftihis impatiently cut in.

"All right already, stop your yapping."

"Was I talking that much? I was just telling you about our house ..."

"Marriage is just one of a whole range of things for us to deal with," Eftihis said importantly, as if delivering a lecture. "Let's not go all soft in the head just because we'll be sharing a bed in a few days ..."

"I didn't say anything wrong ..."

"I'll give you money so you can buy whatever you want ... But before long you're going to have to buckle down and get to work ..."

At a bus stop, Eftihis pulled Mary onto a bus.

"Let's go meet our best man."

"But this dress ... You didn't say anything about ..."

It was strange telling the conductor "two tickets." From now on, he would be saying "two," meaning himself and Mary. He gazed at her fondly in the headlights of the oncoming traffic. She wasn't at all bad-looking. Not like some of those lookers you see, but nice, and bound to improve over time.

When they got off at Omonia, they went into a large, buzzing coffeehouse. Mary was ashamed to have their best man see her looking the way she did, but Eftihis dragged her inside. Thodoros was there. He even happened to be talking with the judge who lived in the house in front. For a split second Eftihis considered turning around and going back out, but instead sat at the next table to let them finish their conversation. At first he paid no attention, thinking they were discussing some business matter. It slowly dawned on him, however, that the judge, Harilaos, was talking about something of great importance.

"Considering he saved your life," Angelos' father went on calmly, "it makes no sense for you to harbor such resentment toward him. I've managed to establish that during the liberation, in Larissa, you were set upon by a mob and they almost ... Correct me if I'm wrong."

Thodoros looked with the eyes of a sleepy bull at this man who kept telling him that he had to remember.

"That's what happened, all right. I verified it, ten different people told me the same story. A little boy discovered you hiding in a barrel. He raised a cry and everyone came running. You tried to escape, you entered a house but they dove in after you and dragged you out again. Then you pulled a gun but they took it from you. The boy remembered you because one night you came to his house with the SS and arrested his father. He was executed in the field next to the house. The boy told me himself, he's in prison now. As I was saying, they made a rush for you and tore your clothes ... You'd denounced more than a few to the Germans. And right then Angelos appeared, with five other partisans. He plunged into the crowd and saved you. He said they were taking the law into their own hands, that the punishment of collaborators was the job of the people's justice. They obeyed him. He led you out of the mob and handed you over to the local command. I learned that later you were able to escape with the aid of the British."

Thodoros still said nothing.

"Tell me the truth: did he save your life or not?"

"I don't know, I don't remember, it was so long ago ..."

"If you're alive today, it's because of him. Yet you're the one responsible for his conviction. The fact is you begged for him to let you go, you confessed everything. Then you testified against him because in your fear you'd laid bare your soul to him ... That's how it was, isn't it?"

"I don't remember ..."

Mary nudged Eftihis to say they should go. Eftihis, without turning, gave her a kick in the shin. He had become so absorbed in the bizarre story at the next table that he'd forgotten she was there. Mary reeled with pain and yelped, but Eftihis grabbed her arm, ready to give it a good yank.

"Quiet, or you'll really catch it."

Thodoros heard the commotion, and Harilaos fell silent. Eftihis stood up and said laughingly that they'd just come in and his fiancée had bumped herself on the iron table, she couldn't see two feet in front of her, she never paid any attention to where she was going.

"Sorry if we disturbed you," he told Thodoros.

Thodoros turned red, puffed himself up and eyed them both with suspicion.

"I saw you from outside so we came in to say hello," Eftihis said. "Is this personal business?"

Harilaos rose.

"That's how it was," he said to Thodoros. "Jog your memory a little and it'll come back to you. It's probably more your conscience that needs looking to. You remember all right. I'm sure you'll be persuaded to do what's right ... You'll be seeing more of me. Think it over ..."

He left without giving any sign of having recognized Eftihis. Thodoros took a deep breath.

"How that man torments me!"

"Business?" Eftihis asked with feigned innocence, to show that he hadn't heard anything.

Mary was relieved that this obese fellow, who was to be their best man, didn't appear to notice her old dress. He had other things on his mind.

"Let me introduce my wife," Eftihis said, to make things easier for him. "All right, so on Thursday ... No big hoopla, let's just get it over with. Then we'll go out some day for a drink. We'll take Andonis along too ... I want us to have a talk ... I've realized the money I have won't be enough. I want you to help me out."

Thodoros nodded his head and looked at Mary. She blushed because she knew he was sizing her up.

They realized they had better leave. They joined hands again and were soon back on the street, walking along in silence. When they'd gone a ways Mary asked him, pleadingly, like a child:

"Buy me some roasted chick-peas ..."

Eftihis bought her a large paper cone of them, taking two or three for himself. At one point he stole a glance at her, and her face looked clear and unblemished.

"We'll get along just fine, you and me," he told her.

"I think so, too."

When they reached her house, Eftihis sent her in to finish the ironing. He wanted their sheets to be clean and fluffy. Before she went in, he held onto her an instant, saying:

"Here, let me give you a kiss now, so we don't make fools of ourselves on Thursday."

THE NEXT DAY, Andonis was back on the streets, trying to convince himself that he had to conduct business as usual. "I'm an active participant in a web of economic interests and interdependencies that lead straight to the prison gate!" A wanted man was essentially a liberated man, and your greatest sense of liberty was when you came to believe you were just like everyone else. Andonis went in for a shave, asked for a newspaper, and informed the barber that all his fears about a new war were wholly unfounded. "Everything will be just fine ..." he said, and the barber responded, "Sir, I admire your optimism." Andonis laughed, and noticed the virtuous tranquility of his face in the mirror. "Everything will be just fine," he repeated with even greater conviction. He had spent the night before in the café at the station. He had learned that at six-twelve the next morning an express train would be leaving for Salonica, and he masterfully led the waiter to believe that he was waiting for a certain lady who was to travel with him. And since it wouldn't have done to let all that time go to waste, he drank three cups of coffee and opened his briefcase in order to polish his article for Yiannopoulos' periodical. The trains blew their whistles and lurched into motion while he sat in his corner writing. In any case, he'd have been doing the same thing at home, so why should it bother him? When the six-twelve arrived, the waiter had told him, "All for nothing, your friend stood you up ..." Andonis concurred with a smile and proceeded to the platform. He merged with the crowd and exited by a different door.

He remembered that the two small-town merchants were staying at a hotel on Athinas Street. He found them seated in the wicker chairs in the lobby, and did a superb job of pretending he just happened to be in the neighborhood and had dropped by out of concern for them. "I knew you wouldn't be up to much. I was hoping to be able to be of some service to you." And he went on quite skillfully about the decisiveness he discerned in their actions, and expressed regret that the talents of such astute merchants should be wasted in the bog of agricultural dealings, while the natural thing was for them to be based in Athens – which he foresaw happening in the near future.

A morning prostitute came out of a room, the washer-woman swept the cracked linoleum, the coffee was sweet as molasses. Andonis persuaded them to find out his prices before buying.

"Why not, what's there to lose?" said the wise guy who had asked Andonis, "And who'll protect us from you?"

The offices of Boufas' company were jammed with people. A workers' committee was demanding to see the owner. The attendant told the committee members to wait, the director would see them shortly.

Andonis asked for the director, Spiros Ioannidis, by name, indicating he was a close friend. He stood to one side to make it clear he was a client there on business. So the strikes were continuing. A strange buzz of vehement conversations, footsteps, and restless movement filled the cramped space. Andonis had encountered the intent stares and the whispering before. One of the workers lost patience: "We didn't come here for a handout. But we didn't drop by just to say hello either ..." "He'll pump us full of his theories again. Let's face it, the man's no good. This is part of his strategy too: just keep them waiting, and when you finally open the door they'll come slinking in without daring to raise their heads." Andonis wondered who there was for him to present demands to.

He was spending a dangerous amount of time on Spiros, and if he didn't watch his step, the two out-of-town merchants would leave. The workers filed into the office, leaving Andonis alone in the corridor. One assistant tried to eavesdrop at the door. Others bustled with studied preoccupation from office to office, their arms full of papers. Andonis peered at the lowered faces of the employees, and suddenly felt like a company accountant himself.

He couldn't rest easy there in the corridor knowing that he might learn news of Vangelia from Ismene, who worked in one of the offices. He approached her with the mute air of someone who's been through the grinder, someone returning after a long adventure. Ismene was taken aback. She at once got up and went into the corridor with him.

"What are you doing here?"

"Have they been by looking for me again?"

Andonis laughed. He was experienced at being "wanted" now, keeping his own secrets and giving no undue weight to this minor imbroglio. But finding that his ludicrous heroism annoyed even himself, he asked Ismene if she had seen Vangelia, and whether she had noticed any suspicion on her part – which would indicate he had been less convincing than he would've liked.

"She seems to be doing all right."

"Would you mind spending a little time with her? She worries about things when she's by herself ... Legal proceedings for financial pendencies are quite vexatious, of course ... A few precautions, however, usually suffice to take care of them ... These days only idiots go to prison for debt ..."

When the committee came out, Andonis took leave of Ismene and proceeded toward the door of the office. He knew how important atmosphere and the initial exchange were to a business meeting. Spiros was on his feet, wiping his glasses and gazing down at the floor.

Andonis had instantly noted the blank expressions on the faces of the committee members as they left, and now the fallen look on Spiros' face led him to conclude that the director was indeed in a difficult position. Andonis weighed the situation in the twinkling of an eye, and went in.

"Well, well, old friend," he said with warm congeniality. "I want you to think upon me as your friend, no matter what happens. I'll always have a place for you in my heart ..."

For all his contrived gusto, Andonis felt a chill at the other's wary formality. He again stressed his feelings of friendship, because he calculated – correctly – that what Spiros needed at that moment was a friend. He spoke of their years at the University, and gave him a quick run-down – since the subject came up – of the whole business with the two out-of-towners.

Spiros promptly buzzed someone in and instructed them to do all they could for Mr. Stefanidis as to prices and choice of merchandise, and to have the invoices sent to his office before tabulating the cost.

"Satisfied?"

"Absolutely. And rest assured I'm always at your service ... What do you say we go out some night together? I bet you're overworked."

From the corridor came the sound of shuffling feet and loud voices. The color again drained from Spiros' face, and he began wiping his glasses. Clio barged in in dismay. Andonis realized it was time to take his leave, since what was happening had nothing to do with him. He pretended not to notice a thing, and in the same congenial tone bid Spiros good-by, as if they were the dearest of friends.

When he opened the door, he saw a large group of employees waiting to go into the office.

THE PRICES ANDONIS OFFERED the merchants proved to be the lowest. They acknowledged as much, and finally decided to buy. He took them directly to the company by cab, and marched into Spiros' office himself. He hastily explained that his clients were outside with the cash. He asked for a discount of over fifteen percent, and wanted to close the deal fast.

"And your own two percent discount on top of that ..."

"I don't want anything."

"Why not?" Spiros said in surprise. "What do you want?"

Andonis bit his lip. He couldn't say exactly what he wanted. Perhaps to wipe the suspicion from the face of the smart aleck who'd said, "And who'll protect us from you?"

Suddenly his eyes lit up. He went up to Spiros and fixed his eyes on him.

"Do you trust me?" he asked.

"To be frank, I don't trust anybody."

"Ah, but you should have a few people you trust."

"Come on, out with it. What do you want?"

"Half the merchandise on credit."

"And who'll sign the loan guarantees?"

"You!" blurted Andonis. "You should trust me."

"Impossible," Spiros answered firmly. "It's not my company."

This truly inflamed Andonis, who went and stood before the desk, ready to gamble everything.

"I am an honest man."

"Quite possibly," Spiros told him with that brittle, insulting politeness of his. "However, that has no bearing on the present circumstances."

"I am an honest man, whereas ..."

Spiros made it clear that the implication wasn't lost on him, but that he was unmoved by Andonis' show of passion.

"How can I guarantee your loans, knowing you as little as I do?"

"In other words, you've forgotten about that mark on your forehead?"

Mr. Ioannides lightly touched the scar digging into one of his eyebrows, looking as if their talk had made him a little dizzy.

"What's that got to do with it?"

"Just so you don't go around saying you don't know what kind of person I am," Andonis said. "Remember that night they threw you in the Merlin Street holding tank, out cold, with your head split open?"

"Sure I remember."

"Then maybe you remember someone who tore up his shirt to use as a bandage, and gave you his last cigarette. Then, since you were feverish, that somebody also gave you his food to help you regain your strength ..."

"That's just it: he's just a somebody to me now."

"That's your right," Andonis answered, beside himself. "But we're talking about trust. If you don't trust me, well then ... A man is consistent in all of his obligations ..."

Andonis faltered, everything swam before his eyes ...

"Let me remind you of something else too. During certain economics finals, who slipped you his blotting paper with the answers on it as he was turning in his exam?"

"But I worked them out for myself."

"That may be. But I was thinking of you. I'm only saying all this because you raised the question of trust."

Andonis didn't stop there, however.

"Suppose I came to you and said, Spiros, loan me a couple of thousand to pay off some interest I owe on a debt, otherwise they're going to throw me in prison, would you give it to me? Not that it's going to happen, something like that could never happen to me, but let's just suppose ... Apparently your only dealings are with crooks, which is why the thought terrifies you ... Economic trust and personal trust," Andonis said, laughing, "have nothing to do with one another ..."

An employee knocked at the door and addressed Spiros with a treacly reverence and stiff formality. Andonis sat back in an armchair and contemplated his next move. The two merchants would pay him in cash. He would keep half the money for himself and sign the drafts. That way he in turn would be able to give them a five to seven percent discount if he saw them making a face. With the cash he kept for himself, he would be able to get the arrest warrant lifted, and have a bit left over to work with. He instantly dubbed the maneuver, "Liquidating by means of extortion the assets of past services freely rendered." By the time the employee made his stiffly-bowing exit, Andonis had worked out all the numbers. It was perfect. He took a draft form out of his briefcase; he always made sure to have useful items along.

Spiros icily signed the forms guaranteeing the drafts.

"Does that make us quits?" he asked Andonis. "For all of it?"

"If that's how you choose to look at it. I think of you as a friend. As to whether or not I'm reliable, just wait and see ... A man's trustworthiness and self-respect are inseparable, in every thing he does ..."

This last bit had a nice ring to it, but Andonis didn't sit pondering it. He shook Spiros' hand with the amiability of someone who'd won, then left him to face Clio, who just then came storming in.

From then on, everything went like clockwork. They selected their merchandise with care. Andonis tacked on a three percent discount of his own, so the two merchants would have no doubt where their best interests lay. He took them out to a grill and worked it all out. In all, they had savings of twenty percent. Then he was a perfect watchdog when it came to picking up their purchases. He arranged all their other business as well, making calls all over town. By afternoon's end, he was hungry but still tireless.

"So what do we owe you?" one of them asked.

"Forget it," Andonis laughed.

This didn't go over well. It hadn't occurred to him that the two merchants might be incapable of understanding why he would go to such lengths to prove he was someone to be trusted – an honest man, no need to feel squeamish about saying it.

"If you're satisfied, I'll be able to serve you whenever you like."

He even managed to find a truck that was headed back to their district empty, and thus was able to arrange for the driver to take them for less. He helped them in and saw them off. He stood waving for a long time, as if they were close family members, not business associates. When the truck was gone, he wiped off his sweat and counted the money he had left. He would be using it to buy his return to the world.

He hurried off to clean up that unpleasant affair with the outstanding debts. Now that he was paying them off, he was afraid of no one. "I guess I'm an honest person after all."

When he arrived at the warrant office, he spoke with all the aplomb of a practiced businessman, and they answered that he would do better to come by in the morning.

"But I'd rather tonight ..."

"Don't worry, it's not like there's any hurry," one of them told him very simply. "What's the big deal, it's not like you're some hardened crook."

"I'd like to take care of it tonight ..."

"Relax, mister ... Is it your first time? What do you know, there are still honest people in the world ... We've been after some of these folks for years ... You'd best come by in the morning ..."

Andonis went off, his mind at rest. The world took on a different aspect. On the way, however, he decided he would do well to hide out for one more night, to avoid any possible complications.

ANGELOS STRETCHED OUT on the newspapers. As soon as Stathis left, he had taken an old one from the stack in the corner. Then another, and another. "It's the only way I'll find any continuity," he reasoned, and soon the whole floor was covered with printed paper. Events and more events, news items, editorials, forecasts. This reverse journey in time was like walking backwards into your own yesterday, and encountering yourself, and the various stages that had brought you to where you were. He took still others, hungrily read through them, and moved farther back, in hopes of discovering which wave it was that had washed him up in this narrow room. At first he knelt on the floor, then read lying on his stomach. "These are all minor causes," he thought, "which, when added up, are somehow equal to my fate, and the fate of others all over the world." The paper had a peculiar smell, as if from the sweat of time, people's struggle to survive.

When he wearied of this, he stretched out his arms and legs on the newspapers and shut his eyes, as if afloat on the world's events, as if rocked by the turmoil, the aspirations and struggles of a sea that had still not found peace. He could feel some of them jutting into his sides, he tossed and turned to get comfortable, but they were like rocks against his back. Exhausted, he gave himself up to the deepening afternoon, the dwindling light. He let his body sink into the thick mattress, with its unfathomable depths. Would he remain like that, abandoned, will-less, until a sleep like death finally stole over him? An obscure death, amid a mute and inscrutable Nature ... "I wasn't always a lost soul, a stolen breath. I may have misspent a million heartbeats, but I never ceased to exist. I remember everything."

The solitude spread out around him in circles which broke against the walls and, rebounding, fell back to engulf him. Huge chunks of night weighed down on his chest, his ears picked up whispers, running footsteps, the ubiquitous roar of the city ... Would they come knocking on his door some evening? And what if they never came? The fact was, he would have to calculate the correct dimensions of things, to reread the papers and try to divine a rhythm there that would help him escape that room, lest he spend his future days prodigally, lest he live a life that was beneath him. The world was filled with people who lived in fear. But what good did they serve? They breathed in only the darkest of corners, they considered the pulse in their veins a noteworthy occurrence, they debased their thoughts. It might still be possible for a desperate person to accomplish something; but a fearful person, never. Such a person was a sick person. None of which meant, of course, that socialism was *not* the humane sequel in the flood of time. Fear wasn't something to be measured in battle, but in that other war whose sole purpose was to turn you into a vegetable.

Angelos reached out and grasped at the scattered newspapers, as if groping for something to cling to.

CHAPTER 10

ON THURSDAY AFTERNOON, all was quiet. Stathis had soundlessly gone off to work, and Vangelia was inside with her door shut. Aliki went into the courtyard and found Eftihis pacing up and down, looking nervous and preoccupied. He greeted her with a smile, as if he had forgotten everything.

"So is today the big day?" she asked.

"I'll find out in an hour," he said, and continued pacing.

Eftihis' getting married meant a change in the courtyard. As of that night, Mary, the tall girl with short curly hair and pimples, would be living there too. Of course, no one would be at the wedding, because a few days before, in the coffeehouse, Eftihis had said for all to hear that it was a strictly personal affair, like having an operation, and there was no need for the whole neighborhood to tag along. "The fact is, fellas, I just don't feel like having to look at all your mugs."

His mother and Mihalis were there waiting. The old lady had come that morning to straighten up and sweep the floor, so the place would be neat and tidy when the newlyweds got back. But the truth was she wanted to be with him when he went to the church, lest the boy feel like a complete orphan. Mihalis had tagged along. Eftihis had promised him something for the errands he'd run, but now, strutting and pacing the courtyard in his squeaky shoes, he seemed to have forgotten. Still, Mihalis looked up to his older brother. He was his own man, someone who always did exactly as he pleased. Indeed, as of today he would be a married man, with his own wife. Mihalis peered in at the double bed in the middle of the room, made up with a lustrous yellow spread of silk and wool, as if waiting to be rumpled once it got dark.

"You'll want me to come pay you a visit now and then, won't you?" he asked his brother.

But he received no answer, and his mother ordered him into the laundry-room to clean off his feet and scrub a bit of grease from his neck – she didn't want anyone saying her two boys had no mother. But Eftihis stopped him.

"Come on," he told him.

He took him by the arm and told his mother they'd be right back. They went over to Mary's house together. Eftihis led Mihalis up to the door and said:

"Tell her father to come outside, it's important. I'll be over at the corner store."

Mihalis held back, but Eftihis shoved him forward. The boy timidly knocked on the door, and Mary opened, her face white, with two rosy spots on her cheeks. "So she's going to be my wife, eh?" Eftihis thought to himself, but he didn't get much of a look at her before the old man, wearing his good shirt, came forward anxiously.

"I'm ready," Eftihis told him.

"God bless you, son," the old man replied.

"At six, right?"

"Right, six ..."

"If you want me to be there, though, we have to take care of that thing you promised."

"What thing?"

"The twenty gold pieces ..."

"I couldn't get them ..."

"Then it's all off. You can take off your shirt and go back to your shop," he snarled at the old man. "It's not the money I care about so much as being made a fool of ..."

"How am I supposed to get them now ..."

"That's your problem. Get them to me at the church, or I won't be going in ..."

Down at the corner, a passing tram let out a screech, as if the rails were howling. Eftihis waited for it to pass, then spoke slowly and distinctly to let the words sink in:

"Bring the twenty sovereigns or the whole deal's off."

"What about Mary?"

"She'll see that her father's someone who breaks his promises."

The old man's eyes widened until they filled the circles of his glasses.

Eftihis left Mary's father in the shop. Was he supposed to sit there and help the old man figure out how to come up with the money? "If I had that kind of advice to hand out, I'd have everything I wanted without anyone's help. The old man can't do without me now."

Back at the house, he told Mihalis and his mother:

"Get ready, we're leaving at six."

He went in and locked the door behind him. Mihalis and the old lady stayed out in the courtyard. It was his house now, he could do as he pleased. Before long he came out in an impeccable new suit with razor-sharp creases, shoes never before worn, a silk shirt, greased-back hair, and a shave as smooth as a mirror. He looked around the courtyard and paused in the doorway, as if wanting people to see he was at a major turning-point in his life. But when he realized that the only eyes watching him were his mother's, he reverted to his old self, stuffing one hand in his pants pocket, and started pacing. The courtyard was clean – flowerpots lined the stairs and the ledge, his freshly painted rooms were filled with new things. Mary would like it. The past few days Eftihis felt as if he had crossed into unknown territory, with new perils at every step of the way. And now it was all happening so fast. He had to gather his energies, tuck into a ball, accurately judge the distance, and make the dangerous leap in such a way as to leave a void behind him, making any return impossible.

When he saw Mihalis in his clean shirt and his mother in her hat, and clutching that ancient handbag of hers, he laughed at the thought that women come into the world with a hat and a handbag, which they hold onto their whole lives through. He laughed a second time seeing their good spirits, and to please them he paid them for all their work. And owing to his own good mood, he gave them a bit extra so they would have a few drachmas to spare for their own fresh starts in life. And just in case they missed the point, he told them:

"There, I guess that makes us quits."

Then he went back inside to make sure they hadn't left any of their own things there, but he really just wanted to see what his new house looked like: the double bed there in the middle, the table against the wall, two chests, three chairs and a coat-rack. That would be plenty. He should have gotten a shade for the overhead bulb, but it was no big deal. He locked the door and thrust the key in his back pocket. Now that's what you call being a real human being.

He glanced at his watch and led the way down the passageway, as if going out for cigarettes.

"Let's get moving," he shouted over his shoulder.

The old lady and Mihalis were taken aback. They were expecting such a moment to be marked by greater ceremony. They followed him out to the street. Ismene was standing at the front gate. Eftihis bid her a curt hello, and marched on. Mihalis came up behind him and whispered that he'd never seen a handsomer bridegroom. His mother heard it, and snapped at him to shut up, she wouldn't have him making a lot of noise. She quickened her pace to catch up with her son. The way that boy swaggered along! She didn't know what went on in his head anymore.

A couple of big lumps came out of the corner coffeehouse and stared, but Eftihis ignored them. His shoes squeaked, his new heels clicked on the pavement. He wanted them all to understand, especially certain sons-of-bitches he could name, that there were more serious things in life than their endless bullshitting, even if he himself acted like it was no big deal.

A little farther on he called a cab over and had everyone climb in. They went by in front of the house again. Ismene was still there at the gate, her face lit crimson by the sinking sun. Her eyes, scowling against the glare, peered up and down the street, as if she were waiting for someone.

WHEN NIGHT FELL, Angelos could feel the cramped and lonely room tightening its grip. He'd glue his eyes to the shutters to enjoy that last image of things before the entire courtyard was engulfed in darkness, before the room grew oppressive with shadows. It was the time of day he liked least, when everything began sinking and dissolving in the waning light. He knew it was a natural and unavoidable occurrence, but that didn't make it any easier to get through the night that bore down so inexorably upon him. Once he had even fixed his eyes on his palm to see the light change, the way one watches a clock trying to see the minute hand move. That evening, he looked on as the sun flared out, then gradually faded on the edge of a glowing cloud visible between the walls of the passageway. The floor was still littered with newspapers – a sea of paper and events that grew calm at this hour, as the wind died down and the days became a flat expanse, as events became indistinguishable from routine commentary.

Ismene slowly crossed the courtyard and knocked on Vangelia's door. She asked somewhat anxiously whether Andonis had returned. "No, he hasn't. The judge asked to see him too. Do you know what he wants?" Vangelia asked her in turn. "Come in, I've got some good news to tell you." Ismene went in and sat down.

"I found a quiet house in Holargos, my aunt's house. It's perfect. She's an old woman, and the house is off by itself, with a garden too ..."

"Could he go stay there?"

"Yes. Does that make you happy? That way you could visit him. You and I could go see it together, if you like."

"Thank you," Ismene said.

"Don't go yet, we haven't set a day. You really should tell him about it."

"But I don't know where he is."

"Why were you in such a big hurry?"

Ismene didn't know what to answer.

"What are you looking at me like that for? As if you felt sorry for me ... It's so obvious. Tell me what you know about me. You seem distracted, afraid of something ..."

"What could I know about you?"

"You don't fool me, though. Andonis tries the same thing ..."

"Thanks for telling me about the house," Ismene said and went out, as if struggling to maintain a false front.

She sat down on the stairs. Everything was so quiet – an overpowering kind of quiet that sucked you in and left you paralyzed. Sitting there on the landing, she looked as she had five years before at Faliron, when they had sat on a rock during their last time together. She was distracted, uncommunicative, as if listening to something far away. The sea was crashing right below them, but Ismene was trying to hear something beyond the sound of the surf. She asked him what the matter was, and he said, "I was just thinking how hard life is going to be for us." The night was windy, her fingers were numb with cold. "And how I love you with every cell in my body," Angelos went on. Ismene wasn't sure how to take it. "Don't go yet. Sit there a little longer, just the way you are, with that scowl on your face. You know, we've barely gotten to know each other." "I never asked you to wait for me." They parted that night, and went five years without seeing each other – up until the other night in the rain. "Try to forgive me for all the grief I'm causing you. It's all I have ..." Ismene went inside and slammed the door.

Angelos' father appeared in his hat and his overcoat. He wore that old silent air of his, the one he had when he would shut himself up alone and not talk to anyone. They would all nod and say, "He's agonizing over one of his court decisions." He was carrying himself like a judge again, like someone given the task of passing judgement. "Maybe this time it's about me," Angelos speculated. Then he remembered that he'd never seen the faces of the judges who'd decided his case. Yet that verdict was meaningless as a judgement, based as it was on a nonexistent event. Maybe his father had come to realize that, for Angelos, the problem had originated later, much later.

Angelos had followed Eftihis' movements all afternoon. Then, stepping over the scattered newspapers, he sat at the table and, without realizing what he was doing, started drawing the mechanism of a lock on some leftover newsprint that Stathis had spread out there. In fact, he was drawing the lock in the wooden green door opposite him – *his* lock, with its bolt and the tongue that clicked into its groove. He drew the springs, the slots, the metal plates. He enjoyed the distraction, but it was the object itself that interested him most. He tried to make all the inner workings of this particular lock come together. But as dusk fell, its thick stain seeped across his drawing and blotted it out. He got up and looked through the shutters at Ismene, and the still-glowing cloud.

At this difficult time of the day, Angelos would stretch out and close his eyes until the dark had taken hold, and the stifling process of change had come to an end. He remembered how, even as a boy, he used to go out on the street at dusk, waiting until his mother had lit their lamp. It was only in the resistance that he hadn't found it an oppressive time of day. Everything had been different then. But now he had no say about either the darkness or his immobility. He couldn't switch on the light. His sketch of the lock lay there on the table as if crushed under a pitch-black hand. Fear was the only constant. Maybe knowing that was what made the night so unbearable. In prison, there's always a guard outside holding the keys, someone on duty to mind you. Your existence isn't a secret, you can sing, curse, even go out into a prison yard of some kind. Here, Stathis was indeed a guard of sorts, but one who unlocked the door and joined him inside. His eyelids were always heavy, and his mulish silence was capable of bringing down mountains. No one ever chose their prison. "The worst thing of all would be for me to forget the reason for my being locked up here." He felt the iron casing of the lock to further familiarize himself with the object he wanted to draw. A system of simple gears made the mechanism sturdy. If you wanted to do an accurate sketch, you had to have the key, or at least to open up the lock and see what kind of key fit it. "If I wanted, I could unscrew the screws and take the thing apart, and see exactly how it works," he thought, and concluded: "Then I'd be free either to draw it, or to leave, since the door would be unlocked." The lock casing was a square of cast iron, and the system of gears inside was properly aligned, since it held the door securely shut. The whole thing functioned thanks to its steady immobility. Angelos rested his forehead against the wood planks of the door, allowing his body to slump against it, as if asleep on his feet.

Vangelia was pacing in the next room; her slow, female tread was unmistakable. That afternoon, Angelos had been sitting at the shutters. Vangelia went into the laundry-room in the courtyard. She left the door ajar, supposing there was no one to see her. She undressed and began bathing herself. Every so often she'd reach over for more water from the tap, and her body would pass in front of the crack in the door: an arm, her shoulder-blade, her hair! Then she'd vanish again. Her arm reappeared, then just as quickly disappeared. Water ran out under the door. Then she came out wrapped in her robe and went back into her room. From that moment on, Angelos had counted her steps and the little noises she made as she moved all unsuspecting around her room. Everything took on gigantic proportions when it entered the four dark walls of that time-devouring space. Angelos couldn't go back to his drawing of the lock. Maybe it was no longer necessary. He couldn't carry through with anything anymore. He collapsed on the bed fully clothed. There was no way of knowing what might crop up, he might have to make another run for it. But aside from that practical reason, the fact was if he undressed and went to bed like a normal person, it meant that, were something to happen, he would have foresworn all hope of avoiding capture. And no matter how cramped the room was, with its single door, it still wasn't easy to accept that a knock on the door meant the end was at hand. Going to bed with his jacket on was kind of like making a loan of hope to your sleep. In his last place, Angelos had been ready when the knock came at dawn. He had clambered down the clay drainage pipe and hid under some boxes at the bottom of the airshaft.

"Why do you lock me in?" Angelos had asked Stathis a few days before.

"Just to be safe."

"For your sake or mine?"

"For both our sakes," Stathis had answered.

Stathis insisted on getting his sleep, with no sense of it being shameful or irresponsible on his part, a disgraceful display of selfishness. He thought of Angelos as just another object in the room. That too was in the by-laws of the prison where Angelos was kept. Stathis had taught him other regulations too, in addition to silence. The other day, when he woke up around noon, Angelos told him, "You know, Stathis, I've been thinking that I could demonstrate mathematically what we were talking about, you know, how socialism is inevitable ... Do you want me to show you how?"

"No need, since I already know it. So what else have you been thinking about?"

There was a touch of mockery in his tone, but Angelos pretended not to notice.

"I didn't have time for anything else, I was too busy."

"Busy doing what?"

"Staying alive."

"But being busy means actually doing something."

Angelos refrained from pointing out that staying alive was indeed a grueling task, similar to the rocks they made them carry back and forth in the political prison camps. Personal action was an added factor, something that sped the coming of socialism. That was old hat. But there were some things that were like melodies you thought you had forgotten, then were delighted to find them still there in your head, intact. The bad part was that it was forbidden to whistle them. One even avoided thinking too clearly, supposing that too was against the rules. That sliver of Vangelia's nakedness he'd glimpsed was another sweet, forbidden memory, which was sealed up, warm and alive, under his closed lids. "I'm alive. If I jab a nail into my arm, I'll feel pain." But could he go on living like that? "Before all else," he told himself, "I must find a way out of this prison. In order to have something to hope for when it's getting dark. There must be a solution."

He heard Vangelia's footsteps again. The quickening bursts of light from the blow torches quivered with impatience. Angelos relinquished himself to his silence, and opened his eyes. The darkness had ripened, it was now fully night. The difficult hour had passed. He had to find a way out – some means of escape.

ALIKI WENT OUT because she couldn't bear to stay closed up inside knowing that there was someone waiting to take her to a dark, thickly wooded area. Was there to be no more gentle, caressing talk, no more gazing into each other's eyes, no more walking hand in hand, or that melting silence when she leaned her head on his shoulder? And if their path were to lead them to a wooded area, they would continue arm in arm, and then, of course, would sit down to rest under a tree ...

Aliki shot a glance at the coffeehouse, and quickly turned the corner. She neither saw nor heard a motorcycle. She stopped by the homes of all her friends, but no one felt like doing anything. When it started getting dark, she found herself back on her own corner. There, in the house next to the corner shop, lived her friend Voula. She went down the narrow entrance way, next to the welder's. She hadn't seen Voula in ages, but they would surely find some way to pass the time. She waited at the door, but there was no answer. From the back came the flicker of blow torches.

The welders worked in a large courtyard. She heard the sound of a motorcycle from the street. If she were to leave now, Pericles would see her. She continued down the narrow passageway. The courtyard was full of wrought-iron railings, staircases, sheet metal, puddles of grease and rust. The white sparks hurt her eyes. A man wearing a cap and dark goggles was holding an iron shield up to his face, like a mask with two square openings. He was welding the joints of a long iron balcony railing. When the flame decreased, Aliki edged up to the crouched figure and asked:

"Isn't anyone at home up front?"

Startled, the man turned the flame lower and straightened up.

"Who you looking for?"

"Voula. Is she out?"

"I don't know. She doesn't tell us where she goes."

The grease-stained man turned up the flame slightly, which became blue-white, like on a gas-stove, and brought it near her face, as if to get a better look at her. Aliki gave a start.

"Move over a bit, you're stepping on the pipe."

Aliki took two short hops to one side.

"So is Voula a friend of yours?"

"An acquaintance."

"She goes out every afternoon."

He seemed young. He kept the goggles on. As if in play, he relit the low flame using the dial on the handle and, taking a huge step, crossed to the other side of the wrought-iron railing.

"Ever seen anyone weld iron before?"

He turned the flame way up and kneeled down to weld a piece of iron low to the ground, just to one side of her foot. Aliki backed away. The man in the mask suddenly straightened up and positioned himself between the wrought iron and the upright oxygen bottles. He kept the flame turned on high, holding it carefully to one side.

"You're a very pretty girl ..."

He came closer and Aliki realized she was trapped. When she'd sprung back in fear, she'd passed through the wrought iron, and now the man was standing at the opening, torch in hand. Aliki backed farther in, and he followed as if leading her. She felt his breathing inches from her cheek.

"Over to the right. Keep your eyes off the flame."

He turned the torch lower. Aliki hesitated. She opened her mouth but nothing came out.

"Don't be scared. Come on. I bet you're even prettier when you laugh ... Don't be afraid ..."

Aliki stood frozen in place, her eyes shut. He turned up the flame again and held it aloft, bathing her in its harsh white light. He admired her for a moment as she cowered in fear, then turned the flame so low they were instantly swallowed in darkness.

"Go on inside."

"No, no," Aliki said, but her cry was stifled before it came out.

"Quiet ... No need to raise your voice ..."

He grabbed her around the waist and she soon found herself in a shed enclosed by a piece of sheet iron and a wall. He set the torch down on an iron bench, its low flame burning blue and dark. The shed was dark too, filled with quick panting, shut off from the whole world.

Over to one side, the torch burned on, melting the iron of the bench.

THE STREET-LIGHTS GLIMMERED like huge stars in the windshield of the pick-up, and Andonis clutched his precious briefcase to his chest. He kept his eyes on the glistening blacktop, and every so often looked out the small window in back to make sure his freight was still there. Tonight he was returning home in triumph. Not only had he put a stop to that ridiculous cat-and-mouse game with the debts, he was also bringing home his own merchandise. And all by virtue of his personal worth. Of course, he'd had to overcome certain foolish quibbles, but it had been his only way out. The truck rumbled along with the other traffic down the central avenues, honking, edging between buses and taxis, while Andonis' chest swelled with pride and emotion. The driver was solemn and taciturn. No doubt he realized that this freight was unlike the others he carried. Now that Andonis had a whole truckload of canned goods, he felt protected on all sides.

"What does a truck like this go for?" he asked the driver.

"Around a hundred and thirty, used. Interested?"

He offered a cigarette to the driver, who seemed like a fine fellow. He asked him how many kilometers to the gallon, and whatever else come to mind, just so he wouldn't have to mutely sit there at this great and joyous moment.

"Give me your address ... I'll have plenty of need for a truck."

Andonis jotted down the number of the garage on his cigarette pack. Merchandise was changing hands at a dizzying rate, and it was precisely that rapid movement that generated profit.

"Turn left here, it's the iron gate after the corner ..."

Andonis jumped nimbly down and ran inside. The courtyard was empty, as usual. Vangelia was sewing, her face luminous and calm.

"I'm back!" he shouted triumphantly from the door.

He slung his briefcase onto the bed and gave her a firm hug. Vangelia had been waiting for him with open arms. "So, we're together at last!"

"You were gone such a long time. How did it go?"

"Well, thank God. Splendidly, as a matter of fact," he said. "Put down what you're doing, Vangelia, and come on outside. I brought some things with me."

"What things?"

"Merchandise!" he said, and felt the word's magic fill his mouth.

Vangelia didn't understand, but she lay her sewing down and followed him out. At the gate, he proudly showed her the truck.

"Canned goods! A sure thing."

And he immediately began hefting the boxes onto his back and stacking them in the passageway. Dripping with sweat and run ragged though he was, he was indomitable when it came to work, insatiable as a starving man holding some scrap of success between his teeth. Still, the boxes were very, very heavy ...

"Let me take one," Vangelia told him.

"It'll only tire you out. Just watch."

Which of course was exactly all she should be doing. She wasn't up to such tasks. As he went by her, he was tempted to drop everything and give her a hug, to sit down beside her and just take it easy, listening to her sweet voice, now that his skin felt chafed raw and his blood was running high. Yes, Vangelia should only watch, lest she have any doubt that Andonis was ready to do a porter's work if that's what it took. He was panting heavily, but one couldn't tell if it was from hard work or emotion.

The cartons were bound with straps sharp as razors, but hell, hands are only hands, so what if they got cut all to pieces.

"Stop and take a rest, man. No need to break your back," the driver advised him.

"Don't worry, I can handle it."

And he loaded up with even more boxes, just to prove he hadn't a thought for himself when it came to using his own muscles. The boxes piled up in the passageway. When he wiped the sweat off his forehead, he left streaks of blood on his face from the cuts on his fingers. But those cans potentially represented his first substantial business venture, and deserved every drop of sweat and blood he shed for them.

"What are you going to do with them?" Vangelia asked.

"Sell them, of course," exclaimed Andonis, astonished at her naivete.

He hurriedly gave her hand a squeeze and went back out to the truck to load up. He himself couldn't understand how he had gotten his hands on so much merchandise. It had been a felicitous maneuver that only went to show it was all a matter of timing. After the out-of-town merchants had left, he had gone by Grigoris' shop to pick up his suitcase. Grigoris was trying to sell a large shipment of canned goods to a customer. Andonis knew how hard up Grigoris was for cash. He felt the roll of bills in his pocket, and when the customer left he flashed it at him. "I'll buy them at half price," he said. "You?" "Yes, me, and right here and now." He discarded a few boxes containing inferior goods, deducted what Grigoris owed him for figuring his taxes, then paid him and called over the pick-up. That's how one conducted business.

"You're sopping wet," Vangelia told him. "What's the rush?"

"I didn't bring you anything from my trip ... But if you ask me, Vangelia, these boxes are the best possible present."

"If you say so ... I have a present for you, too," she whispered.

Once he got them all inside the gate, he slid in his suitcase, sent away the truck, and leaned his body against the boxes. His head lolled back, bumping a sharp corner. Vangelia stood next to him, resting her arm on his shoulders. Then she gently caressed his sweaty forehead and murmured that it was time for him to wash and lie down and get some rest.

"Are you happy tonight?"

"You bet ... It wasn't an easy trip."

The blow torches continued to send out their flickering light, and Andonis felt like his body had cardboard boxes attached to it with metal straps. Up in the sky, a full moon was fighting its way through thick clouds.

"I'm glad you're happy. It's been such a long time ..."

Andonis told her they had to take the goods inside, in case it rained. He would be a little tired by the time he was through, but he wanted to make sure they were safe so he could get a good night's sleep.

"Where will we put them?"

"In our room. They'll fit ... Just for a few days. I'll sell them in no time ..."

"At least come and have a drink of water ..."

She slowly pulled him inside, and he had no strength to resist. No sooner did he step through the door than he froze, his eyes wide, his lips moving soundlessly, as if he'd lost his voice. A baby's garment lying on the table said it all.

"Who is that for, Vangelia?"

Vangelia looked into his eyes, smiling, and softly said:

"Us! I was going to tell you tonight."

Andonis rushed over to the table and raised the knitted cloth in his blood-stained hands, as if to get a better look at it in the light. Vangelia watched expectantly for the least expression on his face. The veins stood out on his forehead, his fingers clenched, his eyes glazed over.

"It's out of the question," he said through gritted teeth. "We can't."

"I'll take care of it."

"No, Vangelia, I told you. Don't even think about it."

"I want it," she told him sharply.

Andonis had become a single swollen vein, ready to burst. Like a maniac he tore at the knitted garment, ripped it to pieces, then bit it, shredding it with his teeth. Then he flung it to the floor.

"I don't want to hear another word about babies."

"I'm going to keep it," Vangelia shouted at him. "It's mine and no one can take it from me."

"You're getting rid of it," Andonis howled. "I'm not letting something like that get in my way now."

"What harm is there in a child?"

"I don't know how long I'll be out, or when they might throw me in prison. That's right, prison. It's not like people are climbing over each other trying to give me money."

"I know that," Vangelia said coldly.

Andonis collapsed exhausted into a chair. He turned to look at Vangelia, but he couldn't find her, as if his eyes wouldn't focus. The gashes in his fingers stung. He suddenly felt poor and powerless again, as if he'd lost something of great value.

"So you know."

"Yes."

"Everything?"

"More or less."

"Then you can see why we can't have it. We're still at the very beginning. What am I saying? We're a step away from utter disaster. Worrying about a child would finish me off. Our future's completely up in the air. What if it were to die of hunger? And I wouldn't be able to fool it either."

He caught sight of Vangelia over in the corner somewhere, standing with her arms crossed, little more than a shadow against the wall. He leaned his head back and shut his eyes. His hands hung useless at his sides.

"None of that has anything to do with our child."

"No way, Vangelia. Just put it out of your mind."

Vangelia looked at him somewhat doubtfully, perhaps even pityingly, seeing his dismay. His face glistened with sweat, his hair stuck to his forehead, and his chest rasped as it heaved. Pity was all he deserved. "So what do you think, now you know everything, Vangelia?"

"What am I supposed to think?"

"Say I went to prison. What would you do then?"

"I don't know, I haven't had a chance to think about it ..."

Andonis sprang up and stormed over to her.

"I want to know what exactly you heard. No more beating around the bush. I owe money, everywhere I look I owe money. These days everybody's in debt, it's no longer considered a crime. So how did you find out?"

"I'm not telling," Vangelia said, digging in her heels. "Each of us can keep what's ours. You keep your debts, and I'll keep my baby ..."

Andonis turned away fuming, and began violently shoving around the furniture, as if in a trance. He had to make room for the boxes. He gathered all their clothes into a heap and dumped them on the wardrobe, which he then pushed noisily into the corner. He dragged the table over, threw aside the embroidered tablecloth, and stacked chairs and whatever else he could find on top. The boxes would go in the corner where Vangelia had been planning to put the cradle, to shelter it from drafts. He pushed their bed up against the wall, shoved the chests under the table, tipped the sofa up on one end, and slung the mattress into the kitchen. The little table where they'd kept the radio and a box with odds and ends – pin cushions, snapshots – he kicked under the bed. As he was pushing and dragging things around, a sob came from the kitchen, like liquid brimming and spilling over. Crying was one thing Andonis could not tolerate. In his irritation, he felt like shouting, but checked himself. "Social progress," he reflected, "began with the division of labor. Each to his own task, crying or no crying."

"Knock it off, and let's get those boxes in here."

Vangelia followed him out into the passageway. So this was his precious merchandise, was it? She mustered all of her strength, picked up a box and, without speaking, took it indoors.

"Over in that corner, next to the bed," he told her, pointing. "It'll be protected there."

She set it down as directed and went back out to get another. As she came and went, she avoided the glazed look in Andonis' eyes. She jumped whenever the cold lightning from the blow torches flashed on the surrounding walls. Andonis had become a shortsighted, terrified, pitiful animal, all arms and back, who wanted to hoard a whole treasure trove in his nest, and who found his way in the dark by sense of touch and smell. His hands were covered with blood – a mere detail – his elbows refused to bend, and his head was incapable of holding anything new.

At some point, when their paths crossed, he asked her:

"If you knew how things stood, why didn't you say anything?"

"I wanted to help you ..."

On her next trip, Vangelia told him,

"My back's so sore."

"Good, maybe you'll lose the child. It's no good to me."

EFTIHIS COULDN'T BREATHE in there. He sat bolt upright in the bed. It felt like he had some kind of noose around his neck. His head was burning up. He cursed out loud when he didn't find his shoes right off, and had to pad barefoot over to the window.

"Where are you going?" Mary asked in a voice he barely recognized, it was so changed.

Every so often, the blow torches lit up the wall across from the bed with stripes of flickering light. The bed creaked. Eftihis turned and saw, for a split second, a bit of Mary's body, lit up and naked as she drew up the covers he'd thrown off in the process of getting up. Lodged in his brain, the image seemed more a smoldering fantasy than a physical body. Mary had insisted on having the lights out, but Eftihis felt as if thick clots of darkness were choking him.

"You want some water?"

"No, just get back in bed."

Eftihis drank a few gulps of water, and looked for something to wipe off his sweat, but everything had changed so much he scarcely knew where he was. He groped around until he found the chair where he'd draped his clothes, hoping there would be a handkerchief in his pants pocket. But there wasn't, so he angrily flung down the pants, and the twenty gold pieces, the ones Mary's father had brought him at the church before the wedding, tumbled out on the floor. He listened to them rolling around, then, keyed up as he already was, got down on all fours to retrieve them. He crawled into all the corners, tucking all he came across into his fist.

"What's taking you so long?"

"I'm looking for something."

He held his face low to the floor as if sniffing them out. He bumped his forehead on one of the bed legs, then he started going around on his knees, sweeping each and every floorboard with his palm. Mary again asked what he was looking for, but he just grunted from the opposite corner of the room, and kept on with what he was doing. It had cooled off in there, and he didn't have a stitch on. "Mary's my wife now," he thought, and it seemed like the strangest thing in the world. Weddings were a breeze, the whole thing was over with before you knew it. He scrambled under the bed, ducking even lower because the springs sagged slightly under her weight. He wrapped his fingers around the wires, even ran his finger along them to see if he could feel the difference. "Now there's someone else living here too," he thought. Mary turned over and the weight shifted.

"You still haven't found it?"

He edged back out. There, he got another one. The wedding had gone quickly, the priest had been in a hurry. There weren't more than six or seven people present. The church had felt empty. Eftihis didn't see anybody, not even Mary. He stared at the candle flame, then noticed an orange pane in the tall narrow window glowing in the sunset. "It'll be over soon," he had told himself. He could hear Thodoros wheezing behind him, and farther back he caught sight of Elpida. She was standing off to one side, the way she did in the warehouse before they all headed out for the day's work. No one paid her any heed. Eftihis was solemn, as befitted the occasion; his behavior seemed to say that having made up his mind and getting this far, the rest was so much poppycock. He cut short the shows of camaraderie and emotion afterwards, taking Mary by the hand and bringing her back here. "I just don't go in for all that phony business," he told her. And now the gold sovereigns lay scattered over the floor, and he was lost on a vast plain of level boards.

Mary raised herself up, and the springs over his head squeaked.

"What did you lose, anyway?"

"There are two missing."

"We'll find them in the morning."

"I think he shortchanged me."

"They probably fell down a crack. Come on, in the morning ..."

"I need to find them, what if they're not all here?"

"You didn't count them?"

"I was trying to be polite. I just shoved them in my pocket so I wouldn't insult the man by counting them in front of everybody, like a money-changer."

"They're all there."

"I don't trust that old man of yours. And I didn't like that look on his face. It was like he'd pulled something off."

"He was just *happy*, couldn't you tell? Come on to bed."

Suddenly Mary jumped up, turned on the light, and sat back down on the bed. Everything froze in place between the four pink walls. Eftihis, stunned as if the light had been a blow to the head, lay face down on the floor, half under the bed. All Mary could see were his legs. Then he backed up a bit, stuck out his head and peered up at her. His hair was wet, his nostrils flared, and his eyes were bloodshot. Mary pulled the sheet to her chin.

"What are you staring at?"

"Fine, there's no rush. You and me are going to be together a long time. So long we'll be sick of each other."

Mary's dark eyes were full of perplexity and surprise.

"Come on."

Eftihis clenched his teeth, and looked her over good, his knuckles pressed to the floor.

"I'm not the kind of person that's easily made a fool of ..." he told her in a precise voice.

"We'll find them in the morning, they probably just rolled into a corner."

"That's not what I'm talking about."

"What are you talking about then?"

"That other thing, the most important. You've been playing the shy little girl with me all night ..."

"What did you say?"

"You didn't have to put on such a big act ... You overdid it."

"Are you crazy?"

"I'm not crazy. I know what I'm talking about," was all Eftihis said. And he immediately resumed searching the floor for the two sovereigns, as if what he'd said was not such a big deal. Why had Mary looked so frightened, as if she'd touched a live wire? Did she have any right to bedevil him by putting on such an act? When he looked back up at her, she was as white as the sheet she clutched tightly at her throat.

"So that's what they told you?"

"Are you saying it's not true?"

"And you believed it?"

"That's my business. But you never said a word to me. Here

we are married, and you still haven't opened your mouth."

"What do you want me to tell you?"

"Cut the crap, Mary. You had an obligation ..."

Mary looked at him wonderingly, as if it were her first glimpse of that kneeling man with the hard face and piercing eyes. What was he getting so wrought up about? A shiver passed through her body, as if cold water were streaming under the sheets. She looked at his feet. Between the heel and ankle was a dark smudge that looked like dirt. The same on the other foot. You could see it between his fingers too. "I'll have to remember to heat water for him in the morning," Mary thought. Why was he looking at her like that, what was he trying to root out of her? Eftihis began crawling around on his knees again. A sovereign glinted next to the table leg. How do you like that – the little bitch had come to rest flush against the wood.

"So did you finally find it?"

"I think it's time you came clean with me, Mary."

"What do you want out of me? There's nothing to say ..."

"Fine ... But I'm not touching you until you tell me. Don't hold your breath. I'm sleeping right here on the floor until you make up your mind ..."

"I don't understand ..."

"You will, someday ..."

Then it was as if something came to him that raised the hair on his neck. He cocked his ear and listened to something far away. He was right. There was a motorcycle approaching. It was still two or three blocks off. He didn't move. Yes, the sound of its engine was getting louder, it was down at the corner, then it halted practically at the gate. Mary's face had drained of color. The engine continued to rumble on the sidewalk. Eftihis abruptly grabbed the sheet and gave it a yank. Naked, Mary gave a shriek.

"Hear that?" he shouted at her.

She hid her face in her hands, as if she were less naked that way. The motorcycle came even closer, it was in the room itself. She heard it drumming distinctly and rhythmically inside her own head.

"You hear it?" Eftihis bellowed again.

"Turn out the light."

"You're the one who turned it on. I like seeing you this way. So it's the light that's bothering you?"

The motorcycle kept running. Eftihis had a mind to go out and give Pericles a punch in the face, but he thought better of it when he recalled he was wearing only his shorts.

"It doesn't remind you of something?"

"What difference does it make what it reminds me of?"

"I'm just asking to make conversation," Eftihis said disingenuously.

"Throw me the covers, I'm cold."

"I'm cold too. Drop it!"

Eftihis went up to her and said, with exaggerated politeness:

"You wouldn't happen to know why that little turd is parked outside our door on his bike, would you?"

"Why don't you go out and ask him?"

"I'm asking you. You're my wife."

He forced her hands away from her face, he shook her by the shoulders and ordered her to look at him. In his anger, he was capable of wringing her pale, soft, dough-like flesh.

"Tell me!"

"Tell you what?"

"The truth."

"What do you want to know for?"

"Just so I know. And don't you worry about what I want to know for."

He gripped her head and tried to pry open her eyelids, thinking it would be easier for her to talk with her eyes open to the light.

"Did you go with him?"

"You already know," she answered, under the force of his badgering. "A trip to Dafni, that's all."

"You want me to call him in here so you can say that to his face?"

"If you think that's the right thing to do, go ahead."

Eftihis quickly pulled on his trousers and went to the door to clear the matter up once and for all. As his hand closed around the doorknob, however, he turned and saw Mary huddled in a ball, a desperate look on her face. He thought he detected a sob under the sheet. He came back, realizing that it wasn't worth making a fool of himself on account of a son-of-a-bitch like Pericles. What was he doing out there, anyway? If Eftihis went out and bashed his head in, it would only draw a crowd. He could settle accounts with him tomorrow. For now, he had Mary to deal with. He wanted to rip up her sheets, to make her see that she had nowhere to hide, no choice but to spit it all out, every last detail. But Mary insisted on keeping her eyes shut, which was like a slap in the face. It meant that she hadn't decided yet to tell the truth. She pulled up the sheet and wrapped herself in it.

"Why get so upset about one little walk in Dafni?" he said sarcastically.

"You're crazy, you don't know what you're talking about ..."

Eftihis sat down on the foot of the bed.

"Listen, Mary," he said with severity. "No one, but no one makes a fool of me unless I want them to ... I know everything because he told me himself."

"So what are you asking me for if you take his word for it?"

"I'd like to hear it from you."

"But if you're so sure you know everything already ..."

"I want you to tell me. Otherwise it won't really be true."

Mary started crying. The bed creaked. The motorcycle was still running out on the sidewalk. Her blubbering infuriated Eftihis even more, so he sprang at her and, digging his fingers into her hair, jerked her head back in an effort to quash her resistance.

"Tell me everything," he demanded insatiably.

Her head, with its short, curly hair, was pinned to the pillow.

"Tell me," he said again.

"You're asking me to tell you something that never happened," she told him, crushed. "You've heard everything."

"What did you two do at Dafni?"

"We took a walk, then came back."

Eftihis shook her hard, slamming her head down again and again, as if truth were something one could be made to spit out. Mary yielded to it, flopping about in his powerful hands like a rag doll.

"What happened at Dafni?"

"Why should I tell you, since you wouldn't believe me anyway?"

He gave her two hard smacks across the face, but the bitch didn't even open her eyes, she seemed unaware of what was going on, as if she'd been drugged. He could still hear the motorcycle at the front gate, its engine throbbing.

"Say something, or I'll tear your hair out. I'll go out and have him come in."

"I don't care," Mary persisted. "Do what you want."

He smacked her again, and howled with malice, aware that there was nothing before him but a soft, white, lifeless sack. What else could he do to her? He put his mouth to her ear and shouted:

"What happened in Dafni? Tell me everything ..."

She didn't even move. Eftihis rocked the whole bed, as Mary's body bounced lifelessly, shuddered, and lay still.

"Tell me, did you lie down with him under a tree?"

"Yes," Mary uttered out of the blue, with a docile effortlessness.

"How many times?"

"Lots, I don't remember ..."

"Tell me everything, right from the beginning. Out with it!"

Mary coughed, as if choking on something. "We went into the woods, and it was like it always is when two people lie down under the pines," she said with closed eyes, in an unrecognizable voice that rolled slowly but unfalteringly off her tongue, as if she were reading a script. She ended by repeating, "Yes, I, Mary, went ..."

"So why didn't you tell me?" Eftihis said in amazement.

"Just to make a fool of you, because I'm a no-good bitch. There, I told you everything, just like you wanted ... I confessed ... But instead of going on torturing me, why don't you just search the floor for the sovereign you're still missing?"

Eftihis scratched his head, and padded around in his bare feet, with mingled fury and embarrassment. Then he sat down on the lower part of the bed and gazed at her for a while. She seemed asleep – loose-limbed and unburdened.

"Mary, I'd have imagined you would have given some thought to what it means to spend the rest of your life with another person ..."

He moved closer, sitting halfway up the bed. He lowered his head and found himself looking at his toes. He instantly hid them under the bed. What with everything else, he never had a chance to wash. Besides, on one's wedding night, everything happened in the dark. No one noticed what the heel of the other's foot looked like. He wondered if Mary had noticed while he was crawling around on the floor. He raised himself over her and studied her, full of curiosity and wonder, trying to understand the change that had come over this girl he used to steal kisses from on street-corners.

"Mary, will you open your eyes so we can talk?"

"What's there to say? Haven't we said it all?"

"Wake up so I can tell you a story that'll help you understand what kind of person you married ..."

"What do you want to go telling stories for?" Mary said. "Come on, turn out the light, the motorcycle's gone ..."

"You're right, it is! I hadn't noticed, I thought I was still hearing the motor ..."

He pulled the covers over her. Her fingers were ice-cold. Her eyelids remained shut.

"You know, Mary," Eftihis began, as if continuing a story from long before, "I'm a child of the war."

"Save the stories for another time," she beseeched him.

"Yeah, you're right. I already forgot what I wanted to tell you ... Anyway, what good are stories? You'll tell me yours one day, won't you?"

"I don't have one," she said with a shrug.

Eftihis stared at her intently for a time, as if going through a box of odds and ends with his eyes, searching for parts to something even he wasn't really sure what to do with.

Mary got up wrapped in the bedclothes and turned out the light. She began sobbing in the dark, she flung herself on him and spoke in short gasps, as she struggled to control herself.

"There's nothing to tell. Trust me. I'm your wife, what more do you want? That's the truth."

"Fine, we'll talk about it another time ... Calm down for now ..." said Eftihis with a note of reproach.

THE CARDBOARD BOXES and packing cases had been carefully arranged, as in a warehouse. "It's a start," Andonis murmured. Vangelia tried to move one of the boxes, but it slipped from her grip and the cans spilled out on the floor. Andonis glowered at her, suspecting her mind was still on the baby. And just to demonstrate the unrelenting pace such work required, he swept up the last two boxes and set them at the very top, as if he'd been a porter all his life. "Tonight, cans are the whole of my existence," he thought to himself.

When he'd squeezed the last one in next to the bed, Andonis spat on the floor, and his spit was full of vexation and dust. He gave the room a dazed look, then rolled up his sleeves to wash.

There was nothing more to say. Vangelia slipped the baby garment into her pocket. She'd really have to fight for that child.

Andonis went into the kitchen and filled the basin with water. His legs looked shorter to her tonight, his back wider and more stooped. When he plunged in his hands, the water darkened with dust and the blood that still oozed from his fingers. The metal straps had sliced his flesh like razors. Panic hovered about him, and he abruptly drained the basin – though not before Vangelia had caught sight of the blood-stained water.

When they were back in the other room, he told her:

"You should feel love for these cans ... You might say they're our foundations. My entire reputation, all of my hopes, are staked on what's inside these boxes."

Then, to thwart her probing gaze, he faced her and declared:

"I have a confession to make, Vangelia. I've been deceiving you. That's right, I tricked you, as if you were just somebody I was doing business with, someone I deceived in order to get their goods for next to nothing – and on credit."

"And what have you gotten from me?"

"I'm afraid I can't tell you that. You'd cut off my line of credit, and then I would have no way to pay back the cash I already owe. I tricked you, that's all I'll say."

"You're not telling me anything I didn't already know," replied Vangelia.

"What? That's not possible ..."

"Open your suitcase," she ordered him.

"But there's nothing in there ..."

"I know for a fact that the clothes you packed for your trip haven't been worn once. Open it ..."

Andonis didn't move, but nor did Vangelia insist.

"You're only saying this because I told you how things stood tonight ..."

"I let you deceive me, I wanted it," Vangelia told him bluntly. "And every time I wanted us to sit down and have a talk, you were too busy with your accounts. But you usually left your papers spread out on the table ... When you went out, I could see they weren't accounts. You were writing down numbers at random ... None of your multiplications were right. I worked them out myself, and they were all wrong ..."

"In other words, you were spying on me?"

"I had to know. But I didn't say anything ... In fact, I tore them all up. They were of no use to you."

Somebody was at the door. Alarmed, Andonis broke off what he was going to say. He was disconcerted to see Angelos' father coming into the room with a smile on his face.

"Good evening," the judge cordially greeted them. "I hope you'll forgive me for stopping in at this time of night. I came by looking for you a few days ago as well ..."

"Yes, I was away on a trip ... Have a seat. I've been so busy these days. But there's no place to sit, is there? You'll have to excuse our disarray ... That's how it is in the world of business ... Sit on the bed, or better yet, over here on these boxes ..."

"I'd like to make an important request of you," the judge said in almost a whisper. "It has to do with my son, Angelos ..."

"They didn't catch him, did they?" Andonis inquired anxiously.

"No," Harilaos answered. "He's doing just fine ... But there's something I'd like to do to help him. I learned from Eftihis that you know a certain Thodoros."

"Thodoros? He's an accused collaborator ... He's no friend of mine. How could a man like that ever be my friend? We've had business dealings, that's all."

"In any case, he was the prime witness at Angelos' trial. Even today, my son's life depends on him. His conviction was due in large part to this man's testimony ..."

"And what can I do?"

"If *you* can help to trigger his conscience, it's possible we can request a review of the trial ..."

"Me, trigger his conscience?'

"If you consider it just, and if you truly want to, you'll find a way," Harilaos said with utmost simplicity. "I wouldn't want to pressure you, nor to influence you ... However, if you share my view, and if your own conscience feels strongly about it ..."

Andonis leaned back against the boxes and folded his arms. He scratched his head, rested his chin in his hand, and gazed tight-lipped at this aged man who was waiting for him to make a promise. Vangelia regarded Andonis intently. The judge had clear, blue eyes, pale white hands, and an air of patient expectancy.

"You think that's such an easy thing to do?"

"Hardly. In fact, I'd say it won't be at all easy. However, I happen to know that you're an exceptionally capable man ... My son was convicted ..."

"I know the whole story," Andonis said. "What I didn't know was that Thodoros was the principal witness ..."

"Ah, so you did know Angelos?" The old man seemed genuinely pleased. "That makes it that much simpler ..."

Andonis went on in a firm tone, as if he had come to some decision:

"It's true. Angelos was a friend, a very dear friend. I never had a chance to tell you, I was always so busy ... And I also didn't want to cause you unnecessary grief by reminding you. I respect Angelos, he's one in a million ... We got to know each other in a number of student groups back under the dictatorship. Later, during the war, we were going to go up and join the resistance together, but I was wounded in an incident here a couple of days beforehand. Remember, Vangelia? A bit farther down, by the tracks ..."

"You don't say!"

Yes ... Now, well, I'm involved in business-matters. I do people's books, odd jobs basically, whatever I can drum up. We all do what we can ... Anyway, you shouldn't worry too much. Angelos' one tough fellow – a real fighter."

"Still, we should do all we can for him," said the old man.

"Agreed," Andonis put in without enthusiasm.

"I trust you ... I know you'll come up with something ... Good-night."

Harilaos got up off the boxes, said good-by to Vangelia and, before leaving, paused in the door and told Andonis:

"I'm so pleased to have finally gotten to know you. Let's hope we manage to get somewhere. We'll have a chance to talk later on. I look forward to hearing the results of your efforts."

“Do you ever see him?” Andonis asked.

“Rarely, and then only with elaborate precautions ... As I’m sure you realize, there’s no point in our meeting unless absolutely necessary ... I’ll let him know I saw you, he’ll be delighted ...”

“Best wait till we have something concrete to report ... Don’t say anything to him yet.”

“But of course, only regards ...”

When he was gone, Andonis stood gazing at Vangelia for a long time.

“So now what?”

Vangelia gave a shrug. At that, Andonis whirled around and started counting the boxes and cans all over again.

CHAPTER 11

WITH THE FIRST LIGHT OF DAWN, Angelos crept up to the chair beside Stathis' pillow and carefully eased the morning paper out of his coat pocket. He went back over to the window, trying not to make noise, because even rustling paper was enough to spark Stathis' ire. But it was still dark, and he couldn't even make out the headlines. He stretched his body out in the chair, propping his head against the wall. "How long am I going to go on this way?" It was a question that, no matter how old it became, remained ever new in that room. What he needed was an escape route. "But where would I go?" he immediately asked himself. This was the courtyard of his house, and it was still redolent of high school anxieties, muffled talk on the stairs up to the roof. If they found him there, he would become a laughingstock. Stathis' sleep was a guardian of silence, an element of the place's reality, like the bed, the shutters, the door, and the old newspapers that were again stacked neatly in the corner.

In all the other houses he'd stayed in, Angelos had believed that the period of anomaly would be brief, that it was something he would be able to get through one day at a time. Whole years had gone by that way. "I can't make the same mistake now," he thought, and decided that what was needed was a complete review of the evidence, beginning with day one. Where had he gone wrong? What would have happened if he hadn't convinced himself that his present situation was only temporary? He had unthinkingly sacrificed the minimum – his daily existence – in order to salvage the maximum – his life – in the belief that the latter was infinitely vast, inexhaustible. Was it the daily cost that had done him in? The maximum and minimum became the same thing in that room smelling of unwashed clothes, dirty feet, and fear, like a military barracks. "I must have been awfully young to have made so free with my life," he said to himself with a smile. "The strange thing is that I still believe it." It couldn't last, though, things would change. He would make sure of that, once it was light enough to read the day's paper.

Noises came from next door. Sleepy steps shuffled across the floor, followed by increasing activity. Then he heard Andonis' voice, clear as day:

"Go back to sleep, I've got some figures to work through here. Correctly this time. I don't need anything, I'll make my own coffee."

Vangelia murmured something but Andonis snapped back at her, saying he had lots to do, and what he needed was quiet and a chance to concentrate.

Ever since Angelos realized who his neighbor was, he had kept his ear cocked to hear all that was said in the next room. His old friend Andonis! He had even promised his father to do something to help Angelos' cause. Of course, it was a bit much to be called "a real fighter," but it was better than being written off entirely. It meant they still had faith in him. Of course, he may just have said it to placate his father, to get rid of him. No, Andonis always spoke his mind, and always carried through with whatever he began. He used to transport arms in a suitcase, which he skillfully smuggled past the checkpoints. He organized strikes and spoke at rallies. "Why," Angelos wondered, "did he talk to Vangelia the way he did? Why didn't he want their child?"

The newspaper was still a uniform gray surface in Angelos' hands, a trap laid to ensnare the first light. From outside came the clatter of shutters, footsteps in nearby courtyards, and other scattered noises as the city hastily prepared to begin the new day. Nothing more was heard from Andonis, who was probably going on with his writing. "I could help him with his calculations," Angelos thought. "I'd work all day, and thank him at night." But that was not to be, the rules governing this peculiar prison of his were strict. Stathis had become the harshest of jailers.

"How long will I go on this way?" he demanded of the mute walls of the room. "Until I pinpoint where I went wrong," he said in answer to his own question. He remembered an old physics professor of his, a short man who told them how Newton had slaved day and night over a single equation. In the eighth year he determined that his labor, from a certain point on – sometime in the second year – had taken a wrong turn. Which meant six years, down the drain. He put aside everything he'd written up till then, and started over. In our day, the same calculations could be done electronically in a matter of hours. But Angelos hadn't kept notes to help him pin down his error. Nor could he avail himself of technological advances in the sciences. But science wasn't the logical working of machines, it was the knowledge of the human mind and hands utilizing the natural and social properties of things. Science was joined to these properties in order for things and for knowledge to be transformed into machinery, tools, theorems ... All these things constituted a "solution" aimed at carrying out specific tasks. It was a way of thinking, not a conclusion. The technical specialists who put methodology into practice served a purpose for posterity, but as yet no science had yet been developed for man in confinement. There was a science of manufacturing, of commerce, of prisons, of war, even of boredom and despair. But Angelos belonged to none of these categories, he had neither chosen nor brought about the situation in which he found himself, nor was he constrained by weakness. In the heart of the age of individualism, it was absurd to talk about the isolation of the individual. "The reason my own problem lacks a solution is that I haven't managed to ascertain the pertinent facts," Angelos reasoned. But what was his problem exactly?

He sank his fingers into his thick beard. His hair too had grown dangerously long. With the resistance, he had gotten to know a cheery fellow who was forever spouting predictions: "In two weeks' time we'll be in Athens," he'd say every so often. Everyone made fun of him, because a year and a half had gone by since he'd started saying it. "I don't know why you find it so funny when I say that in two weeks ..." Then when the Germans left, he was beside himself: "What did I tell you? For two years I tried to convince you, but you wouldn't listen ..." Why should Angelos think of him now? So then, Newton did not discover electronic devices for himself, though he paid dearly for their lack. He'd had the courage to start over from scratch. Anyone who had properly applied a methodology would find Angelos' own problem laughable. Some line of reasoning or effort had come out equaling zero, and rendered his whole system invalid. He had lost his contacts, had forgotten his friends. He'd gone backwards. Were he to meet anyone he knew, he wouldn't know how to speak to them, he might not even understand what they said. Take Andonis. That morning in '43 – March, it would have been – Angelos had gone straight over to Andonis' after eluding the Germans. He'd been studying all night, and had gone to bed exhausted, yet his brain was still awhirl with equations. At dawn, just that time of day, he'd heard the squeal of brakes outside. He had snatched up his pants and a shirt, thrown on his shoes, and at the first knock was already on his way up the stairs to the roof. He jumped over to the next roof, scampered along behind a parapet, cautiously clambered up the tiles – they were wet, and broke at every step – hung down from an iron railing, and ended up in a large courtyard which at the time was an auto shop. He had run down a narrow passage lined with rooms, and came out on the back alley, next to some ruined houses. Then he dashed off to find Andonis. Andonis had burst out laughing when he saw him. He gave him a coat, and off they went together. The whole time he'd been in Stathis' room, he hadn't once heard Andonis laugh. What was the name of the student who used to sit next to him, who was later killed? Then that evening, Angelos found time to go by Ismene's high school when it was letting out. She gave a start when she saw him. "You have to get away, you have to go in hiding," she had told him then as now. "I did get away, as you can see." He learned that his father had suffered a heart attack that morning, when the SS came storming in. He didn't know Angelos had escaped. Ismene kept looking around to make sure they weren't being followed, or that there wasn't a trap of some sort, and Angelos had teased her about it. But she didn't seem to mind, and had asked him in a solemn voice whether there was anything she could do for him. When he'd asked her not to be afraid, Ismene had told him, "Could you do me a favor?" She took a notebook out of her bag and showed him two trigonometry exercises. "I didn't understand a word of today's lesson ... I was too busy thinking ... And now I won't be able to concentrate at all ..." They stood in the light coming from the doorway of a café and he wrote out the answer for her. But she was afraid, and regretted having asked such a huge favor of him. She tugged on his arm trying to get him to leave. But Angelos had shrugged her off, and had done the next problem too without the least difficulty. A little later, near an orchard, she had teasingly asked if he was sure they were correct: "I'm going to copy them just the way they are." "Oh, they're correct all right," Angelos had answered. "When will I see you?" she had asked. "Tomorrow at nine, right here." "You'll be here?" "You better believe it," he'd told her, without for an instant doubting he'd be able to keep his word. The following evening, even though he was across town, he had sprinted over to make it to the orchard on time. "Congratulations, you got an A in trigonometry!" Ismene had told him. "But I'm really just happy you came." He didn't know where he'd be sleeping that night either, but it didn't bother him. All he knew was that the next day he would be back there at the orchard at the same time.

He remembered his rooftop escape as if it'd had been the critical part of the whole ordeal. He retraced his route in his mind, step by step, leap by leap, and ended up feeling a joyous ache, that jumble of emotions that wells up inside you when you successfully evade some great danger. He had walked out from among the ruins into a morning street that was free, empty, and cold. No, not cold, just cool and deserted, with shuttered windows, a gray sky, boundless hope and a reckless freedom that lengthened his stride. But now that first breath of freedom was perhaps not as important as the escape itself. It was a pleasant exercise of memory. Angelos tried to remember more. It was that same morning, two days after the demonstration on the fifth of March. But at some point he lost track. Where had he gone after going across the tiles, and before reaching the auto shop? There was a gap. That part of his escape route must have taken him behind that very room.

He let the newspaper fall to the floor, moved his chair over and sat down at the table to study this problem of memory. He began sketching his route on a piece of newsprint: the stairs, the roof, the parapet, the roof of the adjacent house that looked out on the cross-street, a wash-shed, two wooden grape-arbors, then his hanging down and dropping onto a wall, and from there onto the rooftiles. Then the whole thing over again. He took another sheet of paper – Stathis often left a few on the table. This time he drew with care, trying to keep the size of the structures in proportion to each other. He folded up the first sketch and put it in his pocket. He became absorbed in the wonderful detail of his new effort.

At one point, when Stathis was rolling over, Angelos hid the paper as if it were a forbidden item. When he was sure Stathis was sound asleep, he chuckled at his fear and continued drawing. In order to show the entire route, he lovingly sketched in the ground plan of the surrounding structures. He drew the room he was in, the courtyard, his house, with each of its rooms, Andonis' place, the detached house next door, and a two-story place over to the right. It all came out perfectly! "It's always good to know exactly where you are," he mused.

Andonis pushed back his chair. Apparently he'd completed his calculations. It was time for him to be off. Vangelia asked when he would be back. He reiterated that, as on previous days, he had no idea what might take place by dinner-time.

"Have you done what the judge talked to you about?" Vangelia then asked. "He mentioned it to me again last night. What should I tell him if he stops by again?" "Tell him I'm taking care of it."

"You think that's enough? He's hoping for something more."

"The judge is naive," Andonis barked in reply. "He believes his son's case rests on the testimony of one or even ten witnesses. He doesn't realize that Angelos is being persecuted because of a more general condition, it's not a question of an isolated incident ..."

"Then why did you promise him?"

Andonis mumbled something inaudible.

"So what should I tell him if he comes back?" asked Vangelia.

"Whatever comes into your head ... how should I know?" said Andonis as he shot out the door, briefcase in hand. He was like some frightened deer, bolting into a thicket. For Andonis, at that moment, the street must have seemed the densest of forests. "Andonis is right," Angelos thought. "I'm not an isolated case. My fate doesn't depend on any one witness." He went back to the table and started a new, more detailed sketch, using a fixed scale to keep the dimensions consistent.

Soon Ismene went by, he could tell by her step. She seemed tired, she had lost that girlish spring she used to have. She had become a woman, had come to know only too well the irredeemable nature of time. That night in the rain, he couldn't bring himself to tell her that it might be best if they didn't meet again ... If he had told her that, it would have meant that he accepted the inevitability of his ruin, which would only have added to her sorrow.

He extended his drawing to include the roof behind the house next door. The ground plan was gradually being filled in, each element filled out what went before and led to the next. The whole neighborhood had begun to seem familiar. Behind Andonis' room must have been the large yard where they used to have the auto shop ... Now it was the metal works. Then came the narrow passageway leading to the street parallel to this one. If you made it that far, you were home free ...

Stathis was not an especially effective guard. All one had to do was get the keys out of his pants and leave. "Why does Stathis look at me that way?" Angelos wondered. Everyone looked at him with the same, blank gaze. As if he were just passing through, transitory. Maybe that was the impression he gave, or maybe they knew something he didn't. He thought of the two sisters at Orestes' house, on the side of Likavittos. They used to slip him his food through the cracked door, and scurry away. Luckily, there were French doors out onto the balcony, so when it got dark he could look out at passersby and the corner street-light. There was a cobbler's across the street; next to that lived a girl with blonde hair. Every night a young man would walk her home and they would kiss on her doorstep. No one remembered that Angelos was there. The sisters would laugh and have their friends over, they'd turn on the radio and dance with boys from their set. One night they all went out to take a walk together. It was drizzling, and they burst into laughter the minute they hit the street. Angelos stood motionless, watching the raindrops blurring the glass. In the yellow light from the street lamp, they gleamed like stars. He'd stayed in that house for ten days. It was as if they had excluded him from life, as if he were without rights. Afterwards, he had wandered three or four days until he found his friend Stavros, with whom he'd bunked during the resistance, in Peristeri. "Fine," Stavros had said, "you can sleep in the truck." And he pointed to a large truck covered with a canvas tarp. "No one'll ever know you're there." The house was off by itself, and Stavros kept the truck parked in the yard. The first night Angelos had wrapped himself in a few rag rugs and slept the sleep of the dead. Each morning he would slip into the house, which was all of one room. Stavros' wife worked at a factory in Pireas and came home late. They would leave him the key and Angelos would lock himself in, free to unlock the door whenever he liked. On a couple of different Sundays they'd had friends over. "I'd like you to meet my friend Angelos, he's a great guy," Stavros had said with a wink and a big smile. The rest of them had relaxed, they clinked glasses, swapped banter, and began to feel quite comfortable together. "You really are a great guy, Stavros wasn't fooling," one of them boomed, slapping Angelos on the back. It was good and dark before it broke up, Angelos had said he had work to do. The same friends came back more than once, and it was as if they had known each other for years. Once, when Stavros had the day off, the three of them had gone on an outing together, purely for recreation. That winter, he hadn't even noticed the days growing shorter, then longer again, and he never once felt cold in that truck lashed by rain and wind. One Saturday evening, however, the sound of gunfire disturbed the neighborhood's quiet. Women screamed, kids started bawling. They must have been after somebody, because there was a sound of running feet, and the gunfire got nearer. "Stavros," said a fearful neighbor who happened to be passing by, "there's someone hiding in your truck, I saw them!" Stavros sprang behind the wheel. "Nothing to worry about, it's my assistant. We're leaving tonight on a long trip." And he took off like a bolt of lightning, careening past a number of neighbors talking nervously out on the dirt road. After they had gone a ways, Stavros brought the truck to a stop on a deserted stretch of road. He ran around behind and, raising the flap, said excitedly, "We sure gave them the slip, didn't we?" Angelos climbed out. "Where will you go tonight?" Stavros had asked, stuffing whatever money he had with him into his pocket. "I'll find something," Angelos answered evasively. The truck drove off, leaving him in the middle of the road. He had forgotten to ask where they were. He spent the night curled up in a quarry he stumbled on down the road. He didn't sleep a wink, just stared at the bright lights of Athens in the distance, strewn across the whole width of night. The funny thing was that Stavros had been under the impression

Angelos was sneaking out of the truck, and Angelos hadn't disabused him. Indeed, he had fostered the notion that he went out and met people at night. Yet the truth was he had not once set foot outside of the truck, and the gunfire had had nothing to do with him. The neighbor just chanced to be going past when Angelos lifted a corner of the tarp to see what was happening.

The ground plan was complete. Every square foot of the area was now accounted for. But still he couldn't leave, unlike that time he slipped through the clutches of the SS. He had spent years now in hiding and confinement. He felt old and worn. He had been living under the belief that he would be able to go on putting things off, waiting. And that, by all appearances, was one of his fundamental errors.

HE REVIEWED HIS SKETCH. When you reached the courtyard where the auto shop used to be, you were in the clear.

Suddenly a thought jolted him: What if he were to dig a tunnel?

This solution filled him with joy ... He measured the distance: four meters, five at the most. An underground passage from here over to the edge of the courtyard would cut under Andonis' room, under the corner where the cans were stacked. He *could* escape! Escape his fear! And then he would see about the rest. He was out of time, he could wait no longer ... It was a simple matter, like digging a small drainage ditch. Three cubit meters of dirt, give or take.

Stathis opened his eyes. Angelos quickly folded up the paper and slipped it into his pocket.

"Awake?" he asked awkwardly.

Stathis put his finger to his lips, meaning "Silence."

"Vangelia's out, there's no one there."

"Have you eaten?"

"I was waiting so we could eat together."

Stathis stretched, rubbed his eyes with the back of his hands, and announced he was hungry. A man who worked had every right to be whatever he wanted.

"How about giving me a haircut, Stathis ... My hair's too long ..."

"Why? Planning to go someplace?"

"I just don't like looking like this."

"But who's going to see you?"

"You never know. It might become necessary ... I read just yesterday that there's a chance they'll ease up ..."

"You'll have a lot of haircuts before that happens."

Angelos ignored Stathis' oracle. They opened the parcel of food and set in eating. Eggs, potatoes, cheese – everything tasted good after the work he'd done, and the remembering involved in mapping out his route – all in hopes of coming up with a solution.

"By the way, Stathis, are they building something around here? I thought I heard a cement-mixer ..."

"I don't know. Maybe on the next street over ... There were some old tumbledown places ..."

"Is that auto shop still there? What's behind here, right next to us?"

"What do you care?"

"You never know, someone might hear us ..."

"Bah, it's just another house ..."

"And next to that?"

"A courtyard, they do welding there now ... Why?"

"Just wondering ... There are all these flashes of light every night ... Heard anything about me?"

"Not a word."

"What did Ismene ask you the other afternoon?"

"The usual. Whether I've seen you, where you are ... I let her think I don't know anything. If we start having visiting hours, you may as well start packing."

"You think that'd be best? Would you like me to leave right now?"

"That's up to you. What, you've been hiding all this time for nothing?"

Stathis gave a loud laugh.

"You need some fresh air. Being shut up indoors has had a bad effect on you."

"What's so funny, you think I'm afraid? I've never been afraid. I'm leaving any day now. Right this instant, if that's what you want ..."

"Suit yourself," Stathis said curtly. "All I'm offering you is shelter and safety. But I also don't want any trouble. If you don't like it here, there's always your family's house across the courtyard. You can go over there any time ..."

"I told you, don't go getting the idea I'm afraid or anything ..."

"You're the one who brought it up." Stathis' voice was unusually harsh. "For now, you'll do exactly what I tell you to. Otherwise ..."

"Fine ... Could you at least ask for my books? I need something to read, I'm so far behind ..."

"So read the papers. If I ask her for them, she'll put two and two together and then she'll never stop pestering me. Not a chance. Remember, during the war, when you led me blindfolded to a printing press? I stayed in that basement for three years ... And once, when I asked if I could see Elly, you said no. I heeded you because you were right. I never saw her again ... Do you remember Elly?"

"That's different."

"Of course. But each situation is governed by its own laws, and one has to observe them, right? You spent a whole night back then explaining the rules of the press to me, and I understood perfectly. I resigned myself to living a secret existence. You should do the same. Do you remember Elly at all? I never even said good-by ... Of course, there was nothing between us. I never told her how I felt. What do you think became of her?"

Stathis fell silent, remembering Elly. Then he turned and asked Angelos outright:

"So how long do you think you'll go on living like this?"

"That's what I'm trying to figure out ... Don't think I'm not making a big sacrifice as it is. I told myself, 'I've got to avoid capture,' but now I wonder if I've really managed anything of the sort."

"You're alive, aren't you?"

"Well, in reality ..."

"What is the reality?" Stathis asked.

Angelos put his hand in his pocket and fingered the drawing of his escape.

"Are you happy with your life, Stathis?"

"No, but it doesn't bother me. It seems perfectly natural for me to live the life I do. You should try it – try making up your mind. Either you stay, or you go ..."

"It's kind of hard to picture myself spending the rest of my life in confinement."

"You're in a tougher spot now than when you started. If you go out now, and something happens, it'd be as if all of those years had gone wasted ... You *can't* let them get you. Besides, you're a ..."

"A condemned man, is that what you were going to say?"

"No. A fighter."

"Go ahead, joke about it." Angelos smiled bitterly. "But I've never once let up in my struggle."

"Is that right? What exactly have you been doing?"

"Even if I haven't been doing anything ... I meant just the daily struggle to keep a hold on yourself when there's a sentence hanging over your head ..."

"And where does that get you?"

"If I lose my grip, it's as if the sentence had been carried out."

Vangelia's footsteps from the next room imposed an abrupt silence on them. Stathis began to get dressed, and Angelos once more pulled his chair over by the window.

He had the drawing in his pocket. It was a "solution" of the sort he had long been seeking. If he pulled it off, he would be able to come and go without risk. He looked over at Stathis to see if he could detect any trace of suspicion on his face. Angelos' escape was a secret, a new element of illegality in the room. Three cubic meters of dirt ... What would he find on the other side? The welders worked until eight, ten at the latest. He would have to measure the gap between the floorboards and the ground to find out how deep the tunnel had to be. If he succeeded, he would no longer be afraid.

He went up to Stathis, who was shaving in the broken mirror, and said in his ear:

"Were you making fun of me before when you called me a fighter?"

"No. What, you're not?"

"Being a fighter means taking action, doing something that affects others too ..."

"What else is there?"

"Not losing myself. I'm not sure I've managed to do that."

Stathis shrugged as if Angelos' perplexity were of no concern to him. He finished shaving at his leisure, picked up their breakfast scraps and went to throw them out in the laundry-room. Angelos hid in the corner. A cold breath of freedom swept through the open door. The courtyard was empty, the bright afternoon sun reached to the legs of his chair.

The door closed again. Scrubbed and shaven, Stathis took his leave, locking the door behind him. As always, awaiting him was the news of the world, which his hands would turn into rows of metal type. "Imagine," Angelos thought, "that first night when you roam the streets a free man."

CHAPTER 12

AT DAYBREAK, VANGELIA found him face down in a ledger, his arms spread out on his papers. She sat at the foot of the bed and watched him sleep for a long time, as if trying to trace the changes that had come over him. Then she got up to make coffee and, cramped as things were in there, brushed against him as she edged by. Andonis gave a start, and dashed into the kitchen. He stuck his head under the faucet, as he did every morning, to show Vangelia he wasn't one to lose his stride, even after staying up for days on end. The water in the basin gave back his image, dissolved in its trembling mirror. "I have merchandise now," he thought, and went back to the table to finish what he'd been working on.

"I've lost so much time, Vangelia, I have to make it up somehow. To be honest, I shouldn't sleep at all ... I have to write articles too, and study English, and get more work like this balance sheet here."

He started whistling while drawing some columns with a ruler on a blank piece of paper. At the top, in a looping hand, he wrote "Profits and Losses." Their bed had been pushed into a corner, and during the few short hours that he had lain down, he had seen the dark cardboard boxes rising above him, piled on top of each other like corner-stones. It was as if he'd built himself a castle. Vangelia lacked the proper respect for the materialized value those boxes contained, with their metal strapping and American labels. "I have to teach her the meaning of merchandise. But first, we need to get rid of that child in her womb."

"Why did you stop whistling," she asked.

While he wrote, Vangelia kept her eyes riveted on him. For the past two days, he seemed to have forgotten all about the matter of the baby. Given a few more days, maybe he would get used to the idea. "Just like I've gotten used to having all these boxes in here," she thought. That's why she was being so careful not to talk back to him, or ask him about his work.

"Drink your coffee, it's getting cold."

"Thanks, I'd forgotten all about it. I've got to finish up here, today's the last day for declaring. So tell me the truth, do you feel any love whatsoever toward these boxes?"

"Oh yes," Vangelia replied with a smile, and Andonis rubbed his hands together happily, because he realized that she had given him a credit renewal.

"Why do you love them?"

"Because I can see that you love them. And they represent an important beginning," Vangelia said. "You'll sell them and they'll bring in a profit. Then you'll buy some more and, after a number of similar transactions ... It'll still mean plenty of hard work, but it also means that we'll be able to afford a better life ..."

"Wrong!" Andonis interrupted her strenuously. "Wrong. You're talking like one of those bird-brain females who go around praying for heaven ... What 'other' life is there for us? None whatsoever, just the life we have now ..."

"All right, you don't have to shout. You asked me about the cans ... Who said anything about heaven?"

"It's ridiculous to think that after a certain number of years we'll be any better off, and to talk about the sacrifices we'll have to make. This is our life ... And whatever we do had better happen soon. Don't just sit there with your mouth open, Vangelia, pay attention to what I'm saying ... Would you mind telling Eftihis to come see me?"

Eftihis came in shortly and sat down, somewhat ill-at-ease. Andonis stopped writing and leaned his elbows on the table, with his papers spread out in front of him and the boxes rising up behind. He was secured at last.

"I need your help on something important. I'll give you a good cut to get rid of this stuff fast," Andonis said, pointing over his shoulder with his index finger.

"I've given up that sort of thing," Eftihis said quietly. "I'm interested in something else now, and I asked you ..."

Andonis assured him he was studying the matter continuously, collecting valuable information to ensure their business wouldn't be built on air. But he also made it clear that the cans would have to be sold before any concrete steps were taken.

Andonis gave Eftihis some samples and jotted down the prices.

"So, are we all set then? And I'll take care of planning out your business."

"I'm depending on you, Andonis ... I talked to all sorts of people, but I realized all they care about is using my money to expand their own businesses. Bring the money first, they say, and then we'll arrange the details ..."

"Don't worry about a thing, Eftihis ... So, until this evening ..."

He clapped him on the shoulder and laughed. There were times when he really loved that little rascal. Ask him for a loan, and he stuck his hand right in his pocket. Plus the fact that he always addressed Andonis with respect – which God knows was rare enough – because he knew he had a head teeming with knowledge and ideas.

"We're partners in this, Andonis. I need someone like you. And just so you know, once I hook up with somebody, he's like a brother to me, I mean it ..."

"It'll all work out, Eftihis ..."

"Let's shake on it," Eftihis said.

He gave Andonis' hand a firm squeeze, then took his sample cans and left, not unmoved.

HE SHOWED MARY THE CANS and bid her follow him. "Drop the little princess routine, we've got work to do." She pulled another long face and grumbled how she was tired of tramping all over town, and so on, but Eftihis ignored her, lest she take it into her head that he would fall for her whining. The time for her to cut out the cute stuff was right here and now, at the start.

"I want you along with me," he told her sharply.

Mary came out in the same dress of shimmery blue material she had worn on her wedding day, and followed after him. Ever since they had gotten married, Eftihis had dragged her around with him wherever he went.

He wouldn't talk much along the way, just ask her every so often, "So, what do you think?" Mary would say nothing, which infuriated Eftihis to no end. Then Mary would get into a snit because he didn't talk to her, as if she'd done something to him. "What's more important than choosing which road to take on the most difficult journey in your life?" he told her at one point, exasperated at her inability to conceive, with that thick skull of hers, of the complex problem he was grappling with.

The first few mornings they had stopped at a dairy bar to put something in their stomachs, since they didn't have so much as a *briki* for coffee at home. Mary had worn her shiny blue dress with the pleats and the bow then too, and she would hold her fork with two fingers, trying to act refined. Without consulting her, Eftihis had ordered rusks, butter and honey, and dried toast, and had asked whether she wanted cocoa, and did she like those fluffy pastries shaped like a half moon. And he would clap his hands once or twice, asking for water, or a clean knife, having dropped his in his hurry to chivalrously offer her the plate with the honey. In order to fit in more people, those dairy bars always had small marble tables the size of round baking pans. Mary sat there in a daze, as if all her bows and painted nails had robbed her of her wits. Newlyweds were always like that, hairbrained and clumsy. All she did was smile and stare into a large mirror on the opposite wall, as if she'd suddenly been transported to another world, and had never before seen such wondrous things. Eftihis watched her out of the corner of his eye, trying to make up his mind what kind of person she was, who, out of all the thousands of girls in the world, had chosen him to spend the rest of her life with. He bought her a pastry – did she want *kataifi* or *galaktoboureko*? With or without syrup? Or maybe she'd rather have a cream cake? Which did she like, chocolate or vanilla? And he would ask her about her various preferences, so at least he'd know who she was when it came to food. But Mary wouldn't answer. Her constrained smile was no answer, but Eftihis forgave her since they were still in the early days, and a certain amount of emotion was to be expected. As if he weren't at loose ends himself. There were moments when the world felt transformed, and he couldn't understand why no one else measured time starting with that Thursday evening, as he himself did. He watched the way Mary ate, the way she wiped her mouth and drank water. All these things were great and unfathomable phenomena that required study.

They went around to different people Eftihis knew, and he would ask all kinds of detailed questions about their work. After they left, he would ask Mary if she thought toys were better than plastics, or if Mitsos was more on the level than Tsiroglou. But Mary would only answer:

"I wasn't paying attention. How long do we have to go on walking?"

So Eftihis stopped asking her. They went into assorted businesses, met people in coffeehouses or workshops, until Mary felt quite dizzy. That afternoon, they ate at a restaurant with white tablecloths. Eftihis again did all he could to please her, telling the waiter to bring this, that and the other. So what if up until then he had peddled things on street corners. He was a man of the world, he knew how to talk to merchants, to the police when they took him in, he knew a couple of lawyers, and he had spoken up to them all, like a businessman looking out for his own best interests.

"Mary, dear, do you like your chicken boiled or roasted?"

She laughed, at last! In his delight he clapped his hands, and when the waiter came he didn't know what to say, and in his embarrassment ordered a salad.

As long as the money he got from Thodoros held out, Eftihis was scattering crumpled bills wherever they went. The waiter at the dairy shop got to know them by sight, and would rush over a tray with milk, honey, butter, and those fluffy buns. Mary chewed her food mechanically, as if she'd been fed straw. "She'll settle down," Eftihis would say to himself, looking her over. In three or four days, instead of going to their usual dairy bar, they went to a coffeehouse and had steaming tea served in glass mugs. Eftihis bought a *koulouri* sesame roll from a boy who came by, breaking it in two and giving Mary half.

"This is how it's going to be, kiddo. Until we get the business going, we'll be living like Spartans."

He said it good-humoredly, expecting her to laugh, because then they would be like two buddies sharing their *koulouri* for a good cause. Mary simply dunked hers in her tea and sat there with the same expression frozen on her face. Her nail polish was chipping off, and her blue bows were wrinkled.

They set off again, but Mary halted in the middle of the street like a stubborn mule.

"I'm going home," she said angrily.

"What for?"

"My shoes are killing me. Day after day walking around in heels ..."

"Listen, kiddo, somehow I doubt you've spent your life wearing heels. You should wear your ...."

Then Eftihis remembered they were the only shoes she owned, so he grabbed whatever money he had in his pocket and took her into a shop on Athinas Street to buy a pair of cheap, soft shoes.

"I want you with me, so choose the ones you want and let's get moving ..."

Mary put on her new shoes, and Eftihis was left with just a bit of change. He had decided that as he couldn't take so much as a step by himself, the shoes were a necessary expense, like raw material or a useful tool.

"There'll be no stopping you now," he told her proudly.

He talked to her about the business they would be setting up. Manufacturing of some kind, Andonis had said. Andonis talked too much, but it wasn't as if a thing's value depended on how many words you used to explain it.

"So what do you say, kiddo, do you go along with that?"

"Along with what?"

"With what I just said about our business ..."

"You already asked me that a thousand times today. I give up!"

"Quiet. And step on it or we'll be out here all night," he told her, as if making a joke of it.

They went hungry that night. Eftihis explained to her that it wouldn't do to spend even one of her old man's sovereigns.

"Getting married again to get my hands on another two hundred gold pieces would be a pain in the neck. The same goes for you. Who'd marry you if you didn't have any money?"

They got home late, and once in bed Eftihis tried to have a serious talk with Mary about whether the fellow who made Turkish delight and *halvah* was someone just waiting for a sucker to come along, and whether the best thing would be to set up two or three looms and go into textiles.

"What do you say, Mary? Do you like looms?" "Should I? They make too much noise ..."

Eftihis rolled over and began reading a newspaper. He passed over the stuff about monsters and bombs, and tried to understand a "financial overview," but the problem with newspapers was they made everything so complicated, they only wrote for people with loads of money, not for someone who had barely managed to squeeze a couple hundred gold pieces out of his bride's father.

"So, Mary, what'll it be, textiles or soap?"

"What do you care what I think? You don't love me anyway."

"What makes you think that?"

"Every night you turn your back on me and read ... You don't love me, you don't love me ..."

Mary assumed her whining tone, leaving Eftihis no choice but to clear the air then and there.

"Listen to me, kiddo. What I don't want is to have Pericles' kid. We'll let a little time pass, and then ... I just want to make sure first. Understand?"

Mary burst into a torrent of tears – as if all the taps had been thrown on. Eftihis felt awful.

"I know there's nothing between you two, silly, I just don't want to have to worry about it. I don't want to come out looking like a fool. It'll be better for you too. Just worrying about it would be enough to ruin your life. Not knowing if it was mine or not. Just be patient for a few more days."

"You don't love me, you don't love me," Mary repeated stubbornly.

"Cut it out. You admitted it, didn't you? You want us to go through all that again?"

"So is that why you drag me around with you? Because you're afraid I'll ..."

Eftihis had heard enough. He threw off the covers and raised himself above her, furious.

"Say that one more time, and so help me I'll kill you. I'd like to jam my finger inside your head and yank that thought right out of your rotten little brain ..."

"Then why won't you let me stay home?"

"I want to have someone of my own with me ... You don't like it that I like having you at my side?"

"And who does the housework? Everything's filthy around here, your shirts need washing, the apartment ..."

"I didn't get married just to have someone to do my laundry ..."

"Then why did you, since it wasn't out of love," Mary went on.

"That's another story. Go to sleep now, and just hold on for a little longer. Until we get our business going. And next time I ask you something, I want you to give me a straight answer, and only about what I'm asking about. Like now, what we were saying got all tangled, and I ended up losing my head, all over nothing."

"You're the one that brought it up."

"Go to sleep. And see if you can't tell me in the morning which you like better, textiles or soap."

The next morning, Eftihis didn't ask what her decision was, but then Mary didn't offer to tell him either. They tramped around all day, without stopping at the dairy bar, or even at the coffeehouse for tea. All they did was go by the confectioner's again, and he gave them a bit of the soft paste used in making Turkish delight. Mary popped hers right in her mouth, because she was starving. But it only nauseated her, and she almost threw up. That evening she began complaining again about how hungry she was, like a spoiled child, and Eftihis took his own lump of paste out of his pocket, wrapped in some paper.

"I knew this is how you'd be, so I saved it for you. You're still such a little baby ..."

"What are you going to eat?"

"Don't you worry about me. Come on, eat up."

The following morning, after they picked up the cans from Andonis, Mary immediately asked when they would be getting paid for the job. She felt a sharp pain in her stomach, she said, and her throat was dry. Big deal! When Eftihis told her that they'd probably be able to eat something the next day, Mary stopped in her tracks.

"Tomorrow! Then you can just go on by yourself. My legs won't move another inch."

Eftihis had half a mind to kick her in the shins to teach her what real pain was, but he thought better of it once he remembered they had only been married for ten days. They went into a neighborhood grocery and showed the owner the cans. Mary gaped at the other women shopping and going home with their groceries. The grocer said he was interested, but wanted to see the whole shipment first. Eftihis assured him that it was top-of-the-line, and he had already sold large quantities of it. Then they went to another store, and another, until midday. Mary shuffled along behind him. She told him to find someone to borrow money from, even if only enough for one *koulouri*, otherwise she would go and eat at her father's.

"That's simple," he told her. "Just get a cart and take all your junk, plus the package with the gold pieces, and stay there. And you and me can call it a day."

And so she ended up tagging along with him. It was still just the beginning, she'd shape up. Eftihis had a boundless capacity to forgive her carryings-on. She plopped down on someone's doorstep, exhausted.

"My father gave you those sovereigns to make life easier for us, not so you could starve me to death. Let's cash just one of them and get something to eat ..."

Eftihis was watching a wagon pass, as if he hadn't heard.

"He gave them to you for me, they're mine ..." Mary went on.

Still Eftihis said nothing. He scratched his nose and spat in the street, pacing up and down on the sidewalk. He didn't feel like going through it all over again.

"Don't you have some friend who could give us just a piece of bread or something?"

"Afraid not. If I went crying to someone, I'd never hear the last of it."

"Some friends."

"That's not your problem. Now get up because I'm beginning to lose my temper."

Frightened, Mary did as she was told. She dusted off her dress, smoothed down her hair and went up to him.

"Why can't we open one of the cans?"

"Because they're to sell ..."

"None of the grocers we've been to has opened them. All they care about is the label. What does it matter if it's empty?"

"No one's ever gone around selling canned goods just by showing an empty can."

"Why not?" Mary asked. "It says on the can what's inside."

Mary snatched one of the cans from his arms and tried to run away with it. Eftihis caught her by the shoulder.

"Don't move, or I'll split your head open," he said. They were on the verge of having a brawl, but again Eftihis backed down.

At the next shop, they stopped at, Eftihis showed them the cans and asked them whether they would like a supply of that fine product. When the store manager said something about quality, Eftihis impatiently asked for an opener and pried off the lid: "See for yourself – nothing but the best!" Back outside, he handed the open can to Mary.

"Eat it," he told her.

Mary immediately dug in with her fingers and extracted a chunk of meat. She got it all over her face, and grease dripped onto her shiny wedding dress. Eftihis noticed how predatory her fingers had become, as she stood hunched over the can. Suddenly she spit out the meat and cried:

"It's bad!"

She handed the can back to Eftihis, spitting out what was left in her mouth.

"It's poison!"

"Only in your head," Eftihis told her.

"See for yourself. It's foul!"

Eftihis smelled the can, wrinkled his nose, and tried a bit. He too instantly spit it out.

"It's rotten all right. It must just be this can."

Farther down, he scratched his chin and asked Mary:

"You don't suppose he gave us a bad shipment to get rid of, do you?"

Mary kept spitting out her saliva and asking Eftihis whether people died from food-poisoning.

"Come on, you think it's that easy for someone to die?"

"I think I swallowed a big piece."

"If everyone who ate something rotten died, we'd be dropping like flies. Let's go. I'll sort it out with Andonis, and we'll take it from there."

"What if I get food-poisoning? A neighbor of ours died last year from eating some bad cheese, the very same day!"

"I'll work it out with him, I told you. We'll take care of it tonight ..."

"But I could be dead by then!"

"Come on. I told you, there's nothing to worry about. Believe me, I've seen plenty. So you can drop that 'Help, I'm dying' business, or I'll leave you right here."

"I think we better go home so I can go to bed ..."

Eftihis laughed. He had eaten fruit rinds during the war, rotting grapes and carob pods. He had licked he didn't know how many discarded bones and trampled figs. Mary's stomach must have had a silk lining.

Instead of going home, Eftihis said they would go by the coffee-house in Omonia that Thodoros frequented. He couldn't do anything about the cans of meat until he straightened things out with Andonis. "I'll find out if he was trying to pull a fast one on me."

"Ask Thodoros to loan you some money so we can buy something for food-poisoning. He was our best man, wasn't he?"

Eftihis leaned on a lamp-post and looked at her pityingly as she writhed in misery, convinced her insides were being eaten out. Her blue dress with the bows now was covered with oil-stains – a veritable dish-rag. He stopped giving her derisory looks and rubbed his hands together thoughtfully, as he used to do after stealing a bit of bread dough from his mother. He would roll it between his fingers for hours to keep it from hardening, until he decided what to make out of it. In the end he always came up with something.

"Mary, just drop it. We're going to see Thodoros now, and it's high time you learned how people behave out in the real world. No one's going to know or care if your stomach hurts or if you're starving."

Thodoros was talking to some serious-looking gentlemen, so Eftihis waited. He gave Mary's fingers a hard squeeze to remind her to behave herself. When the others had left, he went up to Thodoros with a show of deference, greeted him respectfully, and sat himself at the table. Thodoros asked what he could get them, and Mary said, "Nothing, thanks." She gave Eftihis a look as if to say, "See, I've learned my lesson."

Eftihis spoke to him briefly and clearly about his business plans, then asked his advice. The whole time he was talking, Thodoros kept looking toward the door, then up at the clock, as if he were hoping to avoid someone who might walk in at any moment.

"It's the most important moment in my life. I have to get something going that isn't going to fail ..."

"I understand, just hurry up and tell me what you want."

"I want your help ... I'm depending on you. I need Andonis because he knows the market. But I'll always ask you before doing anything. I've decided to set up a textile business. It's the best thing around ... Will you help me?"

"Sure," said Thodoros. "Once you've thought out the details, come by and we'll talk it over. But you won't find me here. Come to Syntagma in the morning, the place next to the Ministry. Upstairs ..."

"Is someone after you? Is there anything I can do to help you out?"

Instead of answering, Thodoros got up and picked his way through the tables. Eftihis took Mary's hand, and they went out bewildered and confused.

VANGELIA WAS PLEASED Andonis was home early, but he merely looked over his cans. He set down his briefcase and, rubbing his hands together, said:

"I've got writing to do tonight ..."

He took out his cigarettes, matches, pencils, and finally a small box, which he extended to Vangelia.

"These are for you."

"What is it?"

"You take three of them a day. Just two for now ..."

Vangelia recoiled without touching them. She moved into the corner.

"It's for what we were talking about. Please, I've got so much to do tonight. It's perfectly safe and effective, a top-notch doctor ..."

"I'm not taking them," Vangelia said shortly.

"Come, come, don't be silly. The matter's already been decided. You should have come to that realization on your own ..."

Paying no attention to her objections, he spread out the notes for his study and began writing.

"So, Vangelia, each to his or her assigned task."

"What's mine?"

"To take two of those pills."

Because everything was tremendously rushed tonight, Andonis focused on his papers and started doing an outline for his treatise. But his notes were lamentably rough, so he began reading through his data all over again. He wanted this article to be informed by sound economic thought, not one of those gaseous performances certain buffoons parading as economists were in the habit of dashing off. "The country's been overrun by high-toned good-for-nothings who have an opinion ready on any subject, without once having put their brains through the wringer. All they do is flaunt the terminology and hope they'll make an impression," thought Andonis as he got down to work.

But the hours slipped by and Andonis ripped up one piece of paper after another. The beginning had to be comprehensive yet brief, a straightforward, naturally evolving line of thought. Something with substance.

"Well, Vangelia?"

"Well what?"

"This again? The matter's settled ..."

He was writing whatever came into his head, without order or plan, in hopes that his hand would pick up momentum and free his mind of its heavy inertia.

If Vangelia would only help him out, he would have an easier time of it. He wouldn't have to cope with this numbing inanition, this inner turmoil that was wreaking with his concentration.

"Just do it, honey, and let's get it over with. Really, I'd like to get some writing done."

But since Vangelia just sat there as if paralyzed or deaf, Andonis got up, broke open the small box and got out two white tablets. As he approached her, she got up and went around to the other side of the table. As he came after her, he noticed a spark of terror in her eyes. And she was so fetching tonight, too. He shoved over the whole table to cut off her escape.

Vangelia edged by the cans and shrank from touching them, as if afraid of some antagonistic power lurking in those dark cartons. Where could she run? The room was even more cramped now.

Andonis grabbed hold of her and held her with all his might, trying to force her body to stop its terrified trembling. Vangelia let out a cry, and turned her head away to avoid looking at him. She shoved back his jaw, as if thrusting away some ponderous weight that was bearing down on her.

"I want my child, and I'm going to have it."

"Well, I don't want it."

His neck had become a mass of knotted rope, two bony lumps jutted from his jaw. Vangelia went limp from being squeezed so tightly around the waist. She was afraid his embrace would injure her somehow. Andonis tried forcing the pills into her mouth, but she sealed her lips and shrank back with her hands over her mouth. Suddenly his grip on her changed. He began running his hands up and down her body in a peculiar fashion.

"Don't!" she cried. "I don't want you to touch me."

He gently stroked her hair. He implored her as sweetly as he could to help him out, since it was also to her benefit to resolve the matter peaceably.

"Why are you looking at me with hate in your eyes? I love you, Vangelia. You're all I have. Help me. Please."

"No. I want this child."

He took hold of her under her arms and carried her over to the bed. "Sit down and let's have a talk." Vangelia wasn't listening. She had fixed her eyes on the floor, and sat knotting and unknotting a handkerchief.

"Listen to me, Vangelia: if somebody wants to get ahead in business, he's got to face the fact that he could end up in prison. Otherwise, you're depriving yourself of the chance to develop your abilities to the full, in a world where deception is taken for granted. When you have a child, it's always in the back of your mind, so you lose your edge, you become indecisive – and then it's all over. You become a lousy little salesman, with a briefcase full of samples always in your hand. It's like in the revolution, you have to be ready to sacrifice everything, even your life."

"Are you saying none of them have any children? Even if they *are* ready to sacrifice ..."

"It's not the same, Vangelia. People dying for the cause know their children will be proud of them, but what do the other children say? 'My father died in prison because of his debts.' It doesn't even matter if you've swindled anybody or not."

"So why don't you join the movement again, and let me keep my baby?"

Andonis fell silent. There was a noise from Stathis' room next door, as if somebody had bumped against a wall or tripped over a chair. Vangelia turned at the sound.

"What was that?"

"Nothing. Stathis isn't home this time of night."

"But it sounded like somebody's in there."

"Relax. You're hearing things because you're upset. Why don't you take the pills? It's simple, thousands of women ..."

Andonis began caressing her shoulders again. It hadn't been anything, a shutter maybe, a cat on the roof, or somebody in the courtyard next door. Anything occurring outside his own awkward, stifling perplexity was of no interest or relevance.

"So you really want me to be ruined, eh, Vangelia?"

"I didn't say that, you did."

There was a knock at the door and Eftihis stuck his head in. Vangelia straightened her hair and picked up a chair that had been knocked over. Eftihis noticed nothing. It was their house, they could do what they wanted there. He went up to Andonis and angrily informed him:

"The cans you gave me were rotten! They all but threw the stuff in my face. Why didn't you tell me it was bad?"

"Don't be ridiculous, Eftihis."

"They're rotten, I'm telling you."

"Are you nuts? You think I'd buy cans that had gone bad? You think they could pull that one on me? You just happened to pick a rotten one ..."

"That's what I figured, too," Eftihis agreed.

Vangelia suggested that Eftihis have his wife come over too, and they could make an evening of it. Andonis gave her a furious look, knowing she was just afraid of being alone with him.

"Any chance you've got something for dinner? We've been crazed with hunger today. Mary nearly fainted," Eftihis laughed.

"We'll find something," Vangelia said quickly.

Eftihis went and told Mary there was food, and she promptly came over. Vangelia pulled the table into the middle of the room, and began preparing the food in the kitchen. She seemed pleased to have guests. Andonis gathered up all of his papers, telling himself he would get back to them later on. He put the pills back in his pocket and shot a look at Vangelia to remind her that, stall as she may, this matter would have to be dealt with.

They sat down to eat and Eftihis gave them an animated account of Mary's antics during the day's rounds, how she grumbled from hunger and general wretchedness. He clearly found it all very funny.

"Okay, you can stop kicking me now," he told her. "What, you think they'll start making fun of us behind our backs? There's no law against being hungry. But our gold sovereigns are still all there, and we're going to sink them into something really good. Right, Andonis?"

"Yes, yes, of course ..."

"No one's going to get in the way of my plans," Eftihis said firmly.

"That's how it should be. See how people think out in the world, Vangelia? I've been trying to talk sense to her for days now," Andonis told Eftihis, "but she pretends not to understand."

"Are you going to start a business of your own?" Mary asked them.

"No, it's something different," Andonis said.

Mary was wearing her blue dress with the stains. She ate with relish, focusing all her attention on her plate. She was embarrassed by Eftihis' remarks ... As if it was a crime to want to put some food in your stomach ...

"Kick me one more time, Mary, and you'll end up with a black eye. So as I was saying, we'll live like Spartans until we get this business thing going. We'll get by on handouts, sometimes from you folks, sometimes from somebody else. That's just how it has to be. 'Mary,' I keep telling her, 'if you wanted to live like a princess, you should have married some pansy who parts his hair down the middle.'"

"Cut it out, Eftihis, or I'm leaving."

"Eat your food and keep quiet. Where else are you going to find something to eat?"

Andonis opened one of the cans and emptied its contents onto a plate. He cut the meat into pieces and put one in his mouth. It was rotten. His impulse was to spit it out, but he ate it just to prove that they had been maligning his merchandise.

"You have to watch out, Eftihis. The world's full of crooks today ..."

"You're telling me."

"One can never be sure of another's honesty."

"I'm with you there ..."

" ... since he can't even be sure of his own ..."

Andonis drank some water. So what if he got food-poisoning? If he admitted the cans were rotten, it would be curtains. He'd become a laughingstock. He waited to see who would next reach a fork out to the plate of spoiled food. He felt like the whole wall of cartons was tottering over his head. It wasn't possible. He got up and grabbed another can. In a show of hospitality, he emptied this second one onto the plate. He took the first bite. The foul taste of rotten meat nearly made him vomit. He swallowed it and smiled.

"As a matter of fact, Eftihis, I promised my wife here we'd move to a better place and get some furniture, but I'm asking her for a minor loan of time ... Everything will come together at the first opportunity."

"I haven't asked for anything," Vangelia put in.

"Don't worry, Vangelia," Eftihis said. "Me and Andonis are going to set up shop together, and then you'll see. So, Andonis, have you come up with any good ideas yet?"

Mary cleaned her plate, and reached for the canned food. Andonis didn't answer Eftihis. He was too busy thinking that his whole existence hung on Mary's gesture. Mary jabbed a piece with her fork, and put it in her mouth.

"It's bad!" she cried. "This one's rotten too!"

She spit out her whole mouthful in disgust, making a horrible face.

"You're imagining things, Mary dear!" Andonis said with a smile. "It's excellent. I had some of that one myself, and it was delicious ..."

"But it's rotten."

"You're mistaken. It does have a somewhat strong odor, I'll grant, but that's the kind of meat it is. Many people come to like the flavor, in Australia they eat nothing else ..."

Eftihis smelled the meat and put a small piece in his mouth.

"It's bad all right!" he said.

He tilted back his head and gave Andonis a wry wink, businessman to businessman, to let him know he knew what the other was up to, there was no need to say more.

"It can't be! I think it's delicious!"

"Delicious, my foot! It smells like a rotting corpse."

"Watch," Andonis said, taking a big chunk. He flamboyantly put it in his mouth. He chewed the meat, overcame his revulsion, and smiled.

"Delicious!"

Andonis' ploy began to get on Eftihis' nerves. He eyed Andonis suspiciously, sniffed the whole plateful and asked:

"Are they all this delicious?"

"I don't know what could have happened to your sense of taste. Maybe because you've gone so long without eating."

"He's going to drive me nuts! Vangelia, you try some and see how you like it."

But Vangelia demurred, saying she couldn't eat another bite. Good for her, Andonis thought. She's a trooper. She didn't even give the impression that she believed Eftihis.

"Smell it. I'm telling you it smells worse than a dead cat."

Andonis took another piece and made an even more theatrical demonstration. Mary stared at his mouth. She couldn't believe he didn't throw up. "Man's powers are unlimited," Andonis thought as he swallowed a mouthful with all the naturalness the occasion required. It was paramount that he stick up for his cans. What was a little food-poisoning? "It's impossible for something that belongs to me, something I love the way I love these cans, to make me ill," he said to himself as he gulped down the final portion. He had betrayed neither himself nor his merchandise.

"Brother, you're not human," Eftihis said. "I bet you drink paint-thinner too."

"You'll poison yourself," Mary said in alarm.

"So, Eftihis, have I managed to convince you that your best bet is to go into some line of manufacturing? The commercial world is a vicious circle of mutual deception. All this talk about supply and demand is just a flimsy excuse for petty thievery."

Eftihis watched him closely. What was he to make of people like Andonis, who knew so much and talked a mile a minute. It seemed they were even immune to food-poisoning. They didn't think twice about eating spoiled meat.

"Tell me, Andonis, what do you know about textiles?"

"It's my specialty!" Andonis said proudly. "I worked for years in a textile concern."

"Well, I've made up my mind. We'll get a textile operation going. I think that's the smartest way to go."

"You're absolutely right. There's nothing sounder."

"Do you go along with that?" he asked Mary next.

"Just so long as you get *something* started," Mary said cheerlessly. "I've had all the running around I can take ..."

Andonis was only too happy to detail the ins-and-outs of that particular branch of industry, and Eftihis became all ears and eyes. But they were out of cigarettes. A little wine was in order, too. "What do you say, Vangelia, just a glass or two?" Andonis grabbed an empty bottle. Before leaving, however, he nervously scanned the stack of notes for his essay where he'd left them, then remembered the pills were in his coat, and patted the outside of the pocket just to be sure. He went out the door, calm and smiling. It was chilly on the street. He raised his head and took a deep breath. Stars, it seemed, could be useful things at times.

The taverna was closed, so Andonis filled his bottle with ouzo at Prodromos' coffeehouse. Before going back in, however, he went around the corner and halted near a wall. He stuck his finger down his throat and threw up. He got rid of everything, and afterwards felt much better. That, of course, was a deception of sorts, a kind of business fraud, but he reflected that it would have been mindless idealism for him to subject himself to food-poisoning, since there was no question but that the cans had gone bad. It was just merchandise, and self-immolation was no way of taking their putrefaction upon himself.

He wiped off his mouth and went back inside, in high spirits. He was eager to launch back into his discussion of the textile industry. He triumphantly displayed the full bottle, and Vangelia laughed gaily. But Mary was sleepy and wanted to go.

When Vangelia asked her to please stay longer, Mary began complaining again about the nonstop running around they had been doing for days on end.

"Come on, it's about time you learned how to behave," Eftihis told her. "You don't just wolf down your food and run. We didn't come over just to be fed. You've got to learn some manners, now that we're setting up a business ..."

Vangelia discreetly cleared the plates with the canned food.

Andonis followed her movements without interrupting what he was saying. He saw her empty them into the trash, clearly convinced the meat was bad. As she came back into the room, their eyes met, and Vangelia smiled at him meaningfully, but Andonis pretended not to notice and continued to explain how dependent textile businesses operated, and the various categories they fell into, based on the type of production they engaged in, their size and technical means.

"To your health, Andonis, old friend, you're quite a guy," boomed Eftihis.

Swelling with pride, Andonis emptied his glass. Mary barely wet her lips, just so Eftihis wouldn't berate her for her bad manners. Vangelia didn't even taste hers, and had no intention of doing so, since she knew alcohol could be harmful during a pregnancy. They filled their glasses again. Andonis knocked his off in one gulp. His eyes had begun to glaze over, and his tongue to run away from him.

"So, Eftihis, good friend, I'll set you up an exemplary, highly efficient operation ..."

"I have complete confidence in you. Wasn't I telling you, Mary?"

"And you should," Andonis said with conviction.

He stretched in his chair, and as he leaned back his head touched the boxes. But he jerked it back, as if he'd gotten an electric shock. That dark wall of boxes rising up to the ceiling with its metal strapping, its stamps and colorful foreign lettering, was no longer solid. It was suspect merchandise, which might go off at any moment and blow all his hopes sky high. It was a booby-trap that could easily bury him under its weight.

Andonis refilled his glass, and resolutely drank it down. He scowled, and poured himself another. Then he got up to get some water. He stumbled twice by the time he made the kitchen, but managed to catch himself in the doorway. A loud laugh escaped Mary, but she promptly stifled it when Eftihis jabbed her hard with his elbow.

"Who laughed?" Andonis demanded threateningly. "One of you was making fun of me ..."

No one spoke. Andonis' eyes were vitreous.

"No need to get angry, Andonis," Eftihis said. "I just tickled my wife because she was starting to nod off. Go on about the textile works ..."

Vangelia was ashamed. Something approaching panic rose up in her again. She took hold of Mary's hand.

"Don't leave, please," she said. "Eftihis, tell us a funny story, stay a bit longer. Tell us about the women you peddle things to on the street."

Eftihis good-naturedly tried to distract them by launching into some nonsensical story about being chased by police. He pretended to be drunk himself. Andonis came back from the kitchen doing his best to keep his glass of water from spilling, but half the water went on the floor anyway. He halted in the middle of the room and raised his hand as if about to give a speech.

"The worst thing is not to know what's going on around you. I, however, am an honest man. Honest to the core ... Though maybe it's only being drunk that let's me say so with such confidence. The whole system's rotten ..."

Eftihis, sensing Andonis' speech was headed for no good, got up and began imitating a woman wiggling her hips as she sashayed up to a street vender to buy some sunglasses.

"These, she tells me, have different color glass in each lens. Pardon me? I say. Do you think I'm blind or something? she says. This lens is green, and this one here has a gold tint. Miss, I tell her, that's how all the finest ones are made. Those two colors go together. It's something you of all people should know, beautiful eyes like yours demand just the right colors ..."

Andonis emptied another slug of ouzo on the sly. Vangelia and Mary were laughing at Eftihis' antics, as he demonstrated how he would paw the good-looking girls who came up to his stand, on the pretext of seeing if a blouse fit or not.

In the middle of laughing, they suddenly heard someone singing in a deep, droning voice. Andonis, his head resting up against the boxes and his eyes closed, had begun to sing a melody without words, as if it were a moan issuing from the center of his being. The others stopped laughing and exchanged looks. Vangelia bit her fingers as she saw how ashen his face had become. Mary suggested that they leave. Eftihis went up to him and eyed him curiously.

"Man, you're really stinko! You don't think it was the meat, do you?" he asked the women in a low voice.

"No!" Andonis burst out, bringing his song to an end. "We've already discussed that subject. There's nothing wrong with the meat in these cans, in fact it's delicious. I'm just enjoying myself, in my own way ..."

Vangelia began filling his glass again.

"What are you doing," Eftihis asked her quietly.

She went on filling it, right up to the brim, as if to get him even drunker.

"Cheers, Andonis," she told him and prodded him to drink.

The singing started up again. Eftihis suggested they all sing some cheerful tune together, but everyone ignored him. Vangelia feigned high spirits. She poured Eftihis more ouzo, but when she saw he wasn't drinking it, she discreetly slid it over into Andonis' hand, and he instantly finished it off. She gave a joyless laugh at some new joke of Eftihis', and since she happened to be standing next to Andonis, the easier to refill his glass, she carefully felt his pocket from the outside. She immediately pulled over a chair and sat down near him, trying to follow the tune he was singing. A minute later, as Andonis downed his ouzo, she carefully reached into his pocket and took out the box with the pills in it. No one noticed. Mary was nearly asleep, and Eftihis was spitting an olive pit out in his hand. Vangelia went straight out to the toilet and emptied out the pills. Andonis, bleary-eyed and sluggish, continued rumbling his song.

"Pour me some more," he told Vangelia.

"You've had plenty."

Suddenly there came a soft rapping at the door. Vangelia opened it apprehensively.

"Good evening," Angelos' father said quietly. "Forgive me for disturbing you ..."

Andonis broke off singing, and started to his feet.

"Has something happened?"

"No, I only came to ask if you had anything to report ..."

"Vangelia, get the judge a glass. We're sort of celebrating here tonight, Judge. How about some ouzo? Have a seat."

"Have you spoken to him? What did he say?"

"Unfortunately the right moment never presented itself," Andonis said. "I tried to determine what his feelings were on the matter, but he kept wriggling out of it ... Please, have a seat. If you see him, say hello for me, and tell him to watch out ... Vangelia, you have no idea what a splendid fellow Angelos is ... I'm sorry I don't have anything more helpful to tell you. Even if a friend of his like me can't help you out, I hope you won't take it wrong ..."

"Indeed, I know the problems involved ..."

"I'm always at your service. If I can be of any assistance whatsoever, don't hesitate to ask."

Andonis took a drink of water and continued:

"I hope you're not under the impression those of us on the outside are having a better time of it. What are we doing, anyway?"

"I think there's a degree of difference," the judge observed.

"Certainly. His life is endangered by an actual threat. But let me point out that it's up to him whether his sentence is a fact, or merely an inducement for him to prolong those days of glory."

The judge was not amused.

"So, will you make an effort to have a talk with this gentleman?"

"I gave you my word, your Honor. At the first opportunity ... Don't think that just because I've gotten mixed up with canned goods and inanities like that, that I've forgotten my friends and my ideals. Nowadays it's a question of each of us trying to find a way to put bread on our table. It's not a sell-out. What do you think, is it something to be ashamed of? Sometimes I get so desperate ... Is it possible, I tell myself, that I ... And yet it's true: I, who was brought up on the most glorious of ideas, who even as a youth did all I could with my friends to create a wonderful dream for the world, then fought for it with everything I had – I now spend my day chasing down a few cans of meat or some other business opportunity ..."

"Please," said Harilaos. "Calm yourself. There's no need to defend yourself. No one's accusing you of anything ... I apologize for interrupting your celebration. If you think there are any steps you can take, then do whatever you see fit."

Harilaos bid them good-night and left. Andonis remained standing in the middle of the room. Eftihis went up to him and, peering into his eyes, said with admiration,

"You've sobered up, little brother!"

IN THE DAYS THAT FOLLOWED, Angelos undertook to verify the dimensions of his drawing with regard to all pertinent physical details, and to assemble tools for his undertaking. In a box of odds and ends under the bed, he discovered something resembling a chisel, and quickly tucked it away in his coat pocket. He scraped off a bit of the window shutters to give himself a better view of the courtyard. The tiles allowed him to measure its exact dimensions. He made a note of each new component on the drawing. At night, the blow torch started up again. He opened the windowpane, and studied light from the torch as it flickered against the side of his family's house. It was cut off from below by the jagged profile of the rooftiles on the back wall bordering the garage, which was also the back wall of Andonis' apartment. He noticed that the shadow changed in height, which meant that the source of light was moving forward and backwards. The steps of the winding staircase helped him to calculate the height and degree of change in the projection. His eyes hurt from the intense flashes of light and the effort of making precise measurements. The next night went the same way. He noticed that the shadow had something sticking up from it, a beam or a post of some sort. That too moved horizontally on the wall, thus the welder moved side to side as well. The shadow of the post fell on the edge of the window, then shifted over to the kitchen door on the right. Thus Angelos could estimate the total area of the garage. The next morning, when he knew Stathis was fast asleep, he climbed up on the table and used a chair to measure the room's height, which would be the same as the room next to it.

This whole process took place in silence over a number of days. Now he was ready to begin his computations. When Stathis woke up, he found it strange to see Angelos sitting at the table drawing geometric shapes.

"I'm trying to solve a few trigonometry problems. It's a little like astronomy."

"And what good are they to you?"

"Oh, they're vital," Angelos laughed.

Stathis didn't press him. He gave Angelos a patronizing smile. It seemed quite natural that someone closed up indoors day and night would find something to occupy his time. Indeed, he would have no other choice.

"The other day, it was so clear how much you had loved Elly. I'm sorry for the grief I caused you, with that ludicrous refusal of mine. I had no idea how much it meant to you ... And you didn't insist, you accepted it as if it were the most natural thing in the world ..."

Stathis gave him a pat on the back.

"Forget it, it's ancient history. Back then, we all wanted to do what was right. Right to the bitter end."

Alone again, Angelos continued his computations. He solved the problem, and clapped his hands in excitement. But he instantly reflected that this was a dangerous luxury. That evening, he again studied the flashes of light and shadows on the wall outside.

The following afternoon, when Vangelia left, Angelos moved aside the newspapers and, stamping on the chisel, managed to pry up one of the floorboards. As he pulled it up, a shiver passed through him. The work was beginning in earnest. That crack leading down into the moist darkness below frightened him. It was an undertaking fraught with danger, one that demanded real courage.

There were footsteps on the staircase up to the roof. He hastened over to the window. Lucia was talking with Ismene.

"Want to go to the movies?" Lucia asked.

"No, I'm not in the mood ..."

"Aren't you sick of saying the same things over and over? Just like back then ... the same pathetic tone. If I remember correctly, you used to sleep on the floor without a mattress, because according to you that's how he was sleeping, in the mountains somewhere. Maybe you'd like to be left alone again, so you can go keep him company?"

"What's it to you?"

"Nothing at all. It bothered me back then, but now it just seems absurd ... Let's go have some fun, there's nothing wrong with that, is there? There's a good movie playing."

Ismene again refused, and Lucia stalked off, her heels clicking on the tiles.

Angelos turned back to his task. He easily and soundlessly

pulled up two more planks, and carefully lowered himself down. The floorboards came up to his waist. He would put the dirt into the narrow space under the floor. He took measurements, examined the foundations, repeated the word "escape" several times to himself, then climbed out and nailed the boards back, spreading the newspapers on top. He lay down to think. His head whirled with the momentousness of the step he was about to take. At the same time, it was the simplest of technical exercises.

THE JOY OF MAKING DEALS eclipsed the certainty in Andonis' mind that the meat in his cans was irreparably spoiled. He offered them at a bargain price, hoping only to make back his initial investment. He nearly succeeded with two or three merchants, who manifested an unforgivable gullibility. One wise-guy told him to his face:

"Hell, they're not even worth what it would cost to get rid of them. It's sure death!"

"No one's asking you to eat it!" Andonis shouted in exasperation. "You're supposed to sell it!"

But that two-bit, tight-fisted, suspicious, wily little runt of a merchant couldn't get it through his head that, even granting he was right, quality was relative to price, and refused to discuss the matter. As he did his rounds, Andonis couldn't understand how people knew the cans were bad, despite their nice packaging. There were thousands of defective articles out there. "Every organic compound undergoes modification" he reasoned. "It's as simple as that."

But instead of dashing around doing his thousand and one tasks, Andonis went by Boufas' company and asked to see Mr. Ioannidis. Spiros was in conversation with a very sober-faced gentleman. Andonis kidded him with genial familiarity, and asked if he know where he could pick up some double-width looms at a good price. Then, quite by chance, he learned which bank was holding his drafts, and they chatted about the world market. Spiros remarked, with all the high-priced assurance his office afforded, that the same thing was happening here as elsewhere, that small businesses were going through a crisis period, and would soon be shutting their doors. As an example, he cited a dependent textile works whose equipment Boufas' company would have to impound. Andonis smelled a real opportunity, and paid close attention to the details. Once he had all the information he needed, he abruptly stood up and, raising his finger nearly to Spiros' nose, sprang a question on him.

"What happens if I don't pay back those drafts?"

"Very simple," Spiros said without hesitation. "You go to prison."

"So," laughed Andonis, "you don't trust me."

"Not for a second," Spiros said icily.

"So much the better for you!" cried Andonis amid forced laughter. "That way you'll be prepared. It won't come as a surprise ... Think how hard it would be for me if it meant losing your respect for me ... In other words, it seems quite natural to you?"

Clio's entrance put an end to this serious jest of his.

The sidewalk was thronged with pushing and shoving people. Footsteps mingled, and time marched on. "How did that sleazy little merchant ever figure out there was something wrong with my merchandise?" Andonis wondered, giving his cans a long look, as if he wanted to penetrate the mystery of their putrescence. Everything would be different once he'd gotten rid of those miserable things. If they weren't sold now, would he wander for the rest of his days trying to unload defective goods?

Later he remembered it was time to turn his attention to the baby question. Vangelia had led him along with smiles, subterfuges and obfuscations, while he had wasted precious time trying to work out something with the cans, as if business were nothing more than endless talk. So he darted over to a hospital where an old friend of his was serving as an intern. There they told him that Dr. Papanikolaou was in an operation right then and he would have to wait. The courtyard behind the hospital looked like a factory: incinerators, furnaces, blackened walls, pipes, smoke-stacks, blood-stained linen, ambulances. Nurses whisked from door to door, and seemed to be whispering about some death that was about to take place. Men wearing rubber boots trudged up from the basement carrying laundry bags and garbage cans. That building there must have been where they put the dead bodies, but none of this had anything to do with Andonis, so he pulled out a cigarette pack and started figuring how to get rid of the cans at a reduced price.

Unfortunately, Dr. Papanikolaou was as idealistic as ever. While Andonis spoke to him in a warm and confidential manner about "the matter of Vangelia," the doctor curtly informed him that there was no effective and harmless abortion drug, and that there was nothing that he, as a responsible doctor, could prescribe. Andonis didn't even have it in him to get angry.

Back out on the street, he walked along the endless wall around the hospital. A gray repose wrapped the square, the buildings and trees. The street ran in a straight line down the hill. How was it that everything could seem so cold and indifferent when he and thousands of others were all but going out of their minds amid this irrational calm? He would have to extinguish Vangelia's dream. "Sooner or later," he reflected, "children learn the true story of their parents' lives." How could you face your child once he had discovered that his father was a hustler on the make who played his game dangerously close to the prison gate. "When I become a success, of course, it'll be a different story."

Eftihis was waiting for him in Syntagma with Mary. Andonis explained to him in detail, though with exaggerated optimism, how they would be able to get a good price on the looms Ioannidis was planning to auction off.

"All that's required is a simple, routine act of blackmail, which in our day is called parlaying. He'll sell them to us at any price to avoid the auction. It's a fabulous opportunity!"

Eftihis rubbed his palms together.

"Hear that, Mary? We're going to get us some machinery."

Mary appeared less enthusiastic, but Eftihis pounded Andonis on the back, offered him a cigarette, and warned him not to say anything stupid when they met with Thodoros.

"The other night when you were drunk, you promised the judge all sorts of things. But it's too risky, it could poison the air with Thodoros. Then where would the money come from?"

"Don't worry, I know all about it ..."

Thodoros was upstairs in the coffeehouse, hiding in a corner. He must have been expecting someone, because he kept looking toward the stairs. Andonis launched right in on Eftihis' behalf, explaining how he needed a small loan to purchase a couple of looms.

"If I'd known," Eftihis put in, "I would have tried to get more out of the old man ... Fool that I was, I thought two hundred was a fortune. I didn't know the first thing about real business. You're the only one who can help us, Thodoros ... Then there's nothing I wouldn't do for you ..."

Andonis was afraid Eftihis would put his foot in it, so he interrupted and said he knew where they could get two good setups at bargain prices. It would be a shame not to snap them up.

"If an elderly fellow comes in while we're talking, don't leave. It's this judge who's been harassing me for I don't know how long."

"I saw him once before," Eftihis said. "With white hair, right? What's he want from you?"

"I don't know how to get rid of him," Thodoros said. "He thinks his son ... He talked to me for three hours yesterday ... He follows me wherever I go. I switched cafés, but he came here too ... I tried being polite, I tried scaring him off – nothing worked. And it's around now that he shows up."

"Of course, I haven't the slightest idea what it's about," Andonis timidly volunteered, "but if it's in your power to do something to help him, why not just do it and be rid of him?"

"So, about those looms," Eftihis said, glaring at Andonis. "Will you help us out?"

"Some other time. The judge'll be here at any moment."

Mary was sitting off to one side, paying no attention. Eftihis had instructed her not to butt in while he was discussing business, and now she didn't utter a peep. It was a good sign. It meant she was beginning to adjust.

"Wouldn't it be a shame for all that money to go to waste just because I came up a bit short? I'll pay you all the interest you want."

"All right, all right, but that's enough for now," Thodoros said. "We'll talk it over another time."

"When?"

"When I don't have to worry about this other business ... If you don't find me here, I'll be at my nephew's office. I'm hoping he won't be able to track me down there."

They left and rejoined the bustle on the street.

"So tell me more about the looms," Eftihis said. "When'll we be getting started?"

Andonis realized Eftihis was hungry for dreams – and what could be easier? Without much effort, he had Eftihis excitedly smacking his lips, seeing an entire factory rise before his shining eyes. With Eftihis ready to gobble up such rosy forecasts, it would have been boorish of Andonis to deprive him. He spoke convincingly about multiple shifts, about trucks impatiently waiting for the product out on the street, about industrial "rationalization," about complex machines to cut costs, about finishers and bulk orders. Eftihis was in heaven. He looked Andonis in the eyes.

"A truck!" he exclaimed. "Did you hear that, Mary? We'll have a truck, too!"

"There'll be loads of work. A few greased palms, some undercutting of the competition ... We'll just squeeze by at first ...then later ..."

"Later what?"

"A brand new factory! When the shifts let out, the street'll be flooded with workers! Smokestacks, warehouses, imports ..."

"And what am I going to be doing this whole time?"

"You'll be the factory-owner! You think that's anything to sneeze at?"

"You're all right, Andonis. People say you talk too much, but you have my full confidence! I have no doubt that by this time next year we'll have a full-scale factory up and going!"

WITH HIS NEW MEASUREMENTS and calculations, Angelos drew up an accurate map. Flush with the back wall of Andonis' apartment, in the courtyard that used to be an auto shop, there must have been a small structure, a storage shed or something. It was there he would have to come up. He made fresh calculations to rule out any mistakes. On the far side of the wall lay a distant world that could be reached only after a frighteningly difficult journey.

He sat holding the chisel all afternoon, poised to pry up the boards. Vangelia got into a conversation with Mary – "and we'll have machinery too" – and later with Ismene: "My aunt's expecting us ... You haven't found him yet?"

The next morning, everything was still, and Angelos, his heart thumping, carefully pried up the boards. He poked the dirt under the floor with a stick, then plunged into the dust, cobwebs and moisture. Work had begun. But he had to be on guard for the least little noise. What the task demanded was methodology, precision and patience.

He worked intensively all afternoon, sweating profusely, merging with the darkness and dirt and excitement of having taken the fateful step. "This is more like it," he thought. "I could dig for miles if I had to." He had to utilize every last minute the neighbors granted him with their absence.

When Stathis came home, he went right to sleep. With the first light, Angelos saw that his clothes were white with dirt. He did his best to clean them, but realized he would have to go down naked from then on. How could he explain himself if they caught him at it? "Imagine them arresting me stark naked."

When Stathis woke up, Angelos asked him:

"Would you mind buying me a small present?"

"Like what?"

"A flashlight. It's hard not being able to turn on the light at night. I've been thinking about tacking a blanket over the window, and hanging another one over the bed like a mosquito-net. Then I could read under it."

"Those astronomy problems you were doing the other day?"

"You've got it."

"You'd be better off just going to sleep."

"From six o'clock on? That's when it gets dark."

"Okay, if I happen to think of it ..."

He couldn't do anything all day because Vangelia stayed at home. He put the finishing touches on his plan, and pondered how best to put it into effect. Then he just sat listening to her footsteps. The poor woman lived such a limited existence. It wouldn't be long before that light in her eyes went out. Andonis came back earlier than usual.

"I'll be in the kitchen writing," he told her without enthusiasm. "If the judge comes by, close the door and tell him I'm out. He'd just be wasting my time ..."

Angelos was stung by that last remark, but he explained it away by supposing that Andonis meant he had nothing to tell his father. Still, he didn't have to put it quite like that.

The following morning, Stathis made him a gift of a flashlight.

Now the hours Stathis was asleep passed more swiftly. The newspaper spoke of all the interesting things going on in the world, and everything seemed sure to come out all right. The flowers filled the courtyard with their smell. Ismene watered them in the afternoon. It wouldn't be long now before he'd get to see her. He would give her a day-by-day account of what he'd been doing all those years. Did she remember their first walk together? They had gone as far as the park by foot. Neither of them said anything. They walked the whole way back without exchanging a word. When they found themselves at their starting-point, they looked at each other. "Would you like us to become friends?" "What are we now?" Ismene had asked, surprised. "I mean better friends ..." He had kissed her right as a train went rushing past.

Vangelia finally left.

Angelos lifted the boards and lowered himself in. He rested the flashlight on a joist and, plan in hand, got down to work. He wasted no time in pinpointing the designated spot, and began digging with hard, steady thrusts of the chisel. "I'm not one to sit around like a lump on a log. This way I'll be able to see my family and friends. Who knows, maybe I'll even be of use to somebody." The earth was soft and slightly damp, easy to dig in. Perhaps this underground road would lead him into the light. He scooped out the dirt with his hands and resumed digging.

ISMENE DIDN'T LET UP so much as a moment in her search. She had to find him, had to save him. It would be terrible if his fear got the better of him and he did something crazy out of desperation. She came home exhausted as usual. From the end of the street, her house looked the way it always did. Her shoulders slumped under the burden of waiting. But was there anything left to wait for? Perhaps waiting too had become mere habit. An eddy of wind kicked up everything in its path – proof that it would take the war a long time to end in this corner of the world too. She trudged up the winding stairs. Stathis' door was shut, his room forgotten.

CHAPTER 13

BEFORE DAYBREAK, Angelos sprang up in bed at the usual time. He heard footsteps in the courtyard, and immediately got up to relinquish his place to Stathis. But the key didn't turn in the lock. He waited a little longer. The courtyard was empty. It must have been someone on their way out. He lay back down, but was unable to rest, knowing that Stathis was late. He peered out through the shutters, but the slot of gray sky he could see gave him no clear sense of the time. Then came more steps – Eftihis, coming out to use the bathroom.

Day entered the room with an unwavering, inescapable rhythm. The scattered noises multiplied, objects assumed solid form in his vision.

Day had broken, and Stathis had not come! It was a dramatic and unforeseen development.

He felt himself surrounded by a precarious, mute emptiness, fraught with danger. His problem became more impossible with each passing minute. He'd worn himself out the day before, digging all afternoon, and maybe the trembling that wracked him now was some absurd spasm of fatigue. Maybe Stathis had been tied up at the newspaper, developing events may have forced him to stay on for a special edition. Or maybe he fell ill and had to be taken to the hospital. Whatever it was, it put Angelos in an inconceivably difficult situation. It had come too quickly, before he had things settled in his mind, before he had secured his avenue of escape. The door was locked. The open tunnel awaited continuation. The weather was cold and March-like.

It would have been ridiculous to go on working. The flashlight, the chisel and the spoon no longer served any purpose. He had made considerable progress over the past few days. The tunnel had acquired the length of a man, with just his heels sticking out. What a pity: in two or three weeks it would have been finished. He hunched lower in his chair. The room had become suffocatingly cramped. Stathis hadn't come!

Angelos now felt utterly unprotected. If they found him there, he would be led out through the courtyard, overwhelmed with shame, while his father, Ismene, his mother, Andonis, and Lucia stood on the stairs or at their windows, witnessing his humiliation with a look of unanswerable incomprehension. Stathis' absence may have brought the finale unexpectedly nearer. Perhaps that was what his father had been telling Andonis. No, nobody knew he was there. If something happened, it would be purely by chance. Any steps he took to forestall that coincidence, however, could not be a matter of chance. But the torpor investing his mind wouldn't make that easy.

Vangelia went by, he could tell by her steps. Then Ismene came down the stairs, taut with her many cares. He could detect no change in their faces. Outside, the buses went rumbling down the streets. What was he to do, now that everything had been so suddenly transformed?

THAT MORNING, EFTIHIS woke up in a good mood. He had been talking to Mary since daybreak about the textile works they would be setting up. "You'll have to learn the business too, I need someone I can trust at my side." Mary stretched, yawned, and sighed, "Let's just get started."

He got out of bed, found his cigarettes, made coffee, brought hers over and set it on the chair beside the bed, then began discussing his plans. He saw that Mary wasn't paying attention. Her eyes had glazed over. So, they would get two double-width looms to start with, because they required the same number of operators. They'd get them at half-price, too, Andonis had said so. Then they'd buy a warper. "A warper, Mary, serves ten to twenty looms, so we won't need one right off, we'll take the stuff to somebody else for the time being. Other pieces of auxiliary equipment are spoolers, bobbiners, rotometers – but those can wait until we've gotten things rolling."

"Once the business is going, will you love me?" Mary blurted out.

Eftihis opened the window and thus didn't see the face Mary gave him when he hastily said that he did love her. The courtyard, quiet and clean, was lovely to behold. He whistled as he was putting on his shoes. He kicked aside an old newspaper, combed his hair, and turned to his wife ...

"We'll start living like normal people. The machinery'll be working away, we'll hire workers, maybe even an accountant ... Trust me, Mary. I could sell Bibles to the Turks, I'm not kidding."

To Mary's eyes, he had never looked so handsome. His face was radiant, his eyes limpid. Gaunt from being always on the run, he talked tough but had a heart of gold. She had gotten used to his brusque way of talking to her, the way he looked at her only fleetingly, somewhat askance. The way he was always chalky with the dust of the streets, his nerves tied into knots. As long as he was talking about textiles, his anger left him, his swearing stopped, and his face wore a milder expression. She had never seen him like that.

Suddenly his brow clouded over. He threw on some clothes and knocked on Andonis' door.

"It dawned on me that as long as you've got those cans in there, you can't concentrate on anything else. So I thought I'd call in the people I used to work the streets with. They'll get rid of it before you know it."

"By all means!" said Andonis.

So Eftihis shot over to Monastiraki. He addressed them as a boss who thought of giving them this chance to earn a little something. "Until the real thing gets going." Then, just to give them a jolt, "A textile factory!" he boomed. Glimpsing a certain admiration in Simos' eye, Eftihis felt like he'd grown at least twice as tall. On the other hand, it was also possible that no one believed him, since they didn't even ask for more details – as if nothing were easier than setting up a textile works from one day to the next.

Simos and Iordanis scowled at Fanis, who had suddenly become animated and was all over Eftihis the moment he heard the word textiles. He said he had worked as a knotter. But look how puffed up Eftihis was – that whoring bridegroom who grabbed at his wife's skirts while devouring all her money. That slob who looked upon everyone else as his slave, that sorry excuse for a boss who believed others existed merely to do his bidding. Fanis again tried to get him to say he would hire him. Apparently the dummy had fallen for all Eftihis' hogwash the braggart had been stringing them along with.

"So, factory men from now on, eh?" asked Simos.

"That's right," Eftihis answered firmly. "And if you want to help out with the cans, come on over to my place."

Eftihis set out at once, just so they wouldn't get the idea he was asking them a favor. He raced home and told Mary not to come outside, not even to open the door, because some people would be coming by. They had no need for house guests. Then he told Andonis that it had all been taken care of.

"One of them says he's a knotter. Can we use him?"

"If he's any good, sure."

Eftihis' friends tromped glumly into Andonis' room. The latter was standing amid all his boxes, and had them gather around. As usual, the desire to explain everything possessed him, and he spoke precisely and lucidly about prices and conditions in the marketplace, as if addressing sales representatives who had inquired about his merchandise. He systematically avoided the question of quality.

"Are these them?" interrupted Iordanis. "Give us some samples so we can get started. You can tell us the rest some other time."

Eftihis, standing in the door, was furious that his men had once again behaved like jackasses. On the other hand, Andonis was overdoing it a bit. Simos and Iordanis snatched up the samples and went out into the courtyard. Fanis lingered behind. "You're the knotter?" said Andonis.

"How could you tell?" Eftihis asked admiringly.

"His fingers."

Fanis carefully studied his hands, as if seeing them for the first time. He looked at them from this side and that, then looked Andonis in the eyes, as if pleading with him, as if trying to enter deep into his brain and convince him how much an affirmative answer would mean to him. Fanis' eyes had become virtual wounds. He raised his hands and offered his expert fingers as proof.

"First the cans. Then we'll talk about the other business," Andonis said under his breath.

Fanis reached out his palms to receive the cans, which this unknown man handed him so carefully, as if there were something priceless or highly explosive inside. Andonis reminded him that it had to be taken care of as quickly as possible, then warmly bid them all good luck, giving Vangelia a smile of satisfaction. He held Fanis by the arm, and told him in a confidential tone:

"Be sure you get rid of it, it's absolutely essential. Then come by afterwards and we'll talk about the looms. Don't worry, there'll be a job for you here ..."

At the front gate, Eftihis gave Fanis a slap on the shoulder and told him:

"Let's go sell off this junk, then we can talk textiles. I want to let you in on my plans."

HE SAT BACK DOWN and opened up a newspaper, making a conscious effort to convince himself that nothing had happened, that it was a day just like any other day. He read at random, but the letters grew blurred when he reflected that Stathis had set the letters with his own hands. He tried to remember what Stathis had been like the previous afternoon: thin, not quite awake. His fingers had picked up his bread as usual, his jaws had worked robustly – nothing to foreshadow his sudden disappearance. There had been the usual fatigue in his eyes, as if he were straining to read a gnarled script. Suddenly he had taken Angelos' hand, given it a squeeze, and said: "Courage." At the door, he had raised his hand to his brow, waved good-by, given him a vague smile and locked the door behind him. "Good-by, friend," Angelos had said without being heard.

Some days, Stathis seemed to derive a strange satisfaction from locking him in. Everyone hid an outlaw somewhere deep inside themselves. They shared their bread with him, preserved him, and were afraid to speak even in whispers because of the ever-present danger of being overheard. Angelos covered his face with his hands. "Now I am afraid. Fear is the illegitimacy of my faith in life."

As he sat with the newspaper open, he remembered one day up

in the mountains during the war. Clearing a space in the snow to set up his tent, he made out a boot underneath. He tugged at it, and a whole leg came out, severed at the thigh. He lit a fire. He spent the whole night alone. He'd kept his eyes fixed on the burning chunks of wood, with a severed leg for company. They moved out the following morning. Before leaving, he buried the leg again, so no one would trip over it. He pushed onward through the snow. Wherever someone had walked became a path. Others could go that way after you. But the snow would melt, the footsteps would disappear. That's when there was a danger of getting lost, because you weren't always the first. The others condemned along with him had been lined up one morning and shot at the accustomed place ... Wiping his eyes with his sleeve, Angelos realized he had been holding the newspaper in front of his face the whole time, as if hiding from someone. He wiped his eyes again, and with a shiver pulled the blanket up over his shoulders.

If Stathis didn't turn up soon, Angelos would have to decide, before it got dark, what to do. As long as he sat slumped in that chair, disaster was sure to strike. "I've been putting off the critical battle for so many years now, all that waiting did me in. The trial wasn't the big moment, I wasn't even there for it. Maybe now my case will be decided on its true merits."

Someone was singing in a nearby courtyard, perhaps one of the welders as he adjusted his torch. But Angelos soon knew the song could only have been sung by someone out of work. If you felt that bad, how could you ever go out and look for a job? And how long did the sun shine in countries where such songs were sung? Angelos listened intently, as if to a lecturer who was expounding on an important and abstruse subject. But he couldn't concentrate. What if Stathis didn't come?

LATER THAT AFTERNOON, Eftihis' three friends came by with carts and took away enough boxes to fill the orders they had secured. Everything went off without a hitch. They were good fellows all right. Vangelia watched the proceedings with visible relief. Andonis handed them the boxes, and marked it all down on paper. Fanis asked him something about the textile factory. "Now's not the time," Andonis answered sternly. Eftihis, who was overseeing the distribution and loading, leaned over and whispered in Andonis' ear:

"Looks like we'll get rid of this crap after all. Even if it was dirt inside they could have sold it ..."

He instantly regretted it, however. It was clear his joke had not gone over well. For all of his brains, Andonis still loved the rotten meat in those cans.

When the others had left, Andonis told Vangelia:

"Now that I'm rid of that stuff, let's take a day and go down to Faliron. Just like we used to ..."

Vangelia gave him a dazzling smile. "You mean like in the old days?"

"Uh-huh. Those outings of ours meant a lot to me."

Eftihis happily came over and interrupted them.

"I saw Thodoros and he promised to get some orders for us ... He said he might even put up some money. But not a word about it to anyone, okay? No one's supposed to know ..."

Then Eftihis proudly unveiled his plan. The best thing would be to set the looms up right there, in their rooms. To tear down the dividing walls and join up their two places. They could get rid of the kitchens – who needed them? So, what did Andonis think? It would give them ample space. They would keep only the two end rooms for sleeping. "Who needs a whole damn room for a table and fancy chairs and frilly curtains? Of course, our wives won't go for it, but who cares what they think?"

"We'll see ..." Andonis answered evasively.

He threw his coat on and made for the door.

"You've got more work to do, brother?" Eftihis protested. "I've been waiting for days to have a talk with you, and you're still slipperier than an eel."

"Tonight, I promise," Andonis assured him.

"I'm tired of you putting me off. How long am I going to have to chase around after you?"

"I'll be back early and we can talk about the equipment ..."

Andonis flitted away in his usual manner, and Eftihis swore to himself, looking up at the sky.

The person who sang so plaintively in the neighboring courtyard took up his lament again, annoying Eftihis, whose head was filled with the sounds of his own factory.

LATER THAT EVENING, Eftihis found himself in Petralona. He hesitated on a familiar street, then circled the house without daring to approach. After smoking two or three cigarettes down at the corner, he knocked on Elpida's door.

"It's me, Eftihis. Open up."

She let him in at once, murmuring "Welcome" and standing aside to let him by. Eftihis did his best to act as comfortable with her as ever, as if a day hadn't passed since he used to drop in on her basement apartment every evening. He gave her a pat on the shoulder and asked if she would mind making him a coffee to help clear his head. Why was the light in there so feeble, giving off an orange glow that made everything seem old and mistreated somehow. Elpida looked the same, her shoulders as rounded as ever, her dark, quiet eyes slightly sunken, her hair straight, with a few curls about her cheeks. She always seemed to be waiting for something. Nothing had changed.

"You look a little pale. Is something the matter?" he asked.

"No," she said. "How have you been?"

"Did you look for another place? It's so dank and gloomy in here."

"After so many years ..."

"You've got to move. You must be cold, you're wearing your coat ..."

"No, I just got in."

"Where were you?"

"I'm working in a place that makes boxes ..."

"Without telling me? You should have let me know. Is there someone who means more to you than me? Don't I matter? It's like you don't have anyone to look after you now ..."

Elpida gave him a puzzled look. Why had his cheeks flushed so? What had she said to upset him?

"You're right," he told her. "I abandoned you. I haven't been by in almost two months ..."

"Did I say anything? Wait a second and I'll make your coffee."

"No, thanks. So what are they paying you there?"

"Twenty-five."

"I don't want you to go back there. Do what I tell you. I'm

starting up a new business, and I want you to come work for me. It's going to be a textile factory," Eftihis told her in a quiet voice.

"A textile factory! Congratulations, Eftihis. But I don't know anything about textiles, I've never done any weaving."

"You'll learn. Starting today, you're on the payroll. That's what I came to tell you!"

"But if I don't know how, what am I supposed to do?"

"Hey, I'm hiring you. When it comes right down to it, it's my business, I can hire whoever I like. It'll be getting started a few days from now."

"But what'll I do?"

"Enough of that. Now, could you get me that package I left with you?"

Elpida opened the chest and took out the heavy packet of sovereigns. It was still wrapped in newspaper and tied with a string. It hadn't been touched. Eftihis furiously tore open the wrapping, and once more the gold gleamed in his palms. He took out four gold coins and plunked them down on the table.

"That's your wages. As of today, it's like you were already working."

What was Elpida laughing about, as if she found his anger funny. Then he addressed her quietly and tenderly:

"Tell me something, Elpida. You said you've only been working at the box place for a week. That means you went a month without money, right? But since you knew there was money here, why didn't you just take a bit to help you get by?"

"It was yours, you entrusted it to me ..."

"But what's it worth to me if you were going hungry?"

Again Elpida was baffled by Eftihis' anger. He carefully tied the sovereigns back up and slowly told Elpida how he was planning to set up a couple of looms in his own place.

"Seen anything of Fanis lately?" he asked suddenly.

He looked her squarely in the eye and tried to determine if she was telling the truth.

"I need to talk to him. Any chance you'll be seeing him any time soon?"

"No."

Eftihis stood up.

"Want to take a walk, Elpida?"

"Together?"

"Why not? It wouldn't be the first time."

"It's different now. Where would we go?"

"Just around here. Up to the hill and back."

"Good night, Eftihis. I'll wait for you to tell me when to come about the work ..."

She had already opened the door. Outside, the night was cold. Eftihis realized he could stay no longer. He said good-by without looking at her, then went out the door feeling sheepish, bundling the heavy packet of sovereigns under his arm.

DAY BROKE FOR A SECOND TIME without Stathis coming home. The cool shiver of dawn reached into the room, and the first stirrings of life arose. Angelos listened intently, for it was the most dangerous hour of the day. Then everyone began coming and going, conversing freely, and setting out for their various destinations. Andonis and Eftihis set off together, with the genial optimism of two friends who bolstered each other's morale. Mary promptly began washing down the courtyard.

Angelos rose from his chair and felt the lock. It would be a cinch to unscrew. He touched his face and found that his beard had grown. If only he had a bit of water. There could be no doubt that thirst increased one's fear. The reverse might also be true, of course, but who had time to figure out which came first ... "I wish I knew all there was to know. Then nothing would surprise me." But that was obviously asking too much, especially at a time when nothing at all was certain. He instantly felt that tingling in his brain he used to get when he took exams. But first he would have to shave, and put on a shirt and socks. If he were fully prepared, maybe the right course of action would present itself. He didn't know the latest developments in the news. He stood in front of the bed with his hands on his hips, trying to focus his thoughts. It was the critical moment in his years-old struggle. He felt as if he was standing on a windswept hillside, gazing down on unknown terrain, trying to determine how best to avoid ambush. But all he could see were walls, and his eyes drew back until they were focused on his own chest, in the region of the heart. That's where they aimed for; then came the bright red stain. His dingy undershirt already felt soaked in blood. He tore his eyes away, and checked to see how many screws there were in the lock. It would be a simple matter to escape. But again he could feel that fresh seepage of blood. He touched the spot with his hand, then, to keep from looking at his fingers, snatched up a newspaper lying on the table ... His fingers left no prints on it. But not thinking about it didn't make the possibility any more remote. And where would he go once out on the street? The court decision stipulated a warm carnation on his chest, whose crimson petals unfolded out of a tiny hole. Maybe on his forehead too. But his hand didn't make it up that far. It stopped at his cheek, and he was reminded of his beard.

He discovered an old razor blade, which he sharpened using spit in a cup. In the piece of broken mirror he propped up, his eyes were unnaturally wide from the strain of sleeplessness. The cheek between his stiff fingers was dry and dusty. He too had weathered over the years, like a newspaper yellowed with age. "Only fear never gets old," he murmured, and he felt the urge to laugh, as he did whenever he heard a saying like that. He wondered whether, now that he had lived so long with fear, there was some way for him to control its manifestations, to limit the risk inherent in panic.

He got up and examined the screws of the lock again. He took a knife and tested whether its tip fit the screw heads.

That afternoon, someone knocked softly on the door. Had they come for him? Angelos froze. The knock came again. The doorknob turned a few times. He held his breath. Everything stood still.

"Stathis ... Stathis ..." It was Ismene.

Angelos shut his eyes, listening to the blood throbbing in his veins.

"Stathis, let me in ... There's something I want to tell you ..."

It took all of Angelos' strength to hold back. She knocked again, and Angelos wanted to cry out, but his jaw was clamped tight, not even a groan could escape. Ismene was just a few inches away, the planks of the door were all that separated them. He could feel her warm palm against the wood, her quick breathing. If he cried out, if he so much as whispered for help, his ordeal would be over. Yet how humiliating to have her learn he had been hiding there the whole time.

Her steps faded, and Angelos collapsed exhausted on the chair. She loved him, and was waiting for him. Like him, she was a prisoner, to her years of waiting. Like him, she had sacrificed herself to the hope that some day he would lead a normal life. And he had let her go away in despair.

His eye fell on his undershirt. The red stain was there again, right at his heart. He started to shave his other cheek, the whole time keeping from looking at his forehead in the mirror, especially that spot right above where the eyebrows met.

ANDONIS AND EFTIHIS came back in high spirits that afternoon. They looked at each other with admiration, and recalled how famously they had pulled it all off. They had even had a few quick ouzos in Omonia to toast their future success. Eftihis excitedly told Mary that they had put money down on some machinery, but as she didn't understand right away he raised his voice at her, thinking maybe that way he could penetrate her thick skull.

"Where's Vangelia?" Andonis asked.

"She went to Holargos to visit an aunt of hers," Mary told him.

He and Eftihis went ahead and began making plans.

"If we tear down the walls here, it'll leave us loads of room," Eftihis said.

"It should be plenty."

"I got to hand it to you, friend ... You really did a number on him!"

"It wasn't anything special," Andonis said modestly. "A common act of blackmail. He was in tight straits, and we took advantage of it. What could be simpler?"

"You were fantastic!" Eftihis laughed. "You had him scared out of his pants he'd be thrown in prison. Damn, did you do a good job describing it ... He just caved in when you told him how he'd die in prison from shame ..."

"I was right, wasn't I?"

Eftihis laughed again. So, as it turned out there would be three machines.

"Is there going to be a night-shift?"

"Not at first. It costs too much."

"Right. Plus we've got to sleep sometime. The looms'll be pounding right in our ears ... Big deal, we'll get used to it ... Of course, you can work two double-sized looms with the same number of operators."

Andonis asked Eftihis if he had enough to cover what the poor sap with the looms owed Ioannidis.

"Sure do ..."

"I'll take care of it ... You wouldn't believe what a hard nut my friend Ioannidis is. I've helped him through some tough times, though. I've got him right where I want him."

"So we're all set, then. Our little looms'll be right next door to us here, and we'll be able to get a good night's sleep. In the morning, they'll be cranking away from the crack of dawn. Here come the weavers, you watch over them all day, you're the man in charge. No more running yourself ragged. I'm sick of having to worry all the time. Now it'll just be the warp and the woof, the shuttle going back and forth, and poof, out comes the bread. Isn't that how it works?"

"Something like that ..."

"Now don't start in again with your theorizing. That's how it works all right. And then afterwards I'll put on a suit, and have a night on the town with my friend Andonis. Sometimes we might even take our wives along. And you, my friend, are going to get rid of that briefcase of yours. I'm tired of seeing you always toting that thing around with you. You are solid gold, as far as I'm concerned. I'm confident that one day ... I'm going to give you a free hand. What you say goes. You know what you're doing. I have faith in you ..."

The iron gate creaked open and Simos entered carrying a cardboard box. He walked slowly and sullenly up to them. Iordanis and Fanis weren't far behind. They set their boxes down in front of Andonis' door.

"A shame for all that to go to waste," Simos said in a strangely husky voice.

They brought in the rest. But before they could set them down Eftihis stopped them, enraged, as if threatened by incalculable danger.

"Take them back," he screamed at them. "I don't care what you have to do to get rid of them ... You idiots, you goddamn good-for-nothings ... I don't want to see you back here unless it's with money in your hands."

"There's nothing to shout about," said Iordanis. "Nobody wants them."

"Up yours. By tomorrow, I want every last one of them sold ..."

The three men couldn't understand what he was getting all red in the face about. After all, the cans weren't even his. Mr. Stefanidis, on the other hand, an educated and sensible man, stood there silently, as if at somewhat of a loss, his head tilted back, as if he were short of breath and were trying to get a bit of air.

"I never should have trusted incompetents like you. I'll have to think long and hard about whether I want to use you in my new business ... We put money down on some looms today ..."

Then Andonis spoke up for the first time.

"All right, fellas, just put them down. No need to shout, Eftihis, it's not the end of the world. The gentlemen did all they could, there's nothing to get upset about ..."

They put the cartons down with evident relief. They trudged in with the rest, and soon all the boxes stood stacked in front of Andonis' door. After they'd left, Andonis flung the boxes haphazardly into the room, without saying a thing. Cans spilled out of the torn cartons and went skittering across the floor. Then he went inside, soundlessly shutting the door behind him.

WHEN SHE OPENED THE DOOR, Vangelia was startled to find him sitting hunched over on a carton, his head in his hands. The floor around him was littered with cans and empty boxes. She pushed them out of the way with her foot and went in. Andonis looked up at her, bewildered and lost.

"Don't ask," he told her.

"Should I open the window?"

"Do whatever you like."

At a loss, Vangelia stood beside him, surrounded by scores of round cans with colorful labels.

"Sit down. Just don't look at me."

Nothing could lessen the calamity. The air had been sucked out of the room, leaving only dust to breathe. Everything was sinking into this sea of rotten meat in which he was mired.

Words and things and even the thoughts in one's brain were rotten. All solid objects, whether man-made or natural, gave off the suffocating reek of decomposition. The stench of carrion and sewage clogged his nostrils and formed a knot in his throat.

"What are you carrying on like this for? You knew they were rotten, didn't you?" Vangelia asked with infuriating simplicity.

"Please don't say anything. You can sit here if you want ..."

Vangelia nudged a few cans out of the way with her shoe. What a racket they made! She started to sit down on the carton, but slipped on a can and lost her balance, tripped over another one, and nearly fell. Andonis jumped up to catch her, but he couldn't keep his footing either. He staggered drunkenly across the cans and went down with a clatter. Again there was a clatter of cans, followed by silence. He had ended up at Vangelia's side. What was there to say? "Did you hurt yourself? What time is it outside?" One could spend years like that, sprawled among the cans, gathering dust and cobwebs. Vangelia's foot lay next to the kindly head of an ox from Brazil, who gazed up at her with an awareness of his hopeless situation. He looked as if he were about to lick her shoe.

"So our life consisted of a few cans?" she asked. "And now we're ruined?"

"I don't know. I asked you please not to talk to me ..."

He felt her hand on his shoulder, then on his hair. He thrust it away, it was as if a beetle with long legs had climbed on him to sleep. Decay and humiliation could not be mitigated; they were absolutes, like death.

Andonis wept profusely atop those tin ruins. Suddenly he sat up, steadied himself, and told Vangelia:

"Get up and let's get going."

"Where to?"

"To see the doctor. I want to get it over with today ..."

Vangelia shrank into a corner of the room ... Andonis stumbled toward her, arms outstretched.

"Just because your cans are no good doesn't mean I have to lose my baby."

"I'm begging you, Vangelia, please. I've told you I don't know how many times ..."

"No, we can each keep what's ours. You can keep your cans, and I'll keep my baby."

"You're going to drive me crazy, Vangelia! Help me to get back on my feet, then you can have all the babies you want ... The timing's all wrong. It would be like having a noose around my neck ... My hands would be tied. I'd be dragged off to prison for sure. *Please*, Vangelia. I've always loved you. Why won't you do this to help me? I'm going to gamble everything, even if it means going to prison. But I don't want to be locked away on account of weakness and inaction, and have you come and visit with a child in your arms. It would be twice as humiliating – I couldn't ..."

"No," said Vangelia.

Andonis snapped. He made a lunge for her, but lost his footing and fell. Vangelia darted over to the other corner, behind the table.

"Listen," Andonis harangued, "the issue of the baby concerns us both equally. It's not like we're living in the jungle, we're not stray cats who have babies whenever we're in heat ... Conditions have to be right, and they just aren't now. I can't even promise you anything ... But if you keep this up, I'll just have to walk out and let you fend for yourself ... I'm tired, Vangelia, you don't know what all these promises and extensions have cost me. So, if you want us to go on living together ... Otherwise, I'm taking my briefcase and walking out that door."

Andonis got up, straightened his hair, knotted his tie, and opened the door. The afternoon sun stung his eyes.

"All right, let's go," Vangelia said.

She rose up behind the table, wan and cringing. Her lips trembled, as if she were cold. She may have whispered something, but Andonis wasn't listening.

"Let's go," he said, holding the door open. "This is nearly as hard on me as it is on you. Believe me, it's not how I would have it. But it's the only way."

Vangelia left her corner and, stepping carefully between the cans, slowly went over to the door. She studied his face to see if the emotion in his voice was for real, or just another business ploy.

"And try not to cry."

"Come on," she replied curtly. "But I want you to know, this is the biggest sacrifice I'm going to make for you ... And the last."

"There's nothing to worry about. It's no big deal. Thousands of women ..."

"Keep your speeches to yourself, I don't need convincing ... And don't think I fell for any of that either ... It's a sacrifice, pure and simple ..."

AT THE CLINIC, THE PROCEDURE was, happily, simple and brief. The doctor welcomed them warmly when Andonis reminded him of the engineer's phone call. He asked no questions, and everything was conducted with businesslike and sympathetic complicity. Andonis tried to engage the doctor in conversation, to strike up an acquaintance: "Orestes is a good friend of mine. He's often talked to me about you ..." The doctor, however, left them alone in a waiting room and closed the door. They sat in fraying chairs and stared up at the walls, as if there were nothing to say.

Vangelia sat waiting with her lips tightly sealed. Her coat was shabby. Damn, he should have bought her a new one on credit. To avoid meeting her eyes, however, he picked up an old magazine off the table and became absorbed in it. Doors opened and closed with the rhythm of routine preparations, while a number of white smocks circulated, faceless and voiceless, beyond the glass doors. Vangelia fixed him with her stare, striking fear in his heart. A phrase popped into his head: "The supposedly willing sacrifice of dreams." He wished he could have told it to her. "You have to learn to arrange your defeats so that they lead up to the decisive blow. From that point on, each new defeat, like the one I'm passing on to Vangelia now, brings one irrevocably closer to ruin ..." He threw down the magazine and looked out the window. "But everything is judged by its final outcome," he thought with a certain optimism. A road is a road, nothing more or less. Clouds, cars, pedestrians, buildings ... If he were to tell her: "Let's go, let's keep the child," maybe everything would change. But Andonis didn't have time to think it all out. A door opened ...

"This way," the doctor said softly.

Vangelia got up at once. Before going through the door, she glanced back at Andonis expectantly. Or perhaps she was cursing him, he wasn't sure. Andonis gave her an idiotic smile, and the door closed.

The whole time he was waiting, he could hear the rapid click of metal tools on glass. The tin cans had displaced the child, that much was true. Would Vangelia come out of this alive? What if something were to happen to her? His legs turned to jello at the thought.

He had no sense of how long it was before the doctor opened the door.

"It's over ... Everything was perfectly normal. She'll be awake in an hour or so ..."

Andonis asked the doctor if he could see her. He stole a glance into the room. She was breathing, thank God.

When he next went in, Vangelia was awake, her eyes fixed on the door. She had been waiting for him.

"See! That wasn't so bad now, was it?" he asked.

Vangelia looked him squarely in the eyes and asked:

"So, are you happy, now that you can feel free to go to prison?"

He timidly reached his hand to her forehead, but she pushed it away.

"Fine, fine. Don't talk, you must be exhausted. We'll leave in a bit ... It was all very simple, thousands of women ..."

"You got your way. Now you're free, which is what you wanted ..."

They went home in the rain. The whole way back in the taxi he gently held her head, but the thought came to him that his tenderness might be just another element in the art of the deal. Vangelia seemed dazed, her eyes were unfocused, as if she didn't know where she was. It was raining harder when they got out, so he threw his coat over her. He got her into bed with some difficulty, what with all the cans on the floor. She asked him not to turn the light on. So much the better. Andonis tiptoed toward the door, and quickly went out. And that, for the time being, was the end of that.

THE JUDGE LEARNED that Thodoros frequented a coffeehouse near the post office. He calmly strode inside, scanned the tables on the ground level, then headed up the stairs. When he caught sight of the familiar fat, red face, in back, he could feel his heart racing, but nevertheless managed to act as if he had come in merely to drink his coffee in peace. He sat down with his back to Thodoros, and immediately opened his newspaper, to conceal the pleasurable fatigue he felt coursing through his body. Throughout his search, he was convinced he was carrying out a task of gravest importance. Now he could rest. He would wait to have a word with him once he was finished talking with those two strangers. His presence there was enough. The café was a quiet one, filled with old leather couches and customers conversing in low voices. The chairs were more comfortable than at the place in Omonia. And, for the most part, the customers were people who went on believing that the pace of life was still as they remembered it from the old days.

As Harilaos sat reading his paper, he felt a nervous tap on his back.

"What the hell do you want from me?" Thodoros said, bending over him angrily.

"You know the answer to that. Do you want me to say it again?"

"No, I've already heard it a million times ... How'd you find me this time ?"

"It wasn't hard ... I have the right to go where I choose, don't I? I'm not bothering you ..."

"It makes me nervous to have you follow me everywhere."

"A good sign," said Harilaos imperturbably. "The fact that you're annoyed, even though you know you're in no danger, means that my presence is calling up a response in you."

"What'll it take to get you off of my back?" Thodoros demanded, sitting down next to him.

"It's not for me to say ... In any case, you're the one who came over and started this conversation ..."

"Don't give me that, gramps. When are you going to stop harassing me?..."

"They follow me too ..." Harilaos answered with the hint of a smile, "and I've found it a most unpleasant experience. Which is precisely why I follow you. But their motives are purely malevolent. I came here for *your* sake, to help you remember something. I have only the best intentions toward you, though it also happens to be to my great benefit. Memory, you know, is an exclusively human trait, a privilege that brings with it the issue of conscience."

"Not this again ..."

"I believe we all have our good side, but are often subject to certain mistaken beliefs ... Take you, for example. I encountered all sorts in the course of my legal career. When a criminal's conscience was functioning, I deduced that that person deserved to receive justice, and I took great pains when handing down a sentence. As for the others, I merely imposed the punishment prescribed by the law ..."

"So tell me, were your verdicts always right?"

"Did you by any chance ask that as a way of excusing your own injustice? So has that possibility begun to bother you? Well, well, I guess that means we're making progress!"

"I bet you've sent a lot of people to prison."

"Yes, since you ask, I have. People require laws in order to live, and I enforced them. I believe in justice. Just what law were you enforcing?"

"I don't know anything," said Thodoros angrily. "I told you I don't remember any of that business with your son. I made a deposition ... It was so long ago. You think I don't have anything better to think about? Just leave me alone, will you ..."

"It'll come back to you," Harilaos informed him severely.

He raised his newspaper again and began reading. Thodoros remained beside him, unable to move.

THE THIRD DAY OF STATHIS' absence was coming to a close. The courtyard had been washed down by the rain. "They haven't come for me yet," Angelos thought, curled into a ball on the floor, his head in his hands. But why should they come just because Stathis had not? The two were unrelated. He curled up more tightly. If no one came, he would perish from hunger and neglect. He upended the pitcher just in case there was a drop or two left. The rain was coming down harder. The newspapers and events of the world were stacked neatly in the corner, over the loosened floorboards. His escape route remained unfinished. His parched mouth burned, and he could no longer even bear to lie down on Stathis' old bed with its ragged blanket. How long until daylight? He was entering the most critical time zone now. "Arrests and executions take place at dawn." Someone had said that time was a function of light, but maybe now the opposite was true, maybe now light had become a function of time. Whatever happened, he had arrived at the end unprepared. Why must everyone be so unhappy? The question was naive, at best. He knew very well why he was unhappy, even though the situation in which he found himself could not be called unhappy. He had a friend during the war named Kostas. A tall, slim, light-haired boy who wrote poems in private. One day Kostas said: "I'm not going back to the University until the trumpets of peace sound." He gave away his books and left. A few months later he was arrested and shot. It was even said that the morning he was taken out to be executed, they were all lying face down in the back of the truck, piled one on top of the other. They were singing. The truck drove down the main thoroughfares of Athens. The guards ordered them to stop, or they would bayonet them. Kostas kept on singing and was bayonetted. But what did Kostas' song have to do with Stathis' absence? The rain had begun at dusk. Angelos remembered making his way once through a thick forest, staggering from tree to tree to brace himself, his body numb from the effort of keeping awake and upright.

Deep in his pocket he found the newspaper clipping about his sentencing, tattered and yellow as a dried leaf. He put it back without unfolding it. In his other pocket was the chisel, no longer of any use.

He decided to write a letter to Ismene, and another to his father. It would be humiliating to ask them for help again. Both had expected more from him. "He only remembers me when he needs something," she would say, and she would rip up the letter. And his father would say: "I told you to give it plenty of thought before acting. Now it's too late ..." He tried to think of something to say, but couldn't. If he had made it to that meeting way back in the beginning, everything would be different. He had found his old friends again. He was staying at a house in Kipseli. That afternoon he was bidding an emotional farewell to the kind people who had put him up, when suddenly the doorbell rang and a cousin of the family came in. He hurriedly hid behind a door. The woman, a chatterbox whose high-pitched voice still rang in his ear, stayed until evening. Angelos was trapped behind the door, and thus never met the person waiting for him. The next night he had gone to the same place, but nobody came. And so he was left out on his own.

There were footsteps on the stairs.

Lucia was coming down carrying a sack full of something heavy. Her face – what he could see of it above her raised collar – looked pale. She struggled across the courtyard and went into the laundry-room. As she crossed in front of the window, Angelos realized the bag was full of books and papers. Then she came back out to the door, as if waiting for something. Soon thick, black smoke began billowing out.

"My books!..." Angelos whispered.

The smoke thickened. Yes, they were his books all right, plus he glimpsed some rolled-up drawings ... Lucia slowly backed out, her face tense, her hands in her pockets, shaking with the courage of hopelessness. She stood staunch guard over the fire. "What have I ever done to you?" Angelos thought. The smoke started seeping into the room. Angelos was still glued to the shutters, his nostrils and eyes burning.

Andonis flew into the courtyard in his usual manner, and Lucia stopped him. He approached her with a look of dismay.

"I've been waiting to hear from you for days now," she told him.

"I couldn't do anything, I didn't have time ..."

"This was work too, I would have paid you."

"What are you burning?"

"Some old junk. Just clearing out some of the clutter."

"Nobody sees him, I asked everywhere."

"Never mind. There's no point in it now."

Andonis left. The smoke had become thicker and darker. Lucia stood with her back to the flames. Ismene came into the courtyard. When she caught sight of the smoke, and Lucia standing there, she hesitated a moment. The rain was coming down harder. A suspicion seemed to kindle in her.

"Did you light that fire?"

"Yes," Lucia replied curtly.

Ismene walked over, and Lucia mustered all her strength and stood blocking the doorway. Ismene's eyes flashed. She sprang forward and frantically grappled with Lucia amid the billowing smoke.

Angelos was about to open the window and leap out into the courtyard, but he saw in his mind how ridiculous – not to mention dangerous – it would be for him to suddenly appear at that critical juncture. "Now you come running, when your own things are in danger. Why didn't you open the door all those times I knocked?" Ismene would ask, and would have every right to burn his books herself. By now smoke filled the room. He was wracked by loud coughing. He ran back to the bed and buried his face in the covers. The smoke reeked of disaster. Danger, it seemed, wore many faces.

Lucia stood in the courtyard, as if she'd accomplished what she had set out to do. She straightened her hair and smoothed her coat. Ismene's choking voice came from within.

"He'll need these when he comes back."

"I wish he had come back. But it's too late, I can't wait anymore. I can't forgive or feel sorry for any of you ..."

She went on down the passageway and vanished into the rain. Ismene came out looking disheveled, clutching a few books to her breast. Scattered on the ground were charred remnants, half-burned pages, sooty water and ash. She braced herself in the doorway and stood silently crying, infused with smoke and the rain's desolation.

Angelos watched her through the shutters, stricken. There was nothing he could do. Everything was wrapped in the smoke of disaster. Were he to so much as whisper to her, she would hear. But that would only make matters worse, and complete the disaster. As it was, only a few books had been burned. But by remaining there in the room, wasn't he bringing on his own ruin? What could he do? He inhaled the smell of burnt paper, the smoke filled his eyes with tears. "But how do you know it's only the smoke?"

CHAPTER 14

EARLY SUNDAY MORNING, Eftihis' three friends came over. They were gruff and pushy. Eftihis immediately sensed they were after something. He hurried out into the courtyard still wiping his neck and ears with a towel.

"What are you guys doing here?" he asked without breaking his stride. "I didn't tell you to come over."

"Just paying you a visit. We missed you."

"Kind of early, isn't it?"

"We were afraid we'd miss you ..."

Eftihis realized he would do well to let it pass, there was no point in starting anything. Besides, he was in a good mood today, and had no bones to pick with them. He could afford to be civil, seeing as they depended on him.

"Mary, make some coffee ... Three friends of mine dropped by."

The three of them came forward as a group. They had obviously made up their minds about something. Eftihis studied each of them in turn, without letting them see his surprise. He buttoned his fly in front of them, just so they wouldn't think their being there was any big deal.

"Go on in," he told them.

Inside, they looked the place over as if it were a room in a museum.

"Mary, what have you got for the fellas to eat?"

"Not a thing, and you know it."

The three guests exchanged looks, as if to say "ain't she generous," and, boy, the two of them had their routine down all right, him pretending to ask and her saying nothing doing.

“That’s all right,” Simos said. “We’ll get you some other time.”

Mary looked at Eftihis as if to say, “These are your friends?” She took some clothes off a chair and offered it. Simos sat down on the bed, and Fanis remained leaning in the doorway. When it started raining out again, he came in all the way, but stood a little to one side to show he wasn’t like the other two.

“You always wake up this late?” Simos asked.

“No, we were up early. We’ve just been ... talking.”

The three men again exchanged looks: “Like hell the lovebirds were talking.” Simos gave a sly smile. Mary made coffee and brought it as far as the door without saying a word. Eftihis took the steaming cups from her and passed them around.

“So what’s up,” he asked them brusquely.

“So how long are we going to have to wait, old buddy,” Simos said. “You promised us some sort of work ...”

“We’ve been banking on you ...” added Iordanis.

“That’s what you came about?” Eftihis asked as he tried to button his shirt collar. “It’s all set up, it’s just a matter of putting it in motion. I’ve got it all scoped out, down to the last detail.”

Once again they were unconvinced by his breezy optimism. “So you said before ...” they nodded ironically. But he spoke with the assurance of a boss.

“Besides, I wasn’t at all that happy with your performance the other day ...”

“Now that it’s just us here,” Simos asked, “tell us the truth. Did you really lose your temper or were you just putting on a show for your friend?”

“I wanted him to get rid of that stuff so we could get on with this other business.”

They sipped their coffee and smacked their lips contentedly, concluding that his swearing had been an act.

“So, I told the other two, what do you say we go for some coffee at Eftihis’,” Iordanis said. “He’s married now, he’ll have something to give us ...”

“You sure that’s all you came for?”

“And also so you could have us for lunch.”

“That’ll be kind of tough,” Eftihis answered. “We don’t have any silverware ...”

"They'll give you some over at the grill," Simos told him. "We're telling you straight out: we came to get something to eat."

Eftihis burst out laughing.

"You came to the wrong place."

"We've heard your wife's a hell of a cook. You're the only one of us with any food in the house."

"Besides, you're our boss, you promised us work ... And the other day you dumped bad meat on us, and bitched us out in the same breath."

"Yeah! You owe it to us!"

They laughed at the way they suddenly sprang their trap on him. He was the one with the dowry, he was the one starting up a business – so what was he doing just standing there gaping at them?

"Ask Mary what we've been eating."

The three of them turned to Mary, and their eyes seemed to hold a certain respect for her now. After all, that skinny girl had delivered a whole textile business into Eftihis' hands!

"It's been five days ... All we've had is a bit of tea. Except one night when some friends had us for dinner ..."

They all laughed. Surely this was another one of Eftihis' tricks.

"What about the textile factory?" Fanis asked.

"That's a different story ... Until that gets going, we don't have a drachma to spare ... She's like a mad dog with hunger ..."

"So why not come and work with us in the meantime?"

"He's right," Mary said. "Why not work till we get started?"

Eftihis took the opportunity to chew Mary out, to show his friends he didn't spend all his time gushing over his new bride, that he gave her hell when she went against his wishes.

Iordanis peered into the next room.

"Empty over there, eh?" he said with meaning.

"That's where the machines'll go. There and next door," Eftihis explained. "We got hold of three looms!"

"It'll be summertime by the time you decide to get started ... So you're going to spend every cent your father-in-law gave you ... Tell your wife to bring us some water ..."

They were starting to get to Eftihis. He went into the kitchen himself.

"What's the matter, kiddo?" he asked Mary.

"You sure cut them a lot of slack. Is that how people talk to their boss?"

Eftihis gave her a peck on the cheek and took the water in. The three fell silent when they saw him. Iordanis tried to cover up:

"We were just saying when four people have been through what we've been through together ..."

"Right," Simos pitched in, keeping up the act. "We're as close as brothers ... So when do you think you'll get this thing going?"

"Hold on a second. You and Iordanis don't know a thing about weaving. What would I need you for?"

"Hey, what about that promise you made about giving us all work?"

"You need trained specialists for looms, it's not something just anyone can do. It's not like digging ditches ..."

"You want specialists? I'm your man!" Fanis announced.

His two companions glowered at him turning on them to curry Eftihis' favor. And why had that sleazy bastard been stringing them along anyway, saying he'd have something for all three of them? What did *he* know about machines?

"Eftihis is a good egg," Iordanis said. "He'll take care of us. After all the shoe soles we've gone through together."

They settled down on the floor and started in with the wisecracks, except for Fanis, who got up and walked around the other room, as if looking to see where the looms would go.

Eftihis realized he was in a bind. He walked up and down chewing on his lip. He finally gave Mary money to buy some food.

"What the hell, let's go ahead and feed them, since they're not leaving us any choice. You've been saying you wanted to have people over ..."

"Yes, but not when they're being so pushy about it," Mary said.

"That's just how the world is today ... Plus they're hungry. You wouldn't feel bad just kicking them out in the rain?"

But he immediately tapped his finger to his temple. He had just had an excellent idea. He left Mary in the kitchen and his friends in the other room and knocked on Andonis' door. He found him writing at the table, buried under a pile of papers and books. Vangelia, lying in bed, said nothing.

"Can I interrupt you a moment?" he asked, with a feigned timidity not unmixed with respect.

"What is it?" Andonis asked without looking up.

"When do you figure we'll be picking up the looms?"

"This week, maybe the start of next."

"Couldn't we do it earlier, since we have the money?... What if somebody else gets them first?"

"Don't worry, Eftihis, I'll take care of things directly with Ioannidis."

Eftihis looked around, trying to think of a way to say what he had come to say. Over next to the cans, rain-water was trickling down the wall.

"Your cans are going to get ruined. Are you just going to let them sit there?"

Andonis looked at the moldering wall, and wondered whether Eftihis was just putting him on, knowing they were worthless. Nevertheless he expressed surprise and concern.

"I'll move them first thing. I've got to fix those rooftiles too ... Just think, the cans could rust!..."

Eftihis looked him squarely in the eye and, putting his hands over the papers on his desk, said with a twinkle:

"Look, Andonis, I know a way to straighten everything out ..."

"You do? Did you find a buyer?"

"No. I mean we can get our factory going. Then it'll be easier for you to dump them. We need to get the looms set up ... Come on out and I'll tell you what I've been thinking."

"I can't, I've got too much to do."

Eftihis told him his idea.

"Three friends of mine came by today, you already met them ... They want me to feed them. I'd like to get rid of them, of course, but I figured since I can't just throw them out, we could at least get them to do some work ... Didn't you say that's the only way to turn a profit?"

"What do you want them to do?"

"Tear down the walls, to make room for the looms ..."

"Right now?"

"Right now. It'll be dirt-cheap. One plate of food apiece ... Is that brilliant or what?"

"But I'm swamped with work today."

"Are you getting paid for this?"
"It's my article ..."
"Forget it ... Who'd read it, anyway?"
"Not today, Eftihis. I want to finish up ..."
Eftihis threw all his papers into a pile, snatched away his pencil, and snapped shut his books. "We won't get another chance like this," he told him. Andonis angrily stood up, all set to make a scene, when suddenly he felt like the entire dark wall of boxes was about to come tumbling down on his head.
"Did you hear what Eftihis said, Vangelia? He says we should tear down the walls in here to make room for the looms!"
"What are you telling me for?"
"It's all right with her, she understands ..."
"Do whatever you want ..." Vangelia said.
Eftihis ran over and excitedly informed his friends that he had work for them. He told them to go find picks and shovels so they could tear the walls down. There would be chow, plus ouzo, coffee, and a good time. Maybe even some loose change. Hadn't they come looking for work?
"Get with it!" he boomed jubilantly. "That better thing I promised is starting as of today. Time to get our factory set up!"
His three friends were less enthusiastic. They grumbled about where to find the tools, and so on, but Eftihis dispatched them to various construction sites and yards. He told them to cut the guff and make sure they came back fully equipped.
When they'd left, Eftihis ran into the kitchen and picked Mary up in his arms and gave her a kiss, beside himself with joy.
"We're really getting started! Can you believe it? The factory ... It's getting underway!"
Andonis gathered up his papers. Once again, his article remained unfinished. Yiannopoulos would be expecting him tomorrow, and he would become a standing joke. He should really get it in this issue, so he could show it to Loukis and the others. He would make sure to get it in the next issue, which of course would give him a chance to include more material. Then he tried to explain to Vangelia why it was necessary for him to agree to work with Eftihis. It was a chance for him to manage a manufacturing operation from his home. It could open all sorts of doors for him. He wouldn't even have to give up any of his other major projects.

"Why are you telling me all this?"

"So you'll understand why this disruption is necessary. We'll have to limit ourselves to just this room. We'll be setting up the looms in that room and the kitchen ..."

"Don't ask me, just do what you see fit ..."

Vangelia was still in bed. For the past two days, she hadn't asked for anything, hadn't said anything. You'd think she'd gone in for brain surgery. Andonis asked how she felt, did she want something to eat, should he call a doctor. She responded to everything with a shake of her head. Her dull, languid stare went straight through him the whole time he sat writing at the table, jumbling his thoughts and turning his fingers to ice. "I probably disgust her. She sees everything I do as a pathetic joke, a fraud. I'm not even good at putting on an act any more ..."

Eftihis came in to clear out the room before his friends returned with the picks. They would do best to start with the room with the floor-tiles, it would be stronger. "Didn't you say you needed a solid base?" His own place had a wooden floor – think of the headache it would be to pry up the boards and pour concrete. They could use it for a stockroom. "Come on, let's get this over with." He pushed the table into the corner, shoved the chairs underneath, and hefted the sofa on top. Andonis carefully folded the tablecloth, the napkins – all Vangelia's handiwork. He gathered up the other odds and ends: two pictures, a vase, a little black stuffed cat – a present for Vangelia on her birthday – the curtains and rug. Andonis discerned a glint of fury in Eftihis' eye as he pushed things around ... "A maniac," Andonis thought as he helped slide the table through the door. He looked at Vangelia. "Don't worry, we'll get better furniture when we move to our new place."

Soon the room stood empty. They collected the kitchenware and put it in a hamper, which they stowed in the laundry-room. And that was it. Now they were free to tear down the walls. Nothing could be simpler. But there was still a steady trickle of water running down the wall. The boxes were sure to be soaked on back.

"I have to fix those tiles," Andonis said worriedly.

Eftihis smiled, wondering if Andonis would ever become a normal human being.

Andonis, to demonstrate his faith in the quality and worth of his merchandise, went looking for a raincoat, saying he was climbing right up on the roof.

"Are you nuts?"

"If I don't, the cans'll rust."

Before setting out, he looked over at Vangelia, and felt a rush of pity. He quickly looked away, however; it was like looking in a mirror: his pity redounded onto himself. He went out into the rain. He went across and got a ladder from the coffeehouse, then he went to a building site on the next block. The workers must have felt sorry for him because they were happy to give him cement and a trowel. "I'll bring it right back. My roof's leaking, and I've got some merchandise and a sick wife inside."

He carried the ladder and the rest over to the courtyard. He carefully climbed up onto the roof. He scrambled up on all fours, taking a shortcut over Stathis' room to get to his. The tiles had soaked through, and broke at the least touch. It had rained all through the night. His fingers were numb, water streamed over his forehead and into his eyes. He struggled over to the corner where the cans were. It had to be done – so why did it seem so pitiful? The wind made him feel like he was on a mountain top, which was all the more desolate in the bone-chilling rain. Yet it was only the roof of his humble abode, where his Vangelia lay mired in despair, the seed torn from her womb, robbed of her every dream. How different things had been at the start ... Now here he was knocking himself out to protect a few cans of rotten meat, mostly just to keep up a pretense. He began slapping big dollops of cement on the tile joints and crevices. It took all his strength to hold on. The rain had let up, which made the work easier. But the wind was rising, and it was bitter cold up there.

Lucia, coming through the courtyard, drew up short when she saw Vangelia's room empty. She gingerly approached. Through the half-open door, among the stacked chairs, the bundles and scattered clothes, she saw Vangelia's pallid face, as if jumbled up with everything else. It wasn't until Lucia spoke that she was aware someone had come in.

"Hi, Vangelia ..."

Her distracted gaze livened somewhat, and Lucia squeezed in past the clutter. What in the world was going on?

"You're not moving, are you?" she asked.

"They're putting in a textile factory ... One of Andonis' business things ... Sit here by me, bring the chair over. No, I'm not sick, I'm just resting. It's been so crazy around here ..."

Lucia sat quietly, still trying to grasp the situation. She could hear pounding up on the roof, and the tiles creaking overhead. There was obviously someone up there, but Lucia didn't ask about it. How could anyone live in there? She looked at Vangelia and said:

"I came to say good-by. I'm leaving tomorrow ..."

"Why? You said your husband would be coming ..."

"I'm going home. He's not coming after all ..."

"But you're crying! What's wrong?"

"Anyway, tomorrow I'll be leaving for Karditsa. I've gotten nowhere since coming here. There's no point in staying on. I never found him. I went everywhere, but nobody could tell me anything. All I wanted was to ask him one simple question."

"What about?"

"I can't go on living with that man ... And I've had it with all the mud. If I'd managed to find him ..."

"Angelos, you mean?"

"... I'd have asked him, 'Should I go on living with him out there in the sticks, even if it means going out of my mind?' He's the only one who could have told me. I wanted to hear what he thought. I was nuts to get married ... But at the time everyone had disappeared. A friend of ours used to live in this apartment ... And then Angelos was convicted, and Mother started acting weird, and never went out, not even to the front gate ... I couldn't go on living here. Back then I tried to find him too, but no one would tell me where he was. They all wanted to *protect* him ... 'Tell me what to do!' I would have asked him. 'I know it'll be too much for me here, I'll die if I stay.' But I never found him, and I married someone I scarcely knew ... How can I go back to him?"

"What would you have asked Angelos?"

"What to *do*. Who else could have told me? He's partly to blame for it all ... It's a shame ... They thought I'd get him in trouble, so they hid him. I just can't believe that none of them ever see him. My father sees him all the time, he told us as much. And Ismene does too."

"No," Vangelia said. "I'm sure she doesn't."

"She's lying, I know she is."

"But that wouldn't make any sense. She asked me to find him a place to stay if he needed it. I found the perfect house, but now she doesn't know how to get in touch with him ... There was only one time, a rainy night. They stayed out together all night."

Lucia sat lost in thought. The pounding on the roof continued. She could hear someone walking or crawling around up there.

Andonis crept along, putting cement on the row of tiles along the back wall. Soon the sound of picks reached his ears. Eftihis' friends had returned and had begun tearing down the wall. Andonis' body shrank to a ball, until it took up no space at all – so light and insignificant the tiles no longer broke under his weight. The sound of Eftihis' voice barking orders reached his ears: "Start over on this side. Get moving so we can finish this afternoon." Why all the rush over an act of devastation? Andonis shrank into an even smaller shape and, as if none of it had anything to do with him, began taking extra care in applying the cement. The thud of the pickaxes quickened. He could feel it, hollow, flat and unrelenting, somewhere deep inside him. The cement filled up the crevices.

But he was suddenly struck by the absurdity of what he was doing. It made no sense to take a stand for merchandise that had gone bad, and even more so to try and convince others. Now that the cans were sheltered, their rottenness would be all the more apparent. It would become clear that, out of incompetence, he had gone in for defective goods. Then he would be held responsible for the inevitable consequences.

He raised the trowel and brought it down hard, breaking the corner off a tile. Better the roof should leak, better the cans get soaked. Then it would appear that a natural disaster, not he, was to blame. "They got rusty!" he would say. Who could be held accountable for such an unfortunate turn of events? It would be a brilliant, unlooked-for ruse for him too, in time he might even believe it himself: "What can I say? I bought some canned food, but the cans got rusted in the rain ... A bad break ... So throw me in prison, if you think I'm worth the trouble ..." He flipped over a tile, leaving a gaping hole, and knocked another one loose at the joint, then proceeded to break the entire row above the wall where the cardboard boxes were stacked.

"Andonis, where are you?"

"Up here, fixing the tiles."

"One wall's down ... It's coming right along ..."

"I'll be right down."

"Come over to the edge, the judge wants to talk to you."

Andonis crawled on his knees over to the edge of the tile roof. Harilaos stood in the middle of the courtyard, his raised face streaming with rainwater.

"Any news to report?"

"Unfortunately I haven't tracked him down yet. He's just disappeared," Andonis exclaimed by way of excuse.

"Ah, but I've discovered where he is," the judge declared with pride.

"Where? What did he say?"

"Nothing. I want us to go see him together one of these days ..."

"What was that? I didn't quite ..."

"I said we should go together ... It'd be better if we both talked to him ..." Harilaos repeated.

"Not today anyway. I've got too much to do ... Some other day ..."

"If you would truly like to help," the judge told him reprovingly, "it had better be soon. His behavior indicates he's in some kind of danger. If you're having second thoughts, just tell me so I can let your friend know not to expect anything ..."

"Don't worry, I'll be honest with you. You let me know when you want us to go ..."

"What are you doing up there, anyway?"

Andonis answered so only he could hear, "I'm making a fool of myself, a most solemn and excruciating exercise ..." Then he shouted down:

"I'm fixing the tiles, our roof's leaking ..."

"We'll be in touch," said the judge, and slowly climbed the stairs.

Andonis went back to work, smashing more tiles: "Better disaster than failure." Then he started crawling back the way he came, slapping cement on the tiles he'd broken in passing.

He cautiously climbed down off the roof, and cast a guilty look in through the window of his room. Vangelia was in bed with the door closed. From the next room came the maniacal crash of Eftihis' pickax. He rushed off to return the ladder and trowel.

"Thanks, you saved my life ..." he told them with a grateful smile.

Upon returning, he found that the wall between the kitchen and the middle room was gone. Simos and Iordanis were tossing out the bricks while Fanis shoveled dirt. Eftihis was overseeing, beaming and covered with dust. "We'll be finished by afternoon," he told him.

Andonis did his best to act pleased. He offered a few useful bits of advice – where to put in a beam to support the roof, how to pile up the bricks and dirt. Eftihis took him aside.

"I wonder about you sometimes, Andonis," he told him sharply. "You keep making promises to the judge. But we need Thodoros ... Be careful you don't do anything stupid. If you don't clear all this up soon, I'll have to talk to him myself. We can't let this get in the way of our plans. Watch your step ... You have to choose: either you help the judge, or we get this textile thing going."

Andonis said nothing. In despair he counted the strokes of the picks and calculated how long it took to tear down a house. Simos and Iordanis were working in unison, Fanis never looked up, and Eftihis thoughtfully chewed on a match.

"Nice trick you pulled, getting us to work for nothing," grumbled Simos.

"If you don't like it, just give your pick to Fanis and leave ..."

Simos glumly kept at it, while Iordanis quickened his pace to get on Eftihis' good side. He even turned around and looked at Eftihis to let him know he was giving it everything he had. Andonis wrested open the door between rooms, which was blocked with dirt. Vangelia, motionless, lost, wore the same vacant stare.

"What can I bring you to eat?"

"Nothing."

You could barely move around in there now, everything was so jumbled together. The courtyard glistened with rain. "The rain'll keep up a while longer," Andonis thought, examining the wall of boxes. He tried straightening up a bit and making a space for himself. He pushed his chair over by the wardrobe and spread out his notes. Vangelia couldn't see him when he was sitting there, so he found it easier to relax. But where to begin? Lest he lose any time, he pulled some invoices out of his briefcase and entered them in an accounts book. Then he remembered his essay. But the crashing of the picks, and Vangelia's empty eyes, made work impossible. Across from him loomed the dark cartons full of cans. "I'll think it all through as soon as I catch my breath ..."

When it came time to eat, Eftihis called his friends over. He'd gotten five servings from the grill, spread newspapers in the empty room, and everyone sat down to eat. He shouted to Andonis to join them, but the latter declined, waving his papers.

"Put down the fifty-two forty I paid at the grill. It's our first expense ... Put it under labor."

Andonis didn't eat anything, but that didn't bother him. He wanted to take advantage of the break to collect his thoughts. There was dirt everywhere, dust choked the air, leaving only a gray disorder, like after an air raid. "I wonder what Vangelia makes of all this."

After the men ate and had a smoke, the work recommenced. Iordanis asked Mary for a pie tin or something. He'd barely touched his food. He said he was going to save it for the brats at home.

"You thought I was making it up when I said we hadn't eaten since the last time we worked," he said.

The work went swiftly. Mary's kitchen wall came down next. The hearths and sinks were done away with a single blow of the pick.

"Good going, fellas. I'm proud of you."

Mary brought coffee and a pitcher of water. Once again they stretched out on the floor to rest, and to drink the coffee the boss' wife had made them.

"Got any cigarettes?" Fanis asked Simos.

"Ask your employer ..."

This didn't anger Eftihis because he realized that Simos' gibe concealed a plea. At bottom, isn't that what he was – their employer – since they'd asked him to hire them for his new business? Fanis was silent. He sat leaning against the wall, winding and unwinding a string around his fingers, as if he'd taken refuge in the privacy of his own thoughts. His whole attitude testified to his having done time in prison. Eftihis went over again to check how much space they had now the walls were down. Andonis was standing motionless among the mounds of dirt and bricks, in total bewilderment, as if amid the wreckage of some great disaster.

"What are you doing here?" Eftihis demanded.

"Seeing where the machines will go. It's important to get the arrangement right so we don't waste time with a lot of unnecessary movement ..."

"Tomorrow I'll have them take out the dirt and plaster things up. I want everything to be neat and clean ... We'll need lights, too. So where are we going to put the machines?"

"That's what I'm trying to figure out."

Out of the corner of his eye, Eftihis caught sight of Fanis in the courtyard, heading for the front gate. He immediately took his leave of Andonis, saying "We'll talk tomorrow," and went out. Fanis was keeping close to the walls, his collar turned up and his hands in his pockets. Clearly he was trying to elude Eftihis, which was why he had slunk out. Eftihis kept on his tail. Fanis turned a corner, and started heading for Petralona!

"I've got you this time," Eftihis muttered to himself. They crossed the bridge and Fanis paused, pressed against a wall. What would he do now? Her house was on the next street over. Eftihis hid behind a pole and waited. Then he had to dart into a doorway because Fanis had a change of heart and started to backtrack. Then he stopped, and again began walking toward Elpida's street. But he didn't get past the corner. This time Eftihis leapt behind a pile of crates.

Fanis finally made up his mind. He started down the street toward her door. Eftihis took cover behind a truck. There was light in her little basement window. Why didn't he knock on the pane? How long was he going to stay there, standing flush against the wall? Someone went past. Fanis walked on a bit and came back. "He won't be able to play innocent with me anymore." As soon as her door opened, Eftihis would put a stop to this farce once and for all. Was Elpida expecting him? Fanis stood there for a long time. But in the end he didn't go in. He walked away, passing by the truck Eftihis had hid behind.

"Got you!" Eftihis cried. "You can't weasel out of this one."

Fanis jumped, but in his surprise made no attempt at escape. Eftihis had a firm grip on his shoulder.

"So, old buddy, what have you got to say for yourself?"

"Nothing. I came over, but ..."

Eftihis eyed him closely, without loosening his grip.

"Why didn't you go in? If you're in love with her, why couldn't you bring yourself to knock on her window?"

"Huh?..."

"What if she was expecting you? You go all the way to her door and then just walk off?"

He let go. There was an ember of fear in Fanis' eyes.

"Now we can talk openly, without lying."

"It sounds to me like you're more in love with her than I am, Eftihis."

"That's no concern of yours. Anyway, we're not even in competition."

"We aren't? Then what did you follow me for? What are you doing here?"

"So you do love her? That's all I'm trying to find out. I warned you, you should have let me know. Do whatever you want with her, but I've got to know."

"What I do is my business," Fanis told him flatly.

"You want me to go get her so you can talk to her?"

"If that's what you really want to do ..."

Eftihis grabbed him and together they marched across the empty bridge. A cold wind was blowing, and the moon shone in the rain-cleansed heavens. He asked plainly and calmly, friend to friend:

"Why didn't you knock on her door? What if she was expecting you?"

"She wasn't," Fanis said.

"She's always there alone. Why'd you chicken out? Come on, tell me. I won't hold it against you. Have you ever thought how hard it must be for a single girl living by herself ... But the fact that you had second thoughts, and ended up walking away, means you really do love her. Am I right? Say something! To tell you the truth, I'm glad you're clamming up. I'd like for someone to be in love with Elpida. But really in love, not just messing around ... So tell me what you're thinking."

Fanis still couldn't speak.

"What do you say we go for some wine somewhere," Eftihis suggested.

"Why not just go sit on the hill for a bit."

Once they were seated up on the rocks, Eftihis lost patience and shook the other by the shoulder.

"What are you waiting for? Speak up!" "What do you want me to say?"

Eftihis was feeling expansive. He rested his hand on Fanis' shoulder, and began an old story, and a long one.

"I once had a friend named Kostis ..." He let loose with an unstoppable flood of words: Kostis, the war, Elpida, that German truck, the loaf of bread, his mother ...

"So Elpida is like one of the family to me. It matters to me how she lives and what she eats and where she sleeps. That's why I want you to tell me if you really love her. It'd make me feel a lot better if you did, because right now I feel like I've abandoned her."

Fanis, as if he'd been waiting for just that moment, slowly said:

"I can tell you have the first part of the story right, but you mixed up the last part. You're the one in love with her, and in a bad way too, not just because your friend got killed. It suits you to tell yourself you're protecting her, whereas the fact is you plain love that girl, with or without the rest of it. Aren't I right?"

"You're an idiot, Fanis. You didn't understand a word of what I just said."

"Could be ... But you do love her."

"If I loved her I would have told her. I might even have married her. No, there's no way ... You don't know what you're talking about ... Why wouldn't I have told her?"

"How should I know? Like I know why I didn't knock on her door tonight ..."

"I was sorry you didn't, I mean it. It would have made her happy. Though I'm not sure I would have been able to keep from jumping out and socking you in the jaw – but what would you have cared?"

Fanis stood up and they climbed down the bald, stony hill. Eftihis was sure Fanis had Elpida's smile before him. Eftihis turned to him and told him in a firm voice:

"Once we get the factory going, Elpida will be working there too. You'll see her every day. You'll have to show her the ropes.

But you've got to promise me you'll do right by her. If you're just looking for a good time, you'd better find someone else. The world's full of women."

"You have my word," Fanis said.

They shook hands, as if to close an important deal, and went their separate ways. Eftihis arrived home whistling.

THE COURTYARD WAS EMPTY. Everyone had gone in. Angelos checked to make sure he'd put everything back as it was. There could be nothing testifying to his having been there. The boards had been nailed back in place, the newspapers stood in their corner. He saw things with utmost clarity now. He had squandered so many nights out of fear. But tonight he would leave. He would figure out his next step once he was on the street. It would be suicide to stay there. He tore up the map he'd drawn of the surrounding area. "People don't escape through tunnels in real life," he said aloud, for himself to hear. "All those calculations were a waste of time. They didn't lead anywhere." Once more he wound the scarf around his neck. That was all he had to take with him. He left the flashlight Stathis had given him on the table. He would leave by the window. Unscrewing the lock would only make for needless effort and noise. If the door were found unlocked and the room empty, who knows what suspicions might be aroused. Once on the outside, it would be easier for him to learn what had become of Stathis. "I'd almost gotten used to being alone and desperate," he said to himself as he listened to see if Andonis had gone to sleep.

He opened the shutter. Nothing could be easier. "Don't let me down, brain," he thought, "you're all I have. Don't let me down, I'm depending on you." He stepped through and was in the courtyard. He closed the shutters behind him. The interior of the room seemed empty and very far away. He went into the laundry-room and drank many palmfuls of water, until he felt its cooling influence throughout his body. Then he washed his face and toweled off with the hem of his coat. He moved slowly toward the passageway. His house, the stairs and the flowers were so near he could touch them. Ismene's window was dark. The front gate was open. He felt the night's endless streets drawing him from the stoop ...

Before he could step down, however, someone came barging around the corner and plowed right into him.

It was Stathis.

"Where are you off to?"

"Leaving," Angelos said. "How long did you expect me to wait for you?"

"Come on, I've got some news for you. You can leave later if you want."

He drew him back inside. They crossed the courtyard without being seen. While Stathis searched for his key, a shudder ran through Angelos. Stathis opened the door and turned on the light. Angelos had never seen the room lit up like that. He closed the door behind them, and the turning of the key in the lock struck Angelos as a portent.

"Where've you been all this time," he asked in a whisper.

"Talk naturally," Stathis told him.

"What's going on?"

"I found Elly! That's why I've been away so long ... Were you frightened?"

"Yes," Angelos said for the first time in answer to that crucial question.

"I thought about you, but it couldn't be helped."

There was a knock at the shutter.

"Stathis!" It was Ismene's voice.

Angelos stood behind the door. When Stathis opened it, it concealed him entirely.

"You're back!" she said breathlessly.

"I just got in."

"I saw the light and came straight over. You don't know how many times I've knocked ..."

"I had to leave suddenly for Yannina."

"Any news of Angelos?"

"No ..."

"Did you tell him I wanted to see him? Are you afraid of me finding out about him? You always smile when I ask, as if you're not telling the truth. Are you protecting him? Do you think I'm a danger to him? Look, you're smiling that same way right now ..."

Stathis was no doubt waiting to see if Angelos would stick his head out from behind the door, and he was indeed wearing a smile, imagining Ismene's surprise.

"He's all right," he told her. "I saw him tonight and suggested we come back here together ..."

But Angelos didn't come out. The door stood motionless. Stathis' tone became more serious as he said:

"Don't act like it's my fault. It's not like I have him tied up someplace. He can come see you whenever he likes. It'd be easy ..."

"So why doesn't he?"

Ismene thought Stathis was making fun of her, and broke into tears.

"What should I tell him when I see him," Stathis asked.

"Nothing," Ismene said reproachfully as she went off.

Stathis closed the door, leaving Angelos exposed.

"Why didn't you say anything?"

"Like what? I would have felt so ridiculous."

The room's warmth had vanished with the sound of Ismene's sobbing. Stathis' arrival presented Angelos with a major dilemma. It was as if they were meeting now for the first time after many years. Stathis slapped him on the shoulder – "Hey, sorry I left you all alone like that ..." – and told him to sit down on the very chair he'd all but perished in during those last few horrifying days. The naked bulb hurt his eyes, a thousand hammers were pounding in his head. How could he go on living in this cramped room, especially now that he'd torn up the plans for his escape?

"Why don't I go get us something to eat," Stathis said.

"Forget it, there's nothing open this time of night."

Stathis leaned back on the bed in his clothes, his hands clasped behind his head, and told Angelos to bring his chair over so they could talk. He looked rested, his eyes were radiant. It was the first time he hadn't wanted to go right to sleep.

"I never expected to see Elly again. And by such an incredible coincidence too. She hasn't changed a bit. Oh, sure, it's been twelve years – but imagine, unchanged! She was only twenty when I knew her. You remember her at all?"

"Sure."

"She asked me about you and Vassilis. Naturally, I didn't tell her he was killed, but she guessed as much ... Twelve years ... I couldn't help it, I had to go. Angelos' been in tighter jams before, I told myself ... Haven't you?"

"I guess so."

"Where would you have gone if I hadn't run into you at the gate?"

"I hadn't thought that far ahead."

"Have you ever been on a plane?"

"Never."

"It's wonderful, you're there before you know it. Of course I was afraid I wouldn't get there in time. That afternoon I'd gone to the printing press and started work as usual. At some point they gave me a pile of cables from around the country. The second one was from Yannina. 'Bus number such and such,' it said, 'while completing its run from Yannina to Dodonis, crashed into a ravine twelve meters deep. Among the injured were ...' So while I was setting the names of the injured, my eye suddenly stopped at 'Elly Karela, 32 years old, teacher ...' My fingers froze on the keyboard, I couldn't see straight. I instantly got up. 'I'm leaving,' I told the foreman. Without really knowing what I was doing I called to see when there was a flight for Yannina, and the airline told me there was a bus for the airport in five minutes. I hopped a cab and managed to catch it. I didn't even stop to wash my hands. How could I have contacted you?"

"You couldn't have."

"I spent the night at the hospital because she was in a coma. I recognized her at first glance, even wrapped in bandages the way she was. I didn't see anyone else ask about her. She came to the next day. I told the doctor I was a relative. The funny thing was she remembered me right off. 'Thank you, Stathis,' she whispered, as if not so much as an hour had passed. But how's that for coincidences, eh? If it had been anyone else doing the cables that night ... I might not even have seen it later, because lots of times the small domestic stories get dropped during paste-up when some big new story comes along. We talked some more the following day. Luckily it wasn't anything too serious. A concussion, and a fractured hand. I told her I just happened to be in Yannina, and that I'd read about it in a local paper. Yannina's a pretty place ... She might be down to Athens in a month or so ... She said she'd write ... How long was I gone?"

"Four days."

"I went back to the hospital this afternoon with a big bouquet of flowers. You should have seen the doctor's jaw drop ... I'm sure he knew, but who cares? If she comes down you'll get to see her. She's just the same, after twelve years ..."

Stathis fell silent and closed his eyes, perhaps to contemplate the meaning of those twelve long years. Soon he asked Angelos:

"Hey, what do you say we take a walk? It'll be nice out after all the rain."

"But ..."

"What's the big deal? You were about to go out anyway, weren't you? Without even knowing where you were going ..."

"I was trying to escape ... trying to get away from danger ..."

"Let's go talk some more on the street ... No one'll bother us."

"It's kind of late. Let's just stay here."

Stathis didn't insist. He was feeling pleasantly disoriented. He would go back to work the following day, knowing that Elly would be down in a month.

"So how about you, Angelos?"

"What do you mean?"

"You know, how long are you going to stay in hiding? Are you going to spend the rest of your life here, or in some other room like it? That doesn't sound like the Angelos I knew ..."

"You're right. Only I haven't found the solution yet."

"And what about tonight?"

"I'll stay here a few more days and give it some more thought."

CHAPTER 15

HIS ABSURD WAIT FOR RAIN wore Andonis out. Two weeks had gone by and still not a drop had fallen. Every morning he would check the sky and see clouds massing but, right when it looked like the heavens were about to open up, it seemed to change its mind and instead there would unfold a bright expanse of blue. Then came days of a gray emptiness. The room stood empty. Eftihis' friends had carted out all the debris, done the necessary plastering, and mopped the tile floor. Everything was ready, and still the machinery had not arrived. One small wrinkle remained to be ironed out before they could take possession. Eftihis came and went carrying his sovereigns. The tightly bound parcel was filthy, its newspaper wrapping crumbled in his hands, it looked ready to fall apart at any moment. But he would not hand over a drachma of it until he saw the machines loaded onto the truck.

Andonis decided to resume work as a salesman. He spent most of his time on the cans and a number of other unprofitable tasks. A few days earlier, when the sun was out, he proposed to Vangelia that they take a walk, but she said she wasn't in the mood. "Fine, it's up to you ..." Now that they were without a kitchen, Andonis had brought home prepared food a few times, but they hadn't sat down to eat together and the food went untouched. Other times Vangelia would set a plate before him while he was writing, and he would eat mechanically, wiping his chin with some piece of scrap paper covered with numbers. He went unshaven and unwashed. The room hadn't changed since that Sunday when they had haphazardly piled everything in. Vangelia went in and out without speaking, which may have been why the room seemed so empty, in such disarray. She no longer cared whether his shirt was dirty or if he needed clean socks. She didn't even bother with the tablecloth anymore. There was dirt everywhere, the table was covered with leftovers, their bed was never made. The canned food was ruined beyond salvaging and – what was even worse – without good cause.

"Why did Ismene let the flowers die?"

"I guess she's given up hope."

"So you think they had something to do with Angelos?"

"That was my sense of it."

"Strange ... They made the courtyard so much prettier."

"A lot of things are pretty as long as we love them."

"That's the truth," Andonis said, just to say something.

He stalled a bit longer, then reminded her:

"Don't wait for me this afternoon, I'm not sure when I'll finish up ..."

"Come whenever you like," she said indifferently.

Andonis couldn't stand it anymore.

"Vangelia, how long can we go on like this?"

"I'm not getting in your way, am I? You're completely free. Isn't that how you wanted it?"

"How long can we go on living separate lives? Even if we were just sharing a place, we'd say good morning, and talk about the weather ..."

"Is there something troubling you again? Some outstanding debt? Don't worry, if anyone comes looking for you, I'll tell them you're away on business ..."

Where had her eyes gotten that hard look? As if it were someone else talking, someone he didn't know. Andonis left with his head bowed. "I've lost the battle in here," he thought to himself. "That leaves the streets."

Eftihis called to him in the courtyard, and told him with much gravity that he had discussed the matter of money with Thodoros. "He seems ready and willing to help us."

"On what terms?"

"I couldn't discuss any of that without you ... He'll be expecting us tonight at ten-thirty."

"Where?"

I can't tell you. We'll go together. You're starting to worry me.

I'll meet you at a quarter to. And all we're going to talk about is the loan ... This whole business with the judge has got to stop. If we could get Thodoros off the hook somehow, the loan would be in our pockets."

"Come off it, Eftihis."

"Just to get things rolling. So, I'll see you tonight in Kaningos at a quarter to ten ..."

They parted company, and Andonis was standing at the bus stop when he felt the judge's hand on his back.

"I would deeply appreciate it if you could tell me when you'll be free to pay your friend Thodoros a visit. This evening, perhaps?"

Andonis was at a loss for words. But as the silence dragged on, he decided it would be best to speak openly to the elderly gentleman standing solemnly before him.

"Listen, sir. What would be accomplished by our meeting him? I am a man of business, a man bound by financial obligations. I won't conceal from you the fact that, although I am moved by the whole story with Angelos, I find myself in straitened circumstances right now. At this very moment I am teetering on the brink of disaster ... I am a ... a ..."

"You can have whatever opinion of yourself you like. I, however, happen to need your help ... Have no fear, this is not a financial matter ... Would this afternoon suit you?"

Receiving no answer, Harilaos went on in a confidential tone, choosing each word with great care:

"I saw Angelos a few days ago. I told him that you were acquainted with this vital witness ... I trust Andonis, he told me. If he chooses to get involved, he'll manage to do something, I know it ... He's a true friend ..."

"Angelos said that?"

"Yes, but don't tell anyone. I meet him in secret, no one knows ..."

"It's strange he'd say that," Andonis told him. "Angelos should know that his case doesn't hinge on the testimony of one or even a hundred witnesses. The problem's much more pervasive than that. If that's what he's banking on, he's either become quite naive, or he's let fear get the better of him ..."

"Can that be ruled out, after so many years?"

"No, it's out of the question. Angelos always had exceptionally sound judgement ..."

"In other words, you believe that if there were some slight hope of his getting off, he should disregard it because of general conditions? That's an odd way of looking at things, I must say ... I'll tell Angelos when I see him. He'll be amused. One of these days, perhaps ..."

"No, don't say anything. Just hello from me ... And tell him not to give up ..."

"Fine ... Give it some more thought ... I'll be in Zaharatos' tonight, from seven on. Thodoros spends a good deal of his time at a place near there. If you feel like it, drop by when you're free ... Good day."

The judge went on his way, and Andonis stood there on the street for a while without moving.

THE BLOW TORCH CONTINUED to send out its sharp flashes of light. Now that Aliki had beheld its cold flame with her naked eye, whenever its sharp white light fell flickering on her window, she felt herself strangely troubled. Sometimes it seemed like an invitation tapping at her window. What was the name of the man in the dark goggles? All three of the men working there wore the same caps, and their faces were always covered with dark goggles and grease-marks. One of them smiled at her whenever she walked by, but she couldn't figure out which it had been that afternoon when she found herself trapped by the wrought iron, the tangled oxygen-hoses, and the iron-melting flame.

She slowly went down the long covered passageway and knocked at Voula's door. Someone was working alone in back this time too. No one answered the door. Instead of leaving, Aliki advanced a few more steps and came out in the courtyard. Tonight there was no wrought iron, the shed was dark, and the man in the mask had his back turned. Was he the same one? As she approached , he swung around, startled.

"What are you doing here?"

"I'm looking for Voula ... I'm Aliki."

"No one's inside, they went out."

He kneeled back down and went on with his welding. Hadn't

he recognized her yet? It looked like him, he was almost the same as the one with the flat iron mask and the strong arms.

"Don't look at the flame, it'll blind you."

"I'm Aliki ..."

"You don't want to ruin those pretty eyes of yours, do you?"

"Do you always wear those goggles?"

"Yes, I'd go blind if I didn't ... Especially now I have you in front of me too ..."

"You really mean that?"

"I swear. No matter how dark the glass is, I can see in front of me."

It had been dark the first time, and she hadn't noticed how much handsomer he became when he smiled. After his embrace, she had shut her eyes and hadn't seen anything. Now he was looking at her somewhat strangely. But Aliki took courage.

"What time do you get off?"

"Eight o'clock. Careful you don't step on the tubes."

He knelt back down and lit the torch. The courtyard flickered in its light, and Aliki studied his mouth and the cut of his jaw. He was assuredly the same one. But why didn't he speak to her? Maybe he was angry with her for staying away so long. She stood watching for some time, as he went about his welding. Suddenly he straightened up and, raising his fiery torch, pointed toward the shed. Frightened, she didn't know what to do, she only saw she couldn't escape this enormous man with the sealed face. She tried to say something to him, but as he murmured to her in his gentle voice, his iron arms led her into the shadows.

"You see, I came back!" Aliki told him afterwards.

"Came back? You mean you've been here before?"

"Then it wasn't you? You don't remember me?"

"After tonight, I'll never forget you!" he told her, laughing his gentle laugh, that made the whole shed shake.

ANDONIS SAW BY A LARGE CLOCK that it was seven-thirty.

He hurried over to Syntagma. He saw the judge through the glass of the old coffeehouse, calmly drinking his coffee and watching the door. Andonis hesitated out on the street. He continued on to the next corner, then came back and stopped at one end of the front window. Angelos' father was waiting for him. He should probably go in and ask if they could put off their meeting with Thodoros because something unexpected had come up. "I'd be happy to tomorrow ..."

But as he entered, the judge rose to his feet.

"I knew you'd come ... I'm so pleased to know that you really are a friend. Angelos told me as much ... Let's go catch him before he leaves ..."

The judge's eyes emanated a tranquil joy. He clutched Andonis' arm and led him out onto the sidewalk. He hailed a cab. Now what? "To Patissia," the judge told the driver.

"A true friend ... So there's still hope ... I keep telling my children, there's still such a thing as compassion and honesty in the world, you just have to be willing to dig for it ... By the way, that's one of the peculiarities of our age ... People have tucked their positive qualities away in a safe place, you can't find them out in the business arena ..."

"That's very true ..."

"We old folk are more optimistic. Isn't it strange?"

Harilaos clutched Andonis' hand firmly, smiling and gazing into his eyes. His other hand rested on his shoulder; another moment and he'd be stroking his head. He had difficulty speaking, as if short of breath.

"You look tired ... Don't worry, your troubles will soon be behind you ... I'm so glad ... I knew I could rely on you ... I was convinced of it ... How's your wound, does it ever give you trouble? You should be more careful ... I know what daredevils you all are, but a little prudence never hurt. You've had to cope with so much uncertainty in your lives, all of you ... Was it a serious wound?"

The old man's tone quickly changed.

"How long since you've seen him?"

"Not since back then."

"He hasn't changed. A little haggard, yes, but as for his morale ..."

Andonis bit his lip to keep from screaming. The taxi sped through Omonia. The old man was still holding on to his hand. Andonis couldn't meet his eyes.

"All those years living on the same courtyard and we never met ..." Harilaos said.

"It's just one of those things. I was always so busy ... And I was afraid it would just cause you pain if I reminded you ..." stammered Andonis.

"Ismene was all I had. But now I'm afraid she's gotten tired of waiting too. It's only natural, it's been such a long time ... I've never given up hope, I assure you. Never. What about you, Andonis?"

Andonis didn't know how to answer. He gazed out at the street, the rushing automobiles and people.

"You are all very tired," the old man went on. "Perhaps no generation has had to go through what you've been through ... Which is why you're still so young, I'd even call you children ... My generation was wearing stiff collars and carrying a cane by the age of twenty-five ... So tell me, Andonis, what are your feelings toward Angelos?"

"I love Angelos like a brother, I admire him," Andonis said candidly.

Finally he could meet the old man's eyes. They were avid as a young child's, radiant with the inextinguishable longing of their patient conviction.

"You of course know him better than I do. For all my attempts to get close to my children, I was always their father ... I lost my daughter ... Do you have any idea what Lucia was so angry about? Do you know why she left without saying good-by? Now where was I ... You know him better than I do because the two of you spent your youths together. That's an important distinction. So do you think he's all right?"

"But I thought you said ..."

"Yes, yes, he *is*. What I'm asking is, do you think he's strong enough? Have you ever doubted that he'd pull through?"

"Never."

"That's what I was hoping to hear ... You *are* a true friend!"

Harilaos told the driver to stop. He paid, and they got out and walked down a gloomy sidestreet. The area was new to Andonis, but the old man seemed to know it as if he went there daily.

"This is his brother's house, he comes here a lot," he said, and began knocking on a door.

Andonis went limp. If they found Thodoros, the whole business with Eftihis would be off, and his various promising prospects would evaporate. Worst of all, the last door open to him when the hour of prison struck would close for good. No one seemed to be at home, but the old man wasn't going anywhere.

"Keep your head when you talk to him," he advised. "No need to raise your voice."

He knocked again. Andonis was praying the house would remain silent and dark forever. But Harilaos kept at it.

"They must be out," Andonis said.

"They often eat at a taverna nearby ... Let's go see."

Andonis followed him. At the taverna, the old man was quickly in and out.

"He must be at his attorney's office. His name's Xanthis."

He called another cab. "Akadimias Street," he told the driver, indicating they were in a hurry. He told Andonis that there were a number of matters Thodoros was involved in there and that he stopped by every evening.

"We'll find him, don't worry. He won't slip through our clutches."

"I only have till nine," Andonis said softly. "Then I have to be at a business meeting ..."

"We'll have found him by then." Harilaos again asked the driver to hurry.

The entrance to the building was deserted, as was the hallway of the floor where the elevator let them off. Why do your knees go weak when you are about to knock on certain doors?

"You better go in and ask for him," the judge said. "If I give my name, he'll slip out of here too."

Andonis opened the door, quietly went in, and shut the door after him. There was a girl seated at a typewriter. In the next office, the lawyer sat bent over his large desk, surrounded by bookcases and armchairs. Thodoros was nowhere to be seen.

"Can I help you?" the receptionist asked.

Andonis responded with professional self-assurance.

"I'm offering some exceptional items at incredibly low monthly payments ... Perhaps you'd be interested in ..."

He snapped open his briefcase:

" ... a smart spring dress? Here, I have some samples ..."

"No, thank you."

He quickly left, without insisting. Out in the hallway, he told

Harilaos that Thodoros wasn't there – which was true – nor was he expected.

After that, they went to two or three coffeehouses, a basement *ouzeri*, and finally arrived at Thodoros' house. "Maybe he's sick," said Harilaos. Luckily, however, he wasn't at home either, and Andonis courteously took his leave, giving a false name. He followed the judge everywhere. He couldn't complain. If he were to run into him, on the other hand ... They went to two other offices, where Andonis pulled the same stunt with the clothes samples, but Thodoros was nowhere to be found. Andonis stole glances at his watch, and the judge was visibly perturbed. When they asked in a pastry-shop, the waiter told them the overweight gentleman with the puffy eyes had left just a short while before. "What a pity!" cried Andonis.

"Let's go to Faliron," Harilaos proposed. "He goes there quite often."

"I'd say the odds are against it." Andonis said. "Besides, at nine I've got to ..."

Andonis realized there was no way Thodoros could be in Faliron, since he had an appointment with Eftihis in a quarter of an hour. The two matters, he reasoned, had nothing to do with one another, and he had no business disclosing that he himself would be meeting Thodoros shortly. It was an unrelated matter, of a wholly different nature. That night's meeting was critical. If they could convince him to contribute money, the textile business would really get off the ground, which might prove just the break he'd been waiting for. It would be easier to talk to Thodoros about Angelos' case at some later date. It had already been eight years, and putting it off for another week wouldn't make all that much difference. Besides, he doubted it would have any effect. It was unlikely that Thodoros would be moved to retract his testimony. "I followed wherever the judge led tonight," Angelos told himself. "Is it my fault we didn't find him?"

"Have you seen Angelos recently?" Andonis asked once they were back on the sidewalk.

"He's doing well ... Quite well ..."

"How's he been living? Has he been in hiding all these years?"

"What a dreadful thought, Andonis! How could you think such a thing? Can you imagine Angelos living that way?"

"I mean just for safety's sake."

"That would be the worst possible sentence ..."

Time passed. They would not be finding him that night.

"What now?" asked the old man.

"It's ten past nine. Let's leave it for another time ..."

"I've worn you out, Andonis. But we'll find him one of these days. And who knows, maybe his conscience will have awakened. I believe that everyone hides a grain of humanity inside himself ... As for you, you should take it easier ... I'll tell Angelos about our search tonight. He'll be extremely happy to hear it. He's mentioned you quite often ... I'm anxious to settle this matter before it's too late. And if you see Ismene, do what you can to boost her morale. She's seemed a little discouraged lately. Tell her that Angelos' just fine, that he loves her, and that he'll be home soon ... Emphasize that last part. And as for you, my boy, if you ever need anything at all, don't hesitate to come to me, I'll do whatever I can, even if it's a matter of money. Perhaps you're a little short now ..."

"No, no ..." said Andonis with sudden panic. "I'm all set ..."

"If you need some, please, here, take this ..."

"No, really, thank you," Andonis said quickly. "Good-night."

"Good-night, my boy. And thank you ..."

Andonis headed off in the opposite direction. Had what he'd done with the old man been out-and-out deceit? He tried not to think about it – about the old man, about Angelos, and least of all about himself. He hurriedly made his way to Kaningos Square. He arrived on the button – and there was Eftihis, waiting for him. They met Thodoros a little farther down, and immediately began financial negotiations.

CHAPTER 16

ON SUNDAY, EFTIHIS woke up at daybreak and went directly into the large room to admire his new looms. The machines stood as he had left them the night before. The accessories were still in their boxes or lying on the floor. For the past several days, ever since they were delivered and became officially his, he hadn't slept a wink. He closely examined the iron frames, carefully ran his hand along them without disturbing anything. He felt a reverence for those mysterious yet so precious objects. So what if he still didn't know the first thing about them. The engineer would be there the following day to assemble them, and by week's end the place would be a hive of frenzied activity. Until then, however, it meant lots of fretting and running around.

Eftihis opened the windows. The courtyard was quiet, the sky radiant, the looms solid and comfortably settled in. As soon as he heard noises in the next room, he knocked on the door.

"Come in," came Andonis' voice from within.

Eftihis' jaw dropped when he saw Andonis writing on top of a pile of papers and books. Vangelia was either sleeping or pretending to be, it was all the same to him.

"Didn't you hear me? I've been out here for hours."

"I heard you, I just wanted to finish this article."

Eftihis scowled.

"Come on out and let's have a talk."

Andonis followed him out. They walked silently over to the far end of the room, which now seemed to extend indefinitely.

"What are they giving you for that? I'll pay you to chuck it."

"I'm not expecting to get paid."

"Are you crazy! We're getting a business started here ..."

"I'll explain it to you another time ... Anyway, I've arranged everything: they deliver the thread tomorrow, and I've been running around to all the different departments for permits, plus I'm already lining up orders. What's it to you whether I write or not?"

"Let's get one thing straight, Andonis. This here is our life. Everything's resting on your shoulders. Tell me straight out, are you up for this? It's not just something we're doing to pass the time ... You should be sweating and lying awake over it, thinking about it when you eat and when you take a piss ... It shouldn't be out of your mind for a moment. If you're always writing articles ..."

Andonis assured him he knew his way around the world of textiles, and that everything would be done as efficiently as possible.

"Have you ever started something like this from scratch before? No? Then you don't know squat. I don't need a clerk, they're a dime a dozen ..."

"I know how you feel. We're just at the beginning, and the picture's a little fuzzy yet. Rome wasn't built in a day."

Eftihis' tone softened.

"All right," he said. "So today's the day everyone who wants a job will be coming by for you to interview, like you said. Choose whoever you think is best. Write off anyone who doesn't cut it whether they're friends of mine or not. There's only one girl I want you to be sure to keep."

"Fine ..."

"It's not what you think ... Find something for her to do, something she can learn, just to put her on the payroll."

Then they had a serious talk about orders, raw materials, the finisher and warper, and related topics.

"When are the workers coming?"

"Around eleven."

"That leaves me time to do some more writing ... He's been after me for an article, and I promised him. It'll be good for business too. It's a serious journal ..."

Eftihis laughed and slapped him on the shoulder, as if granting him permission. "So run along and finish it up."

Andonis happily shut himself up in his room again. Eftihis went back inside and found Mary still in bed. He told her the days of lounging in bed and daydreaming were behind them. He paced in the courtyard while she got dressed. Aliki went by. "Hi there, baby-doll," he said to her under his breath. Too bad she doesn't work in a textile mill, he thought. He walked up and down, until he finally went and sat on the step of the laundry-room.

"I'm ready," Mary told him.

"Run off for an hour or two to your father's, or some friend's house, wherever you want ... Come back around noon ... You haven't been over to see your family in quite a while."

Mary went off to find somewhere to pass the time. Eftihis tore open an empty cigarette box and wrote: "Wait here." He pinned it to his door, locked up, and left. He went across to the coffeehouse and sat outside the door basking in the sunshine. He ordered coffee and opened the paper. He had his reasons. He wanted those who came looking for work to understand that the fun and games were over. This was no longer the house of their friend Eftihis, but a factory that would supply them with work, and as such required their respect. If Mary were there, they would start hinting around for her to make them coffee, or they would lounge on the bed and start acting all buddy-buddy. When the shoeshine man came by, Eftihis stuck his feet out without looking up from his reading. He never so much as glanced at the others hanging around the coffeehouse.

Iordanis was the first to show up – he and his wife Varvara. They were neat and clean, as if going to church. Varvara'd had her hair done, which made her look younger. As they approached the corner, Eftihis hid behind his newspaper and waited for them to go in.

Before long, Simos came around the corner, and then Fanis slipped in without noticing him. Then a short but sturdily built fellow hesitated before the gate – someone Eftihis didn't know. The stranger went in.

When he caught sight of Elpida in the distance, Eftihis got up on the pretext of paying Prodromos for his coffee, and stood to one side to get a good look at her. She was the same as ever, with her worn overcoat, her rounded shoulders, but also with that deep serenity she always had about her. It always refreshed you somehow to look at her, with her smooth, ivory forehead, her clear-cut features, her chestnut hair, and her somber eyes with their steady gaze. Was she even aware she had become a woman? Her face wore a hint of a smile, which gave Eftihis a vague sense of satisfaction.

After paying for his coffee, Eftihis didn't go straight home. He took a walk down to the tracks. It was better to have them wait a bit ... But suddenly he remembered that he shouldn't leave Elpida alone in the courtyard with Fanis. He went back nearly at a run.

The courtyard was crowded. Eftihis took them all in at a glance as they turned to look at him. Even his mother was there! What did she want? She was talking to some woman he didn't know. There were two other people there he didn't recognize either. Elpida stood in the passageway. Fanis was over in front of Stathis' window, talking to the stranger he'd seen earlier.

"Everyone just hold on," Eftihis told them.

He went inside and opened Andonis' door.

"Ready? They're here!"

"Why'd you tell so many people to come?"

"There are some I've never seen before ..."

They went into the room where the looms were. Eftihis looked out at the courtyard through the shutters. They were all there for work. His trick with the locked door had worked. They realized this was an important day for them, and they stood around subdued and attentive.

"Tell them to come in," Andonis said.

"No, we have to be systematic about this. Let's get the table for you to sit at. Get some paper so you can take notes."

They brought in the table and set it in the corner, then a chair. "Have you got some paper?" Then another chair for the prospective employee, over to the left. Andonis sat in the chair and tried to act at ease, lighting a cigarette and arranging the paper in front of him.

Eftihis opened the door. Everyone fell silent and attempted to catch his eye. He slowly ran his gaze over each of them in turn, then pointed to the stranger who had been talking to Fanis.

"You first."

His friends' faces froze because he had picked a stranger to go first. The short, sturdy fellow came in and stood before the table.

"What's your name?"

"Yannis Gripakis."

"Who told you about this?" asked Eftihis.

"No one. I happened to walk by when they were unloading the equipment the other day. When I saw the looms, I figured somebody was setting up a business. I asked over at the coffeehouse and decided to come by today, it being Sunday, so I'd be sure to find this Eftihis they told me about."

"That's me!" Eftihis said.

"So, do you need a weaver?"

"What's your experience?" asked Andonis.

"Since '35, I've been at a few different factories."

"Where were you last?"

"At 'Athina,' in Peristeri."

"Why'd you leave?"

"They laid half of us off."

His answer didn't sit well with Eftihis, who was following everything from where he stood leaning on the window sill.

"Let me see your hands."

Mr. Gripakis held out his palms.

"I'm doing roadwork now, with a pickax, which is why I've got these callouses."

Andonis glanced at his hands and immediately found what he was looking for.

"Have a seat, Yannis," Andonis said and bent over to jot something down.

While he was writing – something wholly unrelated to the present circumstances, in fact an idea that suddenly came to him for his article – Gripakis studied his hands trying to figure out why all this was necessary. Eftihis said nothing, just stood there smoking and observing without seeming to. Then Andonis, still bent over his desk, asked a few routine questions, then went with Gripakis over to the looms. He asked him a number of things by way of testing his practical knowledge, and appeared satisfied by his responses. He then went back behind the table and, with the air of a professor administering a university exam, made a cryptic mark beside the name indicating his final judgement.

"Thank you very much, Mr. Gripakis."

"Well?"

"We'll let you know in four or five days."

The sturdily built fellow with the thick eyebrows moved

toward the door, but Andonis stopped him and asked a wholly irrelevant question:

"Where were you during the war?"

"Is that a factor too? Do I have to answer?" he asked without losing his composure.

"Only if you like. Just to give me a fuller picture. What someone was doing back then says worlds about a person."

"I was a *saltadoros*," Eftihis burst in. "I stole bread, gasoline and tires from the Germans."

"I was in the mountains with the resistance," said Gripakis simply. "Anything else?"

"No. Good-by, Mr. Gripakis ..." said Andonis.

Gripakis remained in the courtyard and again struck up a conversation with Fanis. Eftihis stood in the doorway and this time called in his mother. The old lady entered and promptly plopped herself down in the chair.

"As you can see, we have things to do today. It's not a day for social calls. You haven't had a fight with Pavlos' wife, have you?"

"I heard you were hiring. So I came."

"Are you serious? You want to come work for us?"

"I can still work, so why not?"

"That's right, she worked in a textile factory for years," Eftihis said. "Remember when I was just a little kid and you were working somewhere on Kolokinthinou? I had a younger brother then ... When the old man was working, I used to bring the baby over and you'd come out to the entrance to nurse it. Remember that? The poor bastard died later on."

"What's your area of specialty, Mrs. Stamatina?" asked Andonis.

"I'm a weaver, but I can also run a warper, a spinner or a threader. I can tell from the sound of a machine which thread's broken, and I'm right there to tie it back together. No one could switch a shuttle faster. Pit me against any of those young things of yours ..."

"We take your word for it, don't overdo it," her son told her.

"What'll I make?" asked the old lady.

"The standard, what it says in the law."

"Just so I know. I don't like having to depend on my daughter-in-law and my oldest son, that worthless good-for-nothing ..."

"All right, Mother, come on, we've got work to do," Eftihis interrupted. "Run along and we'll let you know ..."

But the old woman didn't budge.

"No one's better at weaving than me, Mr. Andonis. Tell him he should hire people who are going to care about his business. People he doesn't know will take advantage of him until he learns the business himself. And for all the help you'll be giving him, you still can't sit and watch the looms all day long. And there are all sorts of tricks to our trade – slubbing, shrinking, carding ..."

"There are others waiting. Would you mind ..."

Next Eftihis called in Varvara, then one of the women he hadn't recognized.

Mary couldn't believe the number of people massed in the courtyard. She didn't have a key to let herself in, so she asked Iordanis where her husband was. But when she knocked on the door, Eftihis quickly chased her out again. He wouldn't listen. So Mary stood outside along with the others. She saw a woman next to her with light brown hair, and remembered having seen her at the wedding.

"Are you Elpida, by any chance?"

""Why, yes, I am. Why?"

"Eftihis often mentions you, and I've been wanting to meet you ..."

Elpida blushed when she realized she was speaking to Eftihis' wife. She felt like she'd never in her life had the gift of speech.

"Will you be working here too?"

"I don't know, Eftihis left a note telling me to come to his house on Sunday at eleven, and here I am."

"What's your relation to him? At the wedding he said he was only inviting one person 'on his side.' Are you two related?"

"No," Elpida flatly stated. We've known each other for years. I worked with him when we were selling things on the street too."

"That's all?"

"What else would there be?"

Mary nodded as if coming to her own conclusion, then looked Elpida over.

"So you'll be working here?"

"I don't know, I'm waiting for them to call me in."

The murmur of voices in the courtyard fell silent the instant the door opened again. A woman was tearfully pleading to be hired. Eftihis appeared behind her, a sour look on his face. Whimpering and tears were not his cup of tea.

"In three or four days. Now knock it off."

The woman remained standing before the door. Mary left Elpida and went up to her husband. She began telling him in a lowered voice that her father asked him to please send a thousand drachmas by evening, because he had no money to pay the interest on the gold pieces he'd borrowed. This time Eftihis blew up.

"Get out, I mean it!" he snapped. "Tell him he can go slit his throat for all I care."

Stung, Mary retreated. But she had nowhere to go there in the courtyard, because everyone was staring at her after Eftihis bawled her out: "Isn't that the boss' wife?" they were asking each other. The door to her room was locked. Eftihis nodded to Fanis, who was still talking to Gripakis. What were they talking about, had they become friends just like that? Fanis spat – the spit in his mouth would have been plenty bitter by then – and proceeded inside. Once the door closed, the murmur of voices rose again.

"My friend Fanis," Eftihis told Andonis.

"We've met ..."

Andonis asked him various routine questions – age, address, area of expertise – and noted down his response. Fanis answered with his eyes fastened on the looms, as if he were the only one there.

"So, Fanis," Andonis asked brashly, "do you think there's going to be a war?"

"That has nothing to do with weaving," said Fanis.

"Answer the man," Eftihis burst out. "He's got a good reason for asking."

"Just to see how you think," Andonis said by way of excuse.

"That's my business."

"Why won't you answer?"

"Because I don't want to."

Eftihis peered at him closely, as if he were some kind of curiosity. The blood had rushed to Fanis' face. Why was he being so stubborn? Eftihis held his hand to Fanis' forehead, the way one does with a sick person.

"Aren't you the one who was bugging Andonis here, going on

about how you were an expert knotter? So what are you doing, going and clamming up on us?"

"If you'd asked me as a friend, anywhere else, I'd have told you ... I came here to see about getting a job ..."

"Drop it, Eftihis," Andonis said. "I have all I need."

But Eftihis faced him and asked:

"You've been in prison, haven't you? I could tell by the way you were sitting cross-legged on the floor the other day. What were you in for?"

Once more, Fanis refused to answer. Eftihis again asked:

"Tell me, were you in prison or not?"

The question was again met by silence. Fanis' eyes were like red coals. But Eftihis kept at him.

"I never answer when I'm being interrogated," Fanis replied bluntly and with finality.

His answer threw Eftihis off-balance. Andonis quickly changed the subject.

"Okay, then, you'll be our knotter. So what do you think, did we get ourselves some decent looms? They're double-width, with all the accessories."

"They're real nice," said Fanis without hesitation. "You have to be careful with the finisher, though. It's the key to quality work. You need someone who knows how to handle it. And you have to be very careful with the decimater, the razor, the napper, the iron ..."

Fanis now spoke with a different voice. His eyes had returned to normal, his hands had regained their nimbleness. At the start, he said, they should get as many orders as they could – covers, woolens – reliable bulk fabrics. Then, once things got moving, they could start with suits and women's garments. Andonis took the opportunity to discuss a number of technical matters, to show Eftihis that he knew how to talk shop with an expert.

"What other personnel do we need?" Eftihis interrupted.

"A spindle operator," Fanis told him.

"How hard is that to do?"

"Not hard at all. Something a girl without experience could handle. She'd catch on over time."

"Elpida!" Eftihis blurted out. "So, Andonis, do we need one of those?"

"They're indispensable."

Eftihis opened the door and shouted her name. Elpida came in and greeted everyone in a subdued voice. Eftihis led her over to Andonis

"This is the girl I was telling you about. I know her, I'll give you her particulars later. Fanis, why don't you say hello to Elpida? You haven't forgotten all the running around we did, have you?"

"How are you, Elpida?" Fanis asked diffidently.

"So, you'll be the spindle operator ... It's not difficult work. Fanis here will show you. You'll sort of be his assistant ... Put her down, Andonis."

Andonis didn't ask her anything. He gazed at Elpida to get a look at the girl Eftihis wanted to have near him. But Fanis didn't know what to do with himself from the moment Elpida entered the room.

"That'll do," Andonis told the two of them. "You're both hired, you can start tomorrow. Fanis, I'll need you to come test the looms. They'll have to be adjusted ... And make sure you explain to Elpida what her job is ..."

When they were alone, Eftihis rubbed his hands together, pleased at how handily he'd managed things. He sat down to catch his breath.

"This factory of ours is going to be a killer ... We won't need help from any bastard ... Once things get going, we'll sell the stuff, then take our share of the take and our wives and hit the town just like decent folk – one night to a *bouzouki* joint, the next Turkolimano. Have you ever seen how people with money in the bank live?"

He went to the door to call in the next person, but he stiffened.

"Andonis, look who's here."

Thodoros was coming down the passageway. Mary went over to welcome him. Finally there was someone she could talk to.

The others stared indifferently at this obese individual who had arrived by car. They took him to be some big shot, and remained in their places. Only Gripakis went over, intrigued, and studied Thodoros the whole time he was talking to Mary, as if trying to put his finger on something. Mary was bemoaning the fact that, though she often suggested to Eftihis that they go pay

Thodoros a visit, something always came up ..."

Andonis shuddered, and tried to slip back into his room.

"You don't need me. You're better off working things out on your own."

"No, you don't," thundered Eftihis. "What if he brought the money? You're in this too ... You're not afraid of the judge, are you?"

Andonis stood a moment pondering his predicament. Realizing he had no other choice, he sat back down.

Thodoros was in a jolly mood as he strutted in, as if he himself were the boss. Eftihis noted this with displeasure, but didn't dwell on it. What mattered was for him to come up with the loan.

"I came to take a look at the works," Thodoros said self-importantly.

He examined the machines and the work-area, saying everything looked just fine. Mary took the opportunity to slip inside and stand at Eftihis' side. Andonis brought out a chair and told Vangelia to make some coffee.

"Today we're interviewing prospective employees," said Eftihis, as if giving a report. "We didn't want them to drive us crazy straggling in one at a time, so we had them all come at once. And, boy, did they ever. You'd think we were opening a full-scale factory ..."

"You can't be too careful when it comes to selecting your personnel," said Thodoros, as if giving directions. "Are they any good?"

"We haven't signed any of them on yet ..."

"Well, just be careful."

Eftihis told him how they had gone about buying the looms, how many people they had decided to hire, and how all their hopes were riding on him. "We won't get anywhere without your help." This was just what Thodoros liked to hear, as Eftihis well knew. You had to soft-soap someone if you wanted them to dip into their purse. You couldn't do like Andonis, who stood there like a rock the whole time, staring down at his shoes. Where was that famous tongue of his, now that it was time to reel in the catch? "Am I the only one he knows how to talk fancy to?" he wondered. Thodoros, however, who had learned how not to waste time on business deals, informed Eftihis that he had already decided to help, and had brought along the sum he'd asked for.

"Thank you, Thodoros, thank you!"

A number of those still waiting in the courtyard wandered past the door and peered inside. "You'll have to wait," Eftihis told them irritably. "We're busy with something else at the moment." And he slammed the door.

"Now then ..."

"I brought the money."

"Thank you ..."

Thodoros drew from his pocket a piece of paper resembling a contract, with small, typewritten letters.

"It's made out for a hundred fifty gold pieces," he said. "Just sign here and the money's yours."

Eftihis scowled and huddled down as if in a cold wind.

"I thought we said drafts," he noted.

"We're better off with a contract," Thodoros said.

Eftihis snatched the document somewhat roughly off the table top, and handed it to Andonis.

"You read it. I can't make heads or tails of it."

This didn't go over especially well with Thodoros, and yet after years of doing business, he must have known that no one ever signed anything with their eyes closed – not even the Lord's Prayer.

"If you don't want to sign, fine, I'll just leave now, before there are any hard feelings ..."

Andonis started to go through the document with great care. Two forking veins stood out on his forehead. It took him that long to read two pages, he who could absorb a printed page at a glance? He turned back to the first page, coughed, and pretended to be rereading it. He felt the same powerful vice-grip tightening, pressuring him toward some drastic decision. He shut his eyes to size up the situation, then lay the document on the table.

"Well? Should I sign?"

Before he could answer, there came a faint knock at the door.

"Come on, do I sign or don't I?" Eftihis demanded.

"No," Andonis said softly.

But his answer went unnoticed because the knock at the door had become more imperative now, and Eftihis went to see who was there.

It was the judge.

Thodoros sprang up, slammed his fists down on the table, and grunted with rage.

"Get out!" he bellowed. "I can't stand seeing your mug around! Get him out of here or I'll clobber him."

"Here you are!" Harilaos said with a jubilant smile. "What are you getting so wrought up about?"

"How the hell did you find me? Get him out of here!"

Andonis stood between them, just in case Thodoros, whose face had turned purple, lost his head and took a swing at the judge. It was a mess, all right.

"When am I going to be rid of you and your son? Someday I'll get my hands on him and make him pay for the both of you ..."

Harilaos went on in, as Thodoros took a couple of steps backwards. A few of those waiting in the courtyard heard the shouting and approached the door. Gripakis and Fanis joined the others inside.

"You should know by now that wherever you go I'll find you. I don't know why you were trying to hide from me all this time."

"What are you doing here? What do you want?"

"I live here, and you know perfectly well what I want ..."

"Eftihis, Andonis, get this man out of here ..."

Eftihis and Andonis exchanged looks. Now what?

"Get him out, I said!"

"Stop shouting. You know they're not going to kick me out."

No one moved. Thodoros folded up his contract, felt his pocket to make sure the cash was still there, and stomped toward the door. The color drained from Eftihis' face. The critical moment had arrived. If Thodoros were to walk out now, everything would come to a complete standstill. The looms would rust, and perhaps one day be sold as scrap iron. He went up and placed his hands on Thodoros' shoulders, as if restraining a tremendous weight that threatened to crush him.

"Hold on a second, Thodoros, and let's have a talk."

But Thodoros pushed on toward the door.

"Let me out of here."

Even Mary went over and begged him not to go.

Eftihis dropped his hands and turned to the judge.

"I was having a business meeting with Thodoros here ... I have no idea what's between you two ..."

"I wasn't addressing myself to you," the judge sternly informed him. "Nor are your business dealings of the least interest to me. I came to have a word with Andonis here, and who do I stumble across but the man I've been trying to track down for days ... I can wait out in the courtyard until you're finished, if you like ..."

Soundlessly opening her door, Vangelia went over and stood in the corner. Eftihis once again found himself engulfed by the cold void he always felt in the face of danger.

"What have I ever done to you, Judge? I put myself through the wringer trying to get a business going ... I'm not letting anyone foul it up for me now. What have I got to do with your son? Am I the one who condemned him? Do you have anything against me? What have I ever done to bug you or hurt you? Have I ever once come knocking at your door?"

"But I'm not bothering you either."

"Say something, Andonis," Eftihis went on, turning to his friend. "Explain to the judge that our future's hanging on this. Don't act like it doesn't have anything to do with you – it's the big break you've been after for years now ... You know what the alternative is ..."

"I'm leaving," declared Thodoros. "You laid a trap for me. One of you must have tipped him off ..."

"You're mistaken. No one told me anything. This has been my home for the past fifteen years ... Our paths will always cross. You had better get used to the idea ... Last Wednesday, Andonis and I scoured all of Athens looking for you."

"So you're the one, you snake"

"The judge here wanted to meet with you ... We looked all over town, but couldn't find you anywhere."

"Is that what he told you, Judge?" Thodoros asked, roaring with laughter. "Boy, did he pull one on you. What a con-artist ... Last Wednesday and Thursday we were all sitting around drinking wine together in a taverna."

"Is this true?" Harilaos asked Andonis uncertainly.

"Yes," Andonis acknowledged without raising his eyes. "I didn't know where he was at the time. Later on ..."

"I warned you," cried Eftihis. "So you were trying to put one over on me, too?"

The judge turned to Andonis and fixed him with his gaze.

"Have you spoken to him about your friend?"

"No. The discussion was of a purely business nature."

"But you gave me your word."

"I couldn't," Andonis whispered.

Thodoros got up to leave, but Eftihis held him back.

"If you have unsettled business with the judge's son, go find him and kill him. That's just the way it is, Judge ... What do I owe you that I should stand by and let you ruin me? All I want is to get on with my business."

Harilaos ignored him. To Andonis he said:

"Now's your chance. Talk to him so everyone can hear ..."

"And tell him what?"

"What you would have said to him if we had found him."

Andonis made an effort to speak, but couldn't. What could he say? Harilaos' hard gaze passed from one to the other: Andonis standing there mutely; Vangelia at his side, bright red, perhaps from shame; and Eftihis, ready for anything, still trying to work out his next move. Everyone else looked on curiously. They were all in the room by now, the courtyard was deserted. Ismene too had appeared. She immediately grasped the situation, and was filled with dread. So this was the man who held Angelos' fate in his hands? Thodoros, choked with bile, was desperate to escape the endless chaos lurking beyond the judge's eyes ...

"Let me go," he shouted at Eftihis.

Harilaos stood his ground.

"Let go of me, I'll kill him ..."

"What makes you so sure? All by yourself?"

"All by myself. You, too, if I have to."

"I'm at your disposal," the judge told him. "No one's preventing you. The gentlemen here promise not to interfere. What are you waiting for? Of course, it'll be the act of an animal in a blind fury. And even if you eliminate me, you won't be off the hook. You'll just be adding to your list of crimes. If it's the others here you're afraid of, we can go someplace else. Just lead the way ... I was hoping to have one last talk with you ... but what's the point, since your conscience isn't functioning? You've lost the ability to have a normal conversation. All you can do is shout ... You gave false testimony in order to condemn someone who knew too much about you ..."

Harilaos' voice was hard and slashing. One expected to see stripes of blood where his words passed slowly and surely over the other man.

"It's stupid and cowardly to have it in for someone simply because he knows something about you ... Even if everyone abandons him, he'll survive ..."

Ismene came forward. Andonis hunched down even more. Fanis swallowed his bitter spit. Gripakis, a knot of nerves, sprang from the crowd. He went up to Thodoros and, as if not believing his eyes, studied him closely.

"I know this man from somewhere ... I've been wracking my brains from the moment I laid eyes on him ... Aren't you the one we dragged naked out of a barrel in Lamia? It's a crazy world, all right!... Does my face say anything to you?

He turned to the others and asked:

"Have you been talking about Angelos all this time?"

"Yes," Ismene said. "Do you know him?"

"I came looking for a job but you can have it, I'll go back to ditch-digging ... So, as I was saying, this man here ..."

Thodoros made a lunge for the door, but Gripakis held on to him.

"We've got some accounts to settle ..."

Fanis and two or three others moved over by the door to block the exit. They were joined by Stathis, who had come over to see what the noise was all about.

"You've got a lot of people's lives around your neck ..." Gripakis told Thodoros. "Remember the people they hung in the town square? Plus the father of the boy who found you? And the others executed after the trial? And you're still throwing your threats around?"

Thodoros collapsed in a chair like a sack of cement.

"Go on," he grunted. "But you'll live to regret it, too."

"You're lucky Angelos rescued you, because the townspeople were ready to tear you limb from limb ... Afterwards, you confessed to everything, the hangings in the square, that boy's father, the others you had locked up in the camp ... Angelos listened to you all night. I stood sentry at the door. Now do you remember me?"

Thodoros stood up heavily, as if he hadn't heard a word, and pointed at the old man:

"Just so you know, I'm going to get your son ..."

Harilaos suddenly turned pale and braced himself against Ismene, whose blood had run cold at the words. He tried to hide the fact that his vision had blurred.

"I'll root him out myself, I swear to you ... And then ..."

"You'll never find him!" cried Ismene.

Gripakis leaped upon Thodoros, but Fanis and Iordanis held him back. Eftihis wedged himself between them. He let out a howl that shook the windows, and tore at his clothes like a madman.

"Get out!"

In the confusion, Gripakis struggled to get at Thodoros. Eftihis flew into a rage, and Mary shrieked. Someone picked up a chair, but Fanis caught it in midair.

Somebody else came into the room.

He pushed his way through the people at the door. Even those who didn't recognize him sensed that he was somehow mixed up in all this.

"Hold it, everybody! Are you talking about me?"

Everyone froze. It was Angelos. He stopped next to his father, and looked bravely into his eyes: "Here I am, at last." He looked huge, towering, he seemed to fill the whole room. He was as sturdy and vigorous as ever. He ran his gaze over them all. He began by addressing the judge.

"Why are you getting all worked up over this man? He's not worth it."

Harilaos was having difficulty standing. He steadied himself on his son's arm, and it was like a warm, proud embrace. It was Angelos all right, with his strong and sturdy body, his taut energy, his beloved, stalwart stubbornness. Ismene dashed to his side in a flurry of fear.

"So it's you, is it?" Thodoros said.

"That's right. I have nothing to say to you, mister, I don't even care who you are. All I ask is that you use more respect when addressing my father."

"I'm going to get you," Thodoros muttered.

Before he could finish, Gripakis sprang at him, but Angelos checked him.

"Yannis," he said sternly.

"Not again, Angelos! Is that what you came for? To save his life a second time?"

A chill of fear spread through the room. Angelos stared at Thodoros as if he were no more than a stone. How was it that he had turned up right at the critical moment after all these years? No one thought twice about it, it seemed perfectly natural. Of course, his appearance was somewhat unusual: his clothes hanging loosely from his gaunt frame, his eyes somber. He had returned from far away. No, he hadn't been away a single day. Andonis gave him clandestine looks. He had tried to get closer to him, but found he hadn't moved from his spot. Vangelia stood beside him, as if she'd caught a glimpse of someone she knew. Gripakis stood eagle-eyed, coiled tight as a spring, ready to act if the need arose. The air was thick with the scent of danger. How had he dared come to his own home, knowing they were still after him? How far would his rashness take him? Sentenced to death, he lived from moment to moment in the face of grave danger. Yet look how tall he stood!

The judge's body suddenly sagged on his son's arm.

"Let's go," he whispered. "We're through here."

They moved toward the door. The others went with them: Gripakis, Fanis, and a few of the women.

"Thank you," Harilaos told him in a low voice.

"We should get away from here, Father," said Ismene in fright.

"I want to stay," Angelos responded.

The old man, proud and unbowed, took a couple of steps. Then he murmured to his son, "Help me upstairs. And let your mother have a look at you."

On the stairs, Angelos realized his father was having trouble keeping his feet. He grabbed him around the waist and held him up. The old man's head rolled awkwardly, but with great effort he held it steady long enough to look at his son. There were only a few more steps to go. Those still in the courtyard, gazing up after them, were new people, all but unrecognizable, with warm, kindly eyes. Now they understood what it was all about. They remembered everything.

The three men were left alone in the room with the machinery. Andonis started to leave, but Eftihis slammed the door shut in front of him.

"You and me'll settle up later. For now, we need to talk through this business with the loan ..."

"I am leaving," Thodoros shouted. "I walked right into a trap."

Eftihis tried to stop him, but Thodoros persisted. Finally, Eftihis told him in no uncertain terms:

"Fine, so leave – if you've got the guts. Gripakis is out there waiting for you. If he starts laying into you, don't expect me to come to your rescue."

Hence the door remained closed.

THE JUDGE, ANGELOS AND ISMENE reached the kitchen landing. As they went inside, Harilaos called, in a voice hardly his own:

"Ioanna ... I've brought him home to you. You see, I was telling the truth all those years when I told you he'd come ..."

His mother threw her arms around her son. While she showered him with kisses and caresses, Harilaos groped his way forward, holding on to the chairs, the table, the walls. He sat down at his old massive desk and got out the legal file. When the others went in after him, they found him sitting there, bolt upright and solemn. It must have been more or less how he looked when presiding in the court-room.

"I knew you'd come. I never doubted it for a moment ... And now ..."

He tried to say more, no doubt something important and decisive, but his mouth twisted in a sudden spasm, his fingers splayed. He leaned back his head and expired.

Ismene rushed down the stairs and told Stathis, who was still in the courtyard: "Get a doctor! The judge ..." She quickly went back upstairs to see Angelos kissing his father on the forehead and closing his eyes.

Afterwards, everything unfolded with the swift, erratic rhythm imposed by the event. They lay the dead man out on his bed, and Ismene hurried off to see to the various necessary arrangements. Angelos stayed behind with his tearful mother. Stathis brought the doctor. He only stayed for a couple of minutes, just long enough to scribble a short note. They asked the neighbors on the other side to open the glass partition so they could use the wooden stairway in front. The family that had shared the house with them for so many years, none of whom they knew, agreed, and the house reverted to its original form – large yet unknown, filled with new faces. Angelos timidly went through to see the other rooms he used to know: the dining room, the bedroom, the room that had been his father's office. Next to the front door was the coat-hanger and an old framed picture. A woman went out and closed the door behind her. The rooms were full of furniture, everything looked different. The red velvet curtains his mother had sewn, with a yellow-gold border and heavy tassels, were gone. Gone too were the two flower-stands with blue vases, a number of embroideries, and the sofa, its cushions faintly worn and sunken from the many hours of ease the family had spent on them. A man stepped out of the old bedroom.

"And who might you be?"

"Angelos."

"The judge's son!... We'd heard he wasn't around."

"Well, as you can see ..."

"I heard you were dead ..."

Angelos shrugged and went back to his family. He stood at his mother's side and spent a long time gazing at the serene expression on his father's face. The house was open and airy, the curtains swelled with the cross-breeze coming through the open doorways. New faces cropped up at every turn, two women moved through the rooms, nothing closed any longer. And everyone gave him meaningful looks, without saying what was foremost in their minds from the moment they met him. The folder with his court brief lay on the desk. He opened the drawer and returned it to its place. This used to be his room. The stairs up to the roof went right by the window – a mere step away. How many nights had he sat there awake, working through thousands of equations: the science of construction, the durability of material. His father was dead. How could one calculate a man's strength, the durability of dignity, degrees of responsibility, firmness of resolve, the dynamic equilibrium of serenity? Stathis came back upstairs. He handed Ismene some bills, and advised Angelos to leave. Left alone, Angelos told Stathis that when he saw Thodoros, and then heard them all shouting, he couldn't hold back. He'd discovered that the door was unlocked, and went out.

"It was bound to happen sooner or later ..."

"What'll you do now?" Stathis inquired.

"I don't know ..."

"You better start by getting out of here. Go hide out somewhere, then come by the newspaper tonight. They don't need you here. There'll be lots of people here soon. Thodoros is still down with Eftihis – your friend Yannis is making sure he stays there until you leave – but he might not waste any time tipping them off, and next thing you know they'll be over here looking for you ... Protect yourself."

Angelos went as far as the stairs and then came back. He stood over his father again. He was alone with him in the empty room. Suddenly he heard hurried footsteps on the iron stairs, and others coming up the wooden stairs in front. Once again he found himself besieged, defenseless. Panic welled up inexorably in his chest, and he felt himself spinning in a whirlpool of irrational thoughts. He ran into the adjoining room, found it momentarily empty, and without thinking lunged under the bed. He curled into a ball and waited. There were whispers in the room. Vangelia was there, with a neighbor, and those who had come to see about work. Ismene asked first Stathis, then Gripakis and Fanis. "He left," they all told her. "It was the only thing to do ..." someone else said. "He's got to save his skin ..."

The covers on the bed – his bed – reached nearly to the floor. He could see shoes and follow people's movements through a slit. Then the room remained empty except for Ismene, her feet standing motionless in the middle of the floor. Angelos was too ashamed to crawl out. And what if they decided to remove the bed? He would die of shame if they discovered him there ... He couldn't imagine anything more humiliating. Soon the room filled with shoes: dusty shoes, women's shoes, funny-looking shoes, none of which he recognized. Now it was out of the question for him to leave. He lay there shackled and powerless in a dark and bottomless void. He could hear his mother crying, as if it were bubbling up from an inexhaustible spring. "Perhaps she's crying for me as well."

There were other people there, too. At funerals you don't ask the people's names at the door. There were colleagues of his father, retired judges who respected the meaning of justice, and neighbors, women from nearby houses. Most of them talked about the judge's son. No one had forgotten him. Perhaps there were even a few who had come to arrest him. Gripakis talked with Ismene, remembering old times. Andonis was explaining the business with Thodoros and the judge to Eftihis. "In other words, he was really duping the two of us," Eftihis concluded. A low murmur spread throughout.

That night, fewer shoes appeared through the slit, but the room wasn't empty for a moment. In the chair opposite the bed were two feet, pressed tightly together. The bed sagged when two or three people sat on the edge at one time. Fear and shame gnawed at him – the same sickness that had crippled him for years. His hiding there was the ultimate degradation. The judge had died simply and honorably. He had whispered something before he died. "Perhaps it was his final decision about me," thought Angelos. Now that he had returned, after all his wandering, he would have to start over again, figure out his next move. "I'm barely more than a corpse myself," he said, and he could feel his body withering away in its tense immobility. Even his breathing had stopped.

Stathis came home at his usual time, daybreak. He worriedly asked Ismene about Angelos. "What happened? I was expecting him." "I don't know, he left while I was out." The broad wooden stairway creaked whenever someone came up, as it always had. His father would close his door to go over his law briefs; it was the supreme judgement concerning life. "My job brings with it great responsibility," he had once told Angelos "I couldn't bear to become the typical, bureaucratic case-processor."

The next morning, after a long wait, there came a fresh wave of noise, professional footsteps, and despair. The coffin was carried out and the room stood empty. The stairs and front door swallowed up the murmuring crowd. But someone remained behind, he could hear scattered footsteps in the kitchen and in the front rooms. It still wasn't safe to come out. The hush lay heavy on the room, the air had been sucked out.

When they got back, Ioanna softly told Ismene:

"Sneak a look under the bed, he may still be there. I saw him dive under it, but I didn't say anything, I didn't want to embarrass him ..."

Ismene closed the door, so that if he really were in the room, he could come out on his own.

With the room deserted, Angelos crept out from under the bed. He sat in the chair by the window. Ismene opened the door and found him there.

"You're back?"

"I was here the whole time, under there."

"Your eyes are so red. Were you crying?"

"Yes."

"Mother, Angelos came back, he's here now," she told Ioanna a little later.

His mother came into the room.

"You did well to leave, child. There were a few people here I didn't know ... Did you see them, Ismene? They were looking everywhere ... I didn't like it one bit."

They shut the glass partition between the two apartments. "Thank you so much ... I'm afraid we put you out," Ioanna told their next-door neighbors. She locked the door, and the life of the apartment once again turned inward. Angelos was too ashamed to meet their eyes. He kept switching chairs, and could come up with nothing to say. Ismene stayed home from work. She fixed coffee, and prepared a bath for him. They gave him a clean shirt of his father's, socks and underwear. Whenever they heard steps on the stairs, they would shut the door and leave him by himself. Ismene refrained from talking to him, as if everything was already settled in her mind, as if it was all perfectly natural.

That afternoon, after a few latecomers had left, his mother sat down across from him. They looked at each other without saying a word. Ismene was gone for some time. His mother spoke first.

"Once it gets dark, you should very cautiously slip out. Go someplace where you'll be safe, where you can relax some ..."

"I was thinking of staying," Angelos told her.

"No, don't give up ... You can't let them get you. What you need is a good sleep and some peace and quiet. You should take better care of yourself too, you've gotten so thin. If you stayed here, the least little noise would frighten you. You'll be better off someplace else."

"I'm so tired, Mother. That's exactly what I've been doing for years now."

"That's just how it has to be. You'll find somewhere. You had so many friends."

Someone else knocked at the door, and his mother saw how he jumped, his breath catching, his eyes round with fear. A woman who lived nearby went into the next room. Ismene soon returned. She didn't ask him any questions this time either.

"We'll be leaving shortly. I've arranged everything."

"Where to?"

"You'll see. It's perfect."

"This again ..."

"It's the only way."

The neighbor went out. It was the wife of the teacher who used to play chess with the judge. They often came to visit in the evenings, before the war. Ismene told Ioanna that she and Angelos would be leaving as soon as the electricians were finished down at Eftihis' place.

"That's just what I was telling him. It's the best solution ..."

They fell silent again. Ismene went out onto the stairs to check things below.

"With your father gone, there won't be anyone to tell me that you're all right. Send me a message now and then, when you can ..."

Ismene came back in. "Ready?" Angelos kissed his mother and took a last look at the judge's desk, at the room with its old, worn furniture. They turned out the kitchen light and quickly closed the door. Angelos started down, but Ismene took his hand and began leading him up instead. "Come on, don't be afraid." They tiptoed up to the roof. The lights of the city spread out around them. The air was cool. Ismene opened the door of the small shed and motioned for him to step inside:

"Here. Take off your shoes so no one can hear you."

Once they were inside, in the dark, Ismene burst into tears. She smothered her face on his chest to muffle her sobs. Angelos was unsure of his surroundings. He stood motionless, stroking her hair. Then Ismene told him that she had seen to everything. She had laid boards on top of two boxes, with a mattress and clean sheets. "Don't be afraid to sit down. It's a little cramped, but it's clean. I swept and tidied up." She had thought of everything. There was a water pitcher, some bread and sugar, a towel, some biscuits, and two cans of milk. He'd keep the key inside with him. The room had a window out onto the airshaft. "Drop the basket out here with the rope and I'll put in food and whatever else you need. Every night at one-thirty. Am I forgetting anything? It'll do for a few days, until we find something better ..."

Having finished giving him instructions for his new lodgings, Ismene sat down next to him.

"Now let's talk," she said.

He had wanted to put his arms around her and thank her for everything, but he drew back. There was suddenly something hard about her voice. He searched for her face, but could make out nothing. He only sensed her presence, vague and dense there in the encompassing darkness: her quick breathing, and a sharp gaze you could feel coming straight at you, pinning you in place.

"Ismene, I want you to know that I love you now more than ever. I'm sure you have your doubts, and I don't blame you ... Still, I needed to tell you, it might help us later on ..."

"Words! It's all just words."

"You're right. But they're from the heart. Anyway, how else can I talk to you?"

"I never asked you to do anything that would put you in danger. You know I would have given my life to keep you safe."

"Which is exactly what you're doing. What more *could* you do? Believe me, Ismene, I feel like I've got some kind of disease. How can you run when your legs are covered with sores?"

"Nobody's asking an invalid to run."

"But that's what *he* wants. He doesn't have to wait to hear it from others."

Ismene realized their conversation was headed nowhere. Once again her tone changed.

"Where did you go after that night?" she asked him bluntly, as if interrogating him.

"I spent a couple of nights on the street, then I came and stayed in Stathis' room ..."

"His room here in the courtyard?"

"Yes. Thank you for that too, for saving my books. You see, I know everything."

"So why the charade? Were you afraid of me?"

"No, of myself."

"What's that supposed to mean? Would it have been so hard for you to contact me? To say 'Hi, I'm fine, I don't want to see you again, please stop asking about me ...'"

"It wouldn't have been true ..."

"But say you knew I was starving to death somewhere, that I needed your help – just a word from afar, a whistle, a nod – wouldn't you take the trouble to toss me a dry crust?"

Where was her voice coming from? Angelos had lost his sense of his surroundings. He couldn't even extend his hand to find what was next to him. He spoke slowly, as if to himself:

"That night in the rain, I came to ask your help. But when I saw you, I couldn't bring myself to confess to you I didn't have anywhere to go. You gathered as much, of course, but I couldn't bring myself to tell you I was afraid. I feel alive when I'm with you. It meant more to me just to see you than having you go out and find me a place to stay. When I saw how anxious you were, I left. Then I couldn't face having you find out I was hiding in the courtyard of my own house. I watched all of you through the shutters. I can't tell you how many times I wanted to talk to you, but my hand always froze on the latch. I had nothing to offer you, only the devastation that comes from feeling ashamed of yourself. And if I'd opened the door, what would I have said to you? It's no fun to keep asking for help ... Pretty soon we would have both been wondering how long it could go on. What did I have to offer?"

"That was for me to judge."

"Remember what we used to say? True human relationships are always founded on some shared pursuit, some dream or ideal ..."

"That may be true for friends. But I love you," replied Ismene.

"And seeing as I love you, too, it means we have that many more demands to make. We're both looking for something to build our lives on."

"But this way we both end up wasting our lives. When it comes right down to it. We're all sentenced to death. There's no two ways about it. And no one knows when their sentence is going to be carried out."

"What are you trying to say, Ismene?"

"I mean everyone's condemned to death, but that doesn't mean they just throw their lives away. No, they go on living, they even try to make the most of it ..."

"It's not the same thing, Ismene. That's a dangerous oversimplification. It's not that I'm afraid of death. I just don't want to be killed."

"All the more reason for you to avoid capture and get on with your life."

Angelos took a deep breath, and continued with great effort:

"Fear is a disease, Ismene. It jangles your nerves, you can't think straight. All you know is that your insides are quaking. It's a serious disease too. It leaves you paralyzed, brain-dead. It isn't life. Each day you sink deeper and deeper into chaos. The effort to keep going exacts a heavy toll. I can tell you right out: I was afraid. Now I'm at the next stage: I'm ashamed. Last night under the bed ... Would you ever have believed it of me? And tonight, stuck here in this shed like some useless piece of equipment. But turning myself in wouldn't do a bit of good either ..."

Ismene rested the palm of her hand gently on his head. She didn't move it, just held it there, clenching her teeth as if his head were a red-hot slab. Her hand felt heavy to Angelos, but he did his best to bear it, the way a man of conviction undergoes torture without talking. Was it a gesture of pity on her part? Not even Ismene herself could say if it was a caress, or a kind of punishment.

"But there's no reason why we *can't* get on with our lives," she told him firmly.

"How?"

"By going away somewhere. We'll rent a house ... We'll take your mother with us too. No one will know who we are. I'll go on working, and we can find some kind of engineering work for you ..."

"That's no solution, Ismene. Half-measures are dangerous. If I've learned one thing in all this time, it's that. No, what we need is courage and hope. I still don't feel strong enough yet. But I can't stay here either."

"Why not? It's safe ... and we'll be together."

"I'm not sure ... What would I have to offer?"

"You're just being a coward," Ismene cried angrily. "It's just words. You're afraid of living. But things are complicated today, that's all there is to it. And our predicament – your sentence, sickness, fear, defeat, cowardice, whatever you want to call it –

doesn't leave us time to dicker about solutions. That friend of yours with the bushy eyebrows, Yannis, was talking to me all night about how brave and strong you were back then ..."

"And what did you say?"

"That you still were. That you hadn't changed."

"What if you'd known I was hiding under the bed?"

"I still would have said the same thing. I believe it."

"That's what frightens me most of all, Ismene. You have to accept me as I am now. And I'm so dependent on you. On all of you ..."

"But this is something temporary, it's like a sickness that will go away. Yesterday morning when you came in and stood in front of us all, it was just like when you came back from fighting in the mountains. It frightened me at first, but then it seemed quite natural for you to behave that way. I wanted to run up and throw my arms around your neck, the way I used to ..."

"I just couldn't hold back anymore. It was a good thing Stathis left the door unlocked, otherwise I would have broken it down. At that moment, I was capable of anything. Then I realized my problem wasn't Thodoros, or whoever. Those things I can cope with. It was later, when people started coming in, all the footsteps and the opening doors – I panicked ... How could I go live with you when all I'd be doing is shuffling around in one room, talking in whispers so no one could hear?"

"But it won't be like that ..."

"I don't know, Ismene ... Maybe later on ..."

Ismene's temper flared again.

"What have you done with yourself, Angelos? What were all those years of suffering and struggle for? Did you go through all that just to give in now, when no one's even asking you to make a sacrifice? What was the point of putting up a resistance if you only end up retreating from life? What happened to all your ideas? Your strength? Has the sentence been carried out after all? Are you so used up that you don't have anything left to offer – even to yourself?"

"I don't know what to say ... I really wish I did ..."

Ismene got up and opened the door. He could see her body silhouetted in the dark. Around her head glowed a patch of starry sky.

"Think it all through again, from the beginning. Take your time. We'll talk again soon ..."

But before leaving, she turned back and kissed him on the forehead.

"Good-night."

"Good-night, Ismene."

The door closed. All was darkness. "We'll talk again soon."

CHAPTER 17

EVERYTHING WAS GOING SMOOTHLY. The machinery was run-ning, the cloth was selling. The neighboring houses shook wit the steady drumming of looms, a magnificent clatter that fille the air with vitality and power. Each factory has its own way singing, and there's no way to muzzle it. A steady stream of pe ple went in and out, the front gate was never closed, truck unloaded raw material and carted off the finished product. "Se what did I tell you?" During lunch, the workers opened the lunch tins on the long bench their employers had installed ou side, and while they ate the courtyard was filled with jokes ar banter. It had become a veritable garden in there – the flowerpo again burgeoned on all the ledges, with flowers lining the stai all the way to the roof.

From the outset the neighbors complained, with good reaso that they couldn't hear themselves think. To avoid a confront tion, all the windows were closed, which turned the work-are into a suffocating furnace. Wool dust clung to the workers' swea faces, a look of distress crept into all their eyes, and their ove seers began to worry that production would fall. One day Eftih asked Elpida whether the new threads were breaking on her, b he couldn't hear her answer. Her voice was all but gone, her li were parched. He felt so sorry for her that he immediately ga the order for the windows to be opened. "Let them piss a moan," he said, feeling like a real man of business now. "They learn to live with it soon enough." Once more cool air rushed i and everything proceeded like clockwork. And when the neighbo cornered him, mumbling threats and saying how they werer going to let themselves be driven to the madhouse, Eftihis didn't even hear them out: "So go ahead and file a complaint. Just leave me alone."

That evening, during their scheduled meeting, Eftihis told Andonis what he had done. Andonis approved. "Closing those windows was a sign of beginners' weakness," he said, adding that they must rid themselves of such indecision in the future. Each evening, the two partners would outline the day's unfinished business and divvy up the next day's chores, then move on to accounts, dreams, and critiques. Andonis had purchased a thread-counter, and kept track of how many threads per square inch their fabrics contained. He had also assembled a number of books on textiles, which he read on the sly after going to bed. In the morning, he would always lock them away, lest they fall into the wrong hands. He didn't want it going around that he studied by night to play the know-it-all by day. He wasted no time in clarifying his business relationship with Eftihis. "You're the owner. I'm just your factory manager. Once the money starts coming in, I want a percentage ..." "I'm relying on you," Eftihis grumbled. "Why are you getting so slippery all of a sudden?" "It's not my specialty," Andonis told him. "Are you saying you don't have faith in the business?" demanded Eftihis. Andonis assured him that, on the contrary, he took a deep interest in their business. "The proof of my faith is all the time – my most valuable asset – I've already sunk into it ..." They very nearly had a falling out that night, but at last Eftihis backed down, because when it came right down to it, he much preferred being the sole man in charge.

Two days later, Andonis had a real brainstorm. He proposed that Eftihis designate him manager, with power of signature. That way, he explained, he could take out drafts as Andonis Stefanidis, which Eftihis and he himself, as manager, could draw upon at the bank. "It's a fantastic idea!" exclaimed Andonis proudly. "What, are we going in for experiments now?" Eftihis had asked skeptically. But the experiment had succeeded, and after collecting the money, they roared with laughter and bought each other beers. "Fantastic!" Andonis kept saying. Feeling quite pleased with themselves, they went and got their wives, and they all took a walk together, like people of substance and bearing.

For the past several days, Andonis had been wracking his

brains to come up with the most advantageous connections. He never lost sight of the fact that small industrial works like theirs, if they were to be viable, must combine to form larger units. The benefits were obvious. He never stopped thinking about how to create a broader economic nexus, a powerful manufacturing cooperative that would unite smaller, dispersed producers. He still hadn't said a word to anyone. His heart palpitated in the fear that some disruption would occur and ruin his plans. "Perspective, whether right or not, is man's secret pact with time, part of his preparation for the great assault on disaster." When he said something to that effect to Eftihis, the latter burst out laughing as if someone were tickling him.

Their homes had now been united with the factory, and one had to pass through the work-area in order to go out into the courtyard, with its shade, its cardboard boxes, and its waste cotton. How could you get any sleep when work began at 6 a.m.? Andonis was now trying to convince Eftihis that it would be a good idea for them to go half and half on an office. "Isn't that spreading ourselves a little thin?" Eftihis asked. Andonis expounded on the importance of enhancing their business image. "Anyone who walks in here can see we're running a two-bit operation. If we have an office, we can get some business cards printed up with the name of the firm. 'I'm heading over to the factory,' you'll say ... The way things are now, where do you plan to hold your business meetings – in the laundry-room?" Eftihis still wasn't convinced, but would come around.

Eftihis thrived on the commotion and excitement. He loved being surrounded by so many new things, he wanted to learn everything at once, and he often just stopped dead in his tracks and stared at it all, finding it hard to believe that the whole thing had actually gotten off the ground. His eye missed nothing. He would be happily sweating along, then suddenly would burst into a stream of curses that would drown out the sound of the looms. When he swore, his voice became a drawling singsong, and one day Iordanis went up to him and said, "You're not a street-peddler anymore ... Clean up your act a bit, you run a business now." Ever since, Eftihis had kept his swearing to himself. He wandered among the machines, and whenever he saw a pile of discarded thread, he gave advice on conserving resources. Other times he lectured the technicians on avoiding unnecessary movements, as if to remind them that it wouldn't kill them to put a little more of themselves into it. But then he would recall Andonis urging him not to lean too hard on the workers, since forced productivity increases meant defects in the finishing stage, more breakage and waste. So he would always end by saying: "I just don't want you wearing yourself out any more than you have to. Of course, you know what's best ..."

"It's not easy being boss," he told Mary one night, fishing for a bit of admiration, even just a smile or a pat on the head for his achievements. But she merely asked him when, for God's sake, she would be able to buy herself a summer dress. "There's no room for luxuries like that yet," he scolded. Then she complained how he never considered her feelings, whereas that very morning he had raced over to offer "her" – meaning Elpida – a cup of water the moment he noticed she was thirsty. "That's different ... I'm paying her to work for me." But the truth was he must have displayed excessive interest in Elpida, because a few days earlier his mother had also commented: "You've got your eye on that girl. Better watch yourself ..." But it was all nonsense. Just because he was paying her, did that mean he had to forget that she was there more for what she got than what she gave? Besides, Elpida quickly learned her way around and, as his mother herself had remarked, was conscientious. From across the room, Eftihis would watch how Fanis spoke to her, and whether the girl showed any interest. For now, at least, Fanis was devoting most of his attention to his loom, and went home much later than she did. Thus, Eftihis was able to rest easy. The other day at lunch, her hair clung to the sweat on her forehead, and she looked especially pretty. She wore a calm and contented look, no telling why. Eftihis had noticed, and did his best to fathom it. He got nowhere that day, because Mary soon called him in to dinner. At first, he had supposed they would eat with the others on the bench in the courtyard, but later changed his mind. They were better off eating inside, with the door shut, no less. "Otherwise it'll get too familiar. We're running a business here, not having a picnic," he said, and Mary concurred.

The good thing was that the workers all got along, and had put their minds to keeping production up. On the first day, Eftihis told them: "We'll be earning our bread here ..." And when the machines had started up, he couldn't hold back. His eyes filled with tears, and he hurriedly hid himself in the laundry-room. He wept like a baby, and his heart was beating so hard that he grasped his hands to his chest to keep it from bursting. He splashed water on his face, and went out with his eyes swollen and red when they shouted that a truck had arrived with a delivery of thread he had to sign for.

Another big day was when the workers were paid for their first week of work. Andonis again sat in an orderly manner behind the little table, counting out the wages and writing up receipts. He gave each of them their pay – as specified by the law – down to the last cent, and made the appropriate deductions. Although he realized it was a momentous occasion, he tried to act as nonchalant as possible, as if performing the most banal of tasks. Eftihis stood at his side, deeply moved, and gave each worker in turn a slap on the back. His mother kissed him, Elpida thanked him, Iordanis wished him luck, and Fanis looked him in the eyes and shook his hand. It took all his will-power to hold back his tears and not make a fool of himself. When the last worker had been paid, he went around to the front of the table, convinced that he too would be receiving wages. Andonis brought him up short: "You're the owner, you take home the net earnings ..." Eftihis didn't much care for this, but he gave a loud laugh and turned it all into a joke. "Don't I work here too?" he complained. Andonis very deliberately drew a red line in the accounts book and locked up the cash-box. "This is yours," he said, handing him the box. "But you don't get paid." Eftihis scratched his chin irritably, and whispered to Mary that she could forget about the dress. "We only get the earnings, kiddo ... Which means not a penny for the time being ..." Then it dawned on him that in his preoccupation with getting paid, he hadn't noticed if Fanis and Elpida had left together. It would have been a perfect opportunity for them to strike up a conversation and to walk as far as Petralona together. He anxiously went out to the front gate, but there was no sign of them anywhere.

A few days later they handed over their first finished product. While it was true that the blankets came out a little narrow and crooked, after holding conferences, inquiries, and equipment inspections, they concluded that such defects were unavoidable at the start. Thanks to wits, bribery and deceit, Andonis managed to sell it all off. He would go down at daybreak to the warehouse where the deliveries were made, and start buddying up to everyone, buying them cups of coffee and what not. Whatever blankets they yanked out as defective one day, he managed to slip back in the next. Thus there were only a few left over, to be mixed in with the next batch. Eftihis, who couldn't bear the idea of being stuck with seconds, said he would sell them on Eolou Street if it came to that. "*Store liquidation ... Get them while they last*!..." But a few cutting remarks by Andonis kept him from carrying out his plan – without, however, truly convincing him. Eftihis kept two of the blankets for himself – "Why shouldn't we keep warm? We nearly froze to death last winter." He hugged them and wrapped himself in them at night, even though it was already summer. The work orders had come by way of Thodoros. They were from another factory, which had taken on a hefty job with a tight deadline. Hence they weren't overly concerned with quality. The blankets delivered, Eftihis immediately asked Andonis to tally up the profits, but once again Andonis gave him a hard time, and was so short with him that one might have detected a certain malice: "Manufacturing is a matter of a complete circle ..." Another of his excuses was that the factory that gave them the orders would pay them half the amount in thread and the other half in three months' time.

Thodoros helped out considerably. After the judge's death, Eftihis maintained that no one was to blame for that whole fiasco. Thodoros had cursed him and kicked him out. His next visit, Eftihis had whined that there was no point in his being ruined just because of an unfortunate conjunction of events, and that, had he known how much grief the late judge had been causing Thodoros, he would have told the old man how things stood at the outset. Andonis made a timid appearance at one of these meetings, pointing out to Thodoros that his anger was out of place, since the judge was no longer a factor. "I used to know his son, and he thought I might be able to do something to help him." "What," ranted Eftihis, "you want me to hand Angelos over to you? Will that make you happy?" Thodoros didn't respond. At their next meeting, Eftihis blindly signed all the mortgage papers for the looms, and Thodoros gave him the money. Andonis was outraged. Cursing and beating his forehead, he rattled off the risks Eftihis was running. Now Thodoros circulated freely, without fear of the judge popping up and asking him with his impeccable and serene cordiality if his conscience had examined the question of responsibility. "Can you believe it!..." But such discussions did nothing to further business negotiations, so everyone forgot them. Thodoros asked them not to hire that Gripakis fellow because he would only be a troublemaker. And Gripakis, a sharp-witted and practical man, understood immediately when they said they would definitely need him later, once business picked up. He said good-by and went on his way. He came back once or twice, but he went directly to Ismene's door and knocked. She seemed surprised, but later they left together. The others all assumed that they were going to meet Angelos.

Eftihis wandered around in a daze once the noise stopped. It was hard work, demanding that he be constantly on his toes. He told Mary to throw down plenty of water to get rid of the dust. "Have one of the girls do it ..." Mary said, which sent Eftihis into a rage because he knew she meant Elpida. "Starting tomorrow, you go to work at one of the looms. The exercise'll do you good, and it'll get you to use your brain a bit. You seem to be under the impression that you're already the wife of a great industrialist." She silently began mopping the floor, and Eftihis began sermonizing about how when someone doesn't know anything, they go out and try to learn. "You can't go around using the phrase 'I don't know' as if it were your personal privilege. Everybody bends over backwards to learn a trade ... What gives you the right to declare yourself a useless individual and expect others to respect that, huh?"

Eftihis abruptly fell silent. Mary's father was standing in the doorway. He slouched into the room and stood wretchedly before him. "How'd you know which door it was?" Eftihis taunted. Mary came in barefoot, carrying a bucket and a mop.

In a quavering, barely audible voice, the old man began some long story about how interest on the sovereigns he had borrowed for Eftihis the day of the wedding had come due ... "I know you'll come through for me, kids ..." he went on, hoping to gain their pity. Eftihis crossed his arms and coolly heard him out. When he was finished, Eftihis turned to Mary. "Answer the man," he ordered. Mary faltered momentarily, knowing her response would be decisive. Her father went on groveling, until Eftihis lost patience. "Knock it off. Whatever your daughter says goes ... Come on, Mary, speak up." Her father turned his imploring gaze upon her. "Get out!" she shouted at him. Eftihis smiled to himself with satisfaction. "Don't expect anything from us," Mary went on. "We've got a business to run ..." The old man reminded them that it was he who had given them the money for the business, and all he was asking was a very small favor. "If we'd known there was going to be interest on it, we'd have borrowed from somebody else," Mary told him, and Eftihis was amazed to see she was beginning to get the hang of things. "She's right," he told his father-in-law, who all but threw himself at their feet. "They're going to lock me up," he whispered in desperation. "Let them," Mary shouted into his face.

The old man dragged himself out the door and disappeared. Eftihis burst out laughing. "That poor sap! He's downright pathetic the way he carries on ..." Then he turned to his wife, beaming: "Hey, put that mop down, kiddo, and get yourself dressed for a night on the town. You were terrific! We're going to celebrate till the sun comes up ..."

IN THE AFTERNOON, Ismene would water the flowers and sit on her iron landing. Hours went by without her exchanging a word with anyone. She watched who came and went in the courtyard, keeping tabs on strangers. Her nerves were tied to the creaking of the front gate. Sometimes Eftihis asked her with a wink, "Where's hero-boy, did he drop you?" Another time he said, "What are you sitting there all alone for? No date today?" Ismene, of course, never answered, and did her best to conceal the paralyzing fear that welled up in her.

Every since that Sunday, whenever people saw Ismene they thought of Angelos. It was almost as if he were living there, and had always been there, the way he just materialized at the critical moment. And to think he hadn't been afraid to confront that fat fellow. But young fighters like him were never afraid, since they spent their lives cheek to jowl with death. Things were different for them, because they knew that their death was fated, it was only a matter of time. Ismene must have had plenty of guts, too. Imagine loving a condemned man for all those years! It wasn't her loving him that was so strange – everybody loved him – but her waiting for him. She was no doubt thinking about him as she sat there on the winding stairs. What could you say to her? Not the usual patter, to be sure, because it was clear that she didn't fear death either. But what did she want with all those flowers?

When they got off work, the workers greeted her if she happened to be sitting there, at the end of another day.

She had been exhausted lately, with all there was for her to think and worry about. How could she rest when she knew that the person hiding on the roof was counting on her alone? "He needs me now, his life depends on me," she said silently, and stiffened at the thought that some careless act of hers, some imperceptible error, could bring on catastrophe. And she had to do it all by herself, while persuading others that her life went on as before. Coming home from work, she would try to tell at a glance if anything had happened in her absence, looking for some discernible change. Next, she would casually make her way into Eftihis' textile works to see how people looked at her. Most of the time they just greeted her with a "hello" that was lost in the uproar, or even considered that unnecessary, and went on with their work. She would leave with a feeling of relief. One afternoon Eftihis asked, "Are you trying to learn how to work a loom, is that why you're always watching? It's not that easy." Ismene had simply smiled and said she liked watching the machines. Another time she had asked if Vangelia was home, but often one look from someone inside was enough to reassure her that things were as quiet as when she'd left. Only then could she let out her breath and begin to plan for the huge responsibility she'd taken on. She organized her day – errands, shopping for Angelos – so as not to leave the house in the afternoon, because when she did, she was frantic with worry until she got back and assured herself that all was well. Vangelia had asked her to go with her somewhere on a couple of different afternoons, but she had declined. Nowhere did she feel such peace as on that first step of the winding stairs. She sat there like a sentry, huddled and silent. She had to keep her trips up to the roof to a minimum. She also had to keep an eye on everything, in case something were to take on added significance, at which point ... She no longer bought a newspaper in the morning; the judge's glasses never left their case, there on his desk. Fanis would greet her daily: "Morning, Ismene. What's the news?" "Everything's fine," she would answer, and he would go on in to work. If he didn't see her in the morning, he would always find a pretext later on – going out to the laundry-room, or to look at something on the street. Ismene wondered whether his interest concealed anything. What was he expecting to hear? Stathis had asked her once as well, but she replied with obvious irony that she never saw him – wanting to remind Stathis of how he had led her on when she was desperate for news. He never asked after that, and when their paths crossed, they were content to exchange nods.

Night after night, Ismene would wake up at the set hour, switch the kitchen light on and off twice, then wait for him to throw down the rope. That way she could supply his needs, and at the same time it was as if they were exchanging greetings. The last few days he had written her, "I don't need anything, thanks," and she knew he was depressed again, in the grip of a stubborn, proud despair that would have everything hopeless and remote. At first he asked for newspapers, then she sent up his legal brief, which he said he wanted in order to gain a better understanding of his case. Two nights later, however, he sent it back, having no further need of it. Another night he wrote that he needed a ruler, a compass, and some white paper. Apparently he was doing some geometry problems, which beat doing nothing at all. When Ismene knew that her Aunt Amalia would be out the following day, she wrote him to send down his dirty laundry.

The previous evening he had sent her his laundry again. She had hugged the bundle tightly, smelled the sweat, and rubbed her cheek against the warm sheet. She took them to bed with her so they wouldn't be spotted, and fell asleep at dawn clutching them to her breast. When she washed them that afternoon, alone in the house, she sang – how long had it been? – and fondled his flannel undershirt in the deep suds, then rinsed them all again and again with torrents of cool water, till they were spotless. She wanted him to have something that came from her hands next to his body, as an amulet.

When she sprang lightly up to the roof holding the basket of wet laundry, the iron stairs burnt her feet. The walls had soaked up the heat, the rooftiles steamed, and everything wavered before her eyes. She hung out the sheets in front of the door of the small shed, to keep from being seen, then tapped on the wood. The door was unlocked. Angelos, naked from the waist up, lay with his hands behind his head, staring up at the ceiling. Ismene set down the basket and threw herself on him. Angelos gently placed his hands on her hair. She felt weightless, like a feather, or a warm afternoon wind. Then there was the familiar sweat, and the strong, steady beatings of her heart.

They lay for a long time without moving. Ismene, as if waking up, lifted her hair and looked at him.

"Sorry if I scared you. I wanted to see you so bad all morning, I couldn't wait to come ..."

"It's perfectly safe, honey ... Thank you."

Angelos raised himself up on one elbow and leaned against the wall. Ismene put her arms around him and kissed him.

"Do you mind not getting so close," Angelos panted. "It's so hot this time of day," he said, gasping for air.

Ismene's eyes flashed ever so slightly as she got up. Then she bent over the laundry basket. With a certain irritability to her movements, she removed the laundry and pulled a large package from underneath.

"I brought you your books, like you asked. These are all that were left."

She unwrapped the package, revealing the half-burnt books, sooty and crumpled, their charred edges flaking. She set them down on the table. Neither dared to touch them.

"That's all that was left ..." she repeated softly.

"Thank you for saving them ... Don't go yet."

But Ismene did go, a little spitefully perhaps. As the door swung open, Angelos was blinded by the blaze of afternoon light, he could feel the scorching heat on his face. His tiny room, the old store shed, suddenly felt empty. From outside came the wide buzzing murmur of summer. Angelos went over to the window. Here too were shutters, through which he could see a world aflame, a few rooftops and the courtyard. Ismene was hanging out the rest of the laundry – his things. After pinning them on the line, she carefully covered them with the sheets. A few drops fell to the concrete and instantly evaporated. He saw her erect body as it reached for the line, her black hair glistening. When would she be back? He couldn't see her eyes, but he felt sure that anger smoldered there, he could see it in her movements.

HE HAD A BETTER VIEW of the rooftiles from there, making it easier to remember that morning when he had leaped from rooftop to rooftop at the sound of their knock on his door. It would be harder to do this time of day, because the tiles would burn your feet like hot coals. Down in the courtyard, Eftihis' factory was a hive of activity. Andonis came and went in fear and distraction, attempting with energetic procrastination to wrap up unfinished business. It was as if he, too, with his frenetic behavior, were carrying out a sentence of another sort against himself. Like the stifling heat, the rumble of the machines devoured your voice, binding you to the pulse of a motor whose incessant murmur promised you a temporal margin. Andonis likewise hovered in the margins, as if keeping a safe distance from something he was afraid would burn him. Yet once he had belonged to that promising young generation that went to its death with a song on its lips.

The burnt books still lay on the table. Angelos had barely touched them, and that quite gingerly. A few pages had survived intact, scorched only around the edges. He would reread the books, starting at the beginning, like a hardworking student in his first year at the University. Maybe it would provide him with a sort of continuity, a path from which to scout around for the big exception. No battle was ever won by chance, and certainly not from inside a forgotten storage shed. Why had Ismene gone away angry?

Getting up his courage, Angelos took hold of one of the books, scraped away the charred, crumbling edges, and began reading the first page. Why had Lucia been so intent on burning them? She must have felt let down somehow. He remembered how, in the afternoon stillness, the two of them used to steal conserves from their mother's jar. She kept it locked up, to have on hand "in time of need," should any visitors drop in. They would go on barefoot down the freshly-washed floorboards and tiptoe into the bedroom to get the keys from the bedside table. When she noticed the level in the jar sinking, their mother hid some in another cupboard too. How they laughed when they discovered it in a vase! And when they unearthed the bottle of cherry juice in the flour bin, they licked their lips and fingers. "Lucia," he once told her, "someday I'm going to build you a house designed just for you ... Not any old house, but tailor-made, like a piece of custom clothing." Lucia would not have been coming for that house now. Surely she would have understood that it was not his fault that he broke his promise. "I had the best of intentions, but ..." Back then, at mid-day, the streets were empty, the sun pounded on the closed shutters, and the chairs were decked in their sprigged skirts. When the judge came home, he would throw off his stiff collar and his cares and put on a long nightshirt with a reddish braid around the edges. The dairyman, the street-organist, the pumpkin-seed seller and the grocer came by at the same time each day, because everything needed to have its own rhythm. "Lucia, if you don't stop tickling my feet, not only are you going to have all your hair pulled out, but you're going to fail math too." Perhaps she had come on account of some problem she couldn't solve on her own. "Every problem, however, contains its own solution." That maxim went back a long way, to a time when life was simple and orderly. On those afternoons during the war, everything rippled before one's eyes, and as he walked, he would match his stride to the wing-beat of longing inside him. But if he started reminiscing about the old days, he would never get around to reading these books, which had been renewed by fire.

Angelos tried to concentrate. He picked up the ruler and the compass and began working out the first, the most elementary exercise.

FINDING HIMSELF ALONE, Andonis suddenly realized he had no place to be. He had taken care of all of his factory chores, as well as certain other trifling business matters, and was now strolling peacefully along. It was a chance to think. At that time of day, the streets downtown were less crowded, the shops had closed, and those with regular jobs were on their way home. Now that he was no longer being jostled along by the crowds, he sensed how his constant contact with others chafed him. But that sea of faces had receded, leaving the shop windows, the colorful arcades with their closed offices, streets he had walked down thousands of times, doors, the facades of old buildings (urban development had been cut short by the war) side by side with the tinsel glitter of new money, its insolence a testament to how easily it had been acquired; plus a few people lingering at bus-stops, and stores, hundreds of stores filled with merchandise.

A car squealed to a stop abreast of him, and a hand he didn't recognize waved him over. It was Rapas, the engineer, Loukis' friend. Andonis went over diffidently, but the engineer flung open the door.

"Hop in, I need you for something."

So without a second thought Andonis climbed in.

The car sped off. They went past the Zappeion and took Syngrou Street. Better off just keeping quiet and not asking where they were going. They whipped through traffic, clearly in a big hurry to get somewhere. Rapas was a good driver, keeping his eyes on the road while confiding to Andonis.

"You know, Loukis is a big talker. He doesn't have a penny himself, but he still wants to get involved in big-time business operations," Rapas said, as if continuing a conversation from before. "He never has a concrete plan ... He thinks if you get to the ministers' girlfriends, you can get away with anything."

Andonis laughed because that was what was expected of him.

"You're wasting your time with him, Andonis. From the moment I set eyes on you, I realized you had a real grasp of what it means to do business in the world today. Stick with me and you'll see ... If we join forces, there'll be no stopping us ..."

"I'm with you there," Andonis said, casting Rapas an admiring look. "We could really go places together ... That bid we were talking about ..."

"Forget it. I've got my sights on something else now. Something really big ... It's all set up. That's what I want you and me to work on together ... Where was I? Oh yes, so Loukis sees himself as someone gambling in a casino, he's waiting to see what comes up on the wheel."

"What you need is a wheel with only one number," said Andonis

"There you go, Andonis. You hit the nail on the head."

"Luck's only for fools," Andonis went on, taking courage. "And you know something else? It's an excuse to fail. Personally, I've never ... I'd be ashamed, I'd consider it degrading to base my hopes on luck. When you plan something right, every eventuality has to be taken into account ..."

"Exactly. I mean I could open an office and hang out a shingle, and sit around waiting for customers. 'What'll it be, four rooms plus bath?'"

They were heading down toward the sea, as if shot from a cannon. Rapas must have been behind schedule, or expected somewhere. Andonis, ensconced in the seat beside him, sat with his briefcase on his knees, ready to offer his opinion on the delicate matter they were zooming off toward. "He must need my help in some negotiations." They took the turn for Faliron, feeling the cool sea air against their faces. There was no time to enjoy the sight of the boats under sail. How long since he and Vangelia had gone there, as they used to back at the beginning, when they'd walk from one end of the beach to the other?

With an empty road in front of him, Rapas drove even faster. The truth was Andonis knew nothing about him. He had to be under forty. His hands were steady on the wheel. "I wonder what he needs me for," Andonis asked himself, while he talked about the new coastal roads and the relation of transportation to tourism. He spoke familiarly, and tried to offer him a few helpful opinions. That too was a commodity a skilled salesman could dispense in return for certain monthly benefits.

"Orestes," Andonis went on, using Rapas' first name, "the government's policy on investments is going to be revived. The task of reconstruction will be carried out by the private sector. That's the inevitable consequence of the policy they've been pursuing. I set forth this viewpoint, with supporting data, in an article to be published shortly in a financial journal. I'll bring you a copy ... You should pay someone to do your statistical analyses, to leave you free to go out and hunt down contracts, start new projects, make business connections ..."

They passed the airport and in no time had devoured the entire stretch of sun-baked road down to Vouliagmeni. They didn't even stop there.

"Did you mean it before when you said we were friends?"

"Of course," answered Orestes.

Andonis smiled, and looked out the window at the seaside villas. It was a world far from his – the road, the sea, the hot sand. They went past Varkiza too. They sped on without letup. When they arrived at a deserted spot, with nothing but rocks on their right, Rapas suddenly slowed, looked around uncertainly, and stopped.

"Where are we going?" he asked.

The car's interior was suddenly deafeningly quiet, as if they were at the bottom of the sea.

"Where are we going?" Orestes asked again.

"I thought you knew ... You've got somewhere to be."

"And you, Andonis," laughed Rapas, "you never even opened your mouth! We'd have gone all the way to Sunion and driven straight over the edge."

He pulled slowly away. He found a level area and turned around. He tore up the road the whole way back, never saying a word, clutching the steering-wheel with the same grim determination to arrive on time for something or other.

"That was really quite pleasant," Andonis ventured. "It means you needed to get away."

"We're late. I want to be in Ekali by seven."

Andonis kept quiet. He didn't even ask why he had wanted him along. He looked at his watch and said he had urgent business in Kallithea, lest Rapas mistake him for an idle loafer.

When he climbed out of the car, the engineer, screwing up his eyes as if trying to remember something, asked:

"By the way, where do I know you from?"

"I'm Andonis ..."

"Mind telling me when we met?"

"Last winter, once when ..."

"I'll expect to see you at my office ..." Rapas said, and slammed the door, having lost interest in Andonis' explanations.

Once more people went reeling past on the street in the usual muddle. Panic over the indeterminate duration of the temporary made their steps as frantic as a bat's flight. Was money a commodity? Is honesty a convertible currency? What do you think? Answer quickly, without mincing words. But what's more temporary than something permanent that's lost its rhythm? The economies of underdeveloped countries always lacked coherence, existing only on the brink of some cataclysm. "I owe myself years of back-pay." Whoever laid down these twisted streets must have been afraid of looking straight ahead: the age of small businesses. Then came the facade of the bank again, another distinguished-looking gentleman, the sun glaring from the sidewalk. The afternoon crept insensibly down the asphalt. The respite didn't last, however. Each day took place on the brink of some momentous occurrence.

ANOTHER WORKDAY HAD ENDED. The machines and workers had efficiently carried out their assorted duties. Production had increased along predicted lines, and fatigue had come on as gently and naturally as the evening shadows. In the courtyard, the technicians and their assistants washed off the sweat and the fluff, hung up their workclothes in the laundry-room, and quietly set off.

Elpida took the road for Petralona, but at the corner she sensed steps behind her, and soon saw Fanis at her side.

"Are you going straight home?"

"Yes."

"Why the hurry? There's no one waiting for you, is there?"

"You're right, I hadn't thought of that ... So it's only when there's someone waiting for you that you walk quickly?"

"No, but you must be tired. All day in that cage ..."

They went for a couple of blocks without saying anything. Elpida kept her eyes on the ground, as if watching threads on a loom. She was always watching something. Did everything warrant such a wondering gaze? You ended up with sloping shoulders and myopia that way. But here he was, walking alone with Elpida! It hadn't been so hard after all.

"What do you do when you get home?"

"Sit. What else is there to do?"

She was right. It would be difficult for a girl alone in an empty basement apartment to find much to do. He should have thought of that before asking such a dumb question, for which he had no follow-up. A few days earlier, Fanis had decided to speak openly to her. He had spent hours hovering around her street hoping to bump into her. Later he acknowledged to himself how cowardly this was, but that didn't help either. Instead of knocking on her door, he bent down and glanced through her half-open window, which was level with the street. All he saw was the corner of a table, an old chair, and, for a brief instant, her legs in the back of the room. He went away, and the next day he kept looking at her trying to understand how a girl could live in a basement apartment without having even some coward to come knock at her door. He instructed her on the spool and the threads as if she were someone whose name he remembered only when he saw her before her machine.

"So, Elpida, how about if we walk together a ways?"

"Isn't that what we're doing? Sure."

They went through another neighborhood. Everything drooped with heat and fatigue. Women threw water in the street to keep down the dust, or screeched at their kids to go in. Tired wage-earners straggled home with their hands hanging limp at their sides, and a few young women slipped out silently on their way to some rendezvous. The days had grown dry as bone, your steps became careless, you rarely spoke. You worked all day just to make your hands feel useful. The buildings had been built side by side to keep them from falling over. Elpida's dress was old and worn, it made you think she had lived in that basement alone for more years than you could count. The world must not be a very pretty place in her eyes, which was probably why she dragged her feet so often when she walked. She wasn't the only one who had tasted the world's bitterness.

Fanis swallowed. His throat felt knotted up. He tried to match his step with hers.

"We've been seeing each other every day for so long now, and we never spend any time together ... Doesn't that seem strange to you?"

"Not very, since none of you ever ..."

"You mean you'd like to?"

"Of course. Work doesn't keep you company," said Elpida.

He gave her a sidelong glance to see what she was getting at. "I've seen you smile once or twice, and you were so pretty." No, he couldn't say that. He didn't know what it would take to make her happy. Whatever it was, it would require a real effort. All living things were thirsty for something: the lame dog in front of them, those two people talking on the corner, the dusty pepper-trees, even the squeal of the train and the gas burner on the nut-seller's cart, or that fellow strutting down the street. Everything required moisture in order to survive. If his mouth was dry, it was because it had taken him so long to understand that the dryness he felt around him was a permanent state.

"Tomorrow I'll start showing you how to weave all on your own, Elpida ... You need to learn everything if you want to become really good at it ..."

But it was absurd, and probably annoying to her to boot, for him to address her as an expert, as a teacher. Or to bring Eftihis into it. They were in Petralona now, nearing her house.

"Let's go on a bit, it's still early. Up to the hill. It might be cooler up there ..."

Elpida followed him to the parched, barren hill. Everything was wrapped in the blue after-glow of dusk. The rocks were still warm. Lights were coming on here and there, a distant murmur had begun to rise, the shadows to merge. There was a great weight he would have to lift from Elpida's shoulders if he wanted her to smile. Still, she hadn't said that she was tired yet, or wanted to go back. She looked into the distance, at the clear sky, and at Fanis, too, once or twice, then down at the rocks again. It grew darker, the lights thickened in the distance, the silence settled in, and Elpida's face appeared more relaxed.

"Like it here?"

"Yes," she said. "Shall we go up to those trees and look over at the other side?"

ISMENE REALIZED THERE WAS NO POINT in maintaining her huddled vigil at the foot of the iron staircase. Dangerous amounts of time were being lost, they could go on for years and still find themselves in the same boat. Going backwards, in other words, holding their breath every time the gate creaked, every time someone new appeared in the passageway. "I'm tired of being afraid," she said to herself and got up, as if she had just reached an important new decision. She paced the courtyard a while, stole a glance up at the storage shed on the roof, and sat back down on the first step. Then she went up a few more steps and sat down; then a few more. By midnight, she was practically at the top. Yet she didn't knock at the door of the shed. She had spent so many nights there among the flowerpots. It was a sentry duty that didn't allow one a moment's rest. All those years Angelos was away she had been no less sleepless and alert, but back then there had been nothing to guard. Now she had good reason to sit and watch over his sleep.

At the appointed time, she went down and switched the kitchen light on and off. Soon the rope descended. Ismene sent up the package she had prepared earlier, and refilled his pitcher. Angelos wrote her his usual note: "Thank you, good-night." But Ismene didn't sleep a wink.

The next morning, before going to work, she went by her brother Stamatis' house and spoke to him candidly: "You haven't forgotten who I am, have you? This is the first time I've come to ask something of you. I want you to loan me three thousand drachmas." Stamatis, as expected, started in on how he was merely rank and file, "what savings can a department head put aside these days," and besides, he had his family to look after. All she got was a lukewarm promise of a thousand. Then she went to her big sister's and an uncle's. "I don't need advice, I came to ask for money," she yelled when they began to tell her how to live her life. She also stopped by a few friends, sometimes asking for a loan and sometimes venting her rage. Two or three promised to give her something at the start of the month, when they were paid.

At the office, she meticulously thought out her plan. "It's the only solution," she said to herself with conviction, then gaily began toting up the various amounts on index cards: credits and debits, monthly expenses, personal expenses ... What remainder could there be when you were summing up the details of your life? Things had recently taken another turn for the worse at the company, but Ismene ignored the threats from above. There was more talk of a strike at the factory, the office-workers were in a tizzy, Spiros and Clio said menacingly that higher productivity and the corporation were all that mattered. Rumors ran rampant, with everyone desperate to come up with some scrap of useful information. It was the same thing all over again – telegrams, suspicious activity, faces bent over desks, whispers, the numbing chill that made your forehead drip with sweat – it had become every bit as exhausting and precarious as before. But Ismene could not have cared less. If her plans came to pass – and why shouldn't they, since it was to everyone's advantage? – it would mean a fresh start. But she would have to work it all out before presenting it to Angelos.

That afternoon, she ran around doing her usual chores, buying food for the family – which now included Angelos' mother Ioanna – and taking care of Angelos' latest requests: a number of new books and some paper. While in the shop, she asked how much a drawing table cost. When she arrived home, soaked in sweat, she went directly up the stairs, then, half-way to the top, decided she wasn't quite ready yet. Back down in the courtyard, Fanis approached her with his assumed casual air, gave her a wink she didn't understand, and whispered that Thodoros was inside. Upset as she was, she didn't have time to wonder why he had spoken to her like that. She went into the room with the looms without turning to look in back, where Thodoros must have been in conversation with Eftihis, since she could hear his gravelly voice. She went straight into Vangelia's room, which was tidy now, cramped as ever but clean, and with enough room to stand in. It all spoke of a tightly packed disarray, with everything barely squeezed in. Vangelia seemed to have adapted to living in such close quarters, for she again wore that tranquil smile of hers, and her eyes had regained their radiance.

"Remember, Vangelia, when you told me about that aunt of yours in Holargos? Could we go there some afternoon?"

"So you found him? You're seeing him?"

"Yes, I'll tell you all about it ..."

"What are you so upset about? You should feel relieved ... We can go whatever day you like. Is ... *he* all right? I see you sitting on the stairs all the time and I think to myself, Ismene must be worrying again."

"Oh, he's perfectly safe. Can we make it for tomorrow afternoon?"

Vangelia said yes, and Ismene gave her a kiss on the cheek. "You're the only one who knows." On her way out, Thodoros was at the loom nearest the door talking to Elpida. He caught sight of Ismene and instantly saw red.

"It's you, is it? What are you doing here?"

Vangelia angrily stuck her head through the door.

"Is he going to be keeping tabs on us now, Eftihis? Who is he, anyway?"

"You know very well who I am," said Thodoros.

"No need to get excited," Eftihis interjected. "She lives here. You don't really think we need a doorman, do you?"

"This is my business, too," Thodoros snarled at Vangelia. "I need to know what goes on here."

"You're overstating it a bit, don't you think?" Eftihis put in cagily.

"What have I ever done to you? There's no reason for you to blow up at me." Ismene managed to say. "I came here to visit my friend ... Do you have something against me? Why does it annoy you so much to see me? It's up to you to tell me if there's anything behind it."

"Not again!" cried Thodoros. "I already heard all this from someone else – and in exactly that same tone, too. Listen, you, I don't want to see you in here again. Eftihis, I forbid outsiders to enter the work-area ..."

This was too much for Eftihis. He realized that all Thodoros' orders were more than just a joke. He had gone too far this time. Someone had some explaining to do.

"So, friend, exactly what do you mean by 'I forbid'? Whose factory is this, anyway? Who's in charge here?"

"I can't come over here only to have the same people pecking away at me ... Tell her to leave this instant. Kick her out ..."

Ismene stood her ground in the courtyard, looking him squarely in the eyes. In her astonishment, Vangelia concluded that Ismene must have some of the strength and stubbornness of that stalwart young man who had appeared out of the blue that time. After all, she'd had the pluck to wait for him all those years.

Fanis had left his loom running and was standing at her side, with feigned indifference, wiping his hands on a wad of thread-ends. He gave Eftihis an ironic look, as if to say, "So he's the boss, is he, even though you've been passing yourself off as the owner all this time ..." It didn't escape Eftihis that the look of doubt

Thodoros' words had instilled in each and every face was quickly turning to outright mockery.

"I'm the boss here!" Eftihis boomed. "And I decide who can or can't come in. Did you all hear that? I'm the only one giving orders around here!"

"What's this all about?" asked Andonis, who had just come in.

"A small misunderstanding," Eftihis whispered.

But Andonis took one look at the fearless determination imprinted on Ismene's face, and the bags hanging under Thodoros' eyes, and understood instantly. To cut short that dangerous silence, he triumphantly announced:

"Great news! I've secured a sizeable order ... Starting tomorrow, once we seal the deal, we'll be setting up a second shift! Now everyone back to your machines ..."

He took Eftihis and Thodoros by the arm and led them out into the courtyard, where he proudly filled them in on his success. The others returned to their tasks, and Fanis gulped down a clot of bitter spit, angrily flinging down the wadding.

The next afternoon, in good spirits, Ismene and Vangelia set off together. Vangelia had sewn herself a new dress, and was taking greater care with her appearance. She was in all-around better spirits because, however difficult her circumstances – with all the clatter next door and being cramped in that little room – it appeared that the textile business was going well, and Andonis was happy. In recent days, he had stopped telling her lies – she could tell by his tone – and in fact, on two or three occasions, they had even gone out together and had simple conversations, the way they used to, without his making her dizzy with all his promises and agitated prattle, which she found unbearable when he was out to deceive her. On the way, Vangelia told Ismene that, judging by the brief glimpse of him she'd had that one Sunday, Angelos was worth standing up for. "And you were so proud of him ... You were completely transformed ... It did me so much good to see you two together ..." And later she went on: "Andonis talked about him all night. They used to be good friends ... But now Andonis is tired ..."

They arrived at a small house surrounded by a wrought-iron fence draped in greenery. Inside was a quiet, well-tended garden, a couple of steps, then the door. A middle-aged woman cordially welcomed them, and they sat under a grape-arbor. “It’s so lovely here. You have a wonderful yard,” said Ismene. Vangelia wasted no time in calmly addressing the purpose of their visit:

“Aunt, you told me last winter that you had more room than you needed here, and were thinking of renting out two of the rooms. My friend here is interested ... It would be her fiancé and his mother, and, until they get married, which they plan to do very soon, she’d live here with them ... They’re good people, they’d be good company. Her fiancé’s an engineer, he works on industrial drawings all day. He never goes out, and needs peace and quiet.”

“I’m thinking of renting the whole house, as you see it,” Vangelia’s aunt said. “I’m planning on heading back to the island. What’s there for me here? Come on inside and have a look around.”

The house consisted of three clean and spacious rooms with large windows, a kitchen, and a veranda opening onto a quiet, isolated garden. “He’ll like it,” Ismene decided, and thought about where they would set up Angelos’ drawing table, and which room would be Ioanna’s. Vangelia noticed how she passed from room to room, how she opened the door to the courtyard, how she paused at the door – as if it were *her* house, and she were expecting someone to welcome her. She was happy, as if under a spell. Vangelia had never seen her in such speechless transport, her features so radiant. “It’s ... this ... exactly what I wanted,” she murmured.

“And when do you think you’ll come?” asked Vangelia’s aunt.

“In just a few days,” Ismene responded without hesitation. “Maybe next week. Isn’t it perfect, Vangelia?”

She gave her a small deposit on the spot, as much as she had been able to collect, as if to keep her dream from fluttering away. They agreed to come back in a couple of days. “Maybe he’ll come with us!” she said and, moved, took leave of that dear, sweet-spoken woman with the beautiful home that seemed to have been built to house everything Ismene had spent so many years wishing for.

On their way back, the two women both felt ebullient. Ismene couldn’t stop talking about her plans, and her joy infected Vangelia.

“I have a secret, too. You’ll be the only one to know ...”

"What is it?"

"I'm expecting again," Vangelia said. "And this time I'm going to keep it, no matter what. I'm going to have this baby."

"Have you told Andonis?"

"He'll find out when the baby's out of danger. I'm afraid to tell him, anything could happen. Right now things are going well. But tomorrow, who knows?... I'm not putting myself through that again ... I'm right, aren't I? Not for anything ..."

AFTER DARK, ISMENE quietly climbed the stairs carrying a bunch of flowers she had bought on the way home. Angelos had the door open, and was sitting inside, just out of sight. He was quiet and distracted. He didn't know what to make of the flowers. "Put them in the glass," she told him. "It's for decoration."

It would be cooler outside. At that hour, no one would see them. Angelos slid along the wall, and leaned his back against the low parapet so as to keep from view. Ismene sat down next to him, where she could mind the stairs in case anyone came up. She was careful not to touch him, because there had been one other time too, before that sweltering afternoon, when she had leaned against him and felt him recoil. She didn't even tell him of her plan. They sat for a long time in silence. Finally, Angelos told her that he had been reading constantly, that he was pleased to find, after reviewing his old material, that he hadn't forgotten a thing.

"Isn't it odd, Ismene? As if it had only been yesterday ..."

"I think that's how it'll be if we start our lives over again. As if barely a day had passed ..."

"Maybe ... If only it were that easy, Ismene. Has anything changed?"

"It will. We can change it if we just get out of here ... If we're patient, we'll find a way."

"How?"

"Well, let's say we find a nice house with a yard, a quiet, isolated place a ways out of the city. It'll have an iron fence around it overgrown with vines, so no one will see us when we sit in the thick shade of the pine-tree, with all the bushes blooming around us ... Three furnished rooms and a bath ... Your mother will have one of the rooms, you can set up your drawing table in the other, next to the window ..."

"And then?"

"You'll work, you'll make blueprints and do calculations, and I'll go off to the company every morning. I'll come back in the afternoon loaded down with groceries, and the street will be quiet, the house clean and freshly painted. We'll have everything we need. Friends will come visit us – there must be a handful of people we can trust. We'll listen to music, we'll sit on the veranda in the evening, no one will be able to see us through all the vines, I made sure of that. They climb clear to the top, you can't even see it from the street ..."

Angelos leaned his head against the wall, listening. She couldn't make out his expression in the dark.

"And then, Ismene?"

"That's it. All we have to do is decide when to go ... It's furnished, and couldn't be nicer. We'll only take a few things from here ... Vangelia will help us. I've made all the arrangements ..."

"So, if I understand you correctly, Ismene, we'll move out of here and, instead of my being imprisoned in a storage closet, I'll be imprisoned in three rooms with a flower garden ... And instead of it being just me, there'll be three of us locked up together."

"What's wrong with that? Or am I missing something? Are things any better the way they are now?"

"It wouldn't change anything," Angelos said. "If I could go on living here without fear, I'd like that just fine. Of course, having a garden and a country house are all very nice, but can't you see it's not a question of location, or the number of rooms, or whether there are flowers or not ... Even when I was out on the street because I had no other choice, like that night in the rain, I was still a prisoner. Maybe I was even worse off: I was shaking with fear. A house where everyone's afraid will always be a depressing place ... And I would even go so far as to say that anywhere in the city, anywhere in the world, if you live in fear, it's just like being in prison."

"If I were to say that to you, you'd tell me I was wrong, you'd probably even laugh at me. If you still see yourself as a prisoner even when you're out roaming the streets, you better ask yourself if it's because you want to see yourself that way. What's there for you to be afraid of? What more does a man need than to have work and to live with the people he loves?"

"That house of yours is very tempting, Ismene. But I'm afraid it would be a little tough at this juncture. Let me think it over, and we'll see ..."

Ismene kept silent. She didn't tell him that she had already found the house in Holargos, had even put money down on it, and that the woman was expecting them the following week. They stayed on the roof a little longer, without talking, just looking out at the night, with its lights and its stars.

"It's late," Ismene said. "I'm going down."

"Good-night."

"Think about that house in the country with the flowering vine. I want you to give me a clear answer the next time we talk."

"I will," he promised. "Will you let me kiss you, Ismene?"

She returned his kiss, then went slowly down the iron stairs.

CHAPTER 18

THEY HAD STARTED UP a second shift at the factory. The new orders Andonis had brought in were a major breakthrough. Eftihis had agreed to supply, within certain terms and provisions, a specified quantity of goods on a fixed schedule, and thus the pace had picked up. Andonis had worked it all out, fine-tuned it like a clock. Flabbergasted, Eftihis simply looked on with admiration. "That's the whole secret, Mary. You have to fit the different businesses together like the pieces of a puzzle. Is there anything that guy doesn't know? But don't give up, we'll learn in time. The world is full of people who made it in business without being geniuses. We just have to keep asking questions until we find out how money's made ... Just wait, Mary, we'll be living it up before you know it!"

Andonis had amply demonstrated his abilities in the deal. His ulterior motive had been to lessen Thodoros' financial influence, who was trying to get his hands on all aspects of the business. With the new orders, and the others that would follow, they could make it through the critical period and be able to pay off their debts. "I'll set you up a good, solid business," he told Eftihis, and explained that to be a true factory-owner, the means of production had to belong entirely to you. "Keep going, keep going, you're driving me crazy!" Eftihis had cried, drunk with joy. He spent his day inspecting and measuring things. Every now and then, when he caught workers having a laugh among themselves, he would snap, "Would you mind keeping it down?" – just so they wouldn't forget who was boss.

Andonis would come home exhausted, and when Vangelia

wasn't there – where were she and Ismene always running off to anyway? – he would take a chair and sit at one end of the large room. He would rest his briefcase on his knees and watch the workers carrying out their tasks. Work, and more work ... Their experienced, expert hands moved rhythmically and systematically, their eyes and nerve-endings verified and guided: a positive energy, honorably expended. What was cleaner, purer or more precious than the sweat glistening on their faces? Everything was the product of labor, of expended effort, impossible to repay. Was there such a thing as an honest man who didn't work?

He had gotten the new orders from Spiros Ioannidis. He had gone by a few days before to ask about his drafts, and Spiros had mentioned that their factory's productive capacity was unable to meet their obligations. Andonis had jumped at the opportunity, and suggested a friend's operation take over part of the job. He worked out the details with Clio and Boufas, and a few days later Eftihis went himself and signed the papers. The thread arrived, and things got underway. Of course, the rates were lower because it wasn't first hand, but it was still well worthwhile. Another plus for Andonis was that his closer ties with them would make it harder for Spiros to protest his drafts. But nothing was settled yet, there was no telling what might happen. He had all but forgotten the stacks of canned meat in his room. He'd get around to selling it someday. As long as it had a label stating it was something, it could never be a total loss. The only total loss was something without a label, something whose value had not yet been discovered. "A little like me," Andonis said, and grew melancholy at the thought. The workers were hard at it, the machines pounded rhythmically away. Soon this shift would let out, and the next one would arrive. Now there was no letup to the noise, the machines rested only at night. The neighbors complained, the grumbling and fist-shaking started all over again, but Eftihis hit upon the perfect solution. He noticed the old man living behind them made the biggest stink: "It's turned me into a neurasthenic," he'd say, "they're going to lock me up in the loony-bin," and the like. At first Eftihis only lost his temper, then one day he told the neurasthenic, "I bet you're the one whose son is out of work ... I hear him singing those depressing songs of his, and they really get on my nerves ... Tell him to come over and I'll give him a job." And that was the end of their protests, for if anyone said anything, the old man would assail them: "If you've got something against Eftihis, you're going to have to reckon with me first." His son, a tall and curly-headed youth who knew how to run a loom, became devoted to Eftihis and gave up singing. A few days earlier, Andonis had stopped in on Spiros to let him know they needed more thread, and the buffoon, right in the middle of their conversation, had let drop, "The banks gave us notice on those drafts ..." Andonis' blood ran cold, yet he mustered the courage to laugh, to guffaw in fact, as such situations demanded. He arrived home downcast, did a bit of work with Eftihis, and that evening told Vangelia: "We have to look for a new place. You'll crack up if you go on living like this for much longer ... Tomorrow I'll ask an agent I know. We're like rats in a cage. We don't have a moment's peace ... So, by the end of the month ..." Vangelia looked at him with a wary smile. Next he told her that he had decided to rent an office downtown – perhaps even with a telephone – to conduct business, now that things were booming. "Are you in trouble again, Andonis?" asked Vangelia. "Tell me the truth. "No, I mean it ... Haven't we talked about getting a new place? What neighborhood would you prefer?" Why did Vangelia suddenly look so frightened? It wasn't as if he'd given her bad news. "So is it this all over again?" she whispered, turning pale.

A WELDER WEARING DARK GLASSES and a cap raised his torch and greeted Aliki with its flame when he saw her in the passageway. But instead of proceeding into the courtyard, Aliki knocked on the door and was let in by Voula. Three more men with iron masks, their faces streaked with grease, were working in the shop. As Voula got ready to go out, Aliki peered through the window. Three backs were bent over the flame. She still hadn't figured out which was the young man in the shed that first evening. The white glare forced her to shut her eyes. The one man still had on dark glasses and a cap. It was pitch-dark in the room. Had it been the same man both times who led her over with the blow torch? He had strong, powerful arms, that's all she could remember. If he were ever to take hold of her again, she would know him instantly. She asked Voula their names. "Tasos, Nikos, and Bobis.

There was a Lambros, but I haven't seen him for a while." "What's Lambros like?" "Well, like Tasos and Bobis." "Who's the nicest?" "How should I know?" "The strongest?" Voula gave a laugh. "The handsomest?" "They all look so alike with those goggles on." Bobis was heavier, and he walked with a slouch, so it wasn't him. There was someone else standing off to one side. "I don't know that one," said Voula. Nikos had white teeth – he was a more likely candidate. "And Lambros, when does he come?" "What do you care? Do you fancy him?" Aliki observed their movements carefully. Tasos was the most agile, springing from side to side, but Nikos looked taller. At that moment, he was hefting an iron door. She would even know him by his breath, it had been so quick and hot, she could still feel it on her cheek. Of course, it *could* have been Bobis. With those square shoulders of his, he had quietly blocked her path, and she had retreated without even being aware of it. Which of them had it been? They were busy at work, so none of them spoke. As the girls were going out, one of them poked his head out and blinded them with his torch.

"Why don't you talk to me, Aliki?" he demanded angrily.

Aliki turned to look when the light went away, but there was no one there. Which of the two had it been? Which of them should she talk to?

HAVING FINISHED HIS VARIOUS TASKS, Andonis went by Orestes Rapas' office, because it occurred to him that after their high-speed trip down the coast road, the engineer at some point would have figured out where he was going. Andonis found him sweating over a study involving concrete. He couldn't even take the time to talk to him.

"That's wage work, Orestes. In other words, the lowest rung on the scale of paid labor. Work yourself ragged at it, you'll never turn a profit. Profit is when ..."

And he systematically outlined the difference for him.

"What you should be doing is going out and rustling up the work, and leaving the drudgery to others. You're missing out on all sorts of great opportunities, all so you can take an absurd pride in the fact that you're working for a living. Can't you hear the whirr of contracts just waiting to be snapped up out there?"

They discussed a variety of other matters, and Andonis used a hundred and one arguments to get him to open his eyes so they could look around *together* – the magic word! – and pick up some nice government contracts for themselves.

"Do you have anyone who could take these computations of static strength off my hands? You're right, it's a waste of my time."

Andonis' brain rattled like an adding machine, and he said:

"I'll let you know tomorrow. There's one person, really top-notch ..."

Andonis then rushed over to see Ismene at the company offices. Once again the corridors were mobbed – scowls, angry mutterings, a wall of backs – the usual confusion when a group of workers crowds in all at once. Andonis threaded his way through the throng without noticing what demands they were making – "each to his own." Ismene appeared upset. "Why is she so hard on herself," Andonis wondered.

"They're talking about layoffs again ... Every time ..."

"When are you going to see Angelos?" he interrupted.

"I don't know, why?"

"Too bad. I've got a good job for him. It's a real opportunity."

"What is it?"

"You have to go talk to him today, though, tonight, and let me know by tomorrow."

And he went on breathlessly to tell her about Rapas' calculations of static strength.

"It's good work, it'll interest him. The important thing is for us to stick close to this engineer fellow, he's involved in all sorts of big projects. Make sure you see him today. Say hello for me ... I'll expect your answer tomorrow, or better still tonight. Try to persuade him."

"I'll do my best," said Ismene. "Thank you."

Andonis didn't linger. He dove into the crowd and ducked into Spiros' office ahead of the workers' committee. They had become very chummy now. Spiros welcomed him warmly and told the boy posted outside his door he didn't want to be disturbed. They agreed to go out together some night. Then he promised he would have more orders for his friend's business, if he proved to be reliable when it came to meeting deadlines.

"And my draft notes – I don't imagine you've torn them up ..."

"It will all be taken care of," said Spiros.

The conversation broke off when Clio came in. She was furious with the workers, who had picked the worst possible moment to go out on strike, right at the busiest time of year. "It's blackmail, blackmail!" she cried. Then she turned to Andonis with a smile:

"With your help, we won't need them anymore ... We have to meet a strict schedule in the delivery of these shipments. That's why we contracted with your friend to do it ... Let them shout all they want ..."

"So that's it!" cried Andonis, aghast. "You didn't tell me that, Spiros. You should have let me know."

"Would you have refused if you'd known?"

"No. As you know, it's not my operation. Besides, the two activities are unrelated. For us, production is impersonal. Don't worry," Andonis assured him, "your order will be filled no matter what."

A low roar came from without, penetrating the walls and the door cracks to fill that ice-cold office. The workers in the corridor were getting impatient. It was obvious that Spiros had used Andonis only to hold them off and insure that the work got done. He no doubt had anticipated their strike, and distributed his production among a large number of smaller factories. There was a manager with foresight! Now he would be able to assume a different tone with his workers. Seized with sudden panic, Andonis bid them good-by, but before he could leave Spiros hissed:

"And don't forget our unfinished business at the bank. If I find I can't rely on you, things will take their lawful course ...."

Stepping outside the door, Andonis was confronted with a sea of faces. They all seemed to be looking at him. He took a step backwards, only to come up against the hard planks of the door. He slid along the wall and plunged down the stairs, which delivered him, with a chaotic flurry of steps, out into the street.

THAT AFTERNOON, ISMENE returned home drenched in sweat. The fiery summer heat sucked the air from her lungs, and everything gave off a ripple of steam. Her eyes swam as the blaze reached its peak, her shoe soles left prints in the soft blacktop.

The street had become a river of fire, without a scrap of shade, and the walls hovered pink and yellow and blue before her dazzled eyes. If only there were one drop of green in all that, something cool and fresh to loosen the knot that only got tighter, making it harder and harder to breathe. A thousand worries, innumerable concerns and precautions, a swarm of fears darkened the bright air that was engulfing her, melting her. Sometimes she felt a chilling sweat on her forehead, tears dimming her eyes. It was no longer just some vast, cold, implacable danger. The house in Holargos awaited them, and Angelos held back. "I don't know what you're trying to tell me," Ismene had angrily said the other day, and Angelos had been at a loss for an answer. He wiped the sweat from his face, looked down at the page with the problem he had begun, and took a drink of warm water from the pitcher.

In the courtyard, the textile workers were sitting on the ground, leaning against the wall in the shade. Some of them had their eyes closed, to get the most out of their mid-day break. Ismene greeted them, and one or two nodded back. All seemed quiet. She let out her breath and went inside. She promptly took the hamper with the fresh wash up to the roof. But she was too impatient to hang out the sheets in front of the door of the storage shed. No one would see them, everyone was taking their siesta at that hour. The shutters on the surrounding houses were closed.

Angelos was still busy doing his math problems. Stripped to the waist and sweating, there was a certain agitation and fatigue in his eyes. And his little room was a furnace, with the sun beating down on it at all hours.

"Ah, I'm glad you came," he told her.

"Why, have you made up your mind? Are we going to Holargos?"

"Oh, not about that. There's a book I need. And some more paper."

"And what about the house that's waiting for us? You really have to give it a lot of thought. That's the problem you should solve first."

"I've studied it from every angle."

"And?"

"Your solution is just another dead end. It's just a means to buy time. Before long, we'd be faced with another crisis. Spurious solutions merely put off the problem ..."

Ismene fell face down on the bed and burst into tears.

"Words, words ... We're throwing our lives away. What difference does it make, anyway? Aren't you just as afraid here? Why have you been in hiding all these years? This isn't life. You're just deluding yourself. All you do is sit here and tremble, chewing away at your own flesh. *Your* solution means disaster, and that's all. Disaster."

"You think I don't know that? I haven't been able to think about anything else for years."

He reached out to touch her hair.

"Keep your hands off me," Ismene shouted, getting up.

"Cut it out, I didn't do anything."

"I don't want to be humored anymore. I don't need to be given false hope. You're headed straight for disaster. Something bad *did* happen, years ago. How long are you going to let it go on? Your father, when he told us he was seeing you, said it would have been impossible for you to live in hiding, and that if that were the case, it would be the heaviest sentence of all. 'But what if it's true?' I asked him one day. 'Then I'd do everything I could to flush him out, even if it meant his arrest.'"

"He said that?"

"Yes. Maybe that's why he was in such a hurry to complete the brief. I'm not saying you should go live on the streets. Just for us to get away from here, and to start leading a more human life. You're better off being afraid in your own house, with a yard, than here in this closet ..."

Ismene began crying again, and anything he said now would have been superfluous. It was all just words, which of course had no value when there was nothing solid behind them. Yet he was convinced that from the first day in that house of hers, it would be exactly the same as here. Why couldn't he make her see that? He sat down next to her, but she drew back. Then she folded her arms on the table with the geometry problems and put her head down, and it was as if she had withdrawn into that tiny furnace of a room to have a good cry by herself.

The machines started up in the courtyard, and it seemed the afternoon's steel lungs were lurching to life. "Just say I'm sick, exhausted, paralyzed ..." he wanted to tell her.

"When I was at Stathis', Ismene, I started digging a tunnel so I could slip in and out at will ... But I abandoned it because that too was a faulty solution born of panic. The house in the country is pretty much the same ..."

"Stop it! I don't want to hear anymore. I've had it with all your excuses, and all those years you never bothered to get in touch with me, even when you were here in the same courtyard ... It's clear you don't care about me anymore. Who knows, maybe you've even come to see me as a burden."

Ismene abruptly fell silent, hearing steps on the stairs up to the roof. Had they come for him? They exchanged looks, and Angelos glued his eyes to the shutter. Ismene came up beside him. The steps were approaching, the afternoon sun set the houses ablaze. "This is it," Angelos whispered.

The steps kept coming, and Aliki appeared, out of breath. When she reached the top, she looked apprehensively down the stairs, but she didn't have a chance to cry out because Eftihis instantly came into view, his eyes blazing, his neck muscles in knots, hungry, insatiable, his nostrils flaring, his hands spread like grappling irons.

"Not a word," he warned the girl. "Don't even think about crying for help."

Aliki stood in the middle of the roof, hugging herself as if she were cold. Eftihis slowly closed on her, hunched forward slightly, making sure she didn't escape this time. He trapped her over in the corner, where the sun was hottest. When she realized there was no way out, she cowered as if she were stark naked.

"No, leave me alone, please ..."

"Now you're mine!"

He encircled her with his arms in the bright empty space of the roof, as if there were no one else in the world. Her blouse had come open completely, and the sun kept beating down. The rooftop was on fire, Aliki scorched her hand when she touched it. She struggled to get up, gasping for air, but Eftihis, adding his strength to his frenzy, pinned her against the burning tiles.

The whole time, Angelos and Ismene stood side by side, their eyes fastened to the shutter. Not once did they look at each other. They held their breath, and afterwards realized how sweaty they had become when a large drop of common sweat fell from their foreheads where they'd been touching.

When Eftihis released her, Aliki remained on the ground a few moments, her eyes closed. Then she began to cry.

"What's wrong, sugar plum?" Eftihis asked.

"Will you love me?"

"Is that all it is? Hey, you're the prettiest one around, aren't you?"

He straightened his hair, told her, "bye," and went back down the stairs with his slow, steady gait. Aliki sat huddled in the corner. Her tears dried in the heat before even trickling down her face. She straightened her dress, losing herself in the sweltering silence that enfolded her.

Ismene and Angelos stood uncomfortably at the window. It wasn't easy for them to look at each other. An iron crown of thorns tightened at their temples. Their lips were parched, their eyes felt scorched by their riveted attention. When Aliki left, Ismene sat down on an old trunk, turned her back to him and rested her head on a broken chair. Neither was aware of time passing. Angelos remained at the window. He heard the door softly opening, and saw Ismene pass in front of him through the shutters. He watched as she disappeared, going down the steps one at a time.

THE NEXT AFTERNOON, Ismene went back to Holargos. Mount Hymettos was violet-colored, Athens was taking its repose in the deep blueness of the hour, and the little house was quiet, enclosed in its quiet wall of green. Vangelia's aunt told her that she had mopped the tiles, washed the windows and doors, swept the garden and veranda, and watered the flowers.

"The house is ready and waiting for you."

Ismene fought back tears as she went through the rooms again. She went out into the yard, smelled the flowers, and sat on the veranda. Why wouldn't he come? It was so peaceful there, he would be able to rest, to put his mind at ease.

"So when will you be coming?"

"In a few days ..." Ismene answered. "Do you mind if we're a little late?"

"Don't be too late. I'm anxious to be going to Samos ..."

"We'll come. We have to ..."

Ismene returned home. Where else could she go? She sat once more on the iron stairs, as if waiting for something. Isn't that what she had been doing for years? The looms thrummed steadily. Eftihis was bringing in a few packages a truck had unloaded on the sidewalk out front. Aliki went into the courtyard and turned crimson when she saw him. She walked right past him without turning, but then he too acted like he hadn't seen her.

Andonis and Vangelia came back later on, after the looms had fallen silent. Seeing Ismene, Andonis told her he wanted to talk to her, and she hastily followed them into their room. She was startled when he handed her a large roll of paper. She hadn't had a chance to say anything to Angelos the previous afternoon, and hadn't expected Andonis to be bringing anything so soon.

"It's the blueprints for a large building," he told her. "He's to do the static calculations. Everything he needs is here in this envelope. The engineer was reluctant at first, but I snatched it out of his hand. Tell him the sooner the better. He's got time, right?"

"Too much of it," said Ismene.

"There'll be other work from my friend Rapas. I'm trying to steer him away from paperwork, and toward more profitable pursuits. These'll be a snap for Angelos. Give him my best, and tell him I've never forgotten him."

"I will," Ismene said slowly.

When it had gotten dark, and everyone was asleep, she stole up to the roof and tapped on the door of the storage shed. "It's me," she whispered so as not to frighten him. The door was unlocked, and Ismene held it half-open, without crossing the threshold. She gave him the roll of paper and the envelope.

"It's the blueprints for a building. An engineer friend of Andonis wants you to do a static analysis ..."

"Does he know I'm here?" Angelos asked fretfully.

"No, relax. Nobody knows. Tomorrow night, throw down the rope ... Andonis said the engineer was in a hurry ..."

Closing the door, she paused and asked:

"Have you thought over that other thing?"

"Not yet ... Don't pressure me, Ismene."

"You better decide by tomorrow. Otherwise ..."

The door clacked shut, and Ismene was gone.

THE FOLLOWING NIGHT, Ismene switched the kitchen light on and off twice. Soon the rope came slowly down holding the pitcher. There was a note with it: "Tell Andonis many thanks for his gift." Ismene filled the pitcher, tied on a parcel with bread and other food, then attached a note she had written that afternoon: "What have you decided?"

The rope went up. Ismene waited for an answer. Time passed. Then the rope slowly inched its way down, as if hanging back. The note read: "I'm not ready yet. Give me a little time."

Ismene tore some paper off a bag and wrote: "I want an answer *now*. Yes or no." Her hand trembled as she attached it to the rope. Then she gave three jerks on the rope, the signal for him to pull it up.

This time she waited even longer. All was silent.

The rope came back down like a blind worm crawling along the wall. "I can't," the note said. "Please understand. Later on."

Ismene clenched her teeth, held her breath and wrote: "Okay, then. Leave." She hung it to the rope and immediately switched off the light.

A NECESSARY CONDITION FOR TAKING full advantage of an opportunity is not to underestimate any of the factors involved. Andonis kept a different sort of company now, and frequented classier joints. He was relieved that everything was going well at the textile works, and that Spiros was happy. The orders were being delivered on time, and thus the drafts Andonis had taken out remained dormant. Spiros assured Andonis of their friendship, Rapas couldn't go anywhere without him, and Loukis sought his advice on new groupings of clients and projects. The truth of the matter was that other people's work was profitable. He was still at an underdeveloped stage when he was hoping to get something of his own started, since there were people out there offering every service under the sun. He had a briefcase bulging with ideas, legs no amount of running could wear down, and a sharp eye. Someday he would batter down the doors of success. Then he could go into the middle of Omonia Square and shout: "Your money means nothing to me! It just happens to be a measure of success, like applause for an actor or medals for a general." If you wanted to emerge victorious from the deafening battle that raged in the streets and the business sphere, you had to be ready minute by minute to surrender. There's no such thing as heroism in the commercial sector. Clio had recently told him how Boufas had been promising to marry her for the past ten years. But it was always either, "Let's wait and see how business goes," or "Let's get ourselves some new office space, or build a factory, or take out a loan." "And now I'm worried because he's talking about building a second factory, and then he'll start telling me to wait again ..."

Even Thodoros was acting chummy with him. One night he drank a little more than usual and became loquacious: "That poor judge was a good little fellow. He was out to make an honest man of me! It's no small thing to have your conscience pricked. A couple of times I made up my mind to do what he wanted, just to get him off my back, but then I thought better of it. Thodoros, I told myself, don't be a jerk. Conscience is a sucker's game. Once you start getting mixed up in all that, you're screwed. You'll never see the end of it ... You dodged all those bullets with your name on them, and now you're going to let the honorable Harilaos pass judgement on you? I would have been rid of him, sure, but then what? Once you give a little, that's it, you're all washed up. You have to keep on your toes ... If I'd obliged him, I'd have turned into a mellow, saintly old fart. My conscience wouldn't have known when to quit, I'd have ended up giving up everything. No thanks! I know a bum rap when I see one. He was edging me toward the snakepit."

Keeping a close watch on the time, Andonis left at precisely the right moment to allow himself to attend to his other duties. He found himself on the street where he and Angelos had taken part in that demonstration where the calvary had attacked them with swords.

In the lobby of a posh office building, he was surrounded by mirrors. He caught a glimpse of his face, and it looked covered with dust. Later, in the long corridor, he did his best to whistle and lighten his step so as not to frighten anyone when he knocked on the door. His skin felt taut and dry, punished by the chafing passage of air and time. How long would he have to go on dispensing lies from morning to night? "If Angelos was sentenced to death," he thought, "I've been sentenced to self-degradation. But there's a difference ... In my case, the sentence is assured, since my merchandise turned out to be rotten."

He went back to the textile works and reiterated to Vangelia that they would have to see about getting a new place. "Don't give me that look, I really mean it. What, you're going to believe anything I say from now on?" As Vangelia remained silent, Andonis shouted so as to be heard over the thunder of the machines: "I need your smile ... It's not gold, you don't have to hoard it. I *haven't* been telling you lies, do you hear me? I've always told you the truth, as best I could see it ... Don't you care about anything anymore?"

He grew impatient with shouting. Vangelia apparently chose not to understand. He went into the courtyard to discuss the delivery schedule with Eftihis, but just then Ismene appeared in the passageway. The change in her appearance alarmed him; it was as if there were a layer of ash clinging to her sweat.

"What's wrong? Has something happened?"

"No, he's fine, he even said to thank you for 'your gift' ... Here, here's his note."

"But what about you, are you all right?"

Ismene went into the laundry-room, splashed water on her face, drank from her cupped palms, then asked him in a faint voice:

"Is there any chance you need someone with accounting experience in textiles? It's urgent ..."

"No, I'm afraid I do all the accounting here myself ... But I'll keep my eyes open. Who's it for?"

"Me. I was laid off today."

WHEN THE FIRST FLUSH OF DAY found its way into his small room, Angelos would spring up and get to work. He never imagined he would get to start out with such an important job – a seven-story apartment building. But it invigorated him, got his blood flowing again. It was rough going at first, until he found his rhythm, as if there'd been some dead weight he had to shake off. And painful, like running barefoot over thorns. But soon his step became freer, he moved from numbers to their interrelation and significance, and started to enjoy the work. It bore no relation to the endless deliberations that had ravaged him all those years. This was real work! The numbers had become physical realities – loads, pulls, moments and stresses that had to work together as a system of forces that would give the close-knit mass of materials the absolute stability of a building.

Afternoon and evening passed without his leaving his chair. It was all still there, he hadn't forgotten a thing, and his hands that for years he had considered of no use to anyone, could still manage perfectly straight lines and precision drawing. Figuring out a structure's anatomy was an absorbing pastime, an exercise that taught one a great deal. Perhaps it was even a kind of music. To construct any useful object whatsoever was to perform the loveliest and most necessary of functions. It was worth every bit of mental sweat and worry it cost you. And once a building offered its equilibrium as a shelter for someone's life, it became a living thing. If the builder died, or was thrown in prison or even executed, the building still existed because the cement, iron, and stones had been bound together to last a hundred, two hundred, a thousand years. He had always worshiped the world he saw with his eyes – the concrete, material object – and had wanted to construct something of his own. He would surely have died if he had never acquired the ability. His life might have ended in disintegration or suicide. He himself had all but carried out the sentence handed down in absentia. He had often sunk into rank despair at the thought that he would never be able to *make* anything, and still the body he dragged around was rotted through with fear. This, finally, was the moment of truth.

Even before dark, the cycle of night resumed. Ismene's "Leave!" still burned in his mind. "If even Ismene throws me out, there won't be anywhere left to go. I must really be a good-for-nothing, a hopeless case, if even those who sacrificed their lives for me want to punish me. She must be so sick of it by now. Who knows, maybe she even finds me repugnant, maybe it drives her crazy just knowing I'm here, with nothing to offer her, not even acquiescence to one of *her* dreams. Apparently I failed to show her how deeply I love her."

It was dark now, and the drawing and the calculations faded before his eyes. He stretched out on the bed, his mind ablaze, and enjoyed the pleasant fatigue that comes from a good day's work. The scattered cries of evening reached him there. His thoughts were still on the design of his building.

Soon Ismene came up. He recognized her signal, so he wasn't frightened. She tapped on his door, but he didn't let her in. "Maybe it's too soon," he thought. "Maybe I no longer have the right." Her note, with its big letters, hovered before his eyes. The door remained locked – he wanted to show her that he had carried out her command, had accepted the harsh punishment she had levied upon him. Yet there was so much he wanted to tell her about the work he'd been doing.

"Open the door."

There was a hoarseness to her voice he hadn't heard before. At one point, it sounded like she kicked the wooden planks of the door, as if trying to break through and violate its silence.

"Open the door. I have to talk to you."

Angelos sat, stolid as a rock. Ismene went away.

That night, she switched the kitchen light on and off over and over, but Angelos never threw down the rope. His water pitcher was dry, but he felt he had no right to ask for anything. If he stayed, it was because he had nowhere else to go, and because he had to finish the drawings.

WHEN THE CLOCK HANDS neared the hour when she normally would have left for work, Ismene all but ran screaming into the street. Now it hit her how changed her life was, how utterly alone she was in the midst of chaos: with no job, and with Angelos hiding in the storage shed, she was alone in a hostile world. Everything else had been rendered obsolete, dull, flat and inconsequential – it all simply vanished as if it had never been. In a few days, food would become a problem, and there was no one to help her. It was all over for her. And Angelos, with his door locked and the rope coiled under his bed, had no inkling of what was taking place. What if he were to die of hunger? "If he doesn't need me," she reasoned, "it means I am nothing to him. Perhaps he never wants to see me again. That's his right. But he should tell me straight out." Then she was angry with herself for thinking such idiotic thoughts. No one got off that easy, no matter how straightforward they were. What kind of vicious brute would turn his back on the people who love him? Ismene went up and down the stairs, circled the courtyard, and kicked over a flowerpot, which crashed noisily to the ground. The hour passed, and she remained at home.

She locked herself in her room again and wept, lamenting everything. "Don't treat me like I'm sick. I've had it with all your advice and commiseration." Then she went out and aimlessly wandered the streets. There are times when people's faces look black as coal, their eyebrows white, and in the center of their eyes you can see a tiny, snow-white bead, as in photographic negatives. Was it trucks or people or just a strong wind that whooshed past, sucking the air from her lungs? The city lay mutely about her, she could make out nothing but muffled groans, houses and more houses turned upside-down. Didn't anyone think twice about disaster? What did she care? All she ever wanted was a little peace. Where did people find the time to get dressed, where did they learn how to move their mouths, in the mistaken belief they were forming words? Was it asking too much to be willing to trade your whole life for some peace and quiet? People always gave you strange looks, as if you had something horrible on you, and yet you wanted so much to keep them near you. Her body had turned to stone, she no longer felt hunger or thirst, never got sleepy. That was for others. And if she had spent years in waiting, it wasn't out of weakness. She had chosen it, in full knowledge of her actions. It had cost her dearly. She hadn't had a moment's respite since she was in high school. The streets appeared randomly before her, and for all she knew they vanished the moment she passed.

She went back and sat on the stairs. Where else was there to go?

Vangelia came up and spoke to her patiently. In their day, everyone was hanging by a thread. She needn't get overly depressed since she was qualified, and would quickly find something else. "So many thousands of people ..."

"My life's gone," Ismene groaned. "All those years down the drain ..." Patience was not an option in the midst of disaster. They were sure to find him now, he would get desperate and go out hunting for food.

The rope didn't come down that night either. Ismene angrily filled a pitcher with water, wrapped a bit of bread in a napkin, and left them at the door of the shed. If he went hungry and thirsty, he had only his own rash stubbornness to blame.

Now that everything had come to an end, she no longer cared whether it was day or night. That was only for people who actually partook of life, who knew how to keep track of the hour and distinguish one day from the next. She was standing with her face to a high wall. All she could see was a uniform gray. It was futile to ask what came next, or how to escape. And then there was Angelos up there, mired in his sense of hopelessness ... Were she to abandon him, he would perish of hunger and neglect. It would be as if she had carried out the sentence herself.

The next morning, the pitcher was still full, the bread was untouched. When he didn't open the door of his own, she refrained from knocking out of pride. She knew he could see her through the shutters, so she acted as if she'd only come up for a breath of air. How thirsty he must have been, with his lips parched, his throat burning. Was it his way of punishing himself for being unable to accept her solution? The house in Holargos was no dream, as he had supposed. It was not made out of clouds. Its garden fence was made of iron, its walls of solid stone. She sat for a while on the parapet, then as she came down she saw Fanis waiting for her.

"Any news?" he asked.

"Not really," she answered, wondering what he was fishing for.

"You've seemed worried the past few days ... He's all right, isn't he? I keep seeing you going up and down the stairs ..."

"It's cooler up on the roof," Ismene told him.

"You should be more careful ... All sorts of people come in here ... It'd be a shame ..."

"What do you mean?" she asked in alarm.

"Never mind, I think you get my point ..."

He sucked down his spit, and headed back to his loom. Suddenly everything had changed again. There was no keeping it a secret. If one person knew, who knows how many did. Others might have figured it out just as Fanis had. So she hadn't managed to protect him after all. Had some slip-up of hers put him in danger? How could she rest easy now? What if she herself were to bring on his ruin? "So he was right not to want to see me, not even to drink the water I took him. Maybe he realized that I've only done him harm, that I'm not worthy to protect him, to offer him as small a thing as shelter in a storage shed on a roof." He would have to find somewhere else to stay. It would mean her losing him again, but his remaining one more day could be disastrous. But where could he go?

She sat down on the stairs and observed how people looked at her, trying to detect any suspicion or insinuation in their eyes. "Does anyone else know?" she asked Fanis during the lunch break.

"I haven't heard anything. Don't let it worry you ... But just so you'll know, a few days ago, Eftihis chased this girl up onto the roof. You'd gone up a little while before with some laundry. If you'd been there, the two of them wouldn't have stayed up there so long ... So you must have been in the shed. You never hung out your clothes either. And I could see the girl was upset when she came down ..."

"That's all it is? I just didn't see them, I was looking for something in a trunk ..."

"The girl called out for help, but you didn't do anything because you didn't want to give yourself away."

"You've read too many detective novels ..."

"Not a one. I'm right, aren't I? You have nothing to fear from me, I'm just telling you so you'll watch your step ... I'll let you know if I hear anything ... I've also noticed how anxious you look when you come back after being out a while, as if you wanted to find out if anything's happened ... Then sometimes I catch you looking up at the roof ... It's not hard to guess why ... And you always keep an eye on who comes into the courtyard."

"You don't miss much, do you?"

"I like to know what's going on around me, it's something I picked up back in the war ... But don't worry, I'm a friend. There's nothing to be afraid of. You don't even have to say anything to him."

He left her and rejoined the other workers. Who was this new friend? His voice and eyes vouched for his honesty. But regardless of who Fanis was or was not, it was clear that Angelos' presence there had become problematic, even dangerous.

That afternoon, Stathis again asked her about Angelos.

"An old friend of ours is in town and wants to see him. Tell him that Elly's here!"

Ismene, who had never heard the name before, reacted unenthusiastically. She told him the truth – namely that she hadn't seen him in days, and didn't know when she would see him again.

"I want you to meet Elly too ..." Stathis smiled. "She's a good friend ..."

Then he too went off. Ismene sat on the step, wondering which of the many problems crowding in on her to consider first. She felt like she was sinking into a dark morass. Late that night she went up to the roof and knocked on the door. The moon shed its light over everything. She stood for a while with a feeling of desolation. She knocked again. Angelos had come to the shutter.

"Open up, it's an emergency."

When he opened the door, she didn't go in.

"One of the workers knows you're here," she said aridly, as if she had only come to pass on information.

This made little impression on him. He pointed to the chair and told her to sit down.

"I thought maybe you'd come for the engineering study. It's going well, really well. Too bad there isn't a light or I'd show you ... It's a major building project."

"So you're not angry with me?"

"Angry? About what?"

"Because of that stupid note I wrote you the other night."

"But you were right. It seemed a perfectly fitting punishment ... So you're still dwelling on that? Who knows I'm up here?"

"Fanis, one of the workers. You don't think it's serious?"

"Well, it'd be better if he didn't know, but that's how it goes. Anyway, he's a worker. I wouldn't fret over it."

Ismene studied him curiously, as if she were having trouble recognizing him. Moonlight filled half of the tiny room. Angelos sat quietly on the bed, his face placid.

"It cooled off tonight, didn't it?" he said.

"You must have had a horrible time the past few days. And all because of me."

"Not really. I was working."

"And there's something else too ... They laid me off."

His expression changed abruptly, becoming weightier, more serious and thoughtful. He had already told her countless times not to let things get her down, it would sound trite to repeat it now. Ismene remained standing in the doorway, with the whole moonlit night behind her. Angelos stood up and took her arm, leading her out onto the roof. Around them rose the exhalation of the city, the neon signs, the buildings with their open windows. He lifted up her chin with his finger, till their eyes met.

"So, you've given up, now when more than ever ..."

Ismene lowered her head.

"It's true, this is going to be kind of tough. But it's not over yet. Why don't we sit on the ledge a bit."

"Someone might see us ..."

"So what? It's not like we're doing anything unusual."

Angelos had already jumped up onto the low parapet, and for a moment Ismene was afraid he was going to start acting foolish again, just to allay her fear. But instead he calmly gazed out at the night, at the rooftops and the street, and his hand felt firm on her shoulder.

"Now that we've lost that house in Holargos, tell me why you didn't want us to move there."

"There's a right and wrong way of going about things, Ismene ..."

CHAPTER 19

ONE DAY, A SATURDAY, Eftihis and Andonis came back troubled and subdued. They let it be known they didn't want to be disturbed, and went into the room where the boxes of cans were stacked. Their eyes met, and they agreed that things looked bad indeed.

"That Spiros is a real swine," Eftihis said. "Why didn't you let me flatten him?"

"His behavior isn't at all atypical. He didn't need to give us any more orders, he used us as long as he had to, then stopped."

"He promised us five or six months of work," Eftihis told him. "He's a liar and a swine."

"True. But in business, someone who keeps a promise when it goes against his best interests is considered a fool."

"That's a load of crap," shouted Eftihis. "If you ask me, he's got you in his pocket and that's why you went easy on him. Am I right or am I right?"

"But the arrangement was only temporary anyway. He was simply a customer."

Eftihis insisted Spiros was a swine and that he deserved to be punched. "I didn't like his looks from day one. And you just sat there like a lump on a log. What do you owe him?" Andonis assured him that had nothing to do with it. They agreed they would have to lay off the second shift, that very night in fact. "Don't you worry, Eftihis, we'll get other orders ..."

"Who's going to tell them they're fired?"

"You, of course. You're the boss," said Andonis.

It was a simple matter. When the shift was over and the

machines fell silent, Eftihis clapped his hands and Andonis told them, falteringly, that as they had been informed upon hiring, the second shift would last as long as there were rush orders. These had been abruptly terminated ... What else was there for them to do?

He let them draw their own conclusion. A cold silence settled over the room. Andonis did the payroll and saw that everyone was paid. There are few things as poignant as a worker drawing his last pay: a few stunned final words, the hasty clean-up, then the departure with head hung low. Eftihis told them he would let them know the moment the need arose. "That's what they all say," someone muttered. "You'd think they all got it out of the same book."

That night, the same old song came from the next courtyard. Eftihis did his best to ignore it, since it sounded like lament to his ears. He went out with Mary. When they got back, he found Andonis examining various cost factors, and recording the sums to the last digit in various accounts books. They had run out of cash. Spiros would pay them in three months, as they'd agreed, but the accommodation bills they had discounted at the bank came due in a few days, and there were no new orders at the moment. "And the worst of it is we still have a high overhead," Andonis said in closing.

"What you're telling me is we're sunk," said Eftihis.

"Not at all, these are just the usual setbacks encountered in any business ... Don't forget that we're still just at the beginning, and that we started out with virtually nothing."

"In other words, we need cash," Eftihis deduced.

What he couldn't understand was how it was possible for them to work at such a pitch for two whole weeks and still have nothing to show for all their sweat and toil. And then to be in the hole to boot! Strange goings-on, to be sure. Andonis maintained that it all boiled down to cost-factors, and that what they needed was greater system efficiency. "Okay then, give it a shot and we'll see what happens," Eftihis thought to himself.

On Monday morning, once everyone had arrived, Eftihis had them all gather around for a candid talk, since they were practically family. He told them that unexpected difficulties had arisen, that they still owed a bundle of money, and ended by saying that the business had been started as a way for them all to eke out a living. They were therefore obliged to help him out by putting more shoulder into it until their difficulties were behind them. Otherwise their jobs would be in grave danger.

They listened in silence, without showing any special emotion or reaction to his plea, then somewhat numbly and gloomily set to work. Andonis kept assuring Eftihis that it was just a momentary slump, that things would soon be on the rise again. "No business ever follows an uninterrupted upward path. There's always a certain amount of up and down involved." "Sure," Eftihis replied, "but how do you know what's going to hit you next when you're out riding the waves? What if a cliff falls on us and sends us straight to the bottom?" Andonis patiently explained to him that industries always operated with a higher cost of production, and that the initial outlay and the frozen assets took more time to enter the calculation of a product's value. "Put it in your article, I don't want to hear it," said Eftihis as he left for a meeting with Thodoros. The latter would help them. Andonis was full of reservations about him, but a loan was a loan, no matter whose pocket it came out of.

The next morning Elpida arrived before anyone else. She was waiting by her loom when Eftihis entered, and indicated she wanted to have a word with him.

"You seem so worried these days ... Not to mention the problems you told us about yesterday ..."

"Yeah, things aren't working out quite like we planned. But don't worry, even if we only keep to one employee, it'll be you. By the way, congratulations on learning the trade."

"I brought you something ..." she said softly.

She took something out of her pocket, wrapped in a handkerchief. It was the gold chain he had given her the previous winter, and the four gold sovereigns.

"But they're yours."

"You might need them, now that things are a little tight."

"No, you keep them. I gave them to you."

But Elpida dropped them in his hand, and at that moment Mary entered, her suspicions aroused, so he couldn't hand them back. He didn't even have a chance to thank her. In a loud voice, like that of a boss, he asked her about her loom and the thread.

Then the work day began, and he dashed off with Andonis in search of new orders.

The week passed slowly and suspensefully. When Saturday came, Eftihis couldn't contain his anger. He chewed his lip, stormed up and down, and would talk to no one. He would go into the work-area, look at them one at a time, try striking up a conversation on unrelated topics, as if he were no more than a friend – they'd known each other for so many years, and had drunk out of the same cup, so to speak – offered them cigarettes, and swore at the drop of a hat.

Andonis came back dragging his feet, saying he had been unable to come up with so much as a drachma. All the money they had – from Elpida's gold chain and sovereigns – were needed to buy thread on Monday. As the end of the day approached, Eftihis locked himself in the laundry-room and took his head in his hands. But Saturday night wouldn't wait forever. At some point the looms were shut off, the noise abated, everyone wiped the sweat from their hands and foreheads. But realizing that something wasn't right, they delayed before going in to wash.

At that point Eftihis appeared, and somehow found the courage to address them.

"I'm asking a big favor of you tonight. We ran into a bit of trouble ... We're still waiting for some money. Somebody stood us up."

"We'll wait," someone said.

"There's no guarantee he'll come. Don't waste your time."

They were all looking at him: Elpida, his mother, Fanis, Varvara. They were slowly closing in on him.

"How about twenty or so to help us get by," said Iordanis.

"That's kind of tough," Eftihis told him. "We only have enough for the thread. If we can't pay for it, there won't be any work on Monday. Is that what you want? Of course not," he quickly added. "That's out of the question. Production always comes first."

He turned and saw Andonis standing in the corner. Those few seconds of utter silence were critical. Fanis stood facing him, sucking in his spit.

"And if we don't work Monday," he said, "what good will the thread do you?"

"You, Fanis! After all our years of chasing down a few pennies together ..."

"That was different. Back then we were just trying to scrape up a few drachmas here and there. This is real work, it's not the same ..."

His mother suddenly pushed forward.

"The employer always finds a way to come up with money. Who ever heard of workers paying for their own thread ..."

Eftihis felt as if he'd been struck by lightning. Mrs. Stamatina, with her bony features, had apparently forgotten she was addressing her son. She placed her gnarled hands on her hips, and stood there in the courtyard, solid as a tree-trunk.

"I thought you were my mother," he bellowed at her.

"Now he remembers. I'm just a weaver here."

"What are they acting like this for?" Mary asked Vangelia uncomprehendingly. "After all, just a few days ago they didn't even have jobs."

Eftihis broke out of their circle, grabbed Andonis by his collar and gave him a shake.

"Say something. What do I do now?"

Andonis thought for a moment.

"Forgive me for butting in here," he told the workers in the courtyard. "All I would ask is that you believe us when we tell you there was no way of foreseeing this snag, and that it's merely a cash-flow problem. If you could only help us out a little bit, at least now when we're just getting started ..."

"Do you promise we'll get paid on Monday?" Fanis asked.

"I promise," Eftihis declared.

"All right, let's go, if it's only for this once," said Mrs. Stamatina, turning to go.

They proceeded in a group down the passageway. There seemed to be so many of them. Eftihis stood pondering in the middle of the courtyard. He turned to Andonis:

"You didn't warn me about this, friend. Remember that night you were telling me all about manufacturing, that time you offered me the black market job with Thodoros? You were right, you just didn't tell me everything. We're in a hell of a mess."

THE BLUEPRINTS WERE COMING ALONG JUST FINE. The building was slowly taking shape with the solid binding of concrete and steel. Work continued at a relentless pace in that tiny room on the roof. What did sun or sweat or heat matter? Why had it taken him so long to uncover this inexhaustible fund of energy? The mathematical and technical solutions to the various problems involved in the design came to him in a steady flow, since he had already mastered the materials, and had done a minute analysis of the building's dimensions and the resulting interrelation of forces.

The little table had become a drawing-board. Rolls of paper were piled up on the bed and the floor. Angelos would take a drink of warm water from his pitcher, wipe off his sweat, and continue working. His structural drawings took on the solidity of exactitude, of precise calculations, because numbers had the great advantage of being consistent with the dimensions they represented, and could always be validated in relation to other numbers.

Ismene said: "We'll share the bread that's left."

Angelos added: "And the bread we're going to get."

A few times she came at daybreak and spent the entire day at his side. She watched his hand, which had acquired the confidence of the straight line, and his eye, which had regained its clarity. "I'll do that floor plan tomorrow," he said without giving it a second thought, and Ismene noted that he had begun to speak with assurance about what he would do the next day. It was a major step forward. She was inwardly elated, though she said nothing to him, lest she frighten him by pointing out the change. At lunchtime, they shared a tomato salad. "No one's cut out to be a prisoner of silence," he told her, and Ismene laughed. Then he added, almost jokingly, "One becomes a vegetable living in isolation." "Is there anything I can help with?" Ismene asked him. "Of course. In fact, I have a very useful and taxing job for you." "Which is?" "Come sit over here. It's something you know quite well – and are good at too."

He worked without stopping until nightfall, taking advantage of the last glimmer of dusk. After dark, they went out on the roof and sat on the small ledge to rest.

"In two weeks I'll be through," he told her confidently.

THE SITUATION WORSENED the following week at Eftihis' factory. The sounds of grumbling and outright anger were becoming more widespread. Iordanis no longer told his amusing stories at lunch, and there wasn't the same joking and banter. But what really got to Eftihis, what made him want to tear his hair out, was all the whispering that went on. People would break off when they saw him coming, and exchange looks. What a mess! The other weekend's "cash-flow problem" had been solved on Monday by a new loan from Thodoros. Eftihis had moaned and groaned and pleaded. In the end he had signed more documents like the first ones and received the money. All that would be dealt with later. What mattered now was for the looms to be running. The thought that the wonderful clatter he had so come to love might just stop was enough to drive him crazy. The day he saw the factory lying empty and inert was sure to be his last. Andonis made him dizzy with his enumeration of causes – costs, seasonal fluctuations, import practices, competition – but Eftihis knew that these things had always been a part of it, that in the end it was all just so much talk, and that if they only gave one hundred percent, they would pull through. "I'd rather die of hard work," he told Mary, "than of a stroke or a broken heart." With the new loan they had been able to pay half wages for the preceding week. He didn't know what would have happened if Mrs. Stamatina hadn't been his mother. And Fanis rubbed him wrong every time he opened his mouth. Once or twice Andonis started to tell him that they had every right to be angry, they were only asking for their due, but Eftihis only cursed him in return.

More or less the same scene was repeated the following Saturday, but the workers backed down when they were again given half-pay. "Unemployment's as close as the door," Eftihis railed at them from atop a crate. This time, it's true, Andonis helped out by telling them that competition with the large factories was fierce, and that smaller operations like theirs had to be allowed to survive. "You sure have a strange way of putting it," Fanis remarked wryly.

But the stony silence that had set in couldn't last. It became clear that the whispering and the looks were heading for a blowup. Eftihis, who spent his whole day among the workers, grew convinced of this and notified Andonis. It didn't take long for Andonis to grasp the meaning of their behavior. It was all perfectly natural and to be expected, considering they weren't getting paid. He kept this observation to himself, however. Then came a number of notices from the bank, and things got even stickier.

Then, in the middle of all their other worries and woes, the machines suddenly thundered to a stop. Eftihis thought the power had gone out, but when he asked what had happened, the workers formed a wall in front of him and declared:

"We're not working unless you pay us."

"Right now? I can't."

"You gave us your word."

Eftihis called to Andonis:

"Come in here a second, they want something."

But Andonis, who had grasped the situation, was already at the front gate.

"I've got to go to the bank," he said and disappeared.

Eftihis swore at him under his breath, but realized he would have to have it out with the people standing before him as if made out of stone.

"Hey, no need to get violent. Would you mind backing off?... I told you, you'll get paid when they pay us for the merchandise."

They answered this with a roar of common laughter. Letting them see there were no hard feelings, Eftihis stepped over to one side and pointed to the wall.

"Those who don't want to work stand over here, the rest go back inside. One at a time. I want to clear this up once and for all."

Mrs. Stamatina and Fanis immediately went over by the wall, as he had expected. Then came Elpida's turn, and Eftihis smiled because he knew she was on his side. Elpida took two steps and stopped. Then she began calmly walking toward the wall! Eftihis couldn't believe the way the world was crashing down around him.

"Stop," he shouted at the top of his lungs.

Elpida stopped. Her face never lost its placid expression. She was waiting to hear what more he had to say. When she saw he only stood staring at her with his big, bewildered eyes, she went on over and joined Fanis and the old woman.

"You too?"

"Yes," she answered, in the soft voice she always used with him.

Eftihis, as if he'd been given a knock on the head, abandoned his dangerous game. Wiping the sweat off his face, he made a dash for the laundry-room.

"Do whatever you want," he told them. "It's all the same to me."

They dispersed, and he could hear confused discussions, footsteps, commentary. He stuck his head under the faucet to try and clear his thoughts. Then he kicked the door shut.

Two strangers appeared in the passageway – suspicious-looking types unconnected to the textile works. Ismene appeared on the landing with a look of alarm.

"Vangelia," Fanis called. "These gentlemen here would like a word with Andonis."

Vangelia hastened over. They said something to her in a low voice.

"Yes, he lives here," she replied. "But he's away at the moment. He left a few days ago for Larissa. He's on the road a lot, you know ... The moment he comes back I'll let him know."

The two men left, and Vangelia went back in her room and locked the door. Out in the courtyard, nobody moved. Why had Eftihis gone and hid himself? What was he doing in there all this time? A few of them sat on the ground, others paced up and down. But how many were employed there anyway? They had kept such strict accounts, with a stack of books and ledgers, and still Eftihis didn't know how many people there were working for him. A thousand, five thousand, a hundred thousand people?

At some point Eftihis came back out.

"Sorry, I had a dizzy spell. Probably the sun. Anyway, can't you tell when I'm pulling your leg? It's not like we don't kid each other here every day. So, where were we? It's your right to choose whether to work or not ... Who knows a good joke?"

No one would have anything to do with him. He wandered in and out as if nothing were amiss. The machines stood idle. Why hadn't he gone crazy yet? How long would this horrible charade drag on? He stretched out in a corner away from the others. Elpida was sitting in the shade under the stairs. She must not have known what she was doing. What if he crept over there and kissed those shaded eyes of hers? How many thousands of kilometers was it from here to the iron stairs? Who could say whether a whole life would be enough to make that journey? And it was a shame, too, because it would be so nice to know you had years enough to make the trip over, without worrying if you never made it back. It was a little like one of those space-voyages you read about in old newspapers.

Vangelia came out of her room carrying a heavy suitcase.

"Where are you off to, Vangelia?" Eftihis asked.

"They brought me word a cousin of mine is seriously ..."

"That's nothing to get broken up about. Everyone's cousin comes down sick sooner or later."

She was in too much of a hurry to answer. She exchanged a few hasty words with Ismene at the gate, then left, as if she were late for something.

"Elpida!" Eftihis shouted, certain she wouldn't hear.

But strangely enough she came over.

"What is it, Eftihis?"

"Why did you do that?" he asked her softly. "You're all I've got. Even my mother ..."

"Because it was the right thing to do," she told him.

"Why? I don't get it."

"It was bound to happen sooner or later, Eftihis. You've always wanted to protect me. We never talked about anything serious ... There were times it was clear you only wanted to look after me because of Kostis ... I didn't want to live off of my brother's memory. Since I've been working, I've begun seeing things differently ..."

"But I didn't look after you for anyone else's sake," he told her gravely, "but because of how I felt for you ... Please believe me, it was for *you* ..."

"Thank you for saying that ... But it's too late now ..."

"Can we still be friends?"

"Of course," Elpida told him. "We've never stopped being friends."

At that moment Eftihis sprang to his feet because he saw Thodoros coming down the passageway.

"What's going on here? Have you closed up shop?"

Eftihis briefly told him how things stood, and Thodoros began shouting, "You're all fired. I want you out, now ..." But it was obvious he was just joking, and Eftihis followed him inside where they could talk.

Only Thodoros wasn't joking. He shouted that *he* had now put in the most capital and had every right to clean house. Eftihis swore, flung some tools to the ground, and very nearly brought a large wrench down on Thodoros' skull, but then reflected that he stood to gain more from persuasion than violence.

When Andonis came in, he found the workers listening at the windows. "That fat toad wants to fire us," someone said as they clustered around him. There was a plea in their eyes, and he felt an all too familiar breath on his face, scorching him like a flame. A flood of memories rushed through his head.

"All right, all right, calm down," he told them.

He went a little to one side as if to think. Fanis came up to him.

"If they're talking about firing Elpida, please fire me instead ..."

Then the others gathered around him again, and Andonis opened the door and went inside. The two other men apparently jumped on him: "It's your fault, you deal with it." There must have been something pretty serious being said in there; the shouting had stopped, and now all they could hear were whispers.

Then Andonis' voice rang out:

"That's it, that's enough! I won't do it ... I can't ... If you keep pushing me, I'll resign."

The other two must have persisted, because next they heard Andonis flatly declare:

"All right then, I resign! As of this moment, our partnership is dissolved ... Vangelia, Vangelia, I'm a free man!"

He opened the door to their room to make his big announcement, but Vangelia was gone.

THEY HAD BEEN WORKING for three days without eating. There was no more bread or cigarettes or coffee. Angelos was feverish. "I have to finish this," he would say as he inscribed lines and numbers and strange symbols on the plans. Ismene sat at his side, silent and worn out. She didn't miss a day. She left at night and came back at first light. At least they had water. She noticed his hand trembling a few times, but the lines still came out straight and precise. "It's not enough to love your past," he would say. "It's even more important to love your future. All that time I had forgotten there even was such a thing. But there is, for the individual and for the world. The future is our better self. Humanity as a whole has found a solution to its problems. Now it's our turn – those few of us who've been left behind." His lips began quivering, his shoulders twitched, his hand moved to an altogether different rhythm now.

He drew in the final line. "In Athens, on the ..." he wrote, putting in the date. He sat for a few moments, gazing at Ismene, and out at the rooftops – the same ones he had clambered over that morning during the war – then added his signature with a few firm strokes.

"Finished," he announced, and kissed her.

He stood up and opened the window.

EACH MORNING, ANDONIS would set out lonely as an orphan, his briefcase full of samples, and pay calls on one after the other of his old customers. The textile works was still going, but he never once looked inside. Vangelia had been gone a whole week, and he didn't know where she was or whether he would ever see her again.

Once more he wandered the streets of Athens, merging with the crowds.

He pressed the door buzzer with determination. He had been to the same house a few days before and sold some ties and a bottle of cologne to the man who lived there. Someone was playing a piano without letup in the next apartment. "That must drive you crazy," he told the lady who answered the door, with feigned compassion. When he had given her the ties and taken his bit of money, he asked her with sudden interest: "What's that piece they're playing?" "Chopin, the devil take him!" the lady said, raising her eyes to the ceiling as if praying the devil would appear and do just that. The next day, Andonis, despite the thousand and one other things he had to do, looked in an encyclopedia under Chopin and noted down the pertinent facts.

Before ringing at the door, he consulted his index card again.

From inside came the notes of a similar or nearly identical piece. At the sound of the doorbell, the music broke off. A wan-looking girl peered out the peephole at him.

"Good morning, you'll have to forgive me, miss, I never would have presumed, but I felt I had to express my admiration ... I've heard you playing a few times, I often stop in next door ..."

The door remained shut.

"*I love Chopin*!" he exclaimed, "and I've come to congratulate you. Your interpretations!..."

Now the door opened.

"Come in," the girl said timidly.

"I pulled that off," Andonis thought to himself, composedly stepping inside. Once inside the door – the second phase – he continued to laud her playing.

"Of course, I've never met you before, and thus have no reason to flatter you. But the moment I heard you, I said to myself, now there's the real Chopin."

"Please sit down," the girl told him. "So, do you really love music that much?"

"Well, I know a few things about it ... Chopin's a noble voice," Andonis improvised, then stopped for fear of saying something dumb and getting in over his head.

"A lot of people think he was just another romantic," the girl complained.

"They couldn't be more wrong!" Andonis cried indignantly. "He's a genius! Why, his revolt cleared the way for the whole modern movement in music," he added, repeating something he remembered from the encyclopedia. "And he left such a rich body of work! fifty-six mazurkas, seventeen songs, thirteen, I believe it was, waltzes, nineteen nocturnes, fifteen polonaises, and how many etudes? Twenty-seven, that's right, including four fantasies, scherzos, and ballads, three improvisations, and ... and ... what else?"

He fell silent, afraid he sounded too much like an accountant for a subject that brooked no such stockroom approach. But then, as if the numbers were itching at him, he did a hasty addition and declared:

"A total of 190 works! And all in the span of a pitifully short life," he went on without catching his breath, as if her admiration meant nothing to him. "How many of us, miss, perish before we ever accomplish anything at all. What was Chopin's secret? He was happy, that's what. Happy in the living of his life. Are you happy, miss?"

The girl, a potential customer, had difficulty answering. She lowered her eyes. Her fingers, long and bony, numbered among how many tens of thousands that suffered punishment at the keyboard.

"Don't answer," said Andonis. "I didn't mean to upset you ... You know, I once owned a violin. My father died, and I snuck out and sold it during the war. But that's of no interest to you. The important thing is ..."

Andonis abandoned this superfluous line of argument, remembering the briefcase in his hand and the minutes that were ticking away.

"The important thing is for your soul to be nourished by its ideals ..." the pale-looking girl said unexpectedly. "I used to be paralyzed. I spent ten years in bed. All I did was play piano on the sheets with my fingers. I practiced the different pieces without ever hearing them, and told myself when I was able to get up again I would play them all ..."

"And now?"

"Next month I'm going to give a recital ... Will you come?"

"Wouldn't miss it for the world."

A wave of shame washed over Andonis. He edged toward the door with the idea of leaving, but the girl stopped him with a serene smile.

"You know," she said softly, "you too could discover what's most necessary for you to live life ... There must be something that means more to you than anything else ... And it wouldn't be as hard for you, since you're not an invalid ..."

He no longer even dared to look at her. He again told her how much he admired her playing, but the girl told him she didn't care so much about the results, she was just happy to be able to play ...

"And what about you? What do you do?" she asked him.

"I'm a salesman, that's all. Lingerie, neckties, perfume, clothing. I don't think you'd be interested," he said, opening the door. "I used to have ideas too, brilliant ones, which I offered in monthly installments ..."

"Could I see?"

"It's not worth the trouble. It's all extremely cheap. Good-by ..."

He plunged headlong down the stairs and out into the road. How long could he go on walking these endless streets? Run to catch the bus, check the time, collect your change, make a call, buy a paper ... How was one to hold steady when everything was forever changing? What did the late editions say? The trees lining the street made it seem even more thickly inhabited than it was. Vangelia had fled like a hunted animal that hides in a thicket to give birth. "I had become dangerous, and she had already warned me she wouldn't extend me any more credit. She was merely trying to save a child from its father." If he found her, he would tell her of how he had parted ways with Eftihis and Thodoros. "I've been through it all before," he would say. "Remember when I told you about how I left the company? It was the same thing. Thodoros wanted to humiliate me. He reminded me of my debts, the warrants and drafts. But there was really no question in my mind. I didn't have to think twice about it." Thodoros had asked him to fire two of the workers and get the others to work for less pay. "Otherwise, you're through. We don't need you here. That's the way things are these days." Who did they take him for?

He stopped in his tracks and tried to think calmly and systematically. It was something he hadn't yet managed to do. He looked around at the first neon signs blinking on in the gray dusk. People had names and histories, they were all connected by a system of relations as they endlessly trod the streets. He was always lagging behind, like an experienced journeyman who never found out whether he was on the road to success or disaster, never learned how it was that that magical wind, Time, slipped so swiftly through his fingers. He could only feel the tingling numbness its icy draft left in its wake. He could never close his fist fast enough to catch it. Somehow it always managed to slip away.

He stopped in to see Rapas, just in case anything new had turned up. Rapas immediately threw his arms around him.

"Your friend saved my life! He did one hell of a job on those blueprints. Building starts on Monday! I want to meet that fellow. I want to put him in charge of construction."

THE PICK-UP TRUCK JOUNCED ALONG the dirt road, returning empty from the dump. Andonis looked back at that remote spot and gave a sigh of relief. "I should have done it months ago," he told himself. The same driver as before – a good thing he'd hung on to his address – had helped him dump the whole miserable load of rotten meat.

"Are you in a hurry?" Andonis asked the driver.

"No."

"Then let's go over to Holargos."

"A delivery job?"

In recent days, Andonis had been to the houses of all their acquaintances in search of Vangelia. He had just remembered that she used to have an aunt living in Holargos. Maybe she could tell him something.

"You seem in a bad way today," the driver said. "I know, it's no fun tossing out that much merchandise."

When they came to Holargos, Andonis had a flicker of recognition, but it had been so long ago, and the place had changed. He let the truck wait, and went down a quiet street that gave out on a stand of pines. There it was – that little house there. He recognized the fence and the clinging vine. The house was completely enveloped, you couldn't even see the courtyard. He went up to the wrought-iron gate and rapped on it loudly.

Vangelia's aunt came out shortly. He recognized her immediately.

"I'm Andonis," he told her. "I heard Vangelia was here. I don't want to come in. But please just ask her to come out here so I can see her ..."

Her aunt didn't unlock the gate.

"I'll ask if she wants to," she told him and went back inside.

So she was there! He clutched the iron bars of the gate and waited. Vangelia soon appeared. She smiled at him and said hello.

"Come a little closer so we can talk."

Vangelia came nearer.

"You did right to leave," he told her. "I'm not angry at you."

"I want to have this baby. You preferred your cans last time. This time I'm going to have some say in the matter."

"Vangelia, do you remember a girl with light brown hair in

braids who lived in a red-brick house with acacias near the tracks? One night, a man was wounded by a patrol on the street. A door opened, and the girl saved his life ... Do you remember?"

"Yes, I remember," Vangelia struggled to say.

"But later on, Vangelia, that man started feeling tired and afraid. It's a sign of panic, isn't it, to always be on the lookout for a deal? And all those times I made you dizzy with all my talk it was just me trying to deceive myself, using a bit of slight-of-hand to convince myself I was on the way up out of the muck. You were right to run away with our child. All I'd have to teach him is a tangle of lies. And then I was afraid of ending up in prison and having you visit me there. But I guess this is a little like our meeting at visiting hour, isn't it? I spend all day roaming the streets with my briefcase, and now here I am standing behind these bars like a prisoner. Listen, if I get sent to a real prison because of my debts, don't come and see me, and don't say anything to our child. I'd die of shame."

A horn sounded. It was the truck driver, telling him it was time to go.

"Good-by, Vangelia."

And Andonis hurried off, his visiting hour at an end.

CHAPTER 20

ON MONDAY MORNING at daybreak, Angelos came down from the little room on the roof. He washed and shaved, then sat at his father's desk.

"I'm ready. Go get Andonis," he told Ismene.

He took a yellowed newspaper clipping from his pocket. He read it over slowly and carefully. Then he struck a match. He held the clipping until it was engulfed in flames, then dropped it into the ashtray.

Andonis came rushing in, and they immediately embraced with deep feeling – two friends meeting again after how many years? It seemed like yesterday.

"Sit down and let's talk ..."

"So, are you taking that supervising job?"

"Yes."

"We can settle how much you'll be getting for it today."

"Good. And keep as much as you need to pay off your debts."

"Thank you, Angelos."

"It's the least I could do to repay you for your gift."

"So, shall we go?"

"Yes. They start work early at construction sites."

They went down the stairs. There was a commotion in the courtyard. Eftihis and Thodoros were having a row. They broke off when they caught sight of the others.

"Not you again!" Thodoros said to Angelos.

"I don't know you."

"Angelos!" said Eftihis, running up to them. "This bastard's trying to screw me out of my looms. He's out to ruin me! I swear to God I'm going to kill him ..."

"No you won't. Because he's not the real cause ..."

The three of them, Angelos, Ismene and Andonis, slowly proceeded down the passageway.

Angelos halted at the front gate. He leaned against it, as if opening a huge iron gate. It took all of his strength, even though it was unlocked. Then the three of them went on through.

Out in the street, they felt the cool morning breeze against their faces.

ANDREAS FRANGHIAS

Born in Athens in 1921, Andréas Franghias began studying economics but discontinued his studies, because of the Nazi Occupation and his participation in the Resistance. He worked as a journalist and made his literary debut in 1955 with a novel called *People and Houses*. His novels have been translated into German, Rumanian, Hungarian, Russian and French. In 1987 he received the State literary award for his novel *The Crowd*.

MARTIN McKINSEY

Martin McKinsey teaches English at the University of Virginia, U.S.A. He is also the translator of *Late into the Night: The Last Poems of Yannis Ritsos* (Field Translation Series).

WHAT DOES MRS. FREEMAN WANT

Petros Abatzoglou

Here is the portrait of an extraordinary – yet in many ways typical – English couple, as seen through the eyes of a fascinated, ouzo-guzzling Greek narrator, reminiscing on a sun-drenched beach. Under his passionate, yet humorous, scrutiny, Mrs. Freeman and her husband come alive with great vividness, while retaining intact the mystery of their "otherness." The book is much more than the story of Mrs. Freeman's life and times; it also offers an ironical insight into the confrontation of two cultures, two different ways of looking at the world.

FOOL'S GOLD

Maro Douka

"My father, thunderstruck, was demanding to know: but when? This is madness! Impossible. When at last he replaces the receiver in a grand Shakespearean manner – my father has it in the blood – he broke the news to us: Dictatorship. My mother cried out and collapsed in a heap on the sofa. Calliope the maid, as part of her duties, always manages to sense the right moment for a restorative coffee, and set off for the kitchen. May father repeated: Dictatorship, do you hear! I stared at him, shaking off sleep."

This is how Myrsini Panayoutou an Athenian girl about to start university, learns of the coup d'état that brought to power the infamous dictatorship of the "Colonels" in her country in the early hours of Friday, 21st April 1967. The child of a well-to-do family, Myrsini enthusiastically joins the underground resistance, making common cause with a varied cast of characters from backgrounds very different from her own. Afer an early failed love affair she gets engaged to George, a political prisoner, only to find her human instincts increasingly difficult to reconcile with her idealistic philosophy once he is released. The story moves towards its climax as Myrsini becomes involved in the bloody events of 17th November 1973, when tanks were used to evict students from the Athens Polytechnic. At the same time the fortunes of Myrsini's family form a backdrop at once touching and bizarre to an impressionable girl's unflinching search for a true identity, both for herserlf and for her country.

Fool's Gold is a sparkling first nover by a talented writer, one of the foremost of a new generation which grew up under the shadow of the events Maro Douka describes.

ASTRADENI

Eugenia Fakinou

"Grandma Eleni says it's my name, Astradeni, that's to blame, because Astradeni means 'the one who binds the stars.' And who, other than a fairy creature, can bind the stars? I don't tell anyone this, of course..."

Symi, the small island near Rhodes, is where the eleven-year-old heroine of this novel grows up, until financial reasons oblige the family to move to Athens. Astradeni leaves behind a closeknit community, a natural setting that stimulates her imagination, and a rich store of traditional values in which both religion and magic lore have their place. The author lets her tell her own story with winning charm and candour in a style that allows her sensitivity and the sparkle of her intelligence to shine through.

A born storyteller, Astradeni supplies vivid details of the life and human relations on a remote Aegean island, as well as her efforts to adapt to the hard and alienating conditions of city life. For beneath the surface charm of a young girl's narrative the reader is in fact witnessing a painful process of social change, the violence done to the sense of values of individuals experiencing an abrupt transition from a traditional agrarian culture to a competitive, industrialised society of consumers.

THE BUILDERS

Giorgos Heimonas

Giorgos Heimonas was born at Kavala in 1939. He studied psychiatry at the University of Athens and the University of Paris, and he lives in Athens, where he works as a professor, physician, and author. His mysterious and moving narratives have made him one of Greece's most reknowned contemporary writers.

To enter into a Heimonas text is not so much to read the written word as to experience it. His characters repeatedly suggest that the word of their experience flows through the body toward the lips but never reaches speech. Accordingly, Heimonas creates a metamorphosed language and a genre which are neither poetry nor fiction in a conventional sense yet share certain qualities of each. In *The Builders* the protagonist is the herald of a new order of speech and feeling. The text suggests that we cease, as it were, to listen to experience with our neighbour's ear; rather we should feel the world through a sort of language of the nerves. Thus, the narrative does not articulate an idea or situation so much as pulse with sensations of pain, joy, discovery. The feeling of existence becomes its meaning. In Heimonas' words, the world becomes an image and humanity itself the message.

GOOD FRIDAY VIGIL

Yorgos Ioannou

The protagonist in each of these stories is a solitary individual, alienated from society, haunted by memories, fascinated by the disgusting, obsessed with the relationship between love and death, and fetishistically attached to certain objects that bear the traces of traumatic experiences. Ioannou brilliantly highlights the discrepancy between intimate acts of sex and violence, and the way people pretend in public that life can be lived without physicality.

In *Good Friday Vigil* – his last book of stories before his untimely death in 1985 – Ioannou departs from the conversational tone of his earlier work and develops an intricate style whose wanderings evoke the associative meanderings of the memory.

JAGUAR

Alexandros Kotzias

The author has called *The Jaguar* "an extravagant story." He employs an extravagant style to stress the irony of his heroine's attempt to preserve a false image of her moral superiority in the process of promoting selfish ends.

The historical events referred to in Dimitra's account of herself and her family belong to the Second World War period. Dimitra, a mathematics teacher, had been an active member of the leftist resistance movement during the Nazi occupation of Greece and was persecuted as a communist in the civil war era that followed. Years later, she likes to think of herself as an uncompromising individual engaged in a noble struggle to promote the ideals of a socialist revolution.

The unexpected return of the sister-in-law Philio from America to claim an inheritance forces her to take a good look at the past. Her breathless interior monologue throughout the night of her confrontation with Philio reveals Dimitra's obstinate refusal to accept the "bourgeois" compromises she has meanwhile made and has been comfortably living with for the past ten years.

The extravagant melodrama of Dimitra's rhetoric often becomes a caricature of dialectic reasoning, a comic version of double-think paring reality to make it fit within the confines of wishful thinking and self-righteousness. When the verbal torrent is finally spent, the comedy fades leaving a bitter aftertaste of the pathos of self-deception.

In native South American religion the jaguar was regarded as a fierce deity representing forces of war, destruction and human sacrifice.

KOULA

Menis Koumandareas

A "brief encounter" on the Athenian Underground brings together two people, Koula and Dimitris, from entirely different backgrounds and ages. For a few weeks they manage to break loose from their respective shackles and meet in a kind of no man's land of passionate discovery. The couple's emotional fluctuations are charted with remarkable precision and subtlety, in a low-key tone that fully captures the muted drama of their meeting and parting.

THREE SUMMERS

Margarita Liberaki

Three Summers is the story of three sisters growing up in Greece; their first loves, lies, and secrets; their shared childhood experiences and their gradual growing apart. Maria, the oldest, is strong, sensual, keenly aware of society's expectations. Infanta is beautiful, fiercely proud, aloof. Katerina is spirited, independent, off in a dream world of her own. There is also the mysterious Polish grandmother, the wily Captain Andreas, the self-involved Laura Parigori.... Katerina tells the story of these intertwined lives with imagination, humor, deep tenderness, and a certain nostalgia. *Three Summers* is a romance with nature, with our planet. It is the declaration of a young girl in love with life itself.

FAREWELL ANATOLIA

Dido Sotiriou

Farewell Anatolia is a tale of paradise lost and of shattered inocence; a tragic fresco of the fall of Hellenism in Asia Minor; a stinging indictment of Great Power politics, oil-lust and corruption.

Dido Soteriou's novel – a perennial best-seller in Greece since it first appeared in 1962 – tells the story of Manolis Axiotis, a poor but resourceful villager born near the ancient ruins of Ephesus. Axiotis is a fictional protagonist and eyewitness to an authentic nightmare: Greece's "Asia Minor Catastrophe," the death or expulsion of two million Greeks from Turkey by Kemal Attaturk's revolutionary forces in the late summer of 1922.

Manolis Axiotis' chronicle of personal fortitude, betrayed hope, and defeat resonates with the greater tragedy of two nations: Greece, vanquished and humiliated; Turkey, bloodily victorious. Two neighbours linked by bonds of culture and history yet diminished by mutual greed, cruelty and bloodshed.

Farewell Anatolia has been translated into French, Russian, Hungarian. A Turkish translation appeared in 1970, and was hailed as a major contribution to reconciliation between the two neighbours.

ACHILLES' FIANCÉE

Alki Zei

The scene is Paris, sometime after the 1967 military *coup* in Greece. Eleni, together with a group of her friends and fellow political exiles, finds herself working as an extra in a French film: *The Horror Train.* Iti is not the first time Eleni has been caught up in a deadly drama, nor is it her first ride on a "horror train". As the director waves his arms, shouting directions and re-shooting the sequence, Eleni's mind wanders to her first train ride:

"Athens-Piraeus. My first big trip by train.
– You're Eleni? I'm Achilles.
They don't ask which Achilles. One name is enough..."

For the rest of her life, Eleni will be "Achilles' Fiancée," fiancée of the guerilla leader, the brave, handsome *kapetanios* whose code-name is Achilles. In the demonstrations against the German occupiers of Greece, in prison where she waits for a death sentence during the post-war persecution of suspected leftists, in exile in Tashkent where the exiled Greek communists fight amongst themselves, and finally in Paris, she will always be known as "Achilles' Fiancée." But somewhere along the way Eleni becomes an independent character with a mind of her own. As she begins to doubt the slogans that she fought for when she was a blind follower of leaders like her fiancé, Eleni involves us in her own private world of self-discovery. It is a woman's world, where human warmth and deep friendships matter more than abstract ideals, where young girls fall in love and enjoy wearing pretty clothes.

The Greek word for a novel is *mythistorema*, a word that combines "myth" and "history". In her story of a young woman's struggle to survive through an extraordinary period of Greek history, Alki Zei has woven the threads of her own quasimythical life into the stuff of history. The result is a compelling and beautiful novel that opens a new window on modern Greek history.

RED DYED HAIR

Kostas Mourselas

Emmanuel Retsinas (call him Louis) flows like a river in full flood through *Red Dyed Hair* the brilliant first novel by Greek playwright Kostas Mourselas. Louis is the "almost man," once and forever lumpen and anarchocommunist, sometime circus daredevil, part-time yacht captain, full-time subverter of propriety, morals, order. Destroyer, builder, provocateur, catalyst extraordinary.

Spanning four decades of contemporary Greek life as seen from the bottom of the barrel, the novel is an inspired mixture of social satire and political history, a compendium of the bizarre, the erotic, the banal and the unbearable – peopled by a crazed yet touching cross-section of social rejects and climbers, betrayed leftists and police informers, of con-men become businessmen, of whores and bouzouki singers, pimps and greengrocers.

In scene embedded within scene *Red Dyed Hair* spins a tale of social and personal cowardice and treachery against a distant backdrop of courage betrayed at the cost of death. This is the story of a generation that "knocked on the wrong doors, slept in the wrong beds, loved the wrong people, made the wrong choices."

Red Dyed Hair is a hall of ever-receding, endlessly distorting mirrors, a warped (as only art can warp) reflection of the chamber of horrors – the whorehouse – called life. Heraclitan in its flux, self-contained, inconclusive, incisive, *Red Dyed Hair* is like life: vivid, painful; infinitely various and upredictable.